“Any Sherlock Holmes ... tt’s
homage to the great de... *Book Review*

“The star is Holmes, and the narrator is his sidekick. But the Holmes is Mycroft, Sherlock’s older, smarter brother; and the narrator is Paterson Erskine Guthrie, not Dr. Watson. Absorbing.”

—*Publishers Weekly* on *Against the Brotherhood*

“Rousing adventures in fine Sherlockian fashion: on trains, at the edge of cliffs, in dark halls and taverns. Mycroft dons various disguises in order to manipulate events. The tale is true to the Sir Arthur Conan Doyle tradition in the most important way: there’s no doubt the evil is really, truly, unequivocally evil.”

—*The San Jose Mercury News* on *Against the Brotherhood*

“Maintains the integrity of the Sherlock Holmes canon. Fawcett seems to have captured the flavor of Doyle’s work. I would pick up another Mycroft Holmes/Guthrie adventure. My interest is piqued.”

—*The Mystery News* on *Against the Brotherhood*

Tor Books by Quinn Fawcett

Against the Brotherhood
Embassy Row
The Flying Scotsman

Quinn Fawcett

Embassy Row

A MYCROFT HOLMES NOVEL

A TOM DOHERTY ASSOCIATES BOOK
NEW YORK

EMBASSY ROW

A Tor Book
Published by Tom Doherty Associates, LLC
175 Fifth Avenue
New York, NY 10010

www.tor.com

ISBN 0-812-54522-2
Library of Congress Card Catalog Number: 98-23488

First edition: October 1998
First mass market edition: October 1999
Printed in the United States of America

0 9 8 7 6 5 4 3 2 1

The use of the character of Mycroft Holmes is done with the kind permission of Dame Jean Conan Doyle.

For Peter
with thanks for
the loan of
his last name

Prologue

THERE WAS NO other word for it: Mycroft Holmes' evening visits to the Diogenes Club were very much a ritual, adhered to with a regularity that delineated his life. Either Mister Holmes himself, or his double, Edmund Sutton, crossed the road at fifteen minutes before five every afternoon and returned to his flat at seven-forty in a display of reliability that rivaled Big Ben.

I had been in the Diogenes Club rather less frequently since I entered Mister Holmes' employ as his confidential secretary; the place still had the capacity to awe me, and this evening the urgency of my errand served only to make the club more impressive for its silence and its nearly palpable air of undisturbed and profound thought. After explaining the nature of my business to the worthy at the reception desk, I was escorted to the Strangers' Room and informed that Mister Holmes would be with me directly, which news made me more aware of the immediacy of my task. Left to my own devices, I would have gone through the august, musty chambers in search of my employer. As it was, I was given a pony of superior port to ease my wait. It was twenty minutes past six.

"Guthrie, dear boy," said Mycroft Holmes some fifteen minutes later as he came into the Strangers' Room from the *sanctum sanctorum* of the Reading Room; his expression was more perplexed than annoyed at this interruption of his evening rite. "Since it is not your inclination to visit me here, I must suppose that what brings you cannot wait for my return."

"No, sir," I said, hearing my own Scots accent grow stronger for embarrassment; my awareness of it did little to lessen the burr. "The message was specific, and the messenger stressed the need for promptness. Tyers advised me to come at once."

This invocation of the opinion of his trusted, longtime manservant earned me a curt nod from Mister Holmes. "I have never known Tyers to act in a precipitate manner—nor you, for that matter," said he, pulling his lower lip as was his habit when ruminating. His profound grey eyes showed the degree of his concern as his heavy brows drew down over them. He shrugged to demonstrate his ignorance. "I had best have the whole, then. Tell me what brings you, Guthrie."

I drew a heavy envelope from my inner waistcoat pocket and held it out to him. "This came from the Austro-Hungarian embassy; it demands your instant response, we were told in the most emphatic terms. In German," I added out of conscientiousness.

"Always precise," Holmes approved. He took the envelope, turning it over in his big, lean hands with care. He inspected the wafer sealing it. "At least it is only the Austro-Hungarians," he exclaimed with a gesture of relief. "Between all the Japanese and the Bulgarians have been doing this last month, I am prepared to run mad. Either one would be aggravating, but with both of them— If they were acting in concert, I would be utterly distracted. I can almost welcome the Austro-Hungarians."

A more unlikely alliance than the Bulgarians and the Japanese had not been proposed, and I took advantage of his remark to chuckle. "While I share your sentiments, sir," I said as Mycroft Holmes broke the seal on the envelope, "you must forgive me if I find such a notion ludicrous. Indeed, it is more likely that the Turks and the Americans should suddenly become allies."

He paid no heed to anything I said, putting the whole of his attention on the missive I had brought; my minor witticism was ignored. "You would think," he mused aloud, "that they would have had this brought straight here. My habits are well enough established that they . . . Odd of them." He cocked his large, long head.

"Tyers remarked on that, as well," I said, recalling how carefully he had perused the envelope before advising me to take it across the road at once.

"Um," said Mycroft Holmes, removing the paper the envelope contained.

"It seems to me," I went on while he carefully scrutinized the single sheet of heavy parchment, "that this is more irregular than I supposed." The more I thought about it, the less I liked this whole episode.

Mycroft Holmes cut into my thoughts. "What is this packet mentioned? Was it given to you along with—" He held out the sheet to finish his sentence.

"No. There was only the envelope, sir," I said, feeling increasingly uneasy. I knew I was expected to provide all material he might require. "I can return to your flat to see if anything more has been delivered."

At this, Mycroft Holmes' frown deepened. "I doubt that will be necessary," he said in a tone of voice that filled me with foreboding.

"Sir," I began, only to be brusquely interrupted.

"You are a veritable prince of secretaries, Guthrie, truly you are. But I implore you to stop your infernal *sir*-ing," he complained.

"Sorry, si—" I said at once, stopping myself in time. "It's this place. I feel as if I were back in school." I lowered my eyes and was about to find some appropriate way to lessen the offense I had innocently given when the outer door opened and one of the Diogenes Club's porters stepped into the Strangers' Room.

"Yes, Redfern?" Mycroft Holmes said without giving the man more than passing attention.

"There is a packet just been delivered for you, Mister Holmes. I think it may be important. The cove that brought it thought it was. Do you want me to bring it here to you?" He was respectful, even diffident, but I noticed the same straight bearing about him that Philip Tyers displayed, and I suspected that Redfern was another man retired from military service.

"Where is this package?" asked Mycroft Holmes with the attitude of one anticipating risk.

"At the front desk. The fellow wanted to bring it to you himself but as he would not sign the Strangers' Book, I would not permit it." His firmly polite manner did not alter, but I had the distinct impression that Redfern could make such a refusal stick with any but the most belligerent.

Now Mycroft Holmes swung around in alarm. So abrupt and unexpected was this change in him that I did not perceive the cause. I quickly realized that my employer had some specific hazard in mind, for he surged past me and out into the lobby of his club.

I was often astonished at the speed and power with which this apparently portly and indolent man could move when he deemed it necessary. He reached the reception desk and pointed to the paper-wrapped parcel set there. "Is this the package? Tell me, man," he demanded as he reached out for it; I was not far behind him, watching him with increasing apprehension.

Redfern was next to me. "Yes, sir, Mister Holmes," he said, and was about to add something more when Mycroft Holmes seized the package and made for the entrance at a steady run.

"Guthrie!" he shouted to me. "Follow the messenger who brought this!"

"I did not see him," I called after him, acutely aware of disturbing the tranquility of the Diogenes Club.

"Find him!" he ordered as he flung open the door and bolted for the street.

I glanced at Redfern, who remained unperturbed.

"An Austrian uniform, as I recollect. Didn't know the regiment. Parade gear, I think. Forest green and silver." His report was admirably succinct.

"It is enough," I said, more in hope than certainty. But Mycroft Holmes was already into the street by the time I ran out the door of the Diogenes Club; I reached the pavement several strides behind my employer. I paused to look up and down Pall Mall, trying to pierce the gloom of dusk and the crowded traffic of the street for what was probably a forest green Austrian parade uniform. I caught sight of Mycroft Holmes running swiftly toward the corner, the package clutched tightly to his chest. In the next moment he rounded the corner into the alley leading toward the Admiralty.

Then I noticed a flash of a parade tunic in a dark color that might be green, and I was off in pursuit. I did not yell or attempt to gain the man's attention: Mycroft Holmes had taught me that such was folly when truly dangerous events are occurring, and serves only to put your adversary on his mettle. I rushed through the crowd, very nearly knocking over an elderly gentleman making his way with the help of his cane. At another time I would have apologized, but I dared not take my eyes from the man in the uniform for an instant.

It was unfortunate that a sudden, muffled explosion caught the attention of everyone in Pall Mall. The man I supposed must be my target hardly hesitated at the sound, but could not keep from looking back toward the Diogenes Club. In so doing, he noticed me, and surmised my purpose. He began to move more quickly, taking advantage of the sudden confusion on the street. I hastened after him, breaking into a run as the man slipped through the crowd.

At the corner, the man hesitated, as if uncertain which way to go. I took all advantage I could of his uncertainty, closing the gap between us with a burst of speed that surprised even me. As the man dodged between carriages and bolted in the direction of Regent Street, I kept after him, dashing among the carriages, carts, wagons, and hansoms, earning myself a number of round oaths from drivers and pedestrians alike.

We were nearing Charles II Street when I became aware of Mycroft Holmes pelting up behind me. "Saint Albans Mews!" he shouted to me. In the fading light I could see his garments were in disarray and the knuckles of his left hand were scraped and bleeding.

"Sir," I began; I knew Saint Albans Mews was quite near, but on the east side of Regent Street.

"Don't waste breath," he ordered me. "Saint Albans Mews. We'll have him there!"

I knew it was best to comply, and did so as promptly as I could. A dozen strides further on I was secretly pleased to see our quarry stumble. Encouraged, I redoubled my efforts and noticed that Mycroft Holmes did the same; he signaled me to press the man on his left, forcing him to turn east. It would not be easy; though I was fit enough, this sort of chase was taxing for me. Between traffic and poor light, I felt myself at a marked disadvantage.

Ahead, the man veered into the busy thoroughfare, moving to the east side of Regent Street. I did not allow this minor success to diminish my efforts. I continued to force him on his left, so that he would be inclined to go toward Saint Albans Mews; the narrow street was not far ahead now, and I could sense Mycroft Holmes intensifying the hunt. Somehow I summoned up the strength for a sprint.

Saint Albans Mews was surprisingly quiet for being in such proximity to Regent Street. I looked up at the high fronts of the buildings, and noticed a small service alley leading between numbers 4 and 5. The man in the forest green tunic made for it, arms flailing and strides unsteady. I heard Mycroft Holmes come up behind me.

"Follow him, Guthrie!" he shouted. "Don't let him get away!"

I did all that I could to comply, making for the alley at speed, going into the gloom recklessly, and nearly falling over a group of dustbins which the man we were chasing had somehow avoided. I did not like to consider what this might mean, for I was keenly aware that this was an ideal location for an ambush.

"He could be hiding," Mycroft Holmes reminded me as he came down the alley to the service yard behind the houses.

"If he is armed—" I panted.

"You may be sure he is" was Mycroft Holmes' grim answer.

I had already slowed my pace to a steady jog, and I might

have faltered at this unwelcome intelligence, but Mycroft Holmes showed no tendency to hesitate and I was determined to maintain his good opinion.

The service yard was much like all the others in this part of London: It was roughly paved and gave access to the rear of the houses, their stables and kitchens; it was lined with stands of dust-bins and similar receptacles. I peered into the dark, trying to detect any movement ahead of us, but could discern none. "I don't think he can have made it to the next street."

"Nor do I," said Holmes. "Which means he has gone to ground." He tapped his ear. "Listen well, Guthrie."

I did as I was told, making myself breathe through my mouth so that I would not be misled by my own subdued gasping. We walked with caution now, trying to make certain that there was nothing to give our presence away. When we were little more than halfway down the service yard, Mycroft Holmes took hold of my shoulder and pointed to an ajar gate.

"There," he whispered, his hand angling up toward the landing of the first floor. On the ground floor no lights could be discerned; the house appeared deserted.

I could barely detect movement, but I was aware of a shape in the shadows that might have been a man—or a small wardrobe, or a large dog, for that matter. I wanted to make it out before going after it, but Mycroft Holmes was not willing to hesitate. He went to the gate and swung it open silently, then motioned to me to follow him.

Ashamed at my momentary lack of activity, I hurried to climb the stairs, and was rewarded with what must have been an oath in some tongue I did not recognize. I took heart at this and went up the stairs two at a time. Above me, the man made for the second floor.

I continued upward, hearing Mycroft Holmes pounding on

the ground floor door, demanding admittance to the house in the name of Her Majesty's government.

On the second floor, the man I was chasing fell heavily against the landing railing over the service yard. For a moment it seemed he would regain his footing, but then he plummeted downward, landing with a sickening noise of splintering on the high wooden fence. I stood very still, suddenly feeling my muscles turn to jelly. I clung to the banister for the greater part of a minute before I could trust myself to make my way down the stairs.

Mycroft Holmes was standing by the fence; the dead man's upper body hung like a bizarre trophy. He had just completed a cursory examination of the body. "This is most unfortunate, Guthrie. Not that I hold you at fault," he added as I began to offer an apology for my failure to capture the man. "Neither of us could have anticipated this." He indicated the corpse.

There was a sudden spill of light as the kitchen door opened and a small, straight-backed woman of middle years looked out, fear in her deep-set eyes.

"It's Mycroft Holmes, Missus Moss. If you will be kind enough to bring us a lantern?" He spoke calmly and sensibly, and the woman did as he requested.

Half a year ago, I might have remarked on Mycroft Holmes knowing the housekeeper here, but I had become accustomed to his encyclopedic range of information and acquaintances; now all I said was, "She is reliable?"

"Missus Moss? Vastly," said Mycroft Holmes, putting his attention on the dead man again. "Well, one thing we can be sure of: This fellow was no more Austro-Hungarian than I am." He made a gesture of disgust. "I had hoped this would not be difficult, not just now."

"How can you be certain that the man is not—?" I asked, beginning to recover myself a trifle.

"The uniform is a theatrical one. Probably from Covent Garden or the Savoy." He fingered the tunic. "There's even greasepaint on the collar."

I could not conceal my bafflement. "But why would—" I found my own answer. "He was supposed to be identified as being with one of the foreign embassies. Of course. But which one?"

"It hardly matters. The efforts to identify him would provide a distraction," said Mycroft Holmes, looking up as Missus Moss came out bearing a lantern with a tall, narrow chimney and a newly trimmed wick shining brightly. "Thank you," he said as he took the lantern from her. "I am depending on you to keep this incident to yourself. I will tend to this directly."

"Very good, Mister Holmes." She curtsied and withdrew, leaving us with the body.

Holmes gave the lantern to me, indicating where I should hold it to aid him in his efforts. "This is cursory at best. I will have to arrange for the Admiralty to claim the body. There, you see?" he went on. "Greasepaint. And look at the epaulets. I do not need Edmund Sutton to tell me they are for the stage."

I found myself intrigued in spite of my initial revulsion at the sight of the man who lay like a broken soldier doll over the fence. "If he intended to escape notice, this was not a good way to do it," I remarked.

"True enough," said Mycroft Holmes. "Therefore his purpose was to have the blame for the bomb placed at the door of one of our European neighbors." He was inspecting the teeth of the dead man, holding his mouth open with a pencil. "Gold teeth. He was not a peasant, it would appear."

"Bomb?" I repeated as the full impact of his words struck me.

"In the package, dear boy. I was able to get it into one of the mucking barrels behind the Diogenes Club before it exploded. All that it did was spread horse dung from one end of the alley to the next." He indicated the scrape on his knuckles. "And not a moment too soon."

I considered this. "What does this have to do with the Japanese, do you think? Or the Bulgarians?"

"Perhaps nothing," said Mycroft Holmes as he put the pencil back in his breast pocket. "I must assume this was intended to distract us, but from what?"

"Lord knows there are things enough to distract us from," I said, fighting off a sudden wave of nausea.

"It may be something from the past, as well. Not everything I have done has been universally approved." His dry tone was eloquent. He sighed once. "I shall have to send word around to Yvegny Tschersky. He may have information that will help us."

Although I had never met Tschersky, I knew Mycroft Holmes held him in high regard and trusted him as much as he ever trusted a Russian. "Why Tschersky?"

"He hears things, dear boy. He hears things." He straightened up. "Now run along to the Admiralty and make sure someone comes to deal with this. Stress the need for secrecy and haste. Until we know more about this man, I do not want news of it to leak out. The Japanese would not like it. And we are meeting with them day after tomorrow. Anything that suggests scandal would make our position much more precarious than it already is. Cecil would not be pleased if all our work with the Japanese came to naught."

I was glad to be away from the body, but I said as I prepared to go, "Shall I return here with the . . . helpers, or shall I—"

"Make your way back to my flat and put Tyers at ease. We will not see Sutton until quite late. He is rehearsing tonight." He waved me away as if everything were settled, which I knew was not the case. "Do not trouble yourself about Missus Moss," he called after me. "I will explain all to her satisfaction."

"I will see you later," I said loudly enough to be heard, and went down the dark alley as quickly as I could without once again running.

FROM THE PERSONAL JOURNAL OF PHILIP TYERS

I have just returned from handing a private memorandum to Yvegny Tschersky at the Russian embassy on behalf of MH. I was told there would be a reply as soon as possible.

MH came back from the Admiralty but an hour ago, pleased that secrecy of the evening's events seems secure. He informed G that he could go home, but he would be expected at six-thirty in the morning, earlier than usual. G said he would be on time and departed soon after.

A private communication from the PM arrived not ten minutes ago, informing MH that there is to be a greater diplomatic display for the Japanese. MH is not best pleased with this news, to which he is even now writing a protest. I will carry it to Downing Street before I retire for the night.

Chapter One

"THERE'S NO GOOD to come of this: mark my words. These negotiations should be done clandestinely, not in this . . . haphazard way, half diplomacy and half politics. We'll never be able to keep the agreement quiet now," said Mycroft Holmes as he stood before his mirror in his dressing room attempting to fix his cravat in place over his stiff collar. "And the cut of this coat makes me look like a pouter pigeon; Shakespeare's 'good capon line'. Why should the uniform of diplomats be so unflattering to its officers, or the tailors so incompetent? My everyday one is handsomer. Where necessity rules . . ." He turned to me with an exasperated expression. "Thank God I can rely on your discretion. And Tyers' too, for that matter. I am singularly fortunate in my staff and my manservant. I only wish, Guthrie, I could have you at my side to record our discussions, but none of us, save the Japanese, has been permitted to bring his own staff. Never have I had greater need of all your considerable skills, dear boy, and never have I been more systematically frustrated. This was supposed to be a private negotiation, but with Cecil determined to have all the political spectrum represented, men like Lord Brackenheath and that Irish scoundrel Parnell are involved, in order to prevent any claims of underhandedness—" It was apparent he expected no response. He touched the black waistcoat under the deep-grey coat which so annoyed him. "Where did I put my watch?"

"Beside the ewer, sir," I said, used to his curmudgeonliness on this topic now. The first time I heard him complain in this manner I was alarmed, for Holmes was a man prepared to go to any lengths for his duty, as I knew from experience. But that was nearly a year ago now, and I was no longer dismayed. I now understood that he would rather be chased by lunatic occultists and their soldiers than appear publicly in any official government capacity. It was his belief that his effectiveness was compromised every time he was required to present himself in any formal manner.

"Just so," he grumbled, and slipped it into the watch-pocket of the waistcoat, then set the fob in place. It was May, and in the nearly eleven months I had been in Mycroft Holmes' employ as his private secretary and personal assistant I had not known him to enjoy any of the ceremony of diplomacy. It was his contention that by making certain clothes more important than what was being discussed, men were attracted to the diplomatic life for all the wrong reasons. The government was filled with men wanting to undertake the diplomatic life for the grandeur it offered rather than the service. He had, in fact, a marked distaste for all of what he called the "flummery" of court functions, so I was not surprised to hear his animadversions on the one that would begin in an hour. I held my notebook at the ready, prepared to continue with the letter he had been dictating to me. "It shouldn't be necessary to parade about in mufti in order to reach an understanding."

"You might have insisted on less noticeable dress, to keep the meeting—" I reminded him, recalling the three high-ranking officials who visited yesterday afternoon to apprise him of the change in arrangements.

He paid no attention. "Worst of all," he said when he was satisfied with the set of his watchfob, "officially I am not to be there at all. All the Germans or Russians or Austro-Hungarians, or the Americans, for that matter, need to do is wait outside the Swiss embassy and watch for arriving carriages. They will easily recognize half the men involved. These discussions are supposed to be *sub rosa,* though they are starting to look like a military parade, what with Sir Richard King, Sir Garnet Wolseley, and Sir Evelyn Wood for the British Army, Admirals Seymour and Hewett for the Royal Navy. All the more reason not to kit me, or anyone, up this way. We might as well hire a corps of drummers and pipers. But the Prime Minister has decided that we must manage this way, so—" He fixed his stickpin in his cravat and reached for his tall hat. "End the thing with thanks for the discretion that has been shown in regard to this young person; lapses of this sort must be expected of hotheaded young men. Unfortunately. Of course, you need not add my observations, Guthrie," he went on, returning to the letter lying open on his dresser.

I could not hide a wry smile. "I did not plan to."

"A veritable prince of secretaries, as I have maintained from the first," he told me, his aggravation fading a bit. "Make two copies of it, and have it ready for my signature this evening. I should be back before midnight."

"And the files?" I asked, watching him inspect himself in the mirror. "What do you want me to do with them?"

"Reseal them and hand them over to the Admiralty messenger when he arrives. Tell him that it is to be kept available while the negotiations are continuing with the Japanese. Incidentally, I trust your new bootmaker is proving satisfactory."

I had become used to these unexpected and acute insights and so I no longer marveled at them. "He is, sir."

"Excellent. The Italians have a way with leather, have they not?" He smiled slightly. "The glaze on your shoes is Florentine, or I know nothing of the matter." He lifted his head at the sound of the sharp rap on the rear door which Tyers hastened to answer. "Just in time. A useful thing in an actor." With that he turned toward the hall and prepared to meet the new arrival. He strode through his bedroom to the hall door.

"Mister Holmes," said Edmund Sutton, coming through the door as if expecting applause. He paused just over the threshold to be recognized.

"My dear Edmund," said Mycroft Holmes. "How good of you to come again." He put out his hand to the younger man.

Seen side-by-side in this context, I was once again astonished at the actor's skill that transformed him to a double for our employer: Edmund Sutton was as tall and long-headed as Holmes, but a good dozen years younger and four stone lighter and slighter; his thatch of fair hair made his periwinkle-blue eyes more noticeable. Yet with padding of his own invention to make him appear portly and squarer of frame, a wig of grey-shot dark hair cut in the same style as Holmes', and makeup skillfully applied, he would soon present the same appearance as Holmes, and his eyes would somehow have taken on the profound grey color that marked those of Mycroft Holmes. Most remarkable to me, however, was the way in which Sutton would take on Holmes' mannerisms, from his characteristic stride to the way he toyed with his watch-fob or held his cigar. All his own easy flamboyance and gregariousness would vanish once he took on the role he had been engaged to play—the role of Mycroft Holmes.

"Hallo, Guthrie," said Sutton, offering me his hand now that he had greeted Holmes. His smile was open and sincere, his splendid voice pitched to carry only a short distance. That was another of his accomplishments—the way he could change his ringing tones for the soft-spoken rumble of Holmes' voice. Of all the changes he made, Sutton claimed this was the most difficult for him to sustain.

"Good to see you, Sutton," I said. Originally I had found his broad theatrical manner a bit off-putting, but in the last year I had come to like the man and to respect his abilities. In his way, he was as necessary to Holmes' work as Tyers and I were.

"Shall we do the usual routine today?" Sutton asked, nearly laughing, since an essential part of his disguise was the strict maintenance of Holmes' schedule.

"We had better," I answered, finding it less worrisome to jest about his work than I had at first. "So you will take his place in either the study or the sitting room, whichever you prefer." Then I asked what would be a pressing question that day. "What role are you learning now?" since he would fill his hours of going about Holmes' life with the memorizing of a role he was engaged to understudy.

"Just at present, I am memorizing Sir Peter Teazle, from Sheridan's *School for Scandal.* I think you will find it amusing." He looked once more at Mycroft Holmes. "An important affair?"

"It was supposed to be circumspect, and unofficial," said Holmes. "But the Japanese are such sticklers for form."

"The Japanese, is it?" marveled Sutton, adding eagerly, "You might do me a service, should the opportunity come to hand. If you can find a way I might procure one of those magnificent kimonos, with all the layers, I would appreciate it more than I could say." He lowered his eyes. "Not that you haven't better things to do, but in case an opportunity should present itself."

"A full court kimono is a very complicated series of garments," warned Holmes. "The Japanese regard them as treasures."

"Yes, as well they should," said Sutton. "That's why I want one. It is almost impossible to assemble one from other parts, the way I can do with other costumes. The silks alone are unobtainable, and a full garment is beyond my skills to duplicate." He said this in so workmanlike a manner that there was no hint of boasting in it. "It took me almost three years to get a full djellaba, and you know how useful it has been."

"Oh, yes," said Holmes with a burst of amusement. "I probably wouldn't have got out of Munich without it. Very well, my friend. I will do what I can about the kimono." He set his hat upon his head and motioned to me to follow. "Bring my case with you. I will need the documents we discussed."

"I have it prepared," I assured him, and made my way in the general direction of the front door. I noticed once again the strange stain on the framed map of northern India, and wondered if it was, in fact, strong tea, as Holmes claimed, or something more sinister. It was flanked by maps of the Kazan region of Russia and western China, and nine other maps of the Orient. Two of the maps were torn and mended, but only the one of northern India had that ominous, dark stain.

"Look after Sutton," Holmes said in an undervoice as we reached the front of his flat. The large brass Arabian urns had recently been polished and they gleamed softly in the early afternoon light. "This whole negotiation is precarious—more than anyone wishes to admit. If my role is discovered, I fear he may be made to answer for it. That would not be . . . acceptable to me." He put his hand on the latch, not quite looking at me, a sure indication his request was important. "I will not require it, but I would appreciate your remaining here until I return."

"Certainly," I said, and nodded to him to show I was willing to comply.

"If there is any development you believe requires my immediate attention, come yourself to the Swiss embassy. Carry my documents case, so that it will be assumed you are a messenger." He glanced down at the bustle of Pall Mall, indicating the long descent from his second-floor flat. "Make sure you watch Sutton from here when he goes across the road in my stead this evening."

"You are afraid that something might happen," I said.

"Not in any way I can define empirically. But in time one develops a sense of trouble. And these dealings with the Japanese have trouble writ large upon them. There are too many threads in the knot." He shook his head. "What concerns me the most is that the matter should be a simple one—that of establishing the number of Japanese who may attend the Britannia Royal Navy College at Dartmouth—but it is proving to be a vastly more complex problem, and that gives me pause." He saw the hackney cab pull up on the street below. "Well. That will be Sid Hastings for me." The jarvey had almost become Mycroft Holmes' private driver, able to go about the city as anonymously as any cab; he was also a reliable source of information. "I will see you this evening, Guthrie. My thanks to you for all you have done."

"Not needed, sir," I said, and watched as he went down the stairs and into the waiting cab. Satisfied that the vehicle was on its way without incident, I then returned to the spartan bedroom where Edmund Sutton was in the process of taking on the character of Mycroft Holmes. He sat in the single straight-backed Restoration chair, half-dressed, in his padding, trousers, and an open robe while he worked in front of the shaving mirror, a brush in one hand, a small tin in the other, applying a purple-brown paint to the lines of his face to deepen them. He spent a great deal of care in doing what he called "feathering", softening and blurring the edge of the lines so that they would not appear to be painted at all. Already his features were older, the lines hewn into his flesh, and his demeanor had changed. His fair hair looked oddly out-of-place now.

"I realize you dislike feeding me cues, Guthrie, but time is pressing me," said Sutton in a voice far more like our employer's than it had been only a few minutes ago. "I'm sorry to impose in this way. If you are willing to meet me in the study in ten minutes, we should be able to work until luncheon at one-thirty."

Tyers came into the room bearing a tray on which stood a large cup of hot, black coffee, the one personal preference Sutton would not sacrifice to his Holmes role. He put this down in easy reach of the actor and said, "I have arranged for roast pork, onions, and grilled tomatoes. There is a serviceable eighty-year-old Bordeaux that will complement the meal nicely."

"I trust you implicitly, Tyers, and not only because our mutual employer does," said Sutton, becoming more Mycroft Holmes with every breath he drew. "You have not led me wrong before."

Tyers bowed slightly, showing how much he, too, had been convinced by this incomplete transformation.

I permitted myself the luxury of watching Sutton a few minutes more, then retired to the study, and set about putting certain of Holmes' things in order before I began the odd task of prompting Sutton's memorization of lines as Sir Peter Teazle.

"May I have a word with you, Mister Guthrie?" asked Tyers a few minutes later as I made the final sorting of material prior to putting it away in the appropriate cases.

"Certainly," I said, putting one of the cases down on the trestle table where our employer occasionally sat to write out his voluminous notes.

"It is probably nothing, but I cannot get it out of my thoughts, and I decided to consult you." He half-closed the door and looked at the tall, gauze-curtained window as he went on. "When I stepped out this morning, into the service alley, I noticed that there was a new delivery man for the butcher. I thought nothing of it at first, but there was something about him that struck me. I would wager my last ha'penny the man's not English, though I cannot tell you why I think so. He was bringing meat to the two flats below as well as to this one, and he did his work handily enough, but—"

I heard this and waited for anything more he might have to say, for as a retired soldier as well as Holmes' longtime manservant, I knew that Tyers was well-versed in the subtleties of Holmes' work and not given to raising false alarms. When he did not continue, I said to him, "Well, Tyers. Where is the problem?"

"The delivery man was new," he said with greater emphasis, then added, "They have always notified us before when there is to be a new driver."

"Perhaps their usual driver is ill or injured suddenly, and this man is a substitute, brought to the job only this morning; they may have had no time to inform you of the change," I suggested, and wondered why I suddenly felt so exposed. My thoughts carried me back seven months to those terrifying days in Bavaria.

"It doesn't seem right," Tyers persisted. "It is bothersome that Mister Holmes should be starting a delicate mission."

"No," I agreed reluctantly. "It doesn't seem right. Yet it may be nothing more than an unfortunate coincidence, and we are only jumping at shadows." I tried my best to sound convinced of this, and failed miserably.

"That's true," said Tyers in as dismal a tone as I ever hope to hear.

"What should I do?" he asked me.

"You could step round to the butcher's yourself and discover who the delivery man is, if you think it worth the effort. You could address the fellow directly if he comes tomorrow, and discover why he is here. If you are deeply concerned, you could send word to the police and ask if there has been any crime involving butchers' delivery wagons: theft or other pilfering. I could send for Sid Hastings, and ask him what he knows of the fellow. Cab drivers know every delivery man in London." I did not intend to sound sarcastic, but I saw that my words were heard that way.

Tyers nodded. "You're probably right. I am making too much of this new delivery man. But I am left with a malaise where the fellow is concerned. Took me right back to my days in the Crimea and Ethiopia. Cairo, too."

Though I knew little of what actually transpired in Tyers' years of government soldiering, I had learned enough to realize they had often been harrowing, and had left their marks more upon his soul than his body; I knew it was folly to doubt these sensations of his, yet I was not fully convinced. "This is London. But I understand your apprehension. If Mister Holmes were not embarked on this new mission, you would not be so worried about the delivery man," I reminded him as gently as I could, hoping I would persuade us both that we had no occasion for alarm.

"I don't know," said Tyers, making the admission as if to a fondness for opium.

I was about to say something more when Edmund Sutton came into the study. Only it was no longer entirely Edmund Sutton, but Mycroft Holmes, who stood on the threshold, his hand on his watchfob, the other holding two sheaves of paper. "There you are, Guthrie. Can you spare me a minute, dear boy?"

"At your service, sir," I said. I could not keep from offering the man a slight bow as I would to Holmes himself, though, as always, when he first began to play Holmes, he laid the characterization on a little thick, so broad it would carry to a nonexistent balcony. By evening, when he made his visit across the street to Mister Holmes' club, his impersonation would be eerily flawless.

He glanced once at Tyers. "Is there some difficulty of which I should be apprised?"

"No, sir," said Tyers slowly as he retreated from the study.

He permitted Tyers to depart without any reluctance, but as soon as he was gone: "Guthrie? Is anything wrong?" he asked, striding to Holmes' chair and dropping into it. He waited for an answer, his head cocked as if listening for distant sounds as well as anything I had to offer.

"Some question about a new delivery man in the service alley," I said, doing my best to dismiss the matter. "If the fellow is still doing the work tomorrow, Tyers will inquire about him."

"Very good," said Sutton. He held out one of the sheaves of paper to me. "I will rely on your prudence."

"The script?" I said.

"A complete one for you, my sides for me," said Sutton. "I would appreciate it if you would read all the parts in the scenes I've marked. I am beginning to develop Sir Peter's reactions, and for that I must hear all the lines."

Sighing, I opened the script and saw that the play began with a Prologue about rumor and scandal, and then went into a scene between a Lady Sneerwell and someone called Snake. As this scene was not marked, I skipped over it and gave my attention to the next scene, which began with a speech by Sir Peter. "I believe you have the first speech in scene two, sir," I said.

"So Teazle does," said Sutton. His posture shifted in an eerie way, and he was no longer Mycroft Holmes. He began: *"When an old bachelor marries a young wife, what is he to expect? . . ."*

•

FROM THE PERSONAL JOURNAL OF PHILIP TYERS

My visit to the butcher's informed me that the usual delivery man met with an accident two nights ago and is currently being treated for a broken arm. According to the butcher himself he was pressed for time in finding a suitable replacement for his injured driver. The man now doing the delivery is the nephew of the usual delivery man, or so they inform me at the butcher's. While this may be so, I continue to feel a degree of uncertainty that will not leave me. It may be as G says, and

I am overly fashed because of M H's delicate position with the Japanese. I must devote time to observing the new delivery man for as long as he is in this part of London.

I stopped by Baker Street to leave word of M H's current arrangements, as was requested.

M H is still at the Swiss embassy with the Japanese while Sutton takes his place across the street at his club. Fortunately G is here until M H returns this evening. I cannot rid myself of the notion that this place is closely watched; habits of all those long years of active duty prompt my fears, though as yet I have not seen anyone I could directly accuse of such activity, which gives me to worry all the more: Either I am going mad or those watching are experienced and skillful. Neither possibility bodes well.

Chapter Two

BY TEA-TIME, three-thirty in Mycroft Holmes' flat, we had been through *School for Scandal* twice, and I was becoming heartily bored with the mannered text. The only diversion in the whole of the afternoon was the arrival of the messenger from the Admiralty promptly at twenty minutes after three. I handed over the case and Mycroft Holmes' instructions regarding it, and accepted a small file-box with two locks on it in its stead.

LADY TEAZLE: Lud, Sir Peter! would you have me be out of the fashion?

SIR PETER: The fashion, indeed! what had you to do with fashion before you married me?

LADY TEAZLE: For my part, I should think you would like to have your wife thought a woman of taste.

SIR PETER: Ay—there again—taste! Zounds! madame, you had no taste when you married me.

LADY TEAZLE: That's very true, indeed, Sir Peter! and, after having married you, I should never pretend to taste again, I allow. . . .

The first time I read this passage with Edmund Sutton, I found it amusing, but now the wit seemed flat, and I wondered at how Sutton was able to keep the sense of never having heard or spoken the words before so foremost in his thoughts. I was about to finish the line when I saw that Tyers was waiting in the study door; I broke off my reading and went to him.

"The butcher's delivery man was back not ten minutes since," he said, his habitual stoic calm lost to distress. "I would not have seen him had I not been on the back stairs with the seamstress' girl. She was bringing the new shirts for Mister Holmes." He cleared his throat. "I don't know what to say, or to think, sir."

"Are you certain it is the same man?" I could not keep myself from asking.

"There is nothing wrong with my eyes, sir," said Tyers. "And it was not my intention to keep watch for the man. I happened to be where I could observe him without risk."

"What was he doing?" I hoped there would be another, reasonable explanation for the man's presence in the service alley.

"He was smoking a pipe and talking to the dairy carter," Tyers answered, speaking with great care. "He had changed his hat but not his boots. He was not with his delivery wagon."

"It may be that he has driven for the dairy, or knows the man, or is seeking regular employment," I suggested.

"It is possible," said Tyers dubiously. "And it is possible that I am suffering a nerve storm. You are kind enough not to mention it to me, but I am aware that it may be the case."

It was difficult to keep a calm demeanor, given Tyers' anxiety. I pulled at my lower lip as I thought. "If you are right and we are truly under observation, it is essential we give no indication we are aware of what has transpired. We do not want the fellow alerted, for then he might become more suspicious still—"

"And it would not do to have our ruse with Mister Sutton discovered," said Tyers, in agreement. "I take your meaning, Mister Guthrie." He nodded once. "I will attend to the tea and serve it in the sitting room, as is customary."

"Very good," I said, and prepared to return to the study.

"Trouble, Guthrie?" Sutton asked as I entered the room, all signs of Sir Peter Teazle gone. He was once again all Mycroft Holmes. He had risen from his chair and was standing not far from the window. With care he selected a cigar and clipped the end before lighting it, exhaling the smoke with a look of pleasure.

"Best not stand too near the window, sir," I recommended, one hand going to the faint scar on my forehead, the souvenir of a bullet that had smashed through a window in Munich and cut me with the flying glass.

"Is there some reason I shouldn't?" he asked, taking another lungful of smoke.

"You cannot be sure you are not observed," I said, and thought my answer sounded absurd.

"You're too cautious, Guthrie," he said. "The purpose of having me here is to keep up the illusion that Mycroft Holmes is going about his life as he is known to do on all occasions. You will have to permit me to be caught sight of now and again if you wish the illusion to be upheld. And if we are to fulfill our second purpose."

Sutton himself would have winked; as Holmes he gave me a single, decisive nod.

It was uncanny how he could catch Holmes' accents and cadence of speech. I stepped nearer to the window, and allowed myself one quick glance out of it at the rooftop of the house immediately next to this one. It was two stories, one less than this building, and its roof was easily inspected from this vantage point. "I don't see anyone."

"No one there," said Sutton. "I checked already. And you needn't worry that I could not find the man if he were there. I am an actor, and I know when someone is watching me. It's my stock in trade." He left the place by the window and went back to his chair. "Do we remain here or go to the sitting room?" His lack of concern seemed so reckless to me that I could not respond at once.

"Let's go to the sitting room." It was what Holmes and I did at this time almost every day. I watched Sutton stub out his cigar, and allowed him to precede me, as I would have done for our employer.

As we went down the corridor, I found myself listening for unfamiliar noises. Surely the clatter from Pall Mall was more intrusive than it was most afternoons? I imagined I heard more hoofbeats and shouts from below than were usual at this time of day. And the rattle in the service alley behind us was more constant than it ordinarily was? I made myself concentrate on the routine we were supposed to maintain.

The sitting room was the lightest room in the flat, a fine room with tall windows on two sides where Holmes did much of his work, took his meals at a large oak table, and raised a number of plants known for their poisonous properties. It was often more cluttered than it was now, but that would change once Holmes returned home.

"I will plan to go across the road at the usual hour," said Sutton as he sat down at the table. "I would appreciate it if you would watch for anything . . . untoward. I cannot appear to take note of the street, for Holmes never does."

"Certainly," I assured him; I had planned to do so in any case.

"Very good," he approved, and looked up as Tyers came in. "Excellent. Coffee disguised as tea. I thank you for this."

Tyers set his tray down and indicated the pitcher of hot milk. "Use a serviette on the handle when you pour." He had masked his apprehension with the stoic manner expected of a good manservant.

"That I will," said Sutton. He rubbed his hands together as he looked over the tea we had been prepared. There was a basket of scones and hot-cross buns, a jar of fruit compote, another of ginger marmalade, a pot of clotted cream, Scottish shortbread for me, and a small plate of short, savory, broiled sausages. "This is splendid. A proper afternoon tea. One of the real pleasures of this work."

"What would you be doing at this time if you were not here?" I asked, having scant knowledge of how Sutton lived when he was not serving as Holmes' double.

"Oh, we would be ending rehearsal about now, if I were working in a new play. Or I would be resting in preparation for the night's performance, if the play had opened already. In either case I would not have so fine a tea, or the time to enjoy it." He pointed to the sausages. "Even these are welcome. Though I should like to know how Holmes picked up a taste for them."

I did not share Holmes' love of the sausages, but otherwise the tea was a welcome light repast. I had for some time been aware that Sutton was not fond of the sausages, either, but he would eat them, for that is what Mycroft Holmes did, and as long as he was in the role, he would play it as required. I watched as he poured his coffee into a cup and added the hot milk, much as Holmes himself would pour tea and add milk to it.

"It is the little things that are most tricksy," said Sutton as he prepared to take his first sip of coffee. He spoke as if we had been in the middle of a conversation, and were now resuming our discussion. "Those who try to assume another identity often overlook the very things that are most important to convincing others."

"Ah?" I said, putting my cup aside and reaching for a scone. My serviette was spread on my knee and I had taken a small plate from the tray.

"Yes. For example, you would be the very devil to impersonate, Guthrie." He winked very deliberately.

"You mean because my eyes are different colors?" I asked; my right eye is green and my left blue.

"Precisely. One could cover one of the eyes, of course, but that would occasion an explanation for anyone who knew you, which could be more damaging than anything anticipated, because it would draw attention to something distinctive. And, of course, you are left-handed." He sipped his coffee, made a face and set it down again. "Too hot."

"Why is the left-handedness a problem?" I was becoming more curious as I listened.

"You are not aware of how very much you do with your left hand. Those who are right-handed do as much with their right hands, and so automatically. You catch items thrown to you with your left hand when possible, you pick up pencils and spoons and serviettes with your left hand. You open doors with your left hand. You pet dogs with your left hand. Anyone trying to enact you would have to remember to do all those things, constantly, or give himself away completely. Or put your left arm in a sling, but that, too, would occasion comment. You are a challenge."

"What about Holmes is most challenging?" I poured tea for myself from the water jug where Tyers had put it.

Sutton considered his answer carefully. "His constant attitude of thought," he said at last. "Yes. That is by far the most demanding aspect of his character. His intellectual alertness is constant, and not easily conveyed." He put his hands to his forehead as Holmes often did when in pursuit of an idea. "You see? This is not enough. Any fool can ape the gesture. It must be the energy in the eyes. Hardest for me to remember is to keep the voice low, not projected as I have been trained to do, though the accent is simplicity itself, and that is where I must be most vigilant, so that I do not lapse into my old habits, and speak to be heard in the back row."

I watched him with curiosity mingled with respect. When I had first come to work for Mycroft Holmes, I had thought little of actors; I had no understanding of the range of skills the work required. Since knowing Edmund Sutton, my attitude toward the profession and its adherents had changed; I now regard playing a role successfully as an artistic accomplishment equal to the creation of a good painting, and as meticulous in its execution. My own few experiences of attempting to convince others I was someone else had proven vastly more difficult than I had thought they would be, and more dangerous.

Tyers returned carrying the *Times.* "The delivery man has not yet departed. And I think he has company with him." He did not seem upset to tell us this, but there was something that revealed his apprehension. Had I not observed him over the last several months, I would have detected nothing of his state of mind. "I believe they intend to remain here for some while."

"You mean until Holmes returns and I depart?" Said Sutton without any sign of concern. "Let them watch. They will learn nothing."

I was not so sanguine. "There was the matter of the bomb," I reminded him.

"Just my thought," said Tyers. "As we do not know with

whom we are dealing, it would be wisest to err on the side of caution."

"What do you mean to say?" Sutton asked. "Do you think they intend to do more than observe?"

"I think we must consider the possibility," said Tyers. "I fear they may mean mischief."

I recalled the man in the theatrical uniform broken over the wooden fence and I could not wholly suppress a shudder. "There are also residents on the two floors below us," I pointed out, for I was aware there might be other targets of scrutiny.

"A retired High Court judge and a younger son of a Midlands Earl occupy the flats," Tyers said, as if they could be dismissed. "Sir Edgar gambles, they say, but no one would dare to come to his home for such a reason, not when he might reasonably approach the Earl, or could find Sir Edgar at his club. I can think of no reason he should be followed in this clandestine way. His habits are known and his company is established." He shrugged a little. "I have not heard that he is in debt."

"And as you know his servants, you would hear if he were," said Sutton cannily.

"Just so," Tyers agreed.

I thought that Sir Edgar was not the only man of fixed habits in the building: Mycroft Holmes had striven for years to maintain the illusion of his outwardly circumscribed life. "The judge," I pointed out, "might have enemies from his days on the Queen's Bench. He sat on some celebrated cases, as I recall. Someone might still desire retribution. It is possible that the men in the wagon are watching him."

"It is unlikely," said Tyers flatly.

Sutton looked distressed. "Guthrie, you are implying that someone may suspect that Mycroft Holmes is not, in fact, in his flat, and that a ruse is being practiced? You are worried because of what might happen if our deception is discovered? You believe they are watching this flat to determine if I am Holmes or not?" Sutton spoke up, not sounding the least troubled. He chuckled once, his face briefly his own, and his voice raised enough to carry through the room. "What a rare tribute. I have convinced them well enough that they do not know beyond question if Holmes is here or not." He rubbed his hands in ill-disguised glee.

"Which is precisely what you are supposed to do," I reminded him rather more stringently than I had intended. "Convince them beyond question."

"Yes it is. And I hoped I had done a tolerable job of it. But until now, I was not wholly convinced of my success." His pride was so honest and oddly naive that I could not think him immodest.

"You go to the Diogenes Club frequently. Surely you have realized your success before now?" I was startled by the thought that this young man would doubt himself.

Sutton cocked his head self-deprecatingly. "Hardly a test. Holmes is such a fixture there, and his habits so regular that I suspect you, Guthrie, could probably walk a dancing bear across Pall Mall at the correct hour, and the club members would recognize it as Mycroft Holmes because he is the one they expect to see." He made a sweeping gesture with his arm, so wholly unlike the man he played that it jarred my senses. "So I will have to leave by the front today, and in some guise other than my usual." He frowned, though it was apparent he was enjoying himself. "Unless we can mislead them in some way, make them think they are mistaken."

"How?" I asked, worrying what scheme Sutton—an actor fond of dramatics—would present to Tyers and me.

"Well, if we could convince them they are in error, or if we could frighten them sufficiently that they are not likely to continue their observations so brazenly." He was on the edge of an idea, and he struggled to put it into words.

"I think I take your drift," said Tyers. "You want to confuse them, make them distrust what they see."

"Yes!" Sutton exclaimed. "That is precisely it. I want to cause them such consternation that no matter what they see, they will not trust themselves to know what it means." He beamed at Tyers and then at me.

"But how might we do it?" I asked, troubled by the enthusiasm Sutton was showing.

Sutton's blue eyes grew brighter. "I think we must lead them astray. Very much astray." He grinned. "And we must scare them."

I lowered my eyes to the remnants of our tea. "What did you have in mind?"

"Well, I will need a costume of sorts. Something foreign and rather feminine," he said, improvising with relish. "Something not outrageous, but enough to hold their attention." He looked directly at Tyers. "On the rack—there is a Chinese robe. It is a deep golden color, like honey."

"I know the one," said Tyers at once. "The banker's coat." He was about to go off to the kitchen and the room behind it where a large number of disguises hung to retrieve the garment in question.

"Yes. That and the long black wig—the one you used in Cairo. I should be able to put something together with those that will provide a distraction." Sutton rose at once. "And we will work out another deception for tomorrow, if they are not routed today."

"Might it not be prudent to inform Holmes of what we intend to do?" I interjected, not as confident as Sutton of bringing this off. "These men may be very deadly of purpose."

"All the more reason to tend to them ourselves," said Sutton. "He has so much demanding his attention, he need not be bothered with this. We can do this ourselves." There was an air of self-satisfaction about him, and I was aware that he wanted to do something for Mycroft Holmes beyond his regular impersonation. I did not want to dash his hopes, so I quashed my inner doubts and said, "Tell me what you want me to do."

Sutton began to pace, his manner animated. "I will make it appear that Holmes had a possible assignation, one that has just been brought to an end. I will make an exit that will demand their whole attention. While I carry on with you, Guthrie, Tyers can go to observe the men, and discern their purpose. If they think they may have to deal with an hysterical woman, they will reveal themselves." He grinned. "Now, about tomorrow. Tyers, if you can find some opportunities to complain to the other domestics in the building that there are necessary repairs that must be made. Let them know you will have a carpenter the first thing in the morning. My arrival in overalls with tools will not attract anything more than resignation. If the watchers are still here, they will not question what they see."

I realized the wisdom of this part of his plan at once. "Very good. And if there is an apparent disruption in some of Holmes' established habits, they are explained by the presence of the carpenter. He would not be expected to remain here while the hammering and sawing are going on."

"I'll have to generate a bit of noise, to make our duplicity convincing." He was warming to the scenario. "I don't know how much we will disturb the judge, immediately below. I would not like to have him criticize our efforts."

"He will not," said Tyers with purpose. "I'll have a word with his housekeeper tonight, as a courtesy. Then we'll be all right and tight."

"What repairs are being done? Ought we not to agree on them?" I asked, not wanting to be too much caught up in this escapade without sufficient planning.

Sutton did not give me an answer at once but directed his attention to Holmes' manservant. "Tyers, bring me the banker's robe and the wig. I will prepare. My case is—"

"I know where it is," said Tyers, and turned to get the items. Then he spoke directly to me. "There are warped doorframes and doors that need to be rehung. The pocket doors between the parlor and sitting room do not close properly. Holmes remarked upon it last week."

"Can anything truly be done with them?" I asked, knowing that some work must take place if the watchers were to be convinced.

"I've built more than my share of sets and set props. I am a reasonably capable carpenter when I need to be," said Sutton with understandable pride. "I can certainly manage the doors, if it comes to that. And I can build, stain, and varnish everything to match." He smiled with great good humor. "You are prone to underestimate me, the both of you. I wish you would not do that."

I realized his accusation was deserved. "I apologize. You are right, and I have been unfair to you, Sutton."

"Don't poker up, Guthrie," Sutton chided me, sounding amazingly like Mycroft Holmes. "Let us get through today and make ready for tomorrow. I will, of course, bring the wood, as part of my character. I will plan to continue the diversion for three days at least, so Mister Holmes will have more flexibility of time." He went to change the angle of the shutters on the windows, bringing the light from above and effectively cutting off any view from below. "I will now prepare for a scene Sardou would envy." He bowed to Tyers as he returned with the banker's coat and the wig in one hand and Sutton's makeup case in the other. Pushing the last of the dishes away, he took off his jacket, flung away his tie, opened his collar, and sat down again, the makeup case on the chair next to him. He brought out a large mirror and a tin of cleansing cream and set to work.

I watched him as he began yet another transformation, softening his features to an exotic prettiness and changing the line of his brow to an Asiatic slant. In twenty minutes he rose and changed to the banker's coat; his fair hair was now emphatically out of place. He remedied this with the wig, which he had shaped to a kind of disheveled coiffeur. Aside from his height and his light-colored eyes, he might have been an Anglo-Chinese female past her youth but not yet in the grip of age.

"Now what?" I asked as he turned to me, his demeanor entirely changed from what it had been.

"Now you and I will have a dispute on the backstairs while Tyers makes the most of this distraction to determine who is watching this flat, and, if possible, why." He could not keep the amusement from his voice. "You, Guthrie, will call me Missus . . . oh, Swindon. It sounds respectable enough. You will say that Mister Holmes has said I am not to be admitted to the flat again. Offer me money to leave England. Make the whole encounter cold and crass on your part and leave the rest to me." He winked. "You know what to do, Tyers. I won't tell you your business."

Sutton said that so comfortably that I wondered how much he knew of the manservant's history. I had been curious about it for some while but had not been able to learn more than smatterings. Clearly Sutton had more knowledge of the man than I did. "Are we ready?" I asked as I got to my feet. Now that we were embarked on our project I put my misgivings aside. "I hope I will carry my part to your satisfaction, Sutton."

"I believe you will, Guthrie," said Sutton, and then his voice shifted up half an octave and he began to weep as we went into the corridor and along it to the rear of the flat. When we arrived there, Sutton redoubled his weeping and flung the door open, turning back to look at me. "I never thought he could use me so!" he exclaimed amid his tears.

I was vaguely aware that Tyers had gone out the front of the flat; Sutton expected me to respond, so I said, "You know what you must do, Missus Swindon."

"He wants me to do away with myself," he proclaimed dramatically. "I will not let him have the satisfaction. Not after his shabby way with me!"

"You have been offered a generous settlement, Madame. Do yourself a favor and accept it graciously." I noticed Sutton's eyes flashing encouragement, so I went on harshly. "I can do nothing more for you."

"And Mister Holmes will not," said Sutton with awesome finality. "Well, you may be sure I will not permit him to—" The tears became a tempest.

"Madame!" I cried, beginning to be caught up in our little *drama extempore.* I moved as if to close the door.

"No!" Sutton held his head up in defiance, and his voice, unnervingly feminine, was a clarion call. "I am not trash to be tossed into the dustbin."

"Missus Swindon, please. You will embarrass yourself." I was astonished at how very condemning I could sound, how stuffy and condescending.

"I don't care. If Mycroft Holmes is embarrassed, it means nothing to me." Sutton retreated toward the backstairs, taking care not to look down into the service yard below. "I hope the whole world learns of his perfidy."

"Madame!" I thought I saw a flash of movement in the service yard, but kept from looking toward it. "Do not make it necessary for me to summon the authorities."

"Have them in," Sutton countered at once. "Have the whole of London here!"

I was flummoxed by this. "You must go," I said coldly, unable to think of anything more to say.

"You do not know who you are dealing with. I will not let him trifle with me," Sutton insisted passionately.

"There is nothing I can do for you, Missus Swindon," I reiterated, ready to slam the door.

Sutton grabbed hold of my wrist. "You must listen to me, Mister Guthrie. You must. I have given everything to Mister Holmes. He is more than life to me. Do not let him end it like this. It will hurt him, I know it will, as much as it hurts me." The pathos of this declaration struck me: If Sutton had not been acting, I would surely have been moved to compassion.

"Tell me you will intercede for me, Mister Guthrie," Sutton pleaded. "I would thank you every day of my life if you will do this."

"Missus Swindon—" I began.

"Please, Mister Guthrie," he begged. "Tell me you will talk to him. Let him know that I can still forgive him if he will have me back."

I strove to break his grip but could not. "Please leave, Missus Swindon," I said.

He broke his hold abruptly and flung himself away from me, starting toward the stairs in a distraught manner, weeping loudly and occasionally voicing expostulations and profanities that were the more distressing for seeming to come from an attractive, half-Chinese woman.

As I watched Sutton's descent, I saw one of the men in the wagon stick his head out of the back, openly gawking at Sutton. I also noticed that Tyers was standing, very unobtrusively, less than five feet from the wagon. I was reluctant to retreat into the flat, although I supposed it was what was expected of me. Folding my arms as if to bar Sutton's return, I kept my place and watched as he finally reached the service yard, behaving as if he were trying to summon up a few scraps of dignity. Sutton was making his way toward the alley to the street when the man on the driving box caught sight of Tyers, and became distressed.

"You!" the driver shouted, reaching for his whip with the seeming purpose of driving Tyers off by main force.

Tyers moved handily out of the way; the lash of the whip missed him by a good yard and more. It swung around and struck the lead horse on the neck.

The horse whinnied and lurched into a canter, dragging his teammate and the wagon with him, directly at Sutton, who had just entered the alley.

I watched, aghast, as it appeared Sutton must be injured by the runaway wagon.

The wagon careened into the alley, the horses settling into a run in earnest. Sutton was now aware of his danger and looking frantically about for a place to hide. Belatedly I shouted and began to run in the direction of the alley—although what I might do in the event, I could not think. I reached the alley just as I was certain the tragedy must occur.

Then the horses reared, stopping abruptly as a figure appeared at the head of the alley, doing something to arrest the team in mid-plunge. The driver managed to bring his team under control, swearing vituperatively as he did.

Sutton, who had fallen to the ground and now lay huddled in a ball, his arms over his head, his knees drawn up to his chest, his wig askew, slowly recovered, looking bemused to find himself still alive. I came running up just as the driver gave his horses the office and they went out of the alley at a more sedate pace.

Mycroft Holmes stood at the entrance to the alley, his great-coat flapping about him, his expression one of exasperation. "Well," he said as we came up to him, Tyers looking sheepish, Sutton in disarray, and I beginning to experience the pangs of chagrin. "What brought this on?"

Sutton adjusted his wig. "We wanted to find out who was spying on the flat."

"And did you?" Holmes inquired calmly.

"No, sir, we did not," said Tyers in an unruffled way. "Had their horses not bolted, we would have done." A glance passed between him and Holmes that I could not fathom, but it was apparent both men understood his meaning.

"In fact," I said, wanting to make a clean breast of our errors, "we have alerted them to our intentions, which was most unwise."

"I am glad you recognize it," said Mycroft Holmes, a good deal less severely than I thought we deserved. "I am also glad that nothing beyond embarrassment has befallen you." He signaled to Sutton. "You will have to scramble if you are to get out of that rig and across the street by four-fourty-five."

It was less of a reprimand than Sutton anticipated. "Yes. You're right."

"Then get to it, man," he said, adding, "Don't forget to weep and cast more aspersions on my reputation as you go. The neighbors will want to see the end of the act."

Sutton lowered his head, raised his voice half an octave and said, "Thank you, thank you. I knew you could not be so unkind to me."

"Go with him, Tyers, and help him. Guthrie and I will follow directly." Holmes motioned them off and then pulled me aside. "Was this your idea, dear boy?"

"I think we were mutually responsible," I said. "We had a better result in mind."

"No doubt," Holmes agreed, propelling me toward the backstairs. "It may surprise you to know that I do not disapprove of the enterprise you've shown, though the results were not what I would have liked." He made a point of going slowly up the stairs. "I am troubled that you would let it all get out of hand. That isn't like you."

"We did not know the horses would bolt. How could we?" I asked, stung by this unjust accusation.

"You could not, of course," said Holmes as we began to

climb. "The trouble is, as you have already said, that the watchers are now on the alert, and they will be more cautious next time."

"I know," I confessed, shocked that I should have bungled our task so badly.

"The trouble is," said Mycroft Holmes as we reached the first landing, "that we do not know with whom we are dealing, or why. If I had some sense of that, I might be better able to deal with the situation." He was half-way up the next flight when he turned back to me. "If anything should have happened to any of you, I would hold myself accountable."

"Sir—" I exclaimed, trying to find the words that would exonerate him. "It is, in fact, our doing. We did this without consulting you. It is our—"

"Guthrie," Mycroft Holmes interrupted, "you and Tyers and Sutton are in my employ. Had you not been, you would have had no reason to undertake this scheme of yours." He laid his hand on my shoulder. "Your intentions were commendable. But just suppose, Guthrie, that those men are not agents of the Japanese, or the Germans, or the Bulgarians, but part of the Brotherhood. You learned enough about them to know it would be folly to warn them of our intentions. Did you not?"

I had a brief, intense recollection of the sight of a man murdered in one of their loathsome rituals, and I nodded. "But surely—"

"They are still very much with us. And what mischief they might want to make in our dealings with the Japanese or the Bulgarians, I dare not hazard to guess." He resumed climbing. "Until we know what the game is, Guthrie, we had best be very careful of how we play."

I nodded in acknowledgment and went after him. I was trying to think of something to add when he turned around again, saying with such a degree of resignation that I gave him my full attention, "I am sorry I must attend this banquet tonight. If we had more time, I think we might be able to work out a better plan regarding these watchers."

"But the Japanese would not understand," I said, recalling all I had learned about their emphasis on protocol. "Perhaps later."

"I hope. But this is becoming such a public affair, it might not be possible," he said, and reached the landing at the rear of his flat.

FROM THE PERSONAL JOURNAL OF PHILIP TYERS

A packet was delivered at half-eight this evening, from Yvgeny Tschersky. I have put it in M H's study against his return this evening.

I have prepared a note to hand Sid Hastings when he brings M H back tonight. I hope he will have some answers for us in regard to the activities of the butcher's delivery van. After our debacle this afternoon, progress is wanted on that front. If anyone can gain us the intelligence we need, it is Hastings.

A formal case of documents has been delivered here to M H. In a silk-covered chest with the imperial device of Japan—it is, I believe, called a mon—worked into the silk. It is a splendid piece of work. The instructions are that it is only to be opened by M H himself, which just at present is a problem, for Sutton is filling in the role until the banquet concludes, and it is not fitting that he should open the package. So if those watching us are agents of the Japanese, this apparent lack of regard for their delivery may work against us. But as M H is dining with members of the Japanese embassy, I cannot suppose this is very likely. However, the Japanese are more keenly aware of embarrassments than most, which could prove awkward.

Meanwhile I continue my preparations for tomorrow.

The judge's housekeeper has been very helpful. After our little drama this afternoon, I had a few words with her, and as a result she and the judge's manservant will inform Sir Charles that there will be noise in this flat tomorrow, and they will not complain to me, now that

I have assured them that the poor, distracted Missus Swindon will not be returning here. I am relieved that there will be no inquiry regarding M H's activities, for the whole purpose of Sutton being here is to maintain the illusion that M H does not leave his flat but for specific hours and specific destinations. So far this deception has been successful. I must hope it will continue to be.

Chapter Three

MYCROFT HOLMES RETURNED from the banquet at the Swiss embassy at eleven-seventeen that night. He looked tired and exasperated as he shrugged out of his cloak and strode into the study, away from the front of the flat where Edmund Sutton sat in a chair, reading Sir Peter Teazle's lines over again.

"That Ambassador Tochigi will be the death of me, metaphorically if not literally," Holmes exclaimed as he lit a cigar. "I don't know when I have encountered anyone quite so stubborn.

Oh, he is not blatant in his obduracy. Very fastidious about it, he is, as the Japanese always are, but he will not budge. He is determined to have the number of Japanese permitted to attend the Navy College at Dartmouth increased to two hundred, which is patently absurd. The Admiralty is not willing to have so many, for the Japanese would then constitute half the attendees. Nor, I expect, do they want so great a number of their young titled gentlemen away from Japan at the same time and in the same place, be it England or Rio de Janeiro. I have yet to determine why they are seeking so much leeway. When I meet privately with him it will be easier, I hope."

I stood aside so that Tyers could present Holmes with a snifter of four-star brandy. "It sounds difficult."

"There is a package from Tschersky," said Tyers as he made his offering. "And one from the Japanese."

"Tschersky is being remarkably prompt," said Holmes. "What have the Japanese sent now?" he asked of the air before he tossed off his brandy. "Guthrie, I could have used you at my side this evening. No matter. Tomorrow I am arranging for you to accompany me. The Admiralty have already said that James Dewar may observe our negotiations; they cannot reasonably object to you. And given that Tochigi is going to have his secretaries with him, he can hardly protest if I bring mine. It is becoming necessary to have another pair of hands. Eyes, as well, and ears. In the morning, I may send you off to the Admiralty or some such thing." He put the snifter down. "You will, of course, go to the Swiss embassy."

"Actually," I said, taking advantage of the opening he had afforded me, "we have come up with a scheme to deal with that."

"Oh?" Holmes swung around to look at me. "What is it?"

"It is a notion of Sutton's, and it confirms what Tyers already suspects," I said, not wanting to have it said I claimed credit where I was not entitled to any. "It seems that someone may be watching the flat, and Sutton was concerned about concealing his arrival." Quickly I outlined the plan about the carpenter and the doors. "If Sir Charles does not object, I think it would answer handsomely."

"Without doubt," said Holmes. "Quite an excellent idea." He cleared his throat. "We will be able to remain at the Swiss embassy as long as is necessary tomorrow. My absence, and yours, during the day will not be thought remarkable. Edmund can keep my habitual time at the club and anyone determined to watch me—if that is truly what is happening—will be satisfied as to my actions." He took a turn about the study, and ended by coming face to face with Edmund Sutton, who had come in from the sitting room, and was now standing just inside the doorway. He put his snifter aside and extended his hand. "I congratulate you, my dear Edmund, for coming up with so suitable a diversion for us tomorrow. It is so utterly mundane that it should provide perfect deceit."

Sutton's face colored in a most un-Holmes-like manner as he returned the grip. "Pleased to be of service, sir."

"More than service, if you have saved us from discovery." He tapped the ash from his cigar. "No one will wonder that I should be away during necessary repairs. I will ask the Admiralty to send their coach for me, to make it the more convincing that I am about my regular business."

"Would you not simply retire to your club?" I said, indicating the direction of Pall Mall and his club.

"That would occasion remark that none of us want," said Holmes.

"And it would cause the members to make note of the change in habit, and that would make my work far more difficult." Sutton cleared his throat. "Not that I want to tell you your business, Mister Holmes."

"It isn't my business that would be at risk," Holmes pointed out gently. "It's yours."

Sutton nodded his agreement.

Tyers, who had left the room to put down the tray, now returned bearing the large silk-covered case that had been delivered earlier in the evening. He held it out to Holmes. "The instructions are, sir, that only you are to open it." He paused. "If you would rather, I will open it."

Holmes gave a single crack of mirthless laughter. "You mean the Khedive's . . . em . . . present in Cairo?" He looked at the case and shook his head slowly. "No, I doubt it. Scorpions do not seem the right style for the Japanese. That design is the Imperial *Mon,* the *Kiku,* or the chrysanthemum blossom. It would not be honorable for Ambassador Tochigi to do anything so underhanded in the name of his Emperor. In fact, it would bring him total disgrace." He reached out and, using his penknife, pried open the case, lifting the lid with great care.

A large sheet of paper with the mon of Count Tochigi pressed into it lay atop a length of the most exquisite brocade I had ever seen. I heard Sutton give a soft exclamation of admiration.

Only Mycroft Holmes was unimpressed. He swore comprehensively as he lifted the sash—for now that Holmes held it I saw that was what it was—from the case. "I wanted to avoid this," he declared as he looked at the length of shimmering silk. "The ivy is Tochigi's mon," he explained, indicating the design worked in the fabric. "If I refuse his invitation, I insult him personally, and cause him to lose face."

"What are you refusing?" I asked, regarding the sash with some surprise that such a thing should evoke so odd a response from my employer.

He sighed. "The Japanese are to be honored by the Swiss in two nights. There will be a full diplomatic reception. Everyone will be there—French, Italians, Germans, Austrians, Hungarians, Russians, Greeks, the lot of them. Black tie, for Ambassador Tochigi and Prince Jiro, who is currently at Dartmouth."

"It still strikes me as odd, sir," I remarked as I considered what I had heard, "that the Japanese should be so sponsored by the Swiss."

"Ah," said Holmes with a singular smile. "But the Swiss, my dear boy, have no navy, and any arrangements we make with the Japanese cannot possibly encroach on their interests. At the same time, it puts England and Japan in their debt, which serves their purposes very well." He put the sash back in the case and took out the paper. "My invitation. With the added note," he said as he read the neat addendum in French, "that my attendance is to be unofficial; I need not make a formal appearance at the reception line. My name will not appear on the guest list." He tapped the paper reflectively. "Well, that's something. Hisoka Tochigi has not taken complete leave of his good sense. It is something to be grateful to the ambassador for. He has certainly lived up to his personal name. Hisoka means 'reserved' or 'self-contained,' I have been told. Now if only the Admiralty and the Prime Minister will show the same good sense."

Sutton was staring at the card. "What does that say?" He pointed to the Japanese writing that went along the side of the sheet.

"I don't know," Holmes confessed as if admitting to a terrible fault. "I suspect it is a Japanese version of what is written in French on the back. He apologizes that the paper is white and not red, but as the invitation is unofficial, red would not be appropriate." He sighed. "More work for you, Edmund."

"How is that?" Sutton inquired, moving to look Holmes directly in the face. Every sinew of his tall frame expressed curiosity.

It was unnerving to see the two of them standing together this way. With Holmes beside him, the makeup on Sutton's face, which until then had been fully convincing, now appeared to be nothing more than obvious scratchings. It was as if Holmes stood before a faulty mirror in which his reflection was subtly distorted.

"More work because I will need you to continue your . . . charade until the negotiations are concluded, including on the night of the reception, as I will not attend it officially. The routine for you will remain the same. You will have to make my usual appearance across the street, and maintain the fiction that I am at my duties here." He glanced at Tyers. "The driver?"

"He gave up watching about three hours ago, or was replaced by someone I do not yet recognize," Tyers reported. "I will continue to watch."

"Not too obviously," Holmes warned him. "I take it we are talking about the fellow with the German buttons on his coat and the Polish boots. If he wishes to go undetected, he must choose less conspicuous clothes." He accepted Tyers' nod without comment. "It is more important to know whom they represent than to catch them in the act. Once apprehended, their colleagues will be on the alert, and that might not suit my purposes at all." He touched the tips of his fingers together. "If there is a way to follow these watchers, try to do it."

"Certainly," said Tyers. "I have a few tricks left in my repertoire."

Holmes reached for a cigar, preparing to trim the end. "Well and good. Do not, however, put yourself at risk. It is bad enough that we should be subject to this surveillance. It would be far worse if anything should happen to you. Any of you," he added with a gesture as he brought his cigar to his mouth.

I felt a degree of both apprehension and pride—apprehension in that I supposed we were venturing once more into danger; pride in that the trust Mycroft Holmes reposed in the three of us was a compliment of the highest order. "Do you think there is a connection between the Japanese and the fact that you may be being watched?"

"It would be the circumspect thing to do, for the two things are otherwise a coincidence, and you know my lack of faith in coincidences. However, I admit I can discern no commonality between the two factors. That does not mean one does not exist, only that it is not yet known." He smiled as he rocked back on his heels and lit his cigar. "Whoever is watching, and to what purpose, we must, I am convinced, be far more cautious than we often are, and at the same time we must avoid the appearance of increased caution, so that our carelessly dressed spy will not be put on his guard."

"I can contrive to be seen more easily," Sutton offered. "Going to and from your club, for instance."

"No," said Holmes decisively. "That might occasion just the notice we do not want. Continue as you have before." He lowered his eyes and fingered his watchfob. "I wish I knew why we were being watched, for then I would have a fairly good notion of who is doing it."

"Not the other way around?" I asked, for it seemed to me that this would be the more direct approach to the problem.

"Not in this instance, no," replied Holmes. "In this instance the why comes first." He cocked his head in Sutton's direction. "Do you still carry your pistol?"

Again Sutton colored slightly. "Yes. I take your warning very much to heart." He indicated his pockets. "Not while playing you, of course."

Holmes had more of the rum-flavored smoke. "A pity, but it is the wiser course. See that you keep it by you."

"Good gracious, sir," I exclaimed before I could moderate my tone, "do you expect some attempt at violence?"

"It is possible." He gave Sutton a long, thoughtful stare. "I do not want any harm to come to you, Edmund. If you find yourself exposed to danger, I will not expect you to continue with your impersonation of me."

Now the color was very high in Sutton's face, making his makeup appear more than ever like the painted mask it was. "If you think that I would turn from a fight, sir, you are badly mistaken—"

"You might not," agreed Holmes with deceptive affability. "But I would." He had recourse to his cigar again. "Tyers, I want you to be at pains to guard Sutton without being obvious about it."

"I will," said Tyers, his tone revealing that he had already done so and was planning to continue, whatever the circumstances.

"Good," Holmes approved, and indicated the wainscoted corridor leading to the rear of the flat. "In what guise do you leave tonight?" he asked Sutton, regarding him with concern.

"I supposed I might leave by the front carrying a notary's case," said Sutton. "In case anyone is watching the back. I will return by nine in the morning with my carpenter's tools. I have the right gear. You need not worry that I will be recognized."

"That did not even occur to me," said Holmes, and waved Sutton toward the closet near the back of the house where two racks of clothes provided Sutton and his employer with a wide variety of garments. "Guthrie," he added softly as Tyers escorted Sutton out of the study, "I have need of a little more of your time."

"Certainly, sir," I said at once, recognizing the urgency in his request. That undercurrent of hazard that had marked this venture from the beginning became stronger.

"I must rely on your absolute discretion. Is that understood?" He looked at me piercingly. "No word, no hint of what I tell you must escape your lips, now or ever."

Whatever he had to impart, it was most assuredly grave. I took a swift look over my shoulder, and, satisfied that Tyers and Sutton were beyond hearing, I said, "You may depend upon me, sir."

"I know that, Guthrie," said Holmes with a faint smile. "It comforts me more than I deserve." He reached out and knocked the last of the ash from his cigar. "This must go no further: I have it on unimpeachable authority that Prince Jiro has become enamored of an Englishwoman." He shook his head once.

"Dear Lord," I said, keeping my voice low with an effort. "Do you know who it is?"

"No, I do not." He frowned, his profound grey eyes now like stone. "But I will."

"What a terrible scandal there would be," I said, thinking of the public outcry against such a match.

"No one thinks so more than Ambassador Tochigi." He studied his cigar as he stubbed it out. "He has instructions from his Emperor that the liaison is to be ended, no matter what the cost, with total discretion. If one word of this reaches the public, it would end any hope we have of achieving an understanding with the Japanese for the next decade at least."

I could not keep myself from agreeing. Few of the noble houses of England or Europe would look on an alliance with a Japanese—Prince or not—with anything less than dismay. "How long has—"

"—the affaire been going on?" Holmes finished for me. "I have no idea. Tochigi thinks it may be several months." He let the significance of that sink in. "It is not a matter of entertainment for either party, or so Ambassador Tochigi fears. Its very existence is an affront to him, and he wishes to erase the blot on his escutcheon before the Prince returns home. To accomplish this, he intends to hold the resolution of the relationship over the government's head. No agreement will be reached with the Japanese until the question of the Prince and his . . . *bien amie* is resolved. By which, of course, he means ended without a trace of scandal."

"Then that's why there has been a request for so many places at Dartmouth for Japanese." I saw the tactics fairly well. "You would think, though, that given what has happened with Prince Jiro, they would not want any of their young men in this country."

"That would surely put the yellow press on the scent, along with those whose business it is to watch from the shadows," said Holmes. "Ambassador Tochigi is more clever than that. By demanding places for more young Japanese cadets, it protects them from the suspicion that there are doubts about the propriety of conduct—" He stopped as Sutton came back into the corridor. "Very good," he approved.

"Not for daylight, and certainly not up close," said Sutton. "But well enough for tonight. It will get me home. Luckily the arrival of your cab was late enough that it will be supposed that it brought me and I am now, a short while later, departing." He bowed. In his dark frock coat and faintly striped trousers, he had some of the look Holmes had coming out of the cab. "I will use the old cloak, with the worn lining. That should be sufficient to conceal the difference in clothing. And I will carry a hat." He touched his face. "I will remove the paint once I reach home."

"Remember not to go there directly," Holmes said to him. "In case you are followed."

Sutton shrugged. "I will tell Hastings to take me to the address we agreed upon. And then I will make my way to the next street and pick up Hastings again for the rest of the way home." He laughed, and made a sweeping gesture that was almost a bow. I could see he enjoyed the deceptions.

"Very good," said Holmes, and offered the actor his hand. "Thank you for all you are doing for me. Surely we are not paying you enough to compensate for the risks you are undertaking."

"It's not the money, sir," said Sutton with unexpected modesty. "I want to do my bit, you know, and I'm hardly suited to the army or navy." At that he grinned and touched the brim of his hat.

Holmes watched him leave, a speculative look in his eyes. "Say what you will, there goes a very brave man."

"Yes," I agreed, and added in what I hoped was a fair impression of Sutton's manner, "He has told me what it is like to face critics and a bad audience."

Fortunately Holmes chuckled. "Terrifying, no doubt," he said, and signaled me to get my notebook.

FROM THE PERSONAL JOURNAL OF PHILIP TYERS

The groundwork has been laid. The carpenter is coming in the morning, and it is arranged that M H and G will depart for the Admiralty—in actuality the Swiss embassy—upon his arrival. In his persona of the carpenter, Sutton will work a full day on the pocket doors and leave at five-thirty. Sutton will return at six-thirty, as M H and will make his customary visit to his club, then come back to remain here until M H returns from the Swiss embassy.

It is a simple plan, but for that reason has more chance of success, for it has been my experience over the years that the less there is to go wrong the greater the chance of success.

M H has instructed me to make the proper clothes ready for the reception at the Swiss embassy two nights from now. He said that the invitation, unofficial though it may be, is foolish beyond permission. "If our dealings are discovered, all the care we have taken for the last two weeks will be for less than naught, for not only will our efforts be undone, they will be completely undermined."

Tomorrow I am to devote my time to locating whoever is watching this place, and to determine what it is they want to know. I haven't done this since Cairo, but I remember how it is done well enough.

Chapter Four

I ARRIVED IN Pall Mall an hour earlier than was my habit, and was admitted by Mycroft Holmes, who was waiting impatiently for me, once again in the striped trousers and swallowtail coat he so disliked. I, too, had dressed more formally than was my wont, and I carried a black leather portfolio for my notebooks and any papers I was instructed to carry upon our return; it had a small brass lock keeping it closed. The key was in my inner waistcoat pocket.

"There's tea, kippers, and eggs in the sitting room, if you

want a bite of food." He himself held a cup of tea, and was clearly finishing it.

"I've broken my fast already, sir," I said, knowing he was eager to be off, though it was also the truth. In the year I had been in Holmes' employ, I had learned to make myself completely ready before presenting myself to him, and breakfast was part of the preparation.

"Good, good," he said distantly. "Tyers is speaking to the Viscount's servants, alerting them to the carpenter's arrival." He held his cup as he paced. "It is always awkward in these cases," he mused, resuming an interrupted thought. "If only the Prince would tell us who his mistress is. Then we could deal with the situation. The woman would appreciate the impossibility of their . . . liaison and would listen to reason."

"You would threaten her," I said with distaste.

"If she would not accept a more agreeable settlement, yes," said Holmes, and turned on me with a look of chagrin. "Good God, man, I would deny no man his happiness, but this is an untenable romance. It cannot succeed in giving the two of them anything but pain at best and disgrace at worst." He shook his long head. "It is not only that they are endangered by their affaire, they bring far greater risks to their two countries. Any difficulties we might have to resolve can only be exacerbated by this . . . contretemps. I do not think the woman is so lost to propriety and duty that she would remain with the Prince if she understood the magnitude of the problem they have created."

"And the Prince?" I asked, thinking of the unfortunate woman who had so disastrously engaged his affections. "He is the son of the Emperor of Japan. Surely he is not so lost to passion that he is willing to forget his birth. What of his duty?"

"He has refused to discuss the matter with Ambassador Tochigi. And given that the Prince is the Emperor's second son, Tochigi may not press the matter." Holmes shrugged and set his cup aside. "It is a more Medieval society than our own, the Japanese, and more military in character. More proscribed. It is due to their history. They have not been successfully invaded for more than seven hundred years. But though the Normans were the last to conquer, England has a long history of absorbing its conquerors. We have them in our people and our language, layer upon layer of them: Celt, Roman, Saxon, Jute, Angle, Viking, Norman, all have played their part. And that tradition has continued to this day. England has long taken in waves of people fleeing the wars on the Continent—Dutch weavers in Norfolk, Huguenots in the south, Italian intellectuals at Oxford and Cambridge, German and Hungarian musicians with the House of Hanover. We have not turned back those who sought refuge here. Luckily for England."

"So I have grasped from the material you have instructed me to read." I looked about for his case and saw it at the door. "I find much of it baffling."

Mycroft Holmes reached for his cloak. "As do I. Though I am sure many of our best officers would sympathize with the Bushido code."

"The Samurai code? Do you think so? To the point of suicide?" I asked, astonished that Holmes would endorse anything so repellent. "That is what I cannot grasp—a sense of honor that demands self-murder."

Holmes gave me a long, steady look. "There are many kinds of suicide, dear boy. Think a little. Do not assume that those ruined men who blow their brains out to save themselves from scandal are the only suicides in England. They are only the most obvious." He turned as he heard an unexpected sound from the rear of the flat. "Tyers? Is that you?" he called out.

"Mister Holmes" came his answer. A moment later Tyers appeared at the end of the corridor. "Only the baker's delivery wagon is in the back just now. Old Reg is driving, as always. He told me he was thinking about letting his son-in-law take over the work, what with his hands being all gnarled up. I took half the number of scones I usually buy; I remarked that you would be at the Admiralty today and would have your tea there." He regarded me carefully. "The proper coat; very good."

Holmes' grey eyes lit appreciatively. "You will discover how fast that information spreads, won't you?"

"I certainly will," said Tyers, and went to hold the front door for Holmes and me.

I gathered up my portfolio and took an umbrella from the large Chinese vase by the door where Holmes kept several. I was not so much worried about rain as I wanted to have a useful-but-unobvious weapon.

Holmes gave an approving nod. "Wise. Pistols will not be welcome at the Swiss embassy, by either the Swiss or the Japanese. They will claim that we cannot negotiate in good faith if we arrive armed. We will respect their wishes for the time being." Holmes had taken the largest of the umbrellas, the one I knew contained a sword in its shaft. As he led the way down to the street, Holmes said over his shoulder, "The Admiralty carriage will arrive in a short while. I only wish we might use Sid Hasting's cab, but—We must allow time for people to notice our departure."

"How fortunate the morning is sunny," I said, holding my portfolio close against me as we reached the street. "That will make it easier for us to be observed as we make our departure."

"Certainly," said my employer with heavy-handed sarcasm.

Pall Mall was busy at this hour of the morning. Fashionable cabriolets and milord coaches and a few whiskeys and spiders moved along the long curve of the street. Though it was approaching nine, some late delivery wagons mixed with the grander equipages, like fishing smacks among yachts.

The Admiralty coach was a fine modern enclosed brake with a handsome Comtois gelding between the shafts. The driver drew up at the kerb and opened the side panel for us. Mycroft Holmes entered first, I followed and closed the door-panel, making sure that my portfolio was behind my legs against the seat.

"Let me advise you, Guthrie," said Holmes as we started off into the traffic. "The Japanese expect to see a great deal of deference from men of your position, and will not think well of you if you do not show the degree of respect—not to say obsequiousness—their society demands. I realize it is distasteful, but I believe it is also necessary to accommodate them in these matters."

"You wish me to take my model from their secretaries and clerks," I said. "As we did with the Turks in Barcelona last March, is that what's wanted?" I nodded in answer to this rhetorical question, and turned the nod into a bow. "Rest assured, I understand. And I will contrive to do as you request."

"I knew I need not ask," murmured Holmes, and patted his case. "This must be your first concern when you are in my company. No one but you and I are to handle the case and its contents." He leaned back against the squabs. "If I can arrange it, however, I want you to spend some time with the Japanese underlings. It is rumored that the Emperor is seeking more support from the Samurai class, wanting them to endorse his overtures to the West. The servants might well discuss this among themselves; servants usually do. Most of them know some English. And while you are at it, I want you to find out what you can about the character of the Prince."

"Servants' gossip, sir?" I asked, shocked at the suggestion. "How will that help you? Even if I spoke Japanese, I doubt whether the servants would be so indiscreet as to speak out of turn in my presence."

"No, not that, not those whispers that are always passing among servants. I want to know how things stand between Tochigi and the Prince as the Japanese understand it. I want to know what the servants think of the attempts to have more Japanese cadets at

Dartmouth. I want to know if anyone else has been asking similar questions." This last remark turned his face grave. "That may well be the most important of all."

I did my best to appear calm. "I'll do what I can, sir. But from what I have read in the material you gave me, the Japanese are not likely to be very forthcoming with a foreigner like me."

Holmes sighed. "Probably not, but we must make an attempt," he said. "Tochigi is in the position of strength just now."

I stared out the window and watched the jumble of the London streets. We were, I realized, taking a circuitous route to the Swiss embassy. "Strange, isn't it, that a young man's youthful indiscretion should have so much significance."

"Youthful indiscretion, my arse," Mycroft Holmes snapped with unaccustomed ire. "Prince Jiro is going to cause more than scandal, he may well bring about a severing of all relations between the British Empire and the Empire of Japan." He rubbed his jaw—a gesture of marked discontent with him—and said, "Our interests in the Pacific may well be at stake. Consider the unrest in China: We desperately need a strong ally in the Far East if we are not to be damaged by it. Russia now maintains a major fleet at Port Arthur and continues to expand Russian influence with the warlords who control much of central and western China. The prosperity we in these islands all enjoy is the direct result of our trade with the Orient. America is too caught up in itself; there is no other nation on the Pacific Ocean other than the Empire of Japan we can make an alliance with to balance Russia's might."

"I am aware of the troubles in China, sir," I said. "But how can a treaty with Japan bring about the results you seek?"

Holmes looked out into the street, speaking in a remote manner. "The Russians once again appear to be pressing their frontiers. It is an old pattern with them, one used to release the internal pressures of their hybrid country with an outside adventure, which places much of the Orient in danger." He rubbed his chin thoughtfully. "If it were possible, we would deal with their ambitions in another manner. But at this time the English government is not in a position to commit forces so far from Europe in sufficient numbers to maintain a strong presence in Oriental waters. Our obligations in Europe preclude such measures, for it is daily more apparent that humbling France was not the entire purpose of United Germany's intentions. We must continue complete dominance of our seas and the Atlantic or face diplomatic ruin at the hands of an expanding German presence. Therefore we must make common cause with the Japanese to keep the Russian Pacific Fleet from tipping the balance beyond our control. We must also curb any German or Austro-Hungarian schemes to expand their activities into the Orient as they attempt to gain the advantage for themselves. We cannot do this without the help of the Japanese."

"Surely our forces in Singapore and Hong Kong could deal with any German ships straying into their theaters of operation," I protested, remembering a newspaper article I had read in the *Guardian* not long ago. "They haven't a single coaling station anywhere near China, much less India."

"And we have nary a dreadnought among our Far East stations, so the matter may be a moot one, if Germany should put us to the test," Holmes informed me. "Even a single German warship could be enough to dominate the trade-lanes of India and China, with severe economic consequences throughout our Empire. That alone should cause concern in government. Additionally we know that Russia has allocated at least two capital ships to her Port Arthur squadron." His unhappy mood lifted. "But, as the Japanese are more threatened by the Russian fleet than we, they have every reason to enter into this agreement with us. If we can eliminate this one perplexing problem you know about, all will be well and our interests—and theirs—will be protected." He nodded to the pristine white stone façade looming ahead. The handsome

Georgian building and its fenced gardens took up half the block. "Ah. At last."

We had reached the Swiss embassy, and the driver was proceeding toward it with caution, for it had been arranged for us to be let down near the side entrance, away from the porte cochere where our arrival might be noticed.

"All right," I said. "If the opportunity presents itself, I will do what I can to find out how the servants feel about all this, but I must tell you I do not expect much of a response from any of them."

"Very good. I am aware of what you have to deal with." Holmes reached for his case, his umbrella and his cloak in one swift gesture.

The driver turned down a side street and drew up at the kerb near an inconspicuous door in the stone wall of the hundred-year-old building. I gathered up my things and descended from the coach quickly, glancing up and down the street before nodding to my employer. This was the time when I most missed having a pistol with me.

A soft cough from the door caught our attention; the side door stood half-open. Holmes was out of the coach and into the side door as quickly as a man might take a Newmarket hurdle. I followed him at once, trying to make this arrival appear somewhat less secretive than it was.

The servant who greeted us was a small, dapper man with waxed moustaches and a permanent three-cornered smile set on his lips. He bowed. "It is an honor to welcome you to Switzerland, Mister Holmes. I am Andermatt. Please allow me to escort you to the chamber where you are expected."

"Thank you, Andermatt," Holmes said with an expression of approval. "I appreciate all the Swiss are doing to assist England in her dealings with Japan."

Andermatt made a slight gesture which indicated that there

was no effort worth considering. He indicated a flight of stairs. "At the top, the second door on the right." With that he bowed again and went on his way.

As Andermatt left us, Holmes observed, "A most estimable fellow, Andermatt." There was a trace of amusement in his eyes as he turned to me. "You heard him, Guthrie. At the top, second door on the right." Holmes began to climb, taking care not to hurry.

I trod along slightly behind him. "Tell me," I said as we made our way upward, "Whom do you expect today?"

"I suppose it will be Tochigi and one of his two personal secretaries, at least." He reached the top. "The secretaries are Mister Minato and Mister Banadaichi."

Slowly I repeated the names to myself, remembering at the same time to keep my place to the rear of my employer as we arrived at the specified door.

The chamber was good-sized without being overly large. There was elaborate wainscoting with deeply beveled panels rising halfway up the wall with blond wallpaper above it accented with a regular series of straw-colored stripes. Five windows overlooked the largest of the three embassy gardens, their lace curtains delicate as spider webs. I saw that a tray of tea and coffee had been carried up and placed on an occasional table under the windows. So far, it appeared to be untouched.

The Japanese ambassador rose as we entered the room, a dignified man of middle years with the manner of privilege etched into every move and gesture. His whole demeanor was somber, his face gravely expressionless, his blunt hands held at his sides without any offer of a more Western greeting. He was wearing striped trousers and a swallowtail coat. He bowed to Mycroft Holmes, and waited while Holmes returned the courtesy, then took his seat on the far side of a long, glossy table of splendid ash-wood. Separated from him by a single chair on each side, his secretaries remained standing while Mycroft Holmes sat down. "This is my personal secretary, Mister Paterson Erskine Guthrie, of Edinburgh, Scotland."

"You know Mister Banadaichi and Mister Minato; Mister Banadaichi is from Kobe, Mister Minato is from Osaka," said Ambassador Tochigi; the two men bowed and took their places.

Mister Banadaichi and Mister Minato were both fairly young men, not more than a few years older than I. Or perhaps, I thought as I studied them, it was their reserved and respectful manner that made them seem so. Both had straight dark hair, both were clean-shaven, both were dressed in black frock coats and black waistcoats, and both wore trousers with a single stripe down each leg. Mister Minato's face was narrower than Mister Banadaichi's, but otherwise they looked eerily the same to me.

"Let us begin," suggested Mycroft Holmes.

I chose a chair one place away from my employer, put down my portfolio and retrieved my key from my pocket. As I unlocked the portfolio, I saw the look of thunderous disapproval Ambassador Tochigi directed toward me.

"I gave him permission to make ready before we entered the room, as is our English custom," explained Mycroft Holmes at his blandest. "I am certain you have already given your instructions to your secretaries."

Ambassador Tochigi gave a single, curt nod without admitting the accuracy of Holmes' observation. "We are ready."

"As am I, and my secretary," said Holmes as I drew out my notebook and four sharpened pencils. I noticed that Holmes had laid his case on the chair between us. "I received the sash you were gracious enough to send me, with your invitation for the reception tomorrow night."

"Hai?" said Ambassador Tochigi.

"The ambassador questions you in the affirmative," said Mister Minato. His English was almost flawless. I was astonished to hear him, for I realized how great my disadvantage was in knowing no Japanese.

Holmes continued, unperturbed. "I wish the ambassador to know I am very grateful for his invitation—unofficial though it is—but I wonder if we would not serve our countries better by continuing to meet less conspicuously, given the delicacy of our current discussions."

Ambassador Tochigi looked directly at Holmes. "It would insult the Emperor if you were not in attendance."

Holmes turned over his hand as if surrendering his king in chess. "Very well. What can I be but honored."

"Excellent. We will make all necessary arrangements before you leave today. Tomorrow may be a difficult time," said Ambassador Tochigi.

"Your concern is more than I deserve," said Holmes in the same unflustered, deferential tone as before.

"I doubt that," said Ambassador Tochigi, letting sharpness tinge his graciousness.

As I listened, I made a few inconsequential notes, in large part because Messers Minato and Banadaichi were writing steadily and I did not want to appear lax. When I became aware of the growing silence I put my pencil aside. What a strange game this was, I thought, like one of those tales of the American West where adversaries wait for someone to blink before taking sudden action. It was a disconcerting feeling, sitting there so very still and yet as if expecting an explosion.

"I will inform Prince Jiro that he is to meet with us before the reception begins. He will decide if he is willing to do so," said Ambassador Tochigi after the quiet became intolerable.

"That will be most acceptable. We may maintain the discretion we have sought in these dealings with such a meeting," my employer agreed, and went on as if there had been no cessation of conversation or good-will between them. "If my efforts can do anything to assist you in learning the identity—"

"That will not be necessary," said Ambassador Tochigi, and directed Mister Banadaichi to open a chart of the western Pacific Ocean and lay it out on the table. He used his pencil to point out the coast of China. "Now, I think it would be best if we discussed the number of warships your Royal Navy requires to reinforce Australia and Hong Kong, as well as maintain an acceptable presence in the Pacific regions?" His inflection took the command from his suggestion, but not by much.

I could not tell if this sudden change of subjects annoyed him: Mycroft Holmes sat forward on his chair, hands clasped beneath his chin, giving the Japanese his full concentration. I continued to make notes.

FROM THE PERSONAL JOURNAL OF PHILIP TYERS

Sutton is making enough noise to herald Judgment Day. You would think he was demolishing the flat with a hammer and saw for all the thunderous racket he has produced. All of Pall Mall must know that there are repairs being made. It has also provided a superb excuse for me to absent myself from the flat. No one would wonder at my leaving during such cacophony. I have also had the opportunity to complain of this intrusion into our well-ordered lives, and to receive the commiserations of the other servants in this and adjoining houses, all of whom have declared themselves to be wholly opposed to such total intrusions as the one I am currently suffering. I have been offered the comfort of tales of the perfidy of all disruptions to routine, as well as the opportunity to avail myself of the servants' quarters in the ground-floor flat of this building. In turn this has allowed me to remark on the strange behavior of the men in the butcher's delivery van. I must compile all I have heard for M H to peruse on his return.

I did not anticipate the scorn of some other delivery men in re-

gard to the butcher. Few of them thought well of him. One called him lazy, another called him a Nosey Parker, and I began to suspect that this man has recently become unpopular with his comrades. One of the men I questioned shares my belief that the driver was foreign, though he could give me no specific reason for his opinion. I will have to try to garner more tomorrow, when Sutton is at work on the pocket doors. As ruses go, this one is certainly achieving its end, but I cannot help but think that the headache I must endure is a high price for a disguise.

There is a note from Tschersky again, and I gather he is the one making inquiries this time.

Chapter Five

AS WE CLIMBED into Sid Hastings' cab later that evening, Mycroft Holmes said, "I wish I knew what Tochigi is hiding." He consulted his watch. "Ten-thirty. It could be worse."

"Do you think he is hiding something, or that it is his manner that makes you think so? He is very reserved, and I have not yet learned to interpret his silences." I had often found myself baffled during the day, and was not yet convinced that I had any grasp of the actual trouble with the Japanese, other than their determination to put an end to Prince Jiro's unfortunate romance.

"I have thought about that; surely he has a number of tasks to accomplish in his treating with us. The man is less accessible to me than a European would be, and not solely on the grounds of language. He sees the world in a very different light than we of the West do, and I must caution myself against making assumptions that do not consider his character in such perspective," said Holmes quietly as he patted his case. "And in spite of these considerations, I am now tolerably certain that Ambassador Tochigi is evading certain matters, but for what purpose I cannot tell. Allowing for all the formality of Japanese society does not entirely account for Ambassador Tochigi's total reluctance to tell me anything of note he may know of the Prince's paramour. If he is aware of her identity, I doubt he will vouchsafe it to me, though I begin to suspect that he is as ignorant as I on the matter. I can do nothing more without his cooperation, and he is not going to provide any, I fear." He rubbed his face. "Damned frustrating case."

"So it seems to me," I agreed, secretly relieved that Holmes did not have any greater insights into this situation.

We were going along at a good rate—the horse trotting through the half-empty streets—when Sid Hastings swore and drew his horse in. Ahead, just short of the intersection, an omnibus had collided with a house-remover's van, which lay canted on its side. Drivers of both vehicles were on the paving stones, trying to untangle their teams from their harness without causing any more injury to their panicked horses. Frightened passengers on the omnibus pressed their faces to the windows and stared out at the chaos.

Holmes saw all this in an instant; he shouldered out of his cloak and reached for his umbrella, thumbing the release in the handle to free the sword. He motioned to me to be ready.

The same hackles-raising sensation had seized me as well. I

flung out of my coat, then closed my hand around the shaft of my umbrella and wished for something more lethal. Then I readied myself for what was about to happen.

"Now!" As the panels of the cab were pulled back on both sides by men in dark clothing and capes, Holmes rose to his feet and threw himself forward onto the intruder on his side as I rose and kicked hard at the man attempting to gain entrance from my side of the vehicle.

Above us, Sid Hastings swore vitriolically and strove to steady his horse; the cab rocked violently.

I was almost jolted from my feet as the man I had kicked grabbed for my legs and jerked hard. I clung to the inside brace of the hood of the cab with one hand and struck out at him with my umbrella, having the satisfaction of feeling a solid impact and hearing an angry howl.

Mycroft Holmes was hanging precariously on to the cab, his sword flickering deftly in his hand as he kept the man on his side at bay. Once he came dangerously close to being pulled from the cab, but he held on with surprising tenacity. He shouted to me as he fought, "Guthrie! Don't let them get the case! They want the case!"

I realized at once that he was right, for a third man had just begun to climb up the shaft into the front of the cab, a knife glinting in his hand. I slammed my umbrella into his chest and heard the wind go out of him at the same instant I felt the wooden shaft crack and splinter, vanes opening as the tension gave out. I threw the useless thing down and prepared to fend off more of the attackers with my fists and feet. As one of the ruffians seized my leg, I realized I might have been lured into folly, for he twisted my foot with a strength that stunned me. I struggled to pull away, each effort on my part increasing the pain in the sinews of my ankle, the jolt of the pain through my body seeming to unhinge my jaw.

The mare neighed and sidled, sparks coming from where her hooves struck the pavement.

"Watch out! Guthrie!" Holmes shouted as a fourth man joined the assault, hampered by the nervous skittering of the horse, who whickered with distress.

Then Sid Hastings' whip snaked out and flicked the cheek of the new assailant, leaving a bleeding kiss behind. The man clapped his hand to his torn face and screamed. Hastings could not be bothered with this commotion. He used the whip again and the man who was trying to drag me from the cab staggered back.

As quickly as it had begun it was over. The unknown men were routed.

Trying to stave off a residual dizziness I took a firm grip on the panel and pulled it closed again. I had the satisfaction of feeling fingers crunch as I did. As I regained my balance I heard footsteps running away from the cab.

Holmes swung back into the cab once more and pulled his panel to. There was the sheen of perspiration on his brow and he was breathing hard as he shoved the sword back into the umbrella shaft. Then he pulled his handkerchief from his pocket and wiped his forehead. "Well done, Hastings, very well done," he called out before he turned to me. "Are you all right, dear boy?"

"I . . . think so," I answered, aware now that my ankle was throbbing and the palm of my right hand was scraped where I had clung to the frame.

"Not injured, are you?" he demanded.

"Not that I'm aware of, not really, nothing to speak of," I answered, attempting to regain my composure. I did not want to complain of so small an injury as a twisted ankle, for in comparison to the threat, it was an insignificant thing. I gave my foot a tentative waggle; the pain was not too severe. "It was so unexpected."

"That it was," said Holmes grimly. He rapped on the ceiling of the cab. "If you are able to, Hastings, drive on."

"Of course, sir," said Hastings. "Just wanted to give Jenny a chance to settle down." He clucked once to his mare, and the cab moved forward again.

As we picked our way around the wreck, I asked Holmes, "Do you think this was an ambush?"

"It depends on who was doing it," Holmes answered, sounding more apprehensive than he usually did in the face of trouble. "And if it *was* an ambush, our situation is graver than I first anticipated." He stared out into the night-dark street. "I may have underestimated the stakes in this hand."

"How do you mean?" I reached down to make sure our cases were still in place. "What have you underestimated?"

"Those who have an interest in our dealings with Japan, I must hope," he said, rubbing his jaw. "I will have a bruise tomorrow. Damnation." He was breathing sharply still, and I saw that he had one hand pressed against his side.

"Sutton will give you paint to cover it, if you wish to conceal the bruise," I said, certain it was so.

"Good." He remained silent for a short while. "If the Japanese were behind this little escapade, then it would be wise not to reveal any sign of battle. If they did not—" He began to toy with his watchfob. "Tomorrow morning I will send Tyers round to Baker Street, to find out if there are street gangs preying on hackney cabs in this part of town."

"You think it was a street gang? I didn't suppose they would venture beyond The Dials." I was as shocked at this suggestion as I was at the thought that the Japanese might have arranged the attack. I could not shake the growing conviction that the Brotherhood was behind it, for they were Holmes' sworn enemies.

"Nor did I. But we must rule out the possibility before we engage in other speculation." He leaned back against the squabs. "I will want a brandy before I retire. And I must warn Edmund about the increased risk."

"Surely you don't think that he—" I began.

"I don't know what to think, Guthrie, and that is nothing more than the truth." He stuffed his handkerchief back in his pocket and brushed at the front of his cloak as he pulled it around him once again, one hand still firmly in place against his ribs.

I had a thousand questions I still longed to ask him, and I was troubled that he might be hurt, but knew I could receive no answers tonight, nor was I of a mind to pursue the matter now. I did my best to content myself with trying to make myself comfortable for the rest of the ride to Pall Mall.

By the time we alighted, I was feeling chilled and stiff, and I supposed the same was true of my employer, whatever injury he had sustained. My ankle was steadily hurting now and I could feel it swollen in the shoe. I was not certain it could bear my weight. I gathered up the case and portfolio, then waited as Holmes bade Sid Hastings good-night and tipped him handsomely for all he had done. As I swung the panel open, I was reminded afresh that my palm was scraped. I winced.

"Give your Jenny an extra measure of oats," Holmes recommended as he reached the sidewalk. He handed Sid Hastings two pound notes. "She's more than earned them tonight."

"And this will buy the Missus a beef joint to dress as well, thanking your honor for this," said Sid Hastings, accepting the flimsies with a half-salute. With that he signaled his mare the office and went away down the street.

"I didn't realize Hastings was married," I said as we started up to Holmes' flat.

"Oh yes. He's the father of four hopeful children. The youngest is four, the oldest is twelve. He has a daughter, his second child, with a rare aptitude for mathematics. Unfortunately." He did not climb quickly and I began to fear he had received more hurts than I was aware of.

"Why unfortunately?" I asked, not wanting to think of my ankle, which was throbbing painfully.

"A girl with such abilities is nothing more than a freak, particularly in such a household as that of Sid Hastings, where there is little to offer talented children. If one of his sons had such abilities, something might be done for his advancement in more usual ways, but as it is, she will be hard to marry off, most men disliking their women more intelligent than they. And there are no university chairs in mathematics sponsored for females." We reached the first landing. "There is a man who runs a casino on the Continent who might be willing to take her on as a kind of apprentice. If she has the good sense I credit her with having, she will flourish there. I have promised to write to him on Hastings' behalf when the child turns fifteen."

"An apprentice at a casino, who has a talent for mathematics," I said, trying to grasp the full implications and failing.

"Oh, believe me, Guthrie, such abilities are cherished by those who live by setting odds. If she is able to learn the trade she should do very well for herself. And she would be in a position to assist my inquiries from time to time. I am not entirely altruistic, alas." He paused as we reached the second landing, which was dark, giving the impression that Holmes was within, reading, as was his reputed custom. "I hope you will summon Tyers and explain what has happened. I must have a private word with Edmund at once. He is in great danger if his ruse has been discovered."

"Of course," I said.

"Remember about tomorrow morning and Baker Street. My brother will shed some light on these street ruffians." He leaned on the bannister and I could not conceal my alarm.

"Sir, are you—" I started.

He interrupted me wearily. "Knock, Guthrie. Please."

I did as he ordered at once and was relieved to hear footsteps in the hall beyond almost at once.

The door swung open: both Tyers and Sutton stood before us, Tyers holding a lantern. Both of them stared as the light touched us. Gathering from their expressions, we must have been a sight.

"Sir!" exclaimed Tyers. "What on earth—"

"Holmes!" Sutton said at the same breath. He reached out and shouldered the arm of our employer in order to support him into the flat. "Good Lord, what happened?" he asked as Tyers secured the door behind us.

I found myself suddenly too unnerved to talk. I did not want to move the fingers of my scraped hand. My ankle ached abominably, and must have done so since it was injured, but I had not realized the extent of the pain until now, when I no longer had to resist it. I stumbled toward the sitting room, in search of a chair with a hassock. Tyers was right behind me, offering his help.

"Let me get you a brandy, Mister Guthrie," he said in a tone that revealed little. "You're pale as whey."

"Pale, am I?" I asked shakily as I lowered myself into a chair. Had I been a child, I would have wept for the relief this brought. As it was, I shuddered as I carefully elevated my leg and placed my ankle on the hassock. My muscles felt unstrung and every joint was sore as if from prolonged cold.

"Yes, sir. And Mister Holmes, sir, is . . ." He could find no words to describe the condition.

"We were set upon," I said testily, thinking this much should be obvious to the most simple-minded observer. "Coming here in the cab we were attacked. A party of unknown men waylaid us."

"So I gathered," said Tyers with a steadiness of tone that was a lesson to me.

I realized I ought to say more. "A collision caused a delay. While we were waiting to get past it, we were set upon. There were at least three of them, armed. Fortunately Sid Hastings thought quickly. Used that whip of his, too." I turned around to see what had become of Holmes.

Tyers saw this and said, "I think Sutton is attending to him, Mister Guthrie. They have gone to the study."

I was suddenly deeply alarmed. "Will you go and find out what has happened? I know Mister Holmes received some injury, but I don't know its extent, or nature." It bothered me to speak my fears aloud. That they might be justified filled me with dismay.

"I will," said Tyers. "And will take the opportunity to bring you brandy. Then we will see about removing your shoe. From the look of it, your ankle is quite swollen."

Had I not been so concerned for Holmes, this assurance would have filled me with more foreboding than it did. I only nodded and tried as best I could to settle back in the chair. Now that I had the opportunity, I tried to piece together the events of the evening that led to the attack, but try as I might, I could find no commonality to link the Japanese with those who set upon us. But if there was no connection, then what was the reason for the attack, and who had done it? Was the person or persons watching this flat part of the attackers, and if he were, why bother to watch the flat at all, for surely he must know of Sutton's impersonation, and would have no reason to watch the flat if Holmes was his target. I was caught in a tangle and my mind was not calm enough to enable me to find my way out of this labyrinth of my own creation. Who knows how long I might have wrestled futilely with the question? But Tyers came back with a brandy and a report.

"Mister Holmes has received a scrape to his ribs, sir. It is not a dangerous wound, but it has bled and is in need of attention. Sutton is seeing to it now. He is capable and will do as well as anyone to clean and staunch the wound." He watched as I took the snifter he offered. "Mister Holmes asked me to look after you, sir, and make certain you are well enough to get yourself home tonight. If you are not, I am bidden to make a bed for you on the parlor sofa."

"Thank you, Tyers," I said, tasting the brandy. "Let's get to this ankle business." I said this with more certainty than I truly had, for I was well-aware that in removing the shoe, the swelling would be more painful.

"I will get a basin of mustard water, sir, and return." Tyers excused himself again, and I was once more in the feverish throes of speculation, as useless now as it had been a few minutes before. I had been assuming that the attack had been deliberately aimed at Holmes. But what if I was wrong? What if it had been nothing more than an unlucky circumstance, that any cab passing that wreck at that time might have been set upon by these ruffians? But I doubted that the street gangs were as well organized as these men appeared to be, or so set in their purpose. I had the unhappy notion that it had all been part of the plan—the collision of the van and omnibus—for the purpose of making the attack appear to be accidental. But that would imply that there was money and organization at work to arrange such an opportunity. Which once again returned me to who knew of our negotiations with the Japanese, and who would want to put an end to them? To what ends? And who knew enough to realize that Mycroft Holmes was not, in fact, where he was known to be, but out on the London streets—

"Mister Guthrie," said Tyers, cutting into my thoughts. He held a basin and a towel as well as a long-bladed knife. "Shall we get to it?"

I made myself nod, and got a good hold on the arms of the chair.

FROM THE PERSONAL JOURNAL OF PHILIP TYERS

G's ankle was mottled with bruises and much swollen. He soaked it for half an hour in mustard water, and then I bandaged it tightly for him. He is laid down to sleep on the sofa and will return to his rooms in the morning to change and to prepare for the day ahead. I have also applied a medicinal plaster to his hand, though the damage there is less serious.

M H has refused all medication for his scrape but the topical lotion of iodine. Sutton has declared his intention to keep at his side all night in case he should become worse. While I am prepared to fulfill that office, I can see that Sutton is all but distraught, and this will serve to give him the satisfaction of rendering aid, as well as freeing my time in the morning for my regular tasks, which I believe may be crucial. Sutton has some experience in these matters and does not readily panic, for which I am grateful, for I do not relish having to calm Sutton as well as nurse M H. But M H has accepted Sutton's company and assistance willingly and has thanked him for all he has done on M H's behalf. I can only think that the actor is showing a good deal more backbone than I have credited him with in the past.

After breakfast in the morning, I am to go to M H's brother with a list of questions that may shed light on the events of this evening. While I do not have the unrelenting faith in the brother, I am aware his activities take him to places and in company that may have useful information to offer to M H in this coil.

Chapter Six

BY MORNING I was both better and worse. Though my head ached, and my tongue felt like flannel, my funk of the previous night had passed. I discovered that my right hand was only slightly tender; I thanked God I did not need it to write. My leg was stiff and my ankle throbbed, but not so intensely as when Tyers had wrapped it up the night before, which encouraged me to hope that I would not be as lame as I had feared I would be. However, I had a number of bruises I had ignored before which were now making themselves noticed. When I removed the plaster from my palm, the scrape still looked raw. I sat up on the sofa and waited while the room stopped spinning. I had accepted Tyers' offer of a composer last night, and this morning paid the price for having a good night's sleep. At the time it had seemed an excellent notion; now I was not so sure; if it did not go off shortly, I would be concerned. I stared at the window, doing my best to assess the morning.

"I hope I see you well, sir?" said Tyers as he came into the parlor from the sitting room. Sutton's efforts of the previous day had served to restore the pocket doors between the two chambers to full utility.

"As well as can be expected, I suppose," I answered glumly as I did my best to marshal my resources for the day ahead. "But it is not the . . ." I lost track of my thought. "What time is it?"

"It lacks ten minutes of seven, sir," said Tyers. "Mister Holmes woke half an hour ago and is bathing in preparation for having the dressing on his wound changed." He paused, as if there was something more he wished to say, and then thought better of it. "Would you care to join him at breakfast? In the sitting room? You need not worry about clothes, Mister Guthrie. I am certain there is a dressing gown that will serve your purposes among the things on Sutton's rack by the pantry."

I sighed, the need to rise weighing on me. "Since all manner of disguises hang there, no doubt you are correct," I said, trying to lighten my tone and my manner. I had no reason to be curt with Tyers, who had done so much to help me. "Certainly. Choose something for me that isn't too outlandish, and inform Mister Holmes I will be entirely at his service in a matter of ten minutes."

"As you wish," said Tyers, bowing slightly before leaving me to get myself up.

I hobbled about the room, testing my ankle, and knew it

could not be relied upon for much. Little as I liked it, I would have to depend on a cane or a pair of crutches for a day or so until the swelling subsided and my strength returned. Who would have thought so minor a hurt could have such a result? When Tyers brought me a dressing gown of a muted green velvet, I pulled it on and tied its sash, finding it a trifle over-long in the arms, but otherwise unobjectionable. I wondered where Sutton had got it, as I wondered where he had got most of the costumes he supplied to our mutual employer.

"Guthrie," said Holmes as I presented myself to him a few minutes later, realizing how absurd I must seem, in a velvet dressing gown with a notebook and pencil at the ready. "How are you, dear boy? You look a trifle pulled."

"I feel pulled," I allowed. "But if I can procure a cane or crutches, I will do well enough. I am not quite laid up yet."

"Part of being a sensible man," said Holmes, who was looking a trifle pulled himself, what with the large, slate-and-purple bruise on the right side of his jaw, and the general pallor of his countenance, "is knowing one's limitations. Perhaps not so graphically illustrated, but—" He moved stiffly as he sat down, taking care of his left side where the attacker's steel had scraped him.

"Such as you do. Admit your limitations," said Sutton from the other side of the room. He looked appallingly fresh and eager; his blue eyes sparked with amusement. "For I will wager the lead in the Scottish Play that you will not send word to the Japanese that press of work will require you to postpone your meeting until tomorrow."

"Tomorrow is the formal reception," Holmes growled, whether from the circumstances with the Japanese or for being so transparent in his determination to exceed his limitations, I could not guess. "We will have to make an appearance at the Swiss embassy today, if for no other reason to learn how the Japanese want to deal with our procedure for the reception, since, officially, I will not attend. Those who will be there officially will be grand company, indeed." He indicated my notebook. "However, Guthrie, I want you to draft a note to Ambassador Tochigi and tell him that we will be unable to arrive until two in the afternoon. Come up with any explanation that will be acceptable, but not the entire truth, if you please. You might incorporate your injury into what you say, so that there will be no necessity to account for your ankle when we arrive at the Swiss embassy." He watched me write and added, "Then you must make a proper report about last night to be given to the Admiralty messenger this afternoon."

"Are you certain you wish to do that?" Sutton asked him before I could.

"Yes. I am required to tell them of any and all attempts on my person. At such a juncture as we have now, this report becomes doubly important, as it may indicate an attempt to sabotage the whole negotiations, or compromise them at the least." Holmes was looking puzzled. "Why do you question this?"

"Because," said Sutton in his bantering way, "it strikes me you don't yet know who was behind it. As long as you do not know, silence may be the wisest course, for you do not know who among the Japanese may have had a role in your misadventure, if any. That is a possibility. There are others, less pleasant to consider: There could be another reason for the attack altogether, from a group whose purpose and identity are as yet secret. There are men who are party to the negotiations whom you admit do not favor any ties to the Orient beyond what you have now. And there are groups sworn to embarrass England at any cost. You have dealt with such groups in the past, haven't you? And little as you may want to consider it, there could be someone at the Admiralty who is—"

"Good God, man, you sound as if this were a West End melodrama. Are you suggesting there is a conspiracy within the government?" I burst out. "Against the Japanese? Favoring the

Germans? The Russians? Or do you imply that there is an attempt to sabotage these negotiations?"

"Nothing so drastic, sir," said Sutton without a sign of taking umbrage at my accusations. "I am only speculating that just as many of the Japanese are not easy in their minds about England, so there are those in England uneasy about Japan; it may be that they do not all see the advantages of the alliance that you do." He cocked his head to the side, his attitude inquisitive, a visual echo of Holmes himself. "Well, if you *will* have me play you, you must expect me to try to learn your habits of thought. Those habits of thought are the heart of all acting."

Holmes regarded him steadily for the greater part of a minute. Then he sighed and said, "It isn't pleasant to consider what you say, but I agree it is necessary, given all that has transpired. It may sound theatrical, but it may be that this is an instance where life does imitate art." He pulled at his lower lip. "All right." He had made up his mind. "Guthrie, write your report properly, and leave it in my secretary. If there are any questions, say I will want to append my notes to it, and I will do that after the reception, when I have time to assess the situation properly." He shifted in his chair. "Where's Tyers?"

"In the kitchen," said Sutton. "Putting breakfast together."

"Ah, yes," Holmes said. "Well, then, we must ready ourselves for what we must do today." He regarded Sutton a moment. "I will need you to stay on here, for the time I am away from the flat this afternoon." He hesitated, then went on. "Is there some way you could slip out this morning and observe the street for us? As the attack last night was not successful, if there is any connection to those watching this place, I want to know of it. From what Tyers reported to me this morning about that delivery man, I agree he was sent to watch this place, and me. But why? As you reminded me, Edmund, we are still in the dark about motives and identities."

The look of stark intensity in his eyes was unnerving. "Who did it? *Why?*" he repeated.

I had nothing to offer by way of an answer. Instead, I asked, "Would you like me to invent a plausible explanation for our conditions? Something in the order of a mishap, minor enough to be inconsequential, but sufficient to account for our various hurts? What if I should claim that I was hurt when the jarvey's horse bolted last night? And that you ordered me to consult a physician to be certain no bones were broken?"

Holmes shrugged. "As you say, plausible enough. Such things do happen. It would not seem wrong to Ambassador Tochigi that I would give an order of that nature. He expects a man in my position to act responsibly toward my subordinates." He must have read something in my face, for he went on soothingly, "Oh, don't take offense at the word, Guthrie. I do not regard you in the same light as he regards Minato and Banadaichi. I use the term for convenience, not for accuracy." He smiled at Tyers as he brought in the breakfast tray. Holmes' customary sirloin of beef with baked eggs was center on the tray, along with a plate of grilled tomatoes, and a basket of muffins, as was a large pot of tea and a smaller one of coffee, and a jug of hot milk. There were three dishes and three cups-and-saucers for our use.

Ordinarily the sight of such welcome fare would have fired my hunger, but this morning, it had little appeal to me. I looked at the grilled tomatoes and decided I could manage one or two of them, and a plain muffin. I drew up a chair, handling it clumsily. "I will have coffee, Tyers," I said.

"Yes," Tyers said as he went about laying out breakfast.

Sutton pulled up a chair, straddled it and helped himself to the tea. He added sugar and milk, stirring thoughtfully. I watched him, trying to decide what bothered me the most—that he should be so energetically optimistic or that I should be so down-cast. He selected a muffin and broke it in half. "Holmes, if it is all the same to you," he said, so casually that both Holmes and I gave him our full attention, "I think it would be wisest if we send word to Sid Hastings to meet you one or two streets away, say in Jermyn Street or Regent Street. It may be that those watching know his cab on sight."

"It is like most cabs, and there is nothing remarkable about Jenny. The city is full of bay mares. Most people do not know one from another." I knew I sounded too sharp, so I added, "Remember, Holmes cannot move as easily as usual, and I am all but useless. We would make ourselves obvious on the street."

"Precisely," said Sutton.

I stared at him. "You have said you are in agreement that this flat is being watched. What, then, can be the purpose of making ourselves—"

"Let him go on," said Holmes quietly.

"It occurred to me," said Sutton, glancing at me once, "that if you could contrive a suitable disguise to get away from Pall Mall, you could then meet Hastings at Guthrie's rooms. There is less of a chance you would be recognized. It is probably known by the watchers that you have been hurt. Therefore it will be expected that you would make an effort to show extra care. They will expect you to be taken up at the door, not a short way along the street. It could make it possible for you to get away from here without being noticed at all." He gestured toward the window. "If you are certain the watchers are gone, then such precautions aren't necessary, but—" He shrugged eloquently.

"They may not be, but let us observe them in any case." Holmes spoke with more of his usual energy than he had displayed yet this morning. He began to cut himself a slice of the beef, winced once, and found a more comfortable posture to continue his meal. "Tyers, when you go to Baker Street, tell Sid Hastings to meet Guthrie and me at Guthrie's rooms in Curzon Street, at half one. Tell him to come from South Audley Street. Even if Hastings is being followed, he will be coming from the wrong quarter of town to be working at my request." He pressed the meat on his fork into the egg yolk. "We will arrange to have one of the delivery vans take us from here to Curzon Street."

"Providing the watchers do not know where Guthrie's rooms are, sir," said Sutton, finishing his morning repast and setting his serviette beside his plate.

"We will chance it for now," Holmes decided aloud. "You know what to do, Tyers."

"As you wish," said Tyers at his most neutral.

"It is prudent, Tyers," said Sutton quietly. "If I had said nothing, you would have."

At this, Tyers relented. "So I would have," he agreed.

By the time we had finished breakfast, our plans for the morning were complete. Tyers went on his way to execute his errands as Holmes had asked.

"Guthrie, what did you observe last night as we came along Brompton Road, just before the attack took place?" Holmes asked me somewhat later. He had dressed in his diplomatic rig again, his coat another swallow-tail of near-black super-fine. The somber color of his clothing made his bruise appear darker than it was, and Holmes, by contrast, paler. "I have only two more of these. Nothing had better happen tonight."

"I should say not," I answered, and then said, "As we came along Brompton Road, I was thinking that we should have a quick ride down Piccadilly, what with it being so late and the traffic light. To tell you truly, sir, I paid little attention to the road. I was more intent on reviewing the events of your discussion with the Japanese than anything but the speed of the journey."

"Did you not think it suspicious that a house remover should be in that neighborhood at that time of night? Most house removes are done during the day," Holmes inquired. "I have been struck by that oddity, upon reflection."

I considered the question. "Now you mention it, yes, it does seem strange. But I assumed it was on its way to another location. It was traveling on a major street when the collision with the omnibus occurred." As I listened to myself, I found I was becoming distressed at my own thoughts. Perhaps someone had arranged for the accident in anticipation of stopping Holmes on his journey back to his flat. That prospect made me apprehensive.

"I think it might be best if we put you on crutches and claim your injury is more serious than it is. It may give us just the advantage we need, and it will speed your recovery into the bargain. We want these blackguards to think they have succeeded in some regard." He had begun to pace. "If it appears they dealt you a serious blow, then we will be in a better position to discover them."

"Because they will try again?" I asked, feeling abashed that I would have to give them so much credit as admitting my injury at their hands, let alone exaggerating it.

"Because they may become sloppy," said Holmes, as if so much should be obvious. "Think a moment, dear boy: They have attacked us. We drove them off, but today, lo! it seems that they have done more damage than they hoped. They may reveal themselves in any number of ways if they are convinced they have actually brought about real difficulties for me and you." He rocked back on his heels. "I am going to leave this bruise as it is," he went on, indicating the one on the side of his jaw. "It will increase the likelihood that one of our assailants will make a mistake."

"When they try again?" I suggested unhappily.

"That is a possibility," Holmes admitted. "But not so great as the urge to preen or boast. You will have to listen closely to all you hear around you."

"Of course," I assured him, not relishing the notion.

"And tomorrow, I think you had better bring your formal clothing with you when we go to the Swiss embassy at ten. For we will have to do much before the reception begins." He stared hard at the wall. "If only we could discover the identity of the woman with whom Prince Jiro is smitten, our task would be much easier."

I could not help but agree. I had also come to believe that the Japanese would not budge in their patently unrealistic demands until the Prince's indiscretion had been dealt with to their satisfaction. "I will do what I can to discover her name."

"I know I can rely on you, Guthrie," said Holmes as he reached for his diplomatic case. "It is time you were off to your rooms. I will join you there in half an hour. Then we shall be off to the Swiss embassy once again." He indicated the rear portion of the flat. "If you will select a pair of crutches—"

"Sir," I said firmly, "I am not wholly comfortable with this plan . . ." I was unable to find the words to express my doubts about feigning so great an injury.

"Guthrie, dear boy, think a little. We cannot correctly bring arms into the embassy, and yet we are being perused by those who wish us harm." Holmes achieved a grim smile. "A crutch may not be an obvious weapon, but it can serve as an effective bludgeon if it is needed. After what happened last night, I would find such an unassuming weapon most reassuring."

As I heard this, I nodded with understanding. "Yes," I told him, no longer so opposed to the scheme. "I concur, now that I see it. And you're right, sir, it will be reassuring."

"Very good. Keep the secondary purpose in mind when you make your selection," he advised as I made my way down the corridor to the rear of the flat.

FROM THE PERSONAL JOURNAL OF PHILIP TYERS

I have seen M H's brother, who is caught up in an investigation which he warned might hamper the speed of his response to the inquiry I brought. The Swiss embassy has relayed word to Ambassador Tochigi to arrange a delay of today's meeting for M H. I must prepare for the afternoon and evening now. Any change in habitual patterns would put our opponents on the alert, so I will be at pains to maintain the routine with Sutton that is expected.

The butcher's delivery wagon has a new driver.

Chapter Seven

LORD BRACKENHEATH ARRIVED at the Swiss embassy just before tea and made his way noisily to the meeting room the Swiss had provided. He had not bothered to put on the striped trousers and swallowtail coat the occasion demanded. His ruddy face was flushed and his manner was huffy as he brought the case of requested records into the room where Mycroft Holmes was meeting with Ambassador Tochigi.

"I don't mean to mince words with you, Holmes," he said

after he had exchanged the minimally appropriate greetings with the Japanese, "I don't approve of going into the records of the students at Dartmouth in these circumstances. It isn't at all the thing. I wouldn't like it if Englishmen were doing it, but these foreigners—Who knows what use might be made of them?" He shot a quick look at the Japanese, then stared hard at Holmes once more.

"I think," said Holmes at his most even, "that there is no reason to fear that Count Tochigi would be so lost to honor that he would use any information gleaned from the perusal of this material for his advantage. Not that I can immediately discern what that advantage might be." He bowed slightly to Ambassador Tochigi and looked squarely at Lord Brackenheath. "I thank you for your prompt response to my request, my lord."

"Yes. Well." He cleared his throat. "I've served England in government for thirty-eight years, Holmes," Lord Brackenheath announced roundly. "And I can't see how you will turn this to good purpose. And so I have informed our superiors. They have decided to leave the matter in your hands. Since they insist, I must do as my superiors command me." He turned to the Japanese again. "But I have the greatest respect for your Empire, sir. Lady Brackenheath has several pieces of your pottery."

"I see you do respect the Japanese," said Holmes, with a trace of sarcasm in his voice, and covered any possible insult by saying, "It will be a great pleasure to see you and Lady Brackenheath tomorrow night at the reception. They are now referring to it as a gala, as I am sure you are aware."

Lord Brackenheath took the tacit dismissal in good part. "Just so." His heavy dark brows drew down over his bright eyes. "Until then." He bowed to the Japanese once more, his bald pate polished by the lamplight, his fringe of curled hair shining like a slightly slipped halo of white.

Correctly I should have escorted Lord Brackenheath to the

door, but Mister Minato served as my deputy because of my crutches.

"I apologize, Ambassador," said Holmes smoothly once Lord Brackenheath was safely out of the room. "Not all the men working for the government are so maladroit."

I listened, wondering why Lord Brackenheath had been sent on this errand if his feelings were known. I had no doubt that Holmes could have requested someone of a less condemnatory manner than Lord Brackenheath. What had he sought to achieve? What purpose would such an intrusion serve? Perhaps Lord Brackenheath's presence was more a concession to Lord Salisbury than to his own purposes, part of the political maneuvering Holmes so deprecated.

"An awkwardness for you, to have to acknowledge it." The ambassador nodded to show respect for Holmes' admission.

"He is, in fact, a very dedicated man who has given long and laudable service to England." Holmes paused. "But he has decided opinions on the Orient."

"That was apparent," the Japanese ambassador agreed, his tone cordial.

"He suffered certain difficulties in the Crimea and later in China, and it has left its mark. I trust you will make allowances for his immoderation. Not all our diplomats share his sentiments," Holmes said, clearly presenting Ambassador Tochigi an opportunity to be more forthcoming. "As I am sure you are aware."

"A fortunate thing for England," said Ambassador Tochigi, responding to the gambit. "There are many of the same cut in Japan, who believe that it is a weakness to seek treaties with any powers in the West. I am thought eccentric for my support of this treaty, and for liking the society of Englishmen."

I had not been aware until this moment that Ambassador Tochigi had anything but faint contempt for Englishmen. But apparently this admission was part of the game he and Mycroft Holmes were playing. Perhaps Lord Brackenheath's presence was not as importune as I had first assumed. This continued jockeying had been the mark of the whole afternoon and we were all growing weary of it. Still, having so untoward a meeting as the one that had just taken place did not seem to advance the resolution of our disputes, requiring as it did such protracted amends. What possible advantage was there to be gained from this relentless exchange of courtesies? I sat forward on my chair and continued to take notes, most of them inconsequential. I supposed Messers Banadaichi and Minato were doing the same, for both had the same, slightly glazed expression as I knew I wore.

The door opened again, without an announcing knock. Ambassador Tochigi looked furious for an instant, but his manner changed at once. He and his two secretaries rose and bowed to the young man in the Dartmouth cadet's uniform.

Holmes had risen and motioned me to my feet. I had recourse to a crutch to get there. Clearly, I thought, this must be Prince Jiro, the Emperor's second son.

He was taller than Ambassador Tochigi but not more than five-foot-nine, and slight of build, with a handsome, clean-shaven oval face, black hair and eyes. He moved crisply forward, unflustered by the commotion his arrival caused. He gave Holmes his hand to shake before he bowed to Ambassador Tochigi.

"A pleasure to meet you, Mister Holmes," Prince Jiro exclaimed, not quite smiling at Holmes. His English was so perfect it was almost a caricature, like something an American actor would do. "It appears you have suffered a mishap?" This in reference to the bruise on his jaw.

"Just so, your Highness," said Holmes. "A tiresome thing. My secretary, Guthrie here, and I were about to alight from a cab when the horse bolted. I was thrown forward, but my secretary has injured his ankle."

Prince Jiro nodded once. "A bad business. But luckily it will not interfere with your negotiations here, will it?" Now his smile blossomed and I saw that he could undoubtedly be a most engaging young man. "Tell me," he went on to Ambassador Tochigi, still speaking English, "what progress have you made?"

Ambassador Tochigi began his answer in Japanese.

"In English, if you please," said Prince Jiro. "You will cause our friends to become suspicious of us, which is not what we want at all." He looked directly at Holmes. "I hope you will not think badly of us because of this lapse?"

"Why should I?" Holmes replied blandly. "It is fitting that the ambassador address you in the language of your country. Though I am pleased you are willing to have the conversation in English. You are right, Highness. It decreases suspicions to have it so."

The Prince regarded Holmes steadily, taking his measure of the man. He was unintimidated by Holmes' height and breadth of shoulder; Prince Jiro's self-assured manner impressed Holmes as well. "It would be a welcome thing if the agreement could be completed in the next few days, to coincide with the gala reception," he said, directing the weight of this at Ambassador Tochigi. "I would regard it as a personal favor."

Ambassador Tochigi bowed at once.

Prince Jiro made his point a second time, so there could be no possible misunderstanding. "If we could announce the successful resolutions of our differences tomorrow during the gala, I would be deeply grateful to both of you gentlemen." He glanced from Holmes to Ambassador Tochigi. "Between you I know sufficient good-will exists to accomplish the task. And you will do that more effectively if I am out of your way, I am certain of it." He very nearly chuckled as he offered his hand to Holmes once again. "Don't be too put off by our ways, Mister Holmes. We have been our own world for so long that we do not know yet how to accommodate those who are not Japanese, and seek to keep to ourselves. But this is the age of progress, of steel and steam, when the world is changing every hour. I hope you will both make allowances for that. Not all of us think Europeans are barbarians, or that your motives are improper. For my part, I am sure we will deal with you in good faith."

"I will bear that in mind, Highness," said Holmes with a half-bow.

"Excellent. Excellent." He rounded on Ambassador Tochigi. "You heard all I have said to Mister Holmes. I expect you to honor my pledge."

"I am bound to do it," said Ambassador Tochigi, bowing once more.

"I will expect to hear a report of progress before this time tomorrow," said Prince Jiro as he headed toward the door. "I will not be available tonight; you may send word of your progress to my assistant." With that, he caught the latch, swung out the door and was gone.

There was more than forty seconds of silence in the wake of his departure.

"Prince Jiro finds his own path. His personal name is Yukio, for it was known he would make his own way, so he was named for the snow." He looked a bit flustered at this inadvertent gossip. "His family and intimates only use that name. For all the rest, he remains Prince Jiro. To call him by his personal name would offend him." Ambassador Tochigi sat down again, and after a moment, so did Messers Banadaichi and Minato.

"Then, rest assured, we will not do so. The choice of his name strikes me as curious," Holmes said. "He is named for the snow. Because snow goes where it wishes?" he guessed aloud.

"Superficially, yes. There are other . . . ramifications to the name, as well. It has certainly proven apt." Ambassador Tochigi sighed. "We had best resume our work. It would not do for me to fail the Emperor's son."

"Very well," said Holmes, and without recourse to notes, said, "We are in agreement, I think, in regard to the issue of construction. Our yards here will begin laying down the keels for six different classes of ships, once payment for the work is received at the Exchequer. The smallest is to be torpedo boats and the largest will be eight hulls of the dreadnought class, built to the standards of the Royal Navy. Each will carry similar calibers of weaponry to that used on the warships of the Royal Navy. Not only will your Japanese cadets be familiar with the guns, they will be able to exchange ordnance with ships of our fleet if you require it."

"Your Royal Navy maintains the highest standards in the world," said Ambassador Tochigi; I was fairly certain he was sincere.

"And you will have the advantage of those standards," said Holmes. "Further, within six months, naval engineers will begin construction of a modern station and dry dock in a harbor of your Emperor's choice that is capable of supporting these ships once they are completed. Again, your Royal Navy cadets will be able to make the most of this arrangement."

Ambassador Tochigi nodded slowly. "This is in accordance with our requests."

Holmes acknowledged this with a nod. "The ship-building plan will continue for an extended period, with the completion of the last ship expected in 1901. These ships will have access to all British coaling stations for their journey to the Empire of Japan. You are already aware of our arrangements in regard to ordnance so that all these vessels may be maintained in battle-worthy condition. Further, two modern plants capable of producing shot and shell for these warships will be constructed at Osaka and Sasebo for the Emperor. Within ten years Japan will have the nucleus of the most up-to-date navy in the western Pacific region: one that will out-class if not outnumber anything the Russians might harbor at Kamchatka."

"Excellent, yes, this is acceptable." Ambassador Tochigi glanced toward Messrs. Minato and Banadaichi. "All is in accord with your records, is it not?"

The two men nodded as one.

When Holmes spoke again, his voice was so low that all four of us had to listen carefully to hear him. "The unpublished provisions we have agreed upon are more mutually advantageous than those officially outlined." He tapped his fingers on the table to punctuate each point as he recited them. "Both nations agree to respect and mutually protect each other's possessions and citizens. Neither shall render aid, including coaling, to any nation antagonistic to the other. The Empires of Britain and Japan will share with one another all military intelligence relating to the other, and do so in a timely manner. We both agree to make every effort to prevent further expansion of German and Russian influence in the Pacific region, Finally, in return for British recognition and support of your interests in the enumerated islands and Manchuria, your nation agrees to provide military and other assistance should any of our Far Eastern possessions be threatened by another power. We of Britain shall further endeavor to isolate Russia diplomatically should armed conflict arise between Japan and Saint Petersburg."

"Yes," said Ambassador Tochigi. "We are agreed on those unpublished points as well. Though there remains the matter of the enclave at Shanghai, the trading concessions, and the status of the Korean peninsula. These are matters which can be assessed separately from the others and should not prevent our signing the terms in which we are already in accord." He fell silent, providing an opportunity for my employer to speak. He then ducked his head in what I had decided was the Japanese version of a shrug. "But all this may come to nothing if we cannot resolve the matter of Dartmouth cadets."

"I would like to think we can reach a reasonable settlement in that regard," said Holmes.

"The rest hinges on the issue of the cadets," Ambassador Tochigi insisted pleasantly.

"Yes, I suppose it does," said Holmes thoughtfully. "That sums it up." He had been twirling his watchfob for some time. Now he stopped abruptly and said, "I don't know where you would like to begin, but I propose, since it is tea-time as we English view it, that we take an hour to collect our thoughts over tea."

There was a flicker of hesitation in Ambassador Tochigi's response, as if his good manners pained him. "Of course. That is something we can agree upon, Japanese and English—the importance of tea."

Holmes could see this cost the man some effort, so he appended a new observation. "I suppose you find our methods inelegant compared to your own tea ritual. I had the honor to witness an authentic tea ceremony some years ago, when I was a much younger man. I was deeply impressed with the aesthetics of the event."

"Ah. You know the tea ceremony," said Ambassador Tochigi with satisfaction.

"Indeed. And I can see why our baskets of muffins and jars of compote and scones with clotted cream would look unsatisfactory to you, sir." He indicated I should rise. "I have arranged for several varieties of tea to be made. That way we may sample many flavors, and remember the customs observed in other places."

As I rose, so did Messers Minato and Banadaichi. I saw how carefully both of them moved, and I felt the more inept because of my crutches. I laid my portfolio on my chair, as Holmes had instructed me to do, and waited while he placed his notes in his case. He left the case on his chair, as the Japanese had done with their various records. As we left the room, Andermatt appeared as if conjured from the air, and set a lock upon the door.

"Your tea is being served in the White Salon. No one will disturb you there," he informed us with an expression of supreme neutrality. "Enzo will escort you." He indicated a liveried footman hovering at the head of the stairs.

"Thank you, Andermatt," said Holmes, and remarked to me over his shoulder, "Guthrie, you will want to come last, I think."

"Yes, thank you, sir," I answered at once, knowing how inexpertly and slowly I had made my way down his stairs in Pall Mall that morning.

"I am sorry your secretary suffered an injury," said Ambassador Tochigi as he and Holmes descended in the wake of Andermatt and Enzo.

"No more than I, I assure you," Holmes said.

I waited until they had turned down the lower corridor before making my precarious way down the stairs, only to find Mister Minato waiting for me.

"You would like some help?" he offered.

"Need is more the word," I said churlishly, and relented. "Yes, you are right. I may have trouble making my way."

"I will go ahead of you, in case you require support." He bowed slightly. "I ask you not to fall. That would not help either of us."

It took me a moment to realize he was making a joke. "Oh. Exactly. Quite right."

He showed his appreciation by managing a quick smile. "I understand you fought off the attackers."

"Yes. Mister Holmes and I were able to rout them." I found it strange that he should make such an observation but I said nothing, not wishing to offend him accidentally.

"Have a care, Mister Guthrie," said Mister Minato, pointing to where I had placed my crutch. It was near the edge of the tread and could be precarious. Was that, I asked myself, the only thing intended in his warning?

"If you take your time, you will arrive safely," he said with confidence, once again leaving me with the uneasy feeling there was more to his warning than was at first apparent.

When I reached the foot of the stairs he bowed to me and hurried off, I assumed to join the ambassador.

Following him took longer than I had anticipated, and when I arrived at the foot of the stairs, I found myself in an empty corridor of blond wood paneling, hung with a number of lithographic prints of Swiss locales. Nonplussed, I stood for the greater part of a minute, my mind racing, in the hope that someone—perhaps the redoubtable Mr. Minato—would arrive to escort me to the White Salon, for surely I thought they would not want me to wander about the Swiss embassy wholly unattended. When this did not happen, and I remained unescorted, I made my way along the corridor, hoping that I would happen upon the White Salon on my own.

At the end of the corridor there was a tall, open-shuttered window letting in the fading sunlight. It was flanked by two doors. One of them, I supposed, must be the chamber in question. I halted to consider my situation. Selecting on impulse, I rapped on the door on my right and opened it, thinking if it were the wrong room, it would be locked.

I was in error. I stepped, not into the White Salon, but into the library, a chamber of wood paneling, trestle tables, and comfortable chairs, and nary a trace of white to mar the richness of the glossy woods. I saw the ranks of tall cases standing with their ranks of books in German, French, and Italian. And I saw Penelope Gatspy, dressed in the height of French fashion, her fair hair shining, seated at one of the reading tables, poring over an ancient atlas. I could not have been more shocked to find a Hindoo princess at the Albert Hall. What on earth was the Golden Lodge's most successful assassin doing at the Swiss embassy? The answers that sprang to mind were unwelcome.

She looked up at my entrance, and stared. "Guthrie," she said in hushed excitement. "God in Heaven! What are you doing here?"

FROM THE JOURNAL OF PHILIP TYERS

No word yet from Baker Street.

The Admiralty messenger has come and gone for the day, and I have secured the case he brought in the safe at the back of the pantry, for I cannot think it would be wise to place it even in a locked drawer. If our surveillance continues, they will discover nothing about what Holmes is doing, for the documents are well-protected. This way, I may leave the flat in certainty that nothing short of destruction will bring the case to light.

I have been watching the street as covertly as possible, and I fear I am beginning to think every figure a sinister one. Even a crocodile of girls from the French Academy in Regent Street appeared fraught with menace. This cannot continue if I am to acquit myself properly in my assignment. I must get better control of my imagination, or Sutton will decide I am as daft as one of those women in the plays he has performed.

Sutton is thriving on his role. He has worked to make his impersonation flawless, and I must concede he has largely accomplished his goal. I, who have seen him prepare, and who know M H of old, can detect few flaws in his characterization, and they are so minor that were I not in search of them, I would not know they were there. He will soon cross Pall Mall to M H's club, remain there the appointed time and return here. At which point he will resume his study of the role of Sir Peter Teazle. I begin to think he is in his way as agile of brain as many men in government service claim to be.

Chapter Eight

"WHAT AM I doing here?" I countered, hastily closing the door behind me. "What are *you* doing here?" A woman who was an accomplished assassin and operative for the mysterious Golden Lodge did not do many things by happenstance, and certainly not at the Swiss embassy during private meetings between the English and the Japanese. This encounter might well be one that was as much a product of manipulation as the attack on the cab had been.

"My brother works at the English embassy in Switzerland," she said primly.

"So you claimed. Among other things," I reminded her as I made my wary way toward her. The last time I had seen her, we had been in France, making a harrowing escape from members of the Brotherhood, a vast, occult organization dedicated to the ruin of Europe. "Some of them were not true."

If she was aware of my sarcasm she made no indication of it, but stared directly at me. "You have been in trouble again, haven't you?" she said, indicating my crutches.

"An accident," I said, too quickly, for I could not admit to this woman what had actually taken place, for fear she and the Golden Lodge had some connection to the events.

"Accidents are a hazard of our professions, aren't they?" she asked with a winsome smile. "From the look of it, you were lucky."

"Yes," I said, thinking feverishly for a credible explanation for my presence at the Swiss embassy, for surely she would be curious about it.

"I must suppose," she said, abandoning her atlas and coming toward me, "that you are here in regard to tomorrow's gala. Mister Holmes is a demanding employer, is he not, sending you on such a task, given the circumstances."

"I do not find him so," I said firmly, not wanting to have to endure any expressions of false sympathy at this point. "I might say as much for the Golden Lodge, sending a woman like you alone to an occasion like this. Or should I assume there is some reason you are here, beyond the matter of your brother?"

"You may assume what you wish, Mister Guthrie," she said rather primly. She was a remarkably pretty girl in that pale, English way, and we had been in a few close scrapes together not so very long ago. She had lost a colleague to the Brotherhood, and Mycroft Holmes and I had come close to losing a valuable document and a courier. Still, I did not wholly trust her, nor she me. "I understand the son of the Emperor is to attend the gala. The one who's at Dartmouth."

"So he is," I said, feeling remarkably stupid. There was something about Miss Gatspy that made my tongue cleave to the roof of my mouth and my thoughts to dither. "And what interest is that to you?" It was not a gentlemanly challenge, but I could not stop myself.

"The Brotherhood's designs reach as far as the Chrysanthemum Throne and the Vermilion Brush," said Miss Gatspy abruptly. Her references to Japan and China shocked me.

"They cannot want to bring down those empires as well as all of Europe," I said at once. "For one thing, they cannot infiltrate the governments of those places as handily as they can in Europe. China and Japan are chary with foreigners."

She gave me a hard look. "Did you suppose that their ambitions pertained only to Europe, or that their membership limited to Europeans only? Hardly that, Guthrie. Their influence is felt throughout the world, from Iceland to the Argentine, from Vladivostok to New Orleans." If we had not been in this library, I reckoned she would have laughed aloud at me; as it was, her eyes glinted and the corners of her mouth curved. "How better to spread chaos than to set East and West at each other's throats, or pit the New World against the Old? And how greater the vacuum would be that they could occupy in such an eventuality." She glanced at the door. "You will be missed, won't you?"

I was taken aback at her familiarity with my work here. "Why would you think so?" I asked, hoping to cover my dismay with a sharpness of tone I did not feel. I thought my brusqueness would distract her.

I did not succeed. "Well, making full allowances for your crutches, you and I have added several minutes to your journey, and the Swiss are more conscious of time than most. You have not arrived where you are expected, and this could be considered troublesome," she said quietly, unwilling to meet my churlishness with her own. "You had better be about your work. I have things of my own to attend to. Tomorrow evening we will talk again, if circumstances permit."

"So many circumstances," I said in a teasing way, so that she would know I did not think ill of her. "You are planning to attend the gala, then?"

"Most certainly," she said, the angle of her head showing her fine features most admirably. "We of the Golden Lodge take interest in everything that interests the Brotherhood. And this forthcoming gala had the Brotherhood in an uproar. They are eager to embarrass either the English or the Japanese, or barring that, the Swiss, so that the whole negotiations are caught in scandal. It doesn't matter what subverts them so long as the negotiations end in failure."

"No doubt," I said, preparing to withdraw.

She stopped me with a polite phrase. "My regards to Mister Holmes, Guthrie. I am aware that much of the burden of these talks falls on his shoulders. I cannot imagine a more capable man to strive for a solution. And tell him he is more deserving of a knighthood than ever MacMillian was." She offered a playful wave as I closed the door.

In the hall I took a handful of seconds to gather my thoughts before presenting myself in the White Salon. It would not do for me to appear flustered. The Japanese might construe it to our disadvantage.

"Guthrie, dear boy," Mycroft Holmes hailed me from the buffet where he was selecting an array of French pastries. "I was beginning to worry about you. Not enough to call out the Saint Bernards, but perhaps to send a footman looking for you."

I smiled dutifully at his witticism and struggled with the door and my crutches, and happened to catch a glimpse of a man in dark clothing entering the library I had just left. Was Miss Gatspy so brazen that she met her associates within embassy walls? I closed the door before my hesitation could occasion any remark.

The White Salon was certainly deserving of its name: From the lace curtains and linen draperies to the damask upholstery, the room glistened like a Swiss mountain-top, all brilliant with snow. The carpets were a pattern of silver-and-white roses, and the wall-paper was an embossed pattern of white-on-white stripes.

"I took a wrong turn," I said, which was not more than the truth. "And I have only just corrected my error." I looked at Ambassador Tochigi, who was pouring Russian-style tea from a huge brass samovar. This surprised me a bit, and I was about to say something about it when the ambassador himself explained his selection.

"When I was a secretary, like Minato and Banadaichi, I was posted to Russia with the mission there. I developed a taste for the strong, sweet tea the Russians drink. It is a luxury I indulge in whenever I can." He was adding sugar to his cup as he spoke. Then he cut himself a section of Linzertorte, and topped it off with sweet brandied cherries. "How fortunate that Switzerland can choose among three such rich cuisines—French, German, and Italian."

"Yes, it is quite a recommendation," agreed Holmes as he took his seat.

I realized I was at a serious disadvantage, for I could not use my crutches and carry a cup of tea, let alone a plate of pastry, to my seat. I went to Holmes' side. "Sir, I do not wish to offend you, but I would like to request that you permit me to sit at the buffet for tea. Otherwise . . ."

Holmes waved me toward the table. "Have at it, dear boy. I'm certain no one will object."

Ambassador Tochigi looked stuffy at Holmes' answer, and his secretaries carefully made no notice of this exchange whatsoever. I thanked Holmes, made my way across the room, turned a chair toward the buffet in such a place that I could easily watch the others in the room, sank into it and began to select items for my tea. First I filled a cup with good China black, and then bent my mind to choosing between French St. Honoré's cake and Italian zabaglione.

Holmes leaned back and resumed what he had been saying when I came into the room. "What is most pressing, given the potential for disaster in such an . . . association, from what you have said is to discover the woman the Prince has become . . . entangled with, and extricate him without a breath of scandal."

"That is correct," said Ambassador Tochigi. "All other agreements are contingent upon that."

"Understandably," said Holmes.

Ambassador Tochigi took a long sip of his Russian tea. "Has any effort been made to identify the woman?"

"Not successfully, no," admitted Holmes. "If you will forgive me, Count, our hands would not be so completely tied if you were to authorize us to put men to watch the Prince. He would quickly lead us to her."

"That is not acceptable. We have our own men for that purpose." He cleared his throat. "It is not fitting to have a member of the Emperor's family followed by agents of another government. If you will excuse me for making so plain a statement."

"Certainly," Holmes replied affably, "since it will allow me the chance to observe that you are being very short-sighted in this regard, for your men are restricted in their movements about England, and they cannot do the tasks you have assigned them with such restraints."

"Then lift the restraints," said Ambassador Tochigi impatiently.

"It isn't so easily done, Ambassador, if you will forgive me for speaking of it." He watched Ambassador Tochigi. "You would not welcome English guards given leave to make their way unchecked through Japan: No more would England be willing to provide carte blanche to your guards here. The most reasonable compromise would be for you to give permission to us to follow the Prince while he is here. We will not interfere with anything he does at the embassy or in his work with you, but if we are to discover the woman, it is far easier to begin with the man we know than try to settle on a woman we do not know." He paused to enjoy his food.

Ambassador Tochigi gave the matter some thought. "If it were up to me, I would do it, but I must answer to my superiors, as you must answer to yours, and they would not countenance such an act."

"You may underestimate your powers of persuasion, Count Tochigi," said Holmes.

But the ambassador was not willing to listen to flattery. "It would take months if it were to be done at all. And we have little more than a day in which to resolve this question. So I fear we will not be able to put your theory to the test. It is not possible for me to make the request you recommend."

Holmes tried another tack. "I must confess, Count, that I am astonished that given the misadventure of Prince Jiro, your government would want to place so many Japanese cadets at Dartmouth."

Ambassador Tochigi had an answer for him. "Then you have not given the matter much close consideration. It is thought that if there were more Japanese students at the Naval College, there would be greater camaraderie, and the impulse to become involved with foreigners as a balm to loneliness would be less a threat than has been the case with Prince Jiro."

So that was the agreed-upon tale: Prince Jiro had taken up with an Englishwoman because he was homesick for Japan, and could not resist the foreign woman in his loneliness. Therefore, if there had been more Japanese cadets, the Prince would not have strayed. There was a odd logic to the argument, if one accepted the premise that the Prince was seduced. I listened intently as I began on my piece of St. Honoré's cake.

Mister Minato went to the door and glanced out into the hall, then returned silently to his chair. He went on with his tea, and Ambassador Tochigi paid no attention to any of his actions.

"Very well, another two or three would not be unreasonable. But more than that would be apt to lead to the kind of abrasive competition we have made efforts to avoid," Holmes pointed out as calmly as he could.

"It might, but our cadets would be instructed to avoid such unpleasantries." He regarded Holmes with an absence of expression that results in men of the Occident calling men of the Orient inscrutable.

"Young men, proud of their accomplishments and manhood, do not lend themselves to such restraints," Holmes pointed out.

"Perhaps not in the West. It is different in the East." He favored Holmes with an unctuous smile and had more of his tea.

"But you yourself, Count, have had reason to complain of the behavior of your cadets in the West, starting with the Prince himself," said Holmes. "And it may be that there will be those who share his misbehavior rather than preventing it, should your cadets be here in larger numbers."

"That is the wisdom of the West," sighed Ambassador Tochigi. "It is thought that all men will throw off custom and restraints, given the opportunity to do so."

"As history must teach us," Holmes said, and rose to pour himself more tea. He added milk from an antique jug, then returned to his seat.

"Perhaps. But your history seeks to show that this is the way of men, that without fear of punishment—and occasionally with fear of punishment—they will become adventurers and marauders, bringing disgrace to themselves and their families." He looked puzzled. "You call it Original Sin, I believe."

"Not precisely," said Holmes. "But let us not be distracted by discussions on religion. It would serve neither of our purposes."

"No doubt you are correct," said Ambassador Tochigi, and made an abrupt change of subject. "I have read that you have once seen Japan. Is this true?"

"I was much younger then, and my visit was brief. I was told that I should see it in the spring, when it is at its best." Holmes looked directly at Ambassador Tochigi. "I saw Kyoto, and the old harbor at Osaka. But I had only four days in your country."

"Not much time, truly," said Ambassador Tochigi. "I should be most sad if all I could ever see of England was what I could find in four days." He glanced at Holmes. "And your time was not your own."

"No, it was not," Holmes agreed. "In fact, speed was of the essence. Had I been able to discharge my commission in less time, I would have."

A speculative light came into the ambassador's eyes. "Tell me, did this take place just over twenty years ago?"

"It did," said Holmes tersely.

Ambassador Tochigi nodded twice. "I have heard something of that commission. It is remembered with high regard. You were fortunate to escape unscathed." There was reluctant admiration in his voice.

"Not quite unscathed. I have a scar to remind me of the men who wanted to thwart my efforts." Unbidden, his hand went to the top of his collar where the long seam of a scar began.

"Surely you do not hold that against the Japanese?" said Ambassador Tochigi.

"No, I don't. I hold it against the opium lords." He made himself speak more calmly. "It was years ago. Things have changed a great deal since that time."

"To our mutual advantages," said Ambassador Tochigi.

Holmes gave a nod that was almost a bow. "For the time being."

The silence that settled on the White Salon was oddly companionable. I saw that Messers Minato and Banadaichi were looking at Holmes with increased respect, Minato going so far as to duck his head in appreciation. From what I had seen of him, I could not decide if there was any special significance in this greater show of respect than his own very correct sense of conduct.

But these recollections had awakened a number of questions within me. What on earth had Holmes done in those four days, I wondered, that it was still talked about in Japan? He had made no mention of it to me, had, in fact, claimed ignorance in regard to that country. By his standards, I could conceive how a dangerous mission—for surely it had been dangerous—of four days would not constitute any true knowledge of the country. But what had been his purpose then? And what bearing, if any, did it have on the events surrounding us now? I resolved to discuss this further with my employer when we were alone.

I finished my St. Honoré's cake and debated having a little of the zabaglione as well, when Andermatt came into the White Salon, bearing a tray with four impressive bottles and appropriate glasses.

"It is the hour for sherry," he announced, though he was plainly offering more than that. "Sherry, as you see. Russian vodka, almond liqueur, and brandy. You may select whatever pleases you." He put the tray down on the butler's table and waited for requests.

Ambassador Tochigi said, "I will have the vodka, to remember my years in Russia."

Holmes coughed once. "I will have the same."

It was now left to the three secretaries to select our preferences. Messers Banadaichi and Minato both asked for the vodka. So I decided to have something else.

"Is the almond liqueur Italian?" I asked, as if I had some knowledge of the matter.

"Yes, sir. From the Benedictines near Udine. It is not so sweet as most of them."

"I'll try it, then," I said, hoping I would like the stuff. As Andermatt handed me a small sniffer with a generous tot in it, I sniffed at it, finding it oddly harsh in odor. I did my best to show approval. "You're right. It's not sweet."

"I will leave the tray for you gentlemen," said Andermatt. "Your evening meal will be laid for you at eight, if that is convenient?"

"Yes, of course," said Holmes.

At the same time Ambassador Tochigi said, "Most satisfactory."

Andermatt bowed and withdrew.

"An excellent servant," said the ambassador when Andermatt was gone. "The Swiss are always so careful in these matters."

"They have to be, given the nature of their country," said Holmes. "Historically, the French, the Germans, and the Italians have not made very good neighbors, except in Switzerland, where they take great care to get along for the sake of their country."

"A worthy model," said Ambassador Tochigi, "for those who are troubled by their neighbors. Japan, being an island, like England, need not concern itself with such matters."

Holmes shook his head. "Not so. England has seen waves of invaders become English, which Japan has not. We have an obligation to everyone, Norman, Saxon, Angle, Jute, Viking, Roman, Celt, and the rest."

Ambassador Tochigi stared into his vodka. "Not so bad as Russia, but bad enough." He pondered the clear, oily-looking liquid for a moment. "Sometimes when there is an invasion, those invaded accept the newcomers grudgingly, if at all."

"True enough," said Holmes.

I had the oddest sensation that the two of them were suddenly speaking in a code. I touched my tongue to the almond liqueur and listened intently, though I did not know what I expected to hear.

"And where there has been killing, the anger will linger for years—sometimes for more than a lifetime." He drank down his vodka in a single gulp, then poured himself more.

"As you and I have witnessed," said Holmes, and sipped carefully at the vodka in his snifter.

"Exactly," said Ambassador Tochigi.

FROM THE JOURNAL OF PHILIP TYERS

At last. An urchin came around from Baker Street bringing a note saying that none of the street gangs preying on cabs in the manner described has been working north of the Thames. There are no rumors of any new gangs "taking up the lay", and certainly not in Kensington, Chelsea, or Westminster.

However, according to the message the boy carried, there are stories being circulated about a band of malcontents with political ambitions who are not above trying to interfere with negotiations with the Japanese, or any powers beyond the British Empire. They have been trying to stir up public sentiment against the Oriental presence in England, claiming that life would not be safe for good Englishmen. It is expected that they may attempt some demonstration of their position at the Swiss embassy tomorrow night. I have dispatched a note of thanks to M H's brother for his assistance, and given it into the boy's care. He informed me he will call tomorrow afternoon if there are any further developments.

Sutton has almost finished memorizing Sir Peter Teazle, and I am heartily glad of it. What amused me a day ago is now sadly flat, for I have heard it more times than I enjoy. He has just returned from M H's club across Pall Mall, and has settled down in the sitting room, his play in hand.

Sid Hastings has agreed to send his cousin Reginald to pick up M H and G at the conclusion of their dealings. It is hoped that the watchers will not recognize Reginald and his horse, but to add to the strategem, I have recommended that they not return by the Brompton Road, Knightsbridge, Piccadilly route, but travel some other course, and come in from Regent Street, not St. James. It will take longer, but it will be safer, of that I am convinced. I trust Sid Hastings in this, but I know little or nothing of his cousin, who may not be so willing to take this course back from the Swiss embassy.

Tomorrow will be a telling day, no matter how the negotiations fare. I have prepared the formal wear M H will need to take with him upon his departure in the morning. I understand G will do the same.

At least they will be prepared for every possible occurrence.

Chapter Nine

I WOKE BEFORE dawn with the groggy sensation of urgency pulling me awake precipitously. I stumbled out of bed, taking care to support myself on the bureau and then the chair as I made my way to the bedroom door. As I reached for the handle, I heard a sound just beyond the door—the distinctive mew of a cat. My sudden relief was quickly replaced with apprehension. How had a cat got into my rooms? I had taken care to secure the windows and lock all the doors when I returned here last night shortly after eleven. There should be no means for the animal to gain access to the sitting room. With these reflections to caution me, I opened the door a crack and peered out.

This time the cat's cry had the quality of a question, rising at the end of the sound.

"Where are you?" I whispered, not seeing the animal, and being in no mood to chase it on my strapped ankle.

Another mew, this one more confident. I began to hope that however the cat had got in, it would prove to be a minor oversight on my part, and not a warning of more hazards. And if any danger remained, I thought, the cat would surely be silent. The fact that she was crying out meant that there was some degree of safety. I limped out into the sitting room, trying to penetrate the predawn gloom without having recourse to the lamps.

I made my way across my sitting room, hoping that I would not unduly disturb Missus Coopersmith, who served as housekeeper to the six residents of the house. Her quarters were directly below mine and she was known to be a light sleeper.

I heard the cat again, and this time I caught fleeting sight of it—a moving blur of darkness. She had run under the table where I had my meals and did my writing. I pursued her, confident now that I could corner her, and even if the animal was wild, I could contrive to remove it from my rooms. As I steadied myself on the end of the table, I reached for a lucifer. I would need more light on the matter if I were to succeed in getting the cat out of her hiding place. After I adjusted the flame on the lamp, I moved carefully so that I could look under the table without injuring my ankle.

The cat was crouched there, ears back and teeth bared. I noticed that her coat looked matted and it took me a moment to realize it was not blood that marred the cat's fur, but bright red paint, quite fresh, and that smears of it smirched the carpet and floor of the room, a deliberate gesture to tell me that I was not safe here—

that paint could be blood and the cat might as easily have been myself. Whoever had done this was also alerting me that he knew where I lived, and had gained access to my rooms while I lay sleeping. This last thought was no more welcome than the others had been, but I determined to fix my attention on it.

"mrrow," said the cat, timorously trying to get near me.

"I shouldn't wonder," I answered, and decided that I would ask Missus Coopersmith's help in dealing with the cat and the mess she made of the floor and carpets. I would probably have to pay her for the extra service, but given the circumstances, that was more than acceptable to me.

While I shaved, I noticed that the cat began a tentative exploration of her surroundings. I could find it in my heart to pity the poor creature, for it had suffered, through no fault of its own, at the hands of my enemies—Lord, I did not think of myself as a man with enemies! Since I was the cause of its distress and ill usage, I supposed I ought to find it a good home. I certainly owed it that much after it had suffered because of me.

Had I still been engaged to Miss Elizabeth Roedale of Twyford, as I had been at this time last year, I should have asked her to care for it. The thought of Miss Roedale recalled the keen remonstrance my mother had called down upon me when that lady ended our engagement, for it had been my mother's—and Miss Roedale's mother's—dearest wish since the lady and I were children that we should be married. Miss Roedale would not want to have anything from me now, particularly not a stray cat covered in red paint. Now I could think of no one who would be willing to take the cat as an accommodation to me. I frowned over that problem—it was more soluble than determining who put the cat in my room in the first place, and why.

Unbidden, the image of Miss Gatspy rose in my thoughts. What, if anything, was her role in all this? I knew she was capable of killing a man, but I could not imagine her covering a helpless cat in paint. Did the Golden Lodge have anything to do with England's agreements with Japan? Was the Brotherhood interfering in our negotiations? I did my best to recall everything she had said to me at the Swiss embassy, and as I examined her remarks away from the shock of her presence, I was the more confused. What had seemed then a timely warning now held a more sinister intent. I glared at the clothing on my carpenter's valet, as if I might find the answer there.

For an instant I wondered if Penelope Gatspy might be the woman we sought, the one who was enamored of Prince Jiro. I realized at once this was impossible. And while I knew that Miss Gatspy was a very attractive woman in her way, I could not imagine her allowing such a personal entanglement to enter her well-ordered life. Still, I resolved to watch her more closely this evening, to see how she behaved in regard to the Prince. I thought again of Mycroft Holmes' acute interest in my encounter with Miss Gatspy when I related the whole of it to him on the way home last night. To my astonishment, he had professed himself amused to know she was there.

The cat had found a remote corner of my sitting room and was occupied in cleaning her coat. She ignored me most splendidly. I would have liked to make another attempt to pick her up to examine her and reassure myself she had been injured in dignity only, but I could not manage my crutches and an unwilling cat at the same time, and gave up the attempt.

As I prepared to leave, my formal clothes in my valise, and my portfolio's handle looped over my wrist, both of which were devilishly awkward with the crutches, I stopped at Missus Coopersmith's rooms on the ground floor and told her of the cat. "I suppose she is the victim of those bands of young hooligans from Soho who racket about the streets at night, doing mischief."

"In this part of the city?" exclaimed Missus Coopersmith. "You'd think the police would put a stop to it."

I nodded. "It might be wise to be particularly careful for the next few days. There is no saying they might not think of something more . . . unpleasant to do," I told her, wanting to put her on her guard without giving undue alarm.

"How vexing, that such things could happen in Curzon Street. Tell me about the poor animal." Missus Coopersmith was willing to hear me out.

"She is hiding near my bookcase, in the corner, or she was when I left the room. I suspect a little cream will coax her out." I managed to gesture encouragement.

"Cats. People will do such vile things to them." She came up to me and patted my arm. "Do not fret, Mister Guthrie. I will see to the cat. She will take no hurt from me." With that she glanced toward the ceiling. "You said something about paint?"

"Yes. Red paint. I fear it's made something of a mess." As it was intended to, I added to myself. I knew the warning was deliberate. "I am afraid the cat was covered in it. She ran around and the—"

"It is very sad," said Missus Coopersmith, and made a tisking sound. "You need to be on your way, Mister Guthrie. I recall you said you had a function that would keep you out late tonight. I will not be concerned if you do not arrive until the morning hours. And I will tend to your rooms and the cat."

As I watched her bustle upstairs, I was struck again at how much like a grandmother she seemed—round as a dumpling and ruthlessly good-hearted, it was an easy matter to think of her as ancient, when, in reality, I knew she was only six-and-thirty, and was not, in fact, a widow. Her husband was very much alive and posted in India, where he kept three native women as his wives. Missus Coopersmith had found it more tolerable to be a widow than a woman abandoned as she was. She had been given the income from this house by her father-in-law, as much from shame as from affection. She would take excellent care of the cat, and would guard her house diligently.

I made my way out to the kerb and looked along the street for Sid Hastings. I was often amazed at the hours he kept, for he could not have much time with his family given all the hours he devoted to his business. My valise at my side made me feel as if I were off on another adventure at Mycroft Holmes' request rather than venturing to the Swiss embassy for the final stages of our negotiations. For a moment I thought about the cat, and the cryptic warning she was intended to issue. Then I pushed those events firmly to the back of my thoughts.

"Good morning to you, Mister Guthrie," Sid Hastings called out as he brought Jenny to a halt in front of me. It was a good hour earlier than he usually came for me, as arranged. "Have a care getting in. Dare say you're eager to be at it this morning."

"Why, I suppose so," I said as I clambered into the cab, wrestling my portfolio, valise, and crutches under my knees as the vehicle started off for Pall Mall.

"It being the night of the gala, and all," Hastings went on, "I suppose Mister Holmes would like it if the matter were settled by the time the carriages arrive this evening."

"Yes, I suppose he would," I said, "for then he could leave early, as he wishes to do." But that, I thought, was not for the English to decide but the Japanese.

Mycroft Holmes was waiting two blocks from his flat, in Charles II Street. He was engulfed in a cloak and woollen muffler of vast proportions, and he carried a small trunk with him, for all the world like an itinerate salesman of the sort who often sold kitchen utensils to servants. I realized at once I was seeing Edmund Sutton's fine hand in this disguise.

"Cor', sir," said Hastings as Holmes settled himself in the

cab, "you look a right gubber, and that's the truth." He chuckled as he told Jenny to walk on.

"Well, Guthrie, and how are you faring this morning, dear boy?" He pulled at one of the ends of the muffler without any visible effect. "Is your ankle still giving you difficulty, or is it something more?"

I shook my head and told him about the cat.

"Dear me," said Holmes when I had finished and we were nearing the Swiss embassy, "this is very troubling. Very troubling indeed." He stared into the middle distance, which indicated he was caught up in thought. "Red paint, was it?"

"Yes. It may have been red ink, the kind they use in lithography." I wished now I had taken a sample of the stuff to show him.

"Um, bad for the cat," said Holmes, and relapsed into silence, which he maintained until we pulled up at the side of the Swiss embassy. "Leave your things in the cab," he instructed abruptly. "Hastings will drive around to the porte cochere and put them in there, in order to give the impression that we are not expected until later." He prepared to slip into the side door as soon as Andermatt opened it.

"Very well," I said, retrieving my crutches and preparing to join my employer.

The door opened and Andermatt bowed. "If you please?"

We were out of the cab and into the embassy with alacrity. As the door closed behind us, I heard Sid Hastings start his horse moving once more.

"We have footmen at the porte cochere to tend to your things, as we arranged," said Andermatt. "If you will be good enough to come with me, there is breakfast laid out for you and the Japanese in the Morning Room." He paused long enough to relieve us of cloaks and wraps. I saw that Holmes' bruise was developing a yellow-green tinge to its edges; the reason for the muffler was now apparent.

As we made our way to the eastern side of the embassy, I steadied my nerves and said to Andermatt, "Yesterday, when I was looking for the White Salon, I ended up in the library across the hall."

"Yes, sir?" said Andermatt, indicating the open double doors to the Morning Room.

"I met a young woman there, a Miss Gatspy. I was curious about her reason for being here." I glanced at Holmes, who seemed wholly disinterested in my question.

Andermatt achieved a puzzled scowl. "I am sorry, sir, but I am not aware of anyone by that name being admitted to the embassy yesterday. Is it possible you were mistaken?"

Although I had no doubt about Penelope Gatspy herself, I knew it would be best not to challenge Andermatt. "Perhaps I have the name wrong," I said, trying not to sound too forceful. "A handsome young woman, about middle height, pale, rosy hair. Wearing a pine-colored morning ensemble."

"No," said Andermatt. "I cannot recall anyone of that description. I am sorry, Mister Guthrie." With that he bowed and withdrew.

Ambassador Tochigi and his secretaries had not yet arrived, and so Mycroft Holmes and I had the opportunity to discuss our plans for the day.

Holmes helped himself to eggs and sausage while I struggled with a cheese-filled breakfast pastry. "Let me help you, dear boy," he said as he realized how difficult it was to hold a plate and use crutches at the same time.

"Thank you, sir. Just two pastries and tea and I shall do." I sat at the table, feeling awkward that Holmes should assist me.

"Yes," Holmes agreed. "They have been feeding us very well, haven't they?" He poured himself tea and sat down across from me. "About your Miss Gatspy," he began.

For some reason, I answered hotly, "She is not *my* Miss Gatspy."

"Not in that sense, no, certainly not," Holmes soothed. "But you are the one who is forever running into her, aren't you?" He knew I could not truthfully deny this, and so he went on, "I have given the matter some thought, and I think it would be wise for you to find out what has actually brought her here."

"She has already intimated that the Brotherhood is desirous of causing difficulties in Asia as well as Europe," I reminded him. "And we have seen enough of the Brotherhood to know they will stop at nothing to achieve their ends."

"Just so," he responded. "But what has the Golden Lodge to do with it, that is what is troubling me. I cannot bring myself to believe that the Golden Lodge is here merely to observe our activities, with no tasks of their own to fulfill."

I listened to this with increasing apprehension, for I shared his anxieties. "Sir," I said as I stared into my tea, "ought we to warn the Japanese?"

Holmes shrugged his big shoulders. "If we could be certain of what the intentions are of both the Brotherhood and the Golden Lodge, and if we were assured that the loyalty of Ambassador Tochigi was wholly committed to our common interests, then I would say it would be advisable. But as we can speak to neither of these issues, reticence might be our most effective posture for the time being." He leaned forward again. "That is why I think it is so particularly urgent that you speak with Miss Gatspy, to find out as much as you can from her."

"What makes you think she would tell me the truth?" I asked, remembering how skilled she was at dissembling.

Whatever Mycroft Holmes might have answered was lost as Ambassador Tochigi came into the room, his secretaries flanked behind him. All three paused on the threshold to bow. "Good morning," said the ambassador. "I am delighted to start so early. There is much to accomplish."

Holmes had half-risen to return the bow, then sat once again. "I, too, am looking forward to our progress this morning."

Ambassador Tochigi went to select his breakfast, leaving Messers Banadaichi and Minato to stand by the door until he was seated. "At least we have reached accord on Korea and Shanghai, which leaves only the matter of cadets at Dartmouth and the participation of the Japanese navy in the defense of English stations."

"Let us tackle the latter first," Holmes recommended. "It is apt to be the more readily resolved. And though we have not as yet discovered the identity you wish to know, I hope we may find the first answers we seek quickly so that we will have all of the afternoon to work the question of the cadets." He finished his tea and rose to pour more. "I have taken the liberty of informing the Admiralty we will be able to conclude our dealings this evening. They will send Lord Brackenheath and Charles Stewart Parnell along with Robert Cecil, Lord Salisbury himself to prepare the formal document. The choice of Lord Brackenheath and Parnell is so that all Parliament and the government may be adequately represented. Then there will be the military men as well, King, Wolseley, and Seymour at the least, and possibly Hewett and Wood as well."

"I trust you are not being presumptuous," said Ambassador Tochigi. He sat down and his secretaries went about selecting their food. "We may not have concluded all our negotiations by this evening."

"Then let us document those we are agreed upon," Holmes said affably. "It would make the occasion so much more pleasant for all of us."

Ambassador Tochigi considered this. "I cannot promise I will be able to endorse such a document, but I am aware your intentions are of the best, and in accord with the instructions of my Emperor. This is to be a significant occasion, and those attending are of honorable intentions. Further, the agreement is historic. It would be fitting to complete the agreement as a part of the gala."

"Thank you, Mister Ambassador," said Mycroft Holmes. I could hear relief in his voice that was as potent as it was unexpected.

"Yes. Both our governments would be pleased, and the occasion is a splendid one. It would be, as you say, a welcome addition to the evening to complete our dealings." He took a long sip of tea, then said with a wily look, "I take it that you will not present the signed agreement yourself."

"It would not be wise," said Holmes quickly and smoothly. "Best leave it to Brackenheath and the rest."

"Of course." Ambassador Tochigi almost sounded amused.

FROM THE JOURNAL OF PHILIP TYERS

It has been a busy morning, what with a secretary, a Mister Coldene, from the Admiralty coming to the flat with a report for M H which I am about to hand to Sid Hastings to deliver to the Swiss embassy. It would appear that the information sought by the Japanese is not yet available, though much effort has been expended to provide it. I am informed by Coldene that this is rendered especially difficult by the need for confidentiality in all the dealings regarding the Prince.

Sutton is finishing up his study of the Sheridan play, and I am heartily glad of it. He says he is now prepared to review the entirety of the play with actors. I wish him well with it. How anyone is to keep a sense of novelty in a work after such constant repetition, I cannot think. He has indicated his next project will be to memorize the role of Duke Ferdinand in Webster's The Duchess of Malfi. *I have told Sutton that this one he will have to learn on his own, for the next two days may well be filled with activity for M H, which activity will impinge on Sutton as much as on any of us.*

I believe I have found another watcher. This one is a man in in-

conspicuous clothing who has been lingering about in Pall Mall for the last hour. I do not know if I should alert Sutton to the fellow or not. If he is not gone when Sutton goes to M H's club in the evening, I suppose I must. Until that time I will continue to mark this fellow and take care to be at pains to discover his purpose here.

Chapter Ten

"THE ADMIRALTY HAVE taken leave of their senses if it agrees to this!" Lord Brackenheath fumed as he read the rough draught of the agreement reached by Mycroft Holmes and Ambassador Tochigi a scant half hour before.

"It is a reasonable compromise," said Holmes quietly, his manner as politely discreet as anyone would wish. "If you and Parnell will but consider the concessions we have earned, all without providing the Japanese with the one thing they truly seek to know—" He broke off, looking about the White Salon at the three Swiss servants who were laying afternoon tea.

"Yes, yes," said Lord Brackenheath testily. "We must suppose that their concern is not a ploy to give them leverage with England. That is assuming their initial intelligence is correct and the Prince has truly found himself an Englishwoman so lost to propriety that she has been willing to enter into a liaison so repugnant—" He, too, recalled the servants and held his tongue. "Where is the ambassador?"

"He and his secretaries have retired to dress for the evening. As they will be wearing Japanese court dress, their process is rather more complicated than ours." Holmes swung his watchfob, speaking levelly as he did. "I should, perhaps, warn you, Lord Brackenheath, that I am going to advise most strongly that the terms of this agreement be ratified as Ambassador Tochigi and I have agreed to them. I have asked the Admiralty to send over secretaries to make fair copies of the agreement. It would be most . . . impolite to have the terms questioned now."

Lord Brackenheath stared hard at Holmes, his dark brows angling down in a furious glower. "It's men like you who'll be the ruin of England, mark my word."

"That is not for you to decide, my lord," said Holmes, whose courtesy was beginning to wear thin. "I have done what I was charged to do to the best of my ability, and under most difficult circumstances. I should not like to think that so much cooperation and good will might have been for naught."

"Next thing, you'll be saying there should be wogs in Commons," grumbled Lord Brackenheath. "But if the others are willing to go along with this chicanery, who am I to stand against their folly?"

"I am pleased you are willing to cooperate, sir," Holmes said, doing his best to keep the dryness out of his tone.

"Hardly willing, but it has to be done, I suppose. If I do not, some less astute fellow might be duped into believing the nonsense you are espousing." He took a turn about the White Salon. "Pretty place. A trifle too pale for my taste, but well enough." He coughed. "My valet is arriving in an hour, and my wife an hour after that, so that we will all be ready to receive the guests of the evening. As I understand it, you are to have no part in that. You are here for the agreement, not the gala."

"No, I am not, my lord," said Holmes.

"Probably just as well," said Lord Brackenheath. "I would imagine the Admiralty, and the Home Office as well, don't want it known how much you do for them."

"Such is our agreement," Holmes said, and added in a more conversational tone, "I hope your recent travels abroad were satisfactory?"

"Oh, they were tolerable. Those Austrians charge outrageous prices for everything and I was made ill by the waters of Prague, but all in all, it was most . . . instructive."

"I hope Lady Brackenheath was equally pleased," said Holmes.

"She stayed in England" came Lord Brackenheath's blunt retort.

Holmes looked mildly surprised. "Your pardon. I understood you had company on your journey, and I thought—"

"My valet, of course. Good God, man, what kind of jackanapes do you think me, to drag a well-bred girl like Lady Brackenheath all over Europe? Say what you will about modern women wanting to travel, and those foolish females who jaunter off to Africa and Arabia to live among the natives. That's no way for an Englishwoman to behave." His face was ruddy with emotion. "Lady Brackenheath does not hold her reputation so lightly that she would compromise it."

Holmes inclined his long head. "I am sorry I have offended you, Lord Brackenheath. All I can say is that my mistake was not maliciously intended."

"I should hope not." Lord Brackenheath rocked back on his heels. "Very well, I accept your apology on my wife's behalf. But see to it that you do not embroil her in any unseemly conversation this evening."

"As I doubt I shall do more than shake her hand, you may be assured I will not," said Holmes, and smiled as Andermatt appeared once more to review what his staff had done.

"I will see you are escorted to your temporary quarters at the appropriate hour," he said before he signaled his staff to withdraw.

Once they were alone, Lord Brackenheath took up the rough draft of the agreement again. "This matter of Japanese ships defending English naval installations. Do you honestly suppose it will work?"

"I cannot think why not. We have reached accord in all matters regarding ports and warships that will serve England's purposes as well as Japan's, and will ensure our continued might in the Pacific without reducing our capability to respond to any threat the Germans or the Russians might spring on us. What more can we expect from the Empire of Japan, given their position?"

"But what penalties would the Japanese pay if they fail to fulfill their agreement?"

Holmes sighed once. "They would lose face, my lord."

Lord Brackenheath gave Holmes a scornful glance. "As if that were enough!"

"For the Japanese, it is," Holmes informed Lord Brackenheath quietly. "And if we were to question their sincerity, we would insult them mortally."

"Oh, you needn't fear me shoving my oar into your nonsense," Lord Brackenheath said with an air of veiled contempt. "I would have thought you'd ruin it yourself without my help. All I must do is watch." He very nearly smiled at the prospects. "And then steadier plans will prevail, and we will see England on a course she may be proud of."

Holmes bowed slightly. "As you say, my lord."

At that Lord Brackenheath came to confront Mycroft Holmes. "You think I don't know what you're doing? You think I cannot see through your machinations? You will not be drawn into a debate with me, will you? So that we may give the illusion that there is agreement among the English in regard to the Japanese. You will not allow any dispute at this occasion, no matter how reasonable the basis may be."

"Very perceptive, Lord Brackenheath," said Holmes.

"I'm not the noddy you think me, Mister Holmes. I know what o'clock it is." He turned and made his way to the door. "I will retire to change now, for my valet will be here shortly."

As soon as the door was closed, Holmes expostulated, "That arrogant, ignorant, limited old man is planning some mischief for this evening. I can feel it. Damn him! I would wish him at Coventry for his bloody excuse for patriotism." He swung around, chagrined at his intemperate language. "Your pardon, Guthrie. I have no intention to offend you."

"None taken, sir," I told him. "I will do what I can to keep track of the man, if you would like."

"Would you?" asked Holmes. "For I cannot feel comfortable about him. As I have shepherded this agreement so far, I cannot be entirely sanguine until all signatures and seals are affixed to it. There is so much to lose. To have lost the pressure this occasion gives the Japanese to sign the agreement is an opportunity we would be inexcusably foolish to waste. We have the highest officials coming, and Ambassador Tochigi is aware of how great his success would be to have his accomplishment recognized in so distinguished company. He may even forgo the name of the Prince's mistress for the sake of gaining prestige for the agreement, and himself. Should we fail to achieve this end now, it could be months or years before the Japanese are willing to extend themselves again on our behalf. And during that time, who can say what offers might be made to them, from Germany or Russia, or another power we have not yet considered?" He stared blankly at the window, seeing things beyond it that were the product of his imagination. "And if Lord Brackenheath has his way, the agreement will not be signed."

"I'll make sure he is not allowed to interfere, sir," I said, and looked up at the sound of a discreet tap on the door.

Andermatt stepped into the room. "Two secretaries from the Admiralty, Mister Holmes: Mister Hackett and Mister Wright," he announced and stood aside.

"Gentlemen, come in," said Holmes expansively, extending his hand. "Mister . . ."

"Eugene Wright, at your service," said the young man with the fair hair. He flushed deeply before he took a step back.

"And you are Mister Hackett," Holmes said to the second, a small, angular fellow, perhaps five years older than Wright.

"Jeremiah Hackett," he said, taking Holmes' proffered hand. "It is an honor to be part of this historic occasion, Mister Holmes."

Holmes looked at Hackett as if trying to determine if this effusiveness was sincere. "We are depending on you to help it be so. Which of you knows Japanese?"

"I do," said Hackett. "My parents are missionaries in the Far East. I learned Japanese and a little Korean."

"Very good. You will review the Japanese copy of the agreement to ascertain that the translation is as correct as it may be." Holmes made a gesture of approval to the two men. "You will be given space in the meeting room upstairs to begin your labors. Your Japanese counterparts will meet you there—a Mister Minato and a Mister Banadaichi. Both of them are fluent in English, so I trust the copying will go smoothly and well." He held out the draught of the agreement. "As you see, there are one or two items that are not yet wholly complete. You will remain here while those matters are hammered out, and put the necessary information onto the final document." He made a gesture of encouragement and nodded in the direction of the door. "Andermatt will show you the way. Thank you, gentlemen, for being so prompt."

The two secretaries bustled out of the White Salon, and were escorted down the hall by the accommodating Andermatt.

"I trust they will do their work well, considering how much is at stake," said Holmes as the door closed again. He took a turn about the room, pausing at the window to look over the little side-garden.

"Is there any reason to think they would not?" I asked, feeling a start of alarm.

"You heard Lord Brackenheath. Do not dismiss him as a short-sighted fool, though he is. He is not alone in his sentiments. Even within the Admiralty, where it is generally acknowledged that we need better-defined relations with the Japanese, there are those who are opposed to our making any agreements with them, for fear of exposing English ships and English seamen to terrible dangers on behalf of the Empire of Japan. There are even those who cannot believe there is any advantage for England in advancing this agreement, and who would be pleased to help destroy it." Holmes gave a sudden, hard sigh. "Well, fretting will not change anything but my disposition, as my French grandmother used to say." He squared his shoulders, for all the world as if preparing for battle instead of a gala. "So long as we are expected to be in mufti, let us go change for the evening. I would rather be thought previous than laggard."

"As you wish, sir," I said as I got to my feet and reached for my crutches. Little as I wanted to admit it, the ankle was still paining me, though not as severely as before.

Holmes looked around at me. "I want you, as soon as you are

dressed, to find out what Lord Brackenheath is up to. For all his assurances, I do not wholly trust him."

"Nor do I," I confessed as I made my way toward the door behind Holmes.

"Don't be obvious about it, but make certain you know where he is and what he is doing. Make a note of those to whom he speaks." He opened the door and looked down the hall. Satisfied that we were not closely observed, he stepped out and held the door for me.

I cursed my crutches and made my way after him.

We had been allocated a pleasant room on the first floor just above the White Salon overlooking the garden. There was a daybed, a chaise and a writing table from the Napoleonic era, and a more recent armoire. The staff had laid out our clothes and a valet was standing by to assist us, the very model of decorum.

"I will send for the barber if you think it would be wise to shave?" the valet offered.

"Probably a good thing," Holmes muttered. "If matters drag on this evening, it would not do to appear slovenly." He gestured his assent. "Have the barber up, by all means."

The valet left with a bow, and Holmes gestured to me to come closer. "Guthrie, I want you to keep a close eye on our two secretaries. I fear we may have difficulties yet to come, and they might well prove our stumbling blocks."

I was mildly surprised at this warning, and said so. "They are from the Admiralty, sir, and you have always placed faith in their quality of men."

"So I have, so I have," Holmes admitted as he removed his tie and began to work his collar-stud free. "But didn't you notice that Mister Wright had a stub in his waistcoat pocket from a pawnshop? If he is hard-up as that suggests, he would be more open to bribery than many another. And Jeremiah Hackett has stains on his cuffs that could only come from the mixture of oil and ink which I fear indicate he has been operating a printing press—such men often find it difficult to keep secrets if they might enhance journalistic prestige should they be made public." He looked up at the ceiling as if the answer to his doubts would be written there. "I would like to think it were possible to be so trusting now, but I daren't. We have far too much at stake here, and not solely in regard to the Orientals. Not with sentiments so much at odds within the Admiralty itself."

I sat on the chaise near the window and considered the matter. "It is more than just the Japanese, isn't it, sir?"

"Far more, I fear," said Holmes. "It is a question of England's destiny. We are in a position now to set ourselves in the way to being the vanguard of the next century, or we can become mired in the past, and that will drag us down. We must decide now which it is to be. Unfortunately, by embracing the future, we must leave behind certain bastions of outmoded privilege. And if we are to save England from chaos in a decade or two, we must strive now to amend the habits of old that had led us to this coil."

"Mister Holmes," I said, trying not to appear shocked. "Surely you do not mean to compromise the Crown, do you?"

"Hardly," he said sharply. "I am doing all that I can to be certain that the Crown is not compromised. But to do that, I must see that the old notions of how England makes her place in the world are modified to accommodate the realities of today and the years ahead." He put his hands together as he tossed his collar and tie onto the daybed.

"Does Miss Gatspy have anything to do with your concerns?" I asked, my apprehension increasing as I considered the boldness of my inquiry.

"Indirectly, of course she does. I am always troubled when an assassin is present where so many important men are to gather, and for so momentous an occasion. If she is here, then there must be a good reason for it, which cannot but worry me. And that reason undoubtedly concerns the Brotherhood." He began to pace. "If I was certain that the Brotherhood had been discredited in England, I would be less concerned, but I am very much afraid that there are still adherents to the Brotherhood's reprehensible code. Vickers did not escape by good fortune alone. He had help. It is quite possible that he is still in England, working his despicable way into the confidence of those of position and heritage who are unwilling to modify their place in the world, or who are hopeful to gain power in the aftermath of war."

"But surely we would not war with Japan?" I exclaimed.

"No," he said, twiddling his watchfob. "But if the Japanese should come to think that we presented a danger, they might ally themselves with our enemies, and then where should we be?" He sighed. "Then this distress over a Prince's indiscretion would count for nothing."

"In the meantime, however, we must not add fuel to that particular fire." I tested my ankle and was pleased to find it more flexible than it had been, and marginally less sore. "I may be able to manage without the crutches tonight, sir," I said, trying to show him the improvement in my condition.

"Pray, Guthrie, do not," said Holmes. "I would prefer you continue to use them. In case of any . . . misadventure."

I regarded him with intense interest, for the tone of his voice was unlike any I had heard from him before, laden with anxiety and a kind of desperation that seemed to me out of place in the Swiss embassy and on the threshold of so major an accomplishment as this agreement would represent. "Very well. I will continue to use them."

"Thank you," he said with unusual diffidence.

"You anticipate trouble?" I asked, trying not to imagine what his answer might be.

Then there was a soft knock at the door and the valet returned with the barber.

FROM THE JOURNAL OF PHILIP TYERS

Sutton has finally put Webster's tragedy aside and is now taking his tea in the study. He asked me to join him, but I am determined to remain at my post, watching those who are without doubt observing this building. Much as I have tried to dismiss it, I have a growing sense of apprehension that has become more acute with every passing hour. I have recommended to Sutton that he avoid sitting near the windows, for it may be that those who are set to observe us have something more than observations alone in their plans.

The messenger from the Admiralty arrived this afternoon with a small case of documents for M H to examine tonight regarding the current political situation in India. I have put this away against M H's return tonight. I expect the contents will demand a good portion of M H's time this evening.

There is also another missive from Baker Street, this one confirming the first report, that none of the street gangs were involved in the attack on M H and G. This has provided me less comfort than I might have wished.

Chapter Eleven

AMBASSADOR TOCHIGI BOWED as deeply as his splendid full court dress kimono would allow him; the wide fan slipped through his belt hindered this movement, as did the nature of the kimono itself. This magnificent garment was composed of many layers, the outermost being a burnished silk brocade in the pattern of ivy leaves. I stared, recalling that each part of the kimono had significance. What was this array supposed to be telling us, I wondered. I realized that there was an imposing aspect to Ambassador Tochigi that was not apparent when he was wearing trousers and a swallowtail coat.

Behind the ambassador, Messers. Banadaichi and Minato were also in traditional Japanese dress, though neither of their kimonos was as elaborate or grand as Tochigi's. They, too, bowed, more deeply than Ambassador Tochigi.

"Good evening," said Mycroft Holmes, returning their bow. Next to Ambassador Tochigi's gorgeous silks, Holmes' black tie looked sadly lacking, and I felt drab as a mourner in a cortège.

I bowed as much as my crutches would permit me. It was galling to have to seem less able than I knew I was; this pretense was going to be more difficult to sustain than I had first anticipated.

"I am told there is a line where the guests are to be received," said Ambassador Tochigi.

"The Swiss will show you," said Holmes. "I will retire with Guthrie to await you. Our Lord Brackenheath is probably waiting there already."

The Japanese ambassador smiled. "Yes, of course. I had forgotten. You are not here, are you?"

"Not officially," Holmes said with grim amusement.

"Then by all means, be about your tasks." He bowed again and swept on toward the ballroom, his two secretaries following after him, their kimonos glistening in the gaslight.

"What do you think?" I asked as he watched Ambassador Tochigi and his two secretaries continue their stately way down the hall.

"Well," said Holmes drily, "I can see why it is that Edmund wants one of those kimonos." Then his expression changed. "Let us trust that everything goes as smoothly as we have hoped it will." He shook his head as he walked. "I would like to think that we have everything but those last two matters well in hand, but . . ."

We had turned and were now walking in the direction of the

southern wing of the embassy, toward the Terrace Suite which had been set aside for our final negotiations. It was considered by the Japanese the most appropriate of the chambers the Swiss had offered us.

"Did you learn anything watching Lord Brackenheath this afternoon?" asked Holmes in a less weighty tone of voice.

"Only that he had a note from Lady Brackenheath explaining she would be a trifle delayed in her arrival. I didn't discover the reason for it." I still felt embarrassed that I should be party to their personal differences, but I reported the rest dutifully, making an effort to conceal my distaste. "I sense there is some rancor there, for he was most displeased when he read the contents."

"Nothing from anyone else?" Holmes asked.

"Not that I could discover. But he had time to himself." I noticed that the door to the Terrace Suite was flanked by two footmen in the livery of the embassy. "They're going out of their way to ensure the success of this agreement, are the Swiss."

"Hardly out of their way," said Holmes quietly. "They are serving their own best interests. There is little to distinguish between the bankers of Zurich and the Swiss government. If, as they are fond of saying, the business of America is business, the business of Switzerland is money. The greatest threat to those bankers is any disruption in trade. In their vaults are the garnered wealth of many nations. Any war would cause the currencies to be less stable. As it is the nature of bankers to despise things unpredictable, they strive to keep the nations of the world from undertaking any kind of disruption."

"I had no notion that the Swiss were so altruistic," I said, making no excuse for the dubious tone of my voice.

"Oh, as to that, altruism is only a secondary benefit," said Holmes with a nod. "It serves their purposes to place the English and Japanese governments a bit further in their debt, literally and figuratively. With the restive Germans on their border, it pays to have strong friends, and leverage. Prudence is the national Swiss virtue, as you are surely aware." He permitted the footmen to open the doors for us, and passed into the largest of the three rooms of the suite. One wall was French doors and Italiante windows overlooking a broad stone terrace. Just at present the heavy velvet draperies had been closed against the night so that the full impact was modified, but by day this was regarded as one of the handsomest rooms in a handsome building. There were five large canvases in the style of the last century, elaborately framed, for the major decoration. Two sofas had been moved back against the walls and a large writing table had been placed near the center of the room, with a dozen matching chairs drawn up to it. All the lamps were blazing. The doors to the other two interior rooms of the Terrace Suite were closed, but I had been told that both were as well appointed as this one.

"Most gracious," said Holmes by way of approval. "The Japanese might not share the style but they cannot help but admire it."

"If that is important," I said, though I, too, found the room elegant and appropriate to the occasion.

"To the Japanese, it is exceedingly important," said Holmes quietly. "There must be elegance and grace so that everyone may be at ease. Anything less would be offensive to their traditions." He nodded once to show his approval. "Where have they put Wright and Hackett?"

"Just across the hall. I am told that Mister Minato has spent an hour or so with them, going over some of the finer points of Japanese and English for the shared translation." I remembered the harried look on Hackett's face as he and Minato discussed whether the word *obligation* or *responsibility* was the more correct translation of a Japanese word. After watching Lord Brackenheath I had stayed with the secretaries for ten minutes or so, until I perceived my presence was contributing to their anxiety. "I think you may rest assured, sir, that by the time Parnell, King, Wolseley, Hewett, Wood, and Seymour arrive they will find matters well in hand. As will Cecil when he comes for the final signatures."

"Let us hope so," said Holmes, and motioned to the footmen to close the door.

I swung myself the length of the room, all the while wanting to cast my crutches aside and walk, no matter how awkwardly. "Is there any chance you will not reach a full agreement tonight, sir?"

"I devoutly trust not," said Holmes with feeling. "It would be very bad to have a meeting of this sort at such an occasion as this gala and be unable to present the document we all hope to have." He put his hand to his brow—the gesture I had seen Sutton duplicate so well—and said, "If only I knew how far Lord Brackenheath is prepared to go to stop this agreement from being ratified, I would be far more at ease than I am. I fear he may have allied himself with those who have been working to undermine this agreement from its inception, though I have no proof of it."

I was developing an intense dislike for Lord Brackenheath and all those who thought like him, not only for their stubbornness, but their malice. To show my determination I planted my crutches and said, "I will try again to discover if he had any intentions of disrupting this evening's events."

"I may yet ask it of you, Guthrie," said Holmes quietly. He drew out a cigar and brought a lucifer out to light it. As the first blue-grey wraith of smoke escaped him, he said, "If Lord Brackenheath had anything to do with the attack of the other night, I would prefer to know it sooner than later."

I could not conceal my shock. That Lord Brackenheath might try to interfere with the Japanese did not surprise me, but I found it difficult to imagine he would actually try to act directly against Holmes, or any servant of England. "You surely have no reason to suspect him of such perfidy?"

"Not as such, no," said Holmes. "But so many of the alternatives are getting us nowhere that I am forced to consider explanations that I find wholly unacceptable. But I am nonetheless compelled by reason to examine them." He blew out another cloud and then regarded me. "I do not want to be proved right in this instance, but it may be that I am. If that is so, you are going to need all your wits about you. Be careful in what you do. If these men are as desperate as we fear they may be, you will be in danger."

"I am in danger now," I said, thinking of the unfortunate cat and the attack on the cab. "As are you."

"Ah, but I elected to be here," said Holmes with hard amusement lurking in his profound grey eyes. He pulled one of the chairs out and sank into it. "This is going to be a long night—I am certain of it."

I could not cavil. "It will be time well-spent when the seals are fixed and the signatures are in place."

"So I hope," said Holmes, the remoteness returning to his features. "I wish," he said, and blew out another wreath of smoke, "I knew rather more than I do about Lord Brackenheath. How is he fixed in the world. Who he entertains. What amusements he has."

"Once this is over, I will make inquiries for you," I said.

"I think perhaps I should put Tyers on it," he decided aloud, and went to the writing table to take a sheet of paper from the center drawer. There was also an array of pens, and he selected one before taking the standish out. He wrote quickly, and folded the sheet twice before handing it to me. "Have the Admiralty messenger carry this to Tyers at once."

"Certainly," I said, slipping the missive into my inner waistcoat pocket before making my way to the door. The corridor was empty but for the footmen, and I was pleased, for I could take advantage of this privacy to test my ankle. I deliberately put part of my weight on my ankle, and was pleased by how well it held.

The Admiralty messenger, Charles Shotley, was waiting, along with a Japanese and half a dozen Europeans, in the dispatch room next to the porte cochere, opposite to the room where the servants of visitors to the embassy were put. He rose as he saw me coming, a warning look in his glance, as if to remind me to be circumspect in my speech. I drew him aside and gave him the folded sheet, along with Holmes' instructions. "This is most urgent, and must be held in complete confidence, even from your fellows. Wait for an answer, if there is one. Be quick about the work."

"That I will," said the messenger in a soft Suffolk accent. "The man to receive it is Mister Tyers?"

"That's the chap," I said. "A man of middle years, hair going grey. Used to be a soldier. You can tell by the way he stands." I gave him half a crown to speed him on his way. "Report to Mister Holmes when you return."

Shotley offered me a sharp salute and hurried to the door.

Just as he went out, an elegant equipage drew up, a fine enclosed clarence drew up and the footmen of the embassy quickly went to help the occupant to alight and to direct the coachman to the stables.

The woman who emerged from the clarence was uncommonly lovely, with flawless skin, beautifully dressed deep-russet hair, and eyes pale, well-opened, and luminous as aquamarines, shining with intelligence and wit. She moved gracefully without a trace of self-consciousness. But her own beauty was complemented by the way she presented herself: She wore a lustrous satin gown the color of mulberries which showed off her sloping shoulders and deep bosom to admiration. The nipped waist complemented the moderate bustle, the whole making an impression of sleekness and smooth lines at the very vanguard of fashion. A dog-collar of baroque pearls was clasped around her throat and baroque pearls depended from her ears. There was but one ring on her fingers, two hundred years old, to judge by the design, of rubies and brilliants. This radiant creature was no more than five- or six-and-twenty.

One of the English servants hurried up. "Lady Brackenheath!" he exclaimed, and bowed to her.

"Good evening, Thomas," she replied in a voice that was warm with spice.

"Lord Brackenheath is—"

"Waiting impatiently, no doubt," she said, and gathered up her wrap—a long ermine cloak. Her mouth was set in a firm line, the one unbecoming thing about her.

"If you will come this way?" Thomas was already through the door and on his way to the stairs. I stood aside as Lady Brackenheath swept by.

The men in the dispatch room were gazing after her with admiration and yearning, including the Japanese, and I wondered if Lady Brackenheath was aware of the impact she had on men, for surely this was not an isolated incident.

"They say she controls the purse-strings," one of the English servants remarked. "Her old man traded his daughter for a leg up into the aristocracy, but kept his hands on the till. All the money she brought with her remains in her control."

"That's hardly fitting," said one of the foreign servants.

"Married Woman's Property Act," said the first speaker knowingly. "Her Da set up a trust that's tight as a Tyburn cravat."

"Well, it had to be, didn't it? With the tastes his Lordship has, he would run through a fortune as quick as you can say knife."

Although I was at first offended by these remarks, I was also curious, and justified my curiosity by telling myself I was obtaining information of use to Mycroft Holmes. Servants gossiped all the time, and any man who put too much stock in it was a fool. But any man who ignored it was a greater fool. So I remained where I was in the hope I might hear something more that might be of use.

"Trouble is," said another of the English servants, "his Lordship don't take to having his amusements curtailed."

"It was that or drown in the River Tick," said the oldest of the servants in a knowing tone. "He was a right high-flyer just ten years back, gambling and whoring and all the rest of it. Had been for donkey's years."

"Old man Bell weren't no lob-cock, to sign over his purse with his daughter," another of the servants declared. "He knew what he was buying, sure as eggs. He kept his Lordship on a short leash, and let him howl for it."

"And his daughter does the same, they say, little as her lord may like dancing to Dame Fortune's fiddle." The laughter was not quite cruel but certainly unkind.

"What man does? And that to a tune played by a chit younger than his daughter?" asked another.

"Too bad the old man doesn't have children, of her or his first wife," said the oldest servant knowingly.

"No children?" asked one of the other.

"Not acknowledged, any road, though they do say he has a passel from the wrong side of the blanket," said his senior with great certainty. "He didn't take to marriage the first time, either—felt it held him back, as it were. Trouble was, his first wife died young. Took a bad fall on a hunt, so they say. Were some claimed then the fall were more of a push. Anyway, it crippled her up something dreadful. Died the year after from it. His Lordship weren't in no hurry to get fixed again. Lord Brackenheath had her money and his freedom to enjoy for many a long year."

Their easy laughter gave way to speculations that had no place in my work, and I left them to it. I made my way back to the Terrace Suite and allowed the footmen to admit me. "Shotley is off to Pall Mall," I said as I came into my employer's company again.

"Thank you, Guthrie," said Holmes, who was occupying

himself by making notes to himself in his pocket notebook. "But what is it that has you so preoccupied?"

I had not been aware until that moment that I was still mulling the servants' conversation as I made my way here. I shrugged. "Lady Brackenheath arrived as Shotley went off," I said carefully. "She was not what I expected."

Holmes glanced at me. "Did you meet her? I understand she is somewhat younger than her husband."

I was a bit taken aback. "Good gracious, Holmes. You haven't met her?"

"I do not go much into society, as I need not tell you, and I have never aspired to be part of Lord Brackenheath's set with their fondness for riotous living. So, no, Guthrie, I have not met her. Though from what you tell me, it is a pleasure I will anticipate." He closed his notebook and waited for me to go on. When I said nothing, he prompted me. "I have been told her father was an ambitious man with manufactories all over the Midlands. Name of Bell, as I recall: Herbert Bell."

I nodded. "The servants were saying something of the sort. They all seemed to aware of the terms of the marriage contract." I flushed to admit I had listened to their talk. "Not that I solicited—"

Holmes waved my protestations away. "Yes, yes, I know. You did not set yourself to eavesdrop on the servants. I am aware of that. Go on."

"They said her father had tied up her money so that Lord Brackenheath could not gain control of it. She retains her fortune." I made a gesture to show that this might or might not be true. "She is a very beautiful young woman, with considerable bearing and impeccable taste if her clothes for this evening are any indication. She has a most self-assured demeanor." I recalled his earlier question. "I have not actually been introduced to her; I only witnessed her arrival."

"Ah," said Holmes. "Young and beautiful and not a widgeon. Another part of the puzzle is provided. How galling it must have been to Lord Brackenheath to have to accept a clever and wealthy young bride, and from trade, at that. But he had to recoup his fortune. From what I know of the man's past, he must have been desperate indeed to make such an obvious bargain. He might as well declare himself profligate beyond remedy and be done with it." He chuckled once.

"It may have galled her as well, sir, to have such a husband foisted upon her," I said, and added conscientiously, "I doubt she filled her youthful dreams with brusque men her father's age."

"Don't poker up on me, Guthrie. I meant the lady no discredit. But my anxieties are not with her, they are with Lord Brackenheath." He sighed once. "I will have to learn more of Lady Brackenheath, I suppose."

I tried not to feel offended and shamed, but could not entirely hide either of these emotions. I lowered my head and held my tongue until I felt I could speak with proper respect. "I think that will not be necessary, sir. And if I have done anything to bring any scrutiny upon her that would prove the least—"

"Guthrie," Holmes said at a drawl, "I am not going to pillory the woman, I merely want to know how things are disposed of between her and her husband. That was a matter for the parties involved to settle, not I. My concern in the matter is a question of vulnerability, for if Lord Brackenheath wants money, he might have contracted to get some without his wife's knowledge. So if he has control of any of her money, that is significant as knowing he does not. It may also tell us something of her management, if she has any control over her father's fortune." He regarded me in a measuring way.

"There was some intimation from the servants concerning illegitimate children of Lord Brackenheath's," I said at once.

"Not surprising, given his reputation," Holmes concurred. "How good you are to tell me, Guthrie. Yes, I imagine the former Miss Bell would not like to have her money in the hands of her late husband's by-blows."

This crass expression caught me off-guard, and it struck me that my employer knew more of the Brackenheaths than he had intimated. "Nor would anyone wish to countenance such a thing."

Holmes studied me for a full two minutes before speaking. "There must be something quite remarkable about her that you should spring so eagerly to her defense after one sight of her."

To my horror, this time I blushed as deeply as a girl, which only made it worse. "She is very . . . she is most . . ." I could not find words that did not leave me feeling I was an idiot.

"Well, perhaps I will see this paragon for myself later this evening, if she comes with her husband when the seals are affixed to the agreement," he said, and rubbed his chin. "We have less than an hour before all the world comes here, so it behooves us to make the most of this time. Nip across the hall, will you, and discover how the copying is coming. I want to be certain we are all ready for the final negotiations."

"At once," I said, and hastened to do as he bid.

I found Mister Hackett quite alone, two sheets of parchment in front of him. He was painstakingly comparing one—in Japanese—to the other—in English. I saw that he had a pen in his hand.

"Oh. For making note of any questions I might have," he said almost apologetically. "Mister Minato has been most helpful, of course, but I must be certain that I am satisfied the best work possible has been done."

"Where are the others?" I asked, indicating their absence.

"At supper," he answered. "I did not feel I could spare the time to eat, not until this was completed." He frowned at the

Japanese page. "You do not know how difficult this is, trying to find the right word. There are formalities to be observed due to the nature of the occasion, and the language used must reflect that."

"I can imagine," I said, recalling some of the difficulties I had encountered translating English to German. With such a language as Japanese, the difficulty I reckoned increased tenfold.

"When I have completed this work, I will have my soup with the rest," he said to me, his attention still on the page.

"Excellent. I will inform my employer of your progress, and your diligence in this matter." I nodded to him and made my way across the hall, where I told Holmes what I had learned.

"Encouraging, I suppose," said Mycroft Holmes darkly. "I want you to check on Mister Hackett again in twenty minutes."

This indicated a greater concern than I was accustomed to experience in Holmes, so I said, "Is there something you anticipate in this regard?"

"Not specifically, no," said Holmes, a trifle too quickly.

"But you have some reason to fear," I persisted. "What is it?"

"If I knew, I would not be so troubled." He steepled his fingers and regarded me over their tops. "No doubt I am jumping at shadows, but I fear that given the events we have sustained of late, I cannot keep from it. I would rather prove to have been too cautious than not cautious enough."

I wanted to learn more, but the footmen in the corridor flung open the doors, announcing, "His Highness, Prince Jiro."

Immediately behind them, the young man came, his face slightly flushed, his dress uniform of a Dartmouth cadet precise to a pin. His face was set in uncompromising lines. "Mister Holmes. I demand an explanation!"

FROM THE JOURNAL OF PHILIP TYERS

Two of the watchers observed Sutton make his way across the street to his club tonight. I know that he is aware of one of them, but the other has taken up a place in a window three houses along Pall Mall from this one. I cannot like this, for it suggests to me that there are others I have not yet discovered who are watching this flat and Sutton, whom they suppose to be M H.

I have taken to keeping notes regarding these watchers, where they are, at what hours, and what associations, if any, I can discern with others on the street. I am troubled that I have had no success in identifying any of these men, or to discern their purpose beyond surveillance of this place.

My pistol is ready, and I am prepared to use it if it should become necessary, although I trust it will not, for the watchers would seem to prize secrecy, which they cannot sustain once shots have been fired. I have hope that we may yet make our way through this coil unscathed.

Shotley has come from the Swiss embassy with a message from M H, and I have sent back a note saying that I will attend to the inquiries he requires at once. There are references here that will start me on my way, and once Sutton returns, I will have his help as well. By the time M H returns, I will be able to present a fair summary of Lord Brackenheath's life and background. Then M H may tell me what he next requires of me.

Chapter Twelve

MYCROFT HOLMES ROSE and bowed. "Your Highness."

"Never mind all that," said the Prince abruptly, signaling the footmen to close the door, then pacing the room. "What right have you to order anyone to follow me?"

Holmes achieved a look of mild interest. "Even supposing that you are being followed, what makes you suppose that I have ordered it?"

"Because I know it is being done. I have seen someone watching me, and I know why you would want me watched," the Prince fumed. "And I warn you now that it must stop at once. I will not have myself compromised by spies. I will not tolerate this intrusion into my privacy." He tossed his head. "I will not permit the woman you have been trying to identify for so many weeks to be the object of your scrutiny."

"Your Highness, I give you my word as a gentleman, I have not ordered men to follow you."

His single laugh lacked merriment. "Well, *someone* has been following me, and she is not Japanese." He stopped, his hands clenched and his breath coming too fast.

"She?" said Holmes, one of his heavy brows rising speculatively.

"A young woman, very fair, very English. I was able to approach her yesterday, after setting a trap for her. She was wise enough not to deny her mission. When I tried to detain her, she said I should make my inquiries of you, and then fled." His outrage was feeding on itself now, and it was apparent that he might well permit himself to say things he did not generally mean while caught up in his emotions.

I did the unthinkable—I interrupted. "Was she about middle height, slight, fashionably dressed, with light, rosy hair?"

"Then she *is* one of yours!" Prince Jiro pounced on the description. "That is the very woman! Who is—"

I recalled my encounter with Penelope Gatspy at this very embassy, an encounter that now seemed fraught with more significance than I had assumed at the time. "No, she is not one of . . . us," I answered carefully. "Though she is a professional, make no doubt about that. She is part of an organization calling itself the Golden Lodge. She . . . she works all over Europe for this group. She is familiar with some of the tasks Mister Holmes performs for England, and she is not above using this information."

"An obvious diversion," said Prince Jiro.

"Hardly that," said Mycroft Holmes. "Guthrie is telling you the truth, and you should be glad of it."

"Glad? That it has taken a woman to tell me you are abusing the hospitality you have claimed to extend to me?" He paced away and returned to confront Mycroft Holmes. "What possible excuse can you offer for this conduct, sir?" The last word became an insult in his mouth.

Holmes regarded him steadily. "None, nor would I make the attempt if the surveillance were my doing, which, I repeat, it is not. If I were to set spies, as you insist upon calling them, to watch you, Your Highness, I would select them from among your fellow-cadets at Dartmouth, and would encourage them to make a friend of you for the sake of the interest of our two countries. They would not realize they were watching you for me. But I have not done that, nor would I. You will have to accept my word on it, I fear." He glanced at the door. "The others should be arriving directly. I would not like it thought that you and I were—"

Prince Jiro was not to be calmed or distracted. "Whether she is one of yours or not, I want her to stop following me. You are all seeking to discredit me, to bring shame on me, so that you may dictate to me how I am to behave. And *I will not have it!* You are not going to interfere with me again. Is that clear to you?"

"Yes, your Highness, it is clear," said Holmes, and added. "Though I fear I cannot do as you command."

Prince Jiro stood very still, regarding Holmes appraisingly. "If you deserve even half your reputation, Mister Holmes, you will see that my orders are carried out. Do you understand me?"

"Your Highness is very direct." He bowed again, and indicated I should do the same.

"My Highness is deeply offended," Prince Jiro corrected, his manner turning sarcastic with his title. "I will not be followed any more. It will stop. You will see to it." He turned on his heel and went to the doors and rapped once.

The footmen opened the doors so promptly that it was obvious they had been expecting his summons.

Prince Jiro flung out of the room and down the hall.

"Good Lord," I said as the footmen closed the doors once more.

"Precisely," said Holmes, his brow furrowed. "Miss Gatspy appears to have been busy." The last word was condemnation.

"The Golden Lodge has undoubtedly tried to force her to—" I broke off, unable to convince myself of my ill-formed argument.

"Yes," Holmes said measuringly. "The Golden Lodge has mired itself in this affair. And what has the Brotherhood been up to, I wonder?" He fingered his watchfob, and might have begun to twirl it, but the doors were opened again, and this time the Admiralty party came in.

Rear Admiral Sir Richard King was showing his age, though his eyes were keen; his long years with the Indian Squadron had made him something of an expert on Oriental affairs, and he was welcomed for his insights as much as his position. Behind him, Admiral Seymour's thick-set figure was easily discerned. His face looked to be made of seamed leather, tanned as it had been by the Egyptian sun and the waters of the Mediterranean. Immediately after him was Charles Stewart Parnell, his movements eloquent of impatience. He was deep in conversation with Sir Garnet Wolseley, the hero of the Ashantee War. Admiral Hewett brought up the rear of this fine company; the current commander of the East Indian Station was full of energy that belied his more than fifty years.

Lord Brackenheath was the last of the party to arrive, and he presented himself with ill-grace to the men assembled. "The Japanese will join us directly," he declared, as if making an announcement of disaster. "They are still engaged in greeting the arriving guests."

"Excellent," declared Admiral Seymour, answering for all those who had just arrived.

As the question of seating was arranged, Holmes pulled me aside and asked me to check on the four secretaries once again. "We will have need of their services directly. It would be best if you would put them on notice. Make sure that all the copies are secured, as well."

"Three copies, is that correct?" I asked, to be certain.

"Yes. One of the copies written in Japanese, of course. Which is why one of your copyists understands the Japanese language." He turned to acknowledge Sir George Tyrell, whose many journeys through the Orient had made his opinion particularly valuable in these negotiations.

I withdrew from the Terrace Suite and went across the hall once more, this time to find all four men—Wright, Minato, Banadaichi, and Hackett—gathered around the table once more, reviewing their work one more time.

"We're down to the home stretch. The Prime Minister will be along in about two hours. I trust we can conclude our work by then. Is all satisfactory, gentlemen?" I asked, feeling a bit unnecessary, rather like a signal man waving on a moving train.

"Yes," said Mister Wright, attempting to conceal his excitement. "This is an historic occasion, and it is a great honor to be part of this event," he went on, as if to account for the hectic look in his eyes.

"So it is," I agreed, and was about to turn away when I noticed that Mister Banadaichi was frowning portentously. "Is there something the matter?"

"I . . . I suppose not," he answered, his frown unchanged as he stared down at the page. "I thought . . ."

"Thought what?" I pursued, impressions of treachery growing stronger in my thoughts.

"I thought that the ink-cake was not so much used," he said

with an embarrassed glance at his fellow-Japanese, "I suspect it is a trick of the light."

"No doubt," said Mister Minato very quickly. "I noticed this afternoon that the shadows lie long in this room."

"So they do," said Mister Wright, ready to settle the blame somewhere other than on himself. "It's enough to give one the headache."

What, I wondered, had truly bothered Mister Banadaichi? There was no way I could challenge him now without bringing about the embarrassment I had hoped to avoid this evening. I bowed slightly. "What would the significance of less ink be?"

"That the cake has been wet too long," said Mister Banadaichi. "The Japanese copy might be difficult to read. Too much water makes the ink faint."

"I see," I said, though I did not see at all, for I doubted such a minor matter would so distract Mister Banadaichi.

"A minor matter," said Mister Hackett as if reading my thoughts, and stared in the direction of the door. "Not enough to keep you here."

"I would think not," I agreed at once, and allowed myself to be persuaded to leave.

"Is all well?" my employer asked as I returned to his side.

I did not answer at once. "I trust it is," I said at last, with a flatness of tone I hoped would catch Holmes' attention.

His heavy brows lifted, and though he said nothing at that juncture, he clearly indicated to me he was aware that I was bothered. "A matter concerning Prince Jiro, do you suppose?"

"I am uncertain," I admitted, keeping my voice low.

"Did he visit them?" Holmes went on.

"They did not say so," I responded. "It would be unusual if he had taken so improper a step as that."

Holmes nodded. "Just so. Which is one reason I cannot shut it from my mind that he has done more than upbraid me." He glanced over at Lord Brackenheath. "He may still cut up rough over this agreement. I am concerned about him. Having the Prince with a ferret in his drawers is bad enough, but that fool Brackenheath may well try to capitalize on this misfortune and scuttle this agreement for good and all, in spite of the best efforts of King and Seymour and Hewett. And *then* where should we be in the Pacific? We cannot petition the Americans and Canadians to divide their ships and send half of them across the world for England's convenience."

"Is there nothing you can say to him?" I asked, more for form's sake than in the hope of any positive response.

"If I had time I might have done it by contraries—convince him that in supporting the agreement, Lord Brackenheath would hasten the day when England would no longer have to deal with Orientals, but would exert her rightful place in the world, and the rest of that Pukka Sahib blather." He frowned at the tabletop. "But no one warned me."

"Did you suppose they would?" I asked.

"I hoped they would have sense enough to, yes," Holmes replied. He shrugged and added, "They are pouring some excellent Armagnac. How very sensible the Swiss are. I am certain I will be glad to have it before the evening is over. So long as Tyrell doesn't get half-sprung, it should smooth the way for our agreement."

I realized there was no point in pursuing the questions about Lord Brackenheath for the time being, so I followed after him, wishing I did not have to continue to use crutches.

FROM THE JOURNAL OF PHILIP TYERS

Sutton was cautious on his return from M H's club; he informs me that he was aware of two men watching him, one at the junction of Waterloo Place, the other making his way down the street from the south end. He says he is certain they were assigned to him because of how they moved. He claims that he can notice such things in a man's movements.

I will take his word for it, since such things are his stock in trade, but I must reserve judgment until such time as I may observe for myself the men he has mentioned. If they are the same as those I have seen, I will be convinced.

I have had word again from M H, who informs me that he and G might not return until midnight, and I am not to be alarmed by this delay, as it is necessary to accomplish the task before them. Delays are to be expected, he tells me, when the matter is as complex as this one is. He may well issue such instructions, but I cannot school my apprehensions to suit his convenience. With this flat being watched and the reason for it unknown, I cannot banish troublesome thoughts from my mind.

Sid Hastings is standing by to call for M H and G at the Swiss embassy. He has put his cousin's grey gelding between his shafts, so that the watchers will not be alerted by Jenny. I am hopeful that there will be no reason for such precautions, but rather have them and not need them than regret they were not employed.

Chapter Thirteen

"THEN THE WHOLE is settled," said Charles Parnell on behalf of all those gathered. "What a very satisfying resolution for us all. We may get on with the signing of our agreement as soon as Lord Salisbury arrives." His satisfaction was as much for his own key role in advancing Robert Cecil, Lord Salisbury, to the position of Prime Minister as for the successful conclusion of the negotiations with the Japanese. He saw himself as the driving force behind the government and wanted everyone to be aware of it.

"And not a moment before time for him to appear," said Lord Brackenheath in a tone of ill-usage: He disliked Parnell and all those around him, who were, in his eyes, dangerous radicals determined to throw well-ordered society into chaos. "It's gone half eleven. We should have this behind us by midnight."

Seated between Sir Garnet Wolseley and Admiral Hewett, Mycroft Holmes rolled his eyes upward to express dismay at Lord Brackenheath's lamentable conduct.

There was a flurry of activity and the door was flung open by Andermatt, who bowed to the men, and announced the arrival of Robert Cecil, Lord Salisbury and Prime Minister of England.

The men in the Terrace Suite rose and greeted Lord Salisbury in their respective customs: Ambassador Tochigi's bow was deep and held for longer than usual.

"A pleasure," said Lord Salisbury, holding out his hand to the Japanese ambassador. "I thank you for your diligence. All of you. I trust the resolution has been achieved? To everyone's satisfaction?" He took his seat, prepared for the ceremony.

"Yes, I believe the Emperor will be satisfied," said Ambassador Tochigi. "It resolves our differences to our mutual honor and advantage. We are most pleased with the opportunity to gain the invaluable training this will provide our officers. The Royal Navy is foremost in the world, and to enable our men to train with yours on such ships as we will be receiving is appreciated by the Emperor. Additionally, the trade provisions will allow the opening of Chinese ports in a way that adds to our mutual advantage. This will serve to lessen the tensions we have detected in our dealings with certain European interests in the East. Of paramount importance to the Chrysanthemum Throne is peace. With England's help, the Japanese nation will now be assured of receiving the honor and respect properly accorded a modern industrial nation. Our united strength is our best guardian of peace, a peace that will serve the best interests of both our countries."

"I can see no reason to delay, then," said Robert Cecil, Lord Salisbury, who had arrived at the Swiss Embassy twenty minutes before and was now at liberty to give his full attention to the agreement. "Let us have the final terms draughted to the end of the page and we will then sign and seal the copies for our governments. We are prepared to make this official tonight." He smiled diplomatically. "You must be very pleased that our differences have been so painstakingly resolved, Ambassador Tochigi."

"If my Emperor is pleased, I will be honored to have done his bidding." The Ambassador inclined his head.

Lord Salisbury positioned himself at the ambassador's side. "The cooperation of our two nations has already benefited us many times before, so it is doubly suitable that the Occident's greatest monarch and the Orient's most revered Emperor should wish to bind their two nations more surely. This agreement will guarantee the stability of trade in Eastern waters for, I daresay, a century or more. It pleases Her Majesty and her government to endorse the obvious mutual benefits that have made the creation of this agreement so agreeable a process." Here the Prime Minister paused and exchanged a quick look with Mycroft Holmes. "Certainly the British and Japanese Empires will share in the increased wealth and prosperity this agreement assures. As Prime Minister, I welcome this as an encouraging beginning to what will most assuredly be the first step in a growing commonality of our enterprise and our interests in the future."

"We of Japan are also looking forward to an era of greater understanding and broader exchanges between our peoples." Ambassador Tochigi matched Lord Salisbury's tone perfectly.

Holmes turned slightly in his chair in order to say to me, sotto voce, "It's all over now but the dancing and champagne."

Messers. Minato and Banadaichi were watching closely as Messers. Wright and Hackett put the last clauses onto the pages, and then were watched in turn by Mister Hackett as the same was done to the document in Japanese.

Lord Brackenheath rose. "You have no further need of my presence for the nonce. I will return to witness the signatures shortly. I fear I have neglected my wife this evening," he added as he excused himself.

"Neglected his wife," scoffed George Tyrell. "It has nothing to do with his wife. He wants to put as much distance between this agreement and himself as he can. I wonder that he was invited at all."

"He had to be included," said Holmes to the distinguished traveler. "If we did not allow him, or some other associate of his who shares his view, the whole of this agreement would be endlessly debated in Parliament, to no one's eventual good, and the possible discrediting of the agreement itself. With him here, there can be no claim that their point of view was not represented."

Tyrell snorted but nodded his agreement. "A sad state of affairs."

"Well, he is out of the room now, so we can get on with this signing," said the Prime Minister. "Billstowe, get the seals for us, will you, please?" His secretary, a man of such careful neutrality that he was almost invisible, hurried to fulfill his commission.

Ambassador Tochigi leaned forward in his place and said, "I thank you on behalf of my Emperor for your diligence in bringing this agreement about."

"No thanks to Brackenheath," interjected Tyrell with deliberate sarcasm. "The man is positively antediluvian in his attitudes."

"Certainly," allowed the ambassador. "But we have men of his stripe in Japan as well, and Mister Holmes is right, if they are ignored they do more mischief than if they are included in such negotiations."

"Good to spike such guns," said Sir Garnet Wolseley.

"It is necessary to do it, soon or late," said the Prime Minister as he got to his feet. "Better to keep an eye on him, as you indicated, and then be assured that there are no covert acts set to bring all these efforts to failure."

"Still, it is awkward to have him about," said Tyrell, determined to have his notions endorsed by someone among the company.

"Oh, without doubt," said the Prime Minister. "But necessary."

Holmes had risen with the rest, and exchanged bows and handshakes with the Japanese. He signaled to me again. "Once the seals are fixed, I want you to go in search of Lord Brackenheath. We need his witnessing signature, and he is likely to complain a great deal about this agreement if we allow him to roam loose tonight."

"As you wish," I said, not relishing keeping watch over Lord Brackenheath for any purpose whatsoever.

"I know this is not wholly to your liking, Guthrie, but I would account it a great favor if you would be willing to make note of those to whom Brackenheath talks tonight." Holmes was being more accommodating to me than he usually was, and it made me suspicious of him.

"Do you expect interference?" I asked.

"I don't know what to expect," said Holmes bluntly. "That is the problem as I see it. I have only my . . . guesses, for they are no more than that, but I cannot ignore the dangers we still face."

"All right," I said, and patted my crutches. "But I'm not going to be much use slinking about."

"Do your best, Guthrie. That's all I can ask of you, or of anyone." He sighed again, and I had the uneasy feeling that he was privy to some intelligence he had not shared with me. At a less public occasion, I might have pursued the matter. As it was, I accepted his instruction with as much grace as I could muster—

which was not much—and prepared to go in search of our dissatisfied Lord Brackenheath.

"You may remain for a short while," Holmes assured me. "I do not want your actions to appear too obvious."

I would have liked to make a pointed observation on the matter, but I quickly saw that there would be no use to it. This evening was proving to be as demanding as I feared it might be, and I was aware that I was becoming testy of humor because of my long inactivity and a small-but-persistent headache which gnawed at the back of my eyes. It was useless to debate orders with Mycroft Holmes, and I knew it.

The gala was in full progress. I could hear a company of musicians playing one of the minuets from Handel's *Water Music,* though it was mixed with the clamor of conversation. I went down the corridor toward the ballroom in the hope of catching sight of Lord Brackenheath. It would be most upsetting, I thought, to have him elude me at such a gathering as this.

As I made my way along the corridor, I noticed a man in a regimental uniform from Germany or Austria hovering in the doorway to the ballroom. I had not noticed him earlier, and I supposed that the incident at the Diogenes Club with the unknown fellow in the theatrical uniform made me more suspicious of this chap. I observed him until he glanced my way, at which point I entered the ballroom.

Stepping over the threshold I paused to get my bearings and noticed that Prince Jiro had just offered Lady Brackenheath a glass of champagne. I looked around, hoping that Lord Brackenheath was not in the ballroom, for he would be apt to take offense if he saw his wife with Prince Jiro. Which, I decided, was probably why the Prince had done it. I allowed to myself that I could not blame Prince Jiro for his gallantry, for Lady Brackenheath was surely the most elegant woman in the whole ballroom.

Lady Brackenheath smiled at Prince Jiro as she accepted the

wine from him, and I thought Lord Brackenheath would surely be outraged if he saw such cordiality between them. Then I realized with a start that Lady Brackenheath was only two or three years older than Prince Jiro. No wonder she was enjoying his company, for not only was he the center of the occasion, he was her contemporary, a pleasant change for her.

Andermatt appeared at my side. "Mister Guthrie, may I assist you in any way? I have a little time to spare, and it is fully at your disposal."

It was on the tip of my tongue to ask about the fellow in the European uniform, but I knew it would not be appropriate. I made myself pleasant. "That is very kind of you, but no thank you. I am on an errand for my employer."

"Ah, yes. Mister Holmes, who is not officially here tonight. It would be awkward if he were to be seen in the ballroom." He was about to go on when he stopped and said, "There was an inquiry at the messengers' room about him, half an hour ago or so. His presence was denied, of course. Perhaps it should have been mentioned."

"Was it from the Admiralty?" I asked in some alarm.

"No. A gentleman came and asked if Mister Holmes was attending the gala, given he has done so much work on arranging this agreement with the Japanese. Of course, no message was left." He said it as calmly as he might announce dinner.

I felt my bones go cold. No one was supposed to know Holmes was here at all, in any capacity. We had been at great pains to keep up the appearances that his routine had not deviated. Now this, which meant our meticulous plans had been for naught. To have such a question asked shook our carefully maintained fabrication to the foundations. "And what did you say?"

"I was not there. However, the man was informed that no one of that name had been here at any time today, or was in any way connected with this gala." Had he not possessed such formidable dignity, I would have sworn he smirked. "The staff here knows how to do the work expected of it."

"So I should hope," I said, sighing once. "Thank you, Andermatt. I will tell my employer of this incident."

"Very good," said Andermatt, and began to move away from me.

The musicians had switched from Handel to Strauss, and the opening bars of the *Village Swallows Waltz* summoned couples onto the floor.

"One last thing," I said, reclaiming his attention. "Have you seen Lord Brackenheath?"

Andermatt turned back to me. "He told me he was going out into the Terrace Garden to smoke in peace."

"I see," I said, thinking that he might have more sinister purposes than that. "When was that?"

"Not long ago—about ten minutes, I should think." This time Andermatt was gone before I could frame another question.

There were French doors on the far side of the room leading onto the terrace. Since the direct route lay across the occupied dance floor, I made my way in that direction circuitously, only to be waylaid by Penelope Gatspy, looking delectable in a gorgeous gown of a color between amber and rose, which must have been made for her in Paris and which showed off her charms to admiration.

"Mister Guthrie," she said, coming up beside me and plucking at my sleeve. "How fortunate to see you here."

"Miss Gatspy," I said as I turned toward her, not quite smiling at her, but expressing a modicum of pleasure. "I fear I cannot linger. I am currently on an errand."

"No doubt. For Mister Holmes, of course. But I want to speak to you about a development of which he should be aware."

She looked around as if we might be overheard, though in the noise of the room, I supposed if we shouted we should not attract any attention.

"Tell me what it is," I said, hoping she would be brief.

She drew me a little out of the way, and waited a moment as she looked over the dance floor. "There," she said, pointing to one of the pairs on the floor.

"The Russian? Do you see him?" She did not do anything as obvious as pointing, but cocked her chin in the direction she wanted me to look.

"You mean the Grodno Hussar?" I asked, picking out the one obviously Russian uniform on the dance floor.

"Yes." She watched him swirl his partner around the end of the ballroom and then start the long, twisting way back. "I doubt he's Russian at all. I have been watching him, and I am certain he is not what he seems."

I heard this with a mixture of disbelief and annoyance, for it seemed a minor matter at best. "Why do you think that?"

"Because he swears in Hungarian," she said. "I heard him."

I shrugged. "His family is Hungarian on his mother's side," I suggested, "or he has a superior officer who has banned profanity, and so he has found a safe way to curse without having to deal with disfavor, or he has occupied a post in Hungary in the past, perhaps at the Russian embassy there, and has learned a few words to curse with." All three suggestions were given sensibly, and I was satisfied would account for the man's behavior. "Besides, there are Hungarians present. He could as well have been part of their contingent if he is Hungarian."

"I don't like it," she said with feeling. "The man makes me . . . worry."

With a quick smile I looked down at her. She was really quite stunning tonight, I thought. It was a pity she had thrown in her lot with the Golden Lodge as she had, for she and I would forever be adversaries, and that was unfortunate for both of us. Or so I felt at this moment. "I will keep an eye on him."

"I'm doing that," she said in exasperation. "I think he ought to be watched. He may be up to no good."

I caught the edge in her words, and I became apprehensive. "Tell me—do you have specific information I should share?"

"No, I do not," she answered. "I have only the observations I have made and my own conviction that there is more to this occasion than is obvious." She gave me a single, hard look, then directed her gaze toward the door to the corridor. "The meetings going on here are the true reason for these festivities, aren't they? It isn't simply a matter of the Swiss wanting to honor the Japanese."

"You know I—" I began uncomfortably.

"—can't talk about it," she finished for me. "Yes. I am aware of that." She made an impatient gesture. "And you cannot linger either, can you? You are doing the bidding of Mister Holmes. Who is not on the guest list, I have discovered. But I doubt you would be here if he was not."

"Miss Gatspy," I protested.

"Oh, never mind, Guthrie," she said bluntly, and took a step away from me. "Mind the Russian-who-is-not-Russian." And with that she was gone into the confusion at the edge of the dance floor.

I could not help but watch the man she had indicated swing elegantly in the fast-paced waltz with his pretty Austrian partner. How could Miss Gatspy be so certain about the man? And was swearing in Hungarian so different from swearing in Russian that she could tell the difference between them? Had she truly intended to warn me or was her intention to distract me from my purpose? I hardly knew how to regard her actions, though in retrospect they filled me with misgivings. With these uncomfortable notions to goad me, I resumed my progress toward the terrace doors, hoping that Lord Brackenheath had not left while I was speaking with Miss Gatspy.

The night air was chilly after the heat of the ballroom. I steadied myself on my crutches and made my way through the spill of light from the open doors to the edge of the terrace. I saw no one, and heard only the music and conversation behind me as I approached the steps leading down into the garden. I did not relish descending to the graveled paths at night, which might well bring me to another fall. As I pegged my way down the first few steps, I longed for a torch or a lamp to pierce the deep shadow of the stairs. I used my crutches to feel my way, testing them carefully as I placed them on the broad stone treads.

Then I became aware of a bundle at the foot of the steps, like a large sack of laundry. I made my way to it carefully, thinking that this could be a trap, perhaps the sack hid a bomb or something worse. I could swear the hackles rose on my neck, for I certainly felt a sudden presence of danger. After a quick look about me, in case I should be set upon while making my way down the stairs, I descended, my breathing harsh in my throat, half-expecting a bullet, knife, bludgeon, or other attacker upon me on the instant.

With an effort I got down to inspect the shape, feeling with both hands in the hope that I might not put myself in too much danger if I did not actually upset whatever-it-was, lying there in the dark. For an instant I thought of the insurrectionist bombs left in sacks in Ireland for the unwary to trigger, and wondered if this could be one. I touched what was certainly good cloth, but it was wet and slightly sticky. The breath caught in my throat. I suppose that I realized what this was upon the instant, but I would not permit myself to own it. Then I felt a sleeve, and as I pulled on it, the body rolled slightly, and in the faint lume from the lamps in the street beyond the garden I could just make out the pain-contorted features of Lord Brackenheath.

FROM THE JOURNAL OF PHILIP TYERS

I have asked Sid Hastings to send his oldest boy around in the morning. I want to put him to work in the access court behind the house, to watch who comes and goes from the place. I am afraid those who are keeping this place under surveillance are on guard against me, and are likely to conceal themselves if they think I am watching as intently as they are. But a child, and a scruffy child at that, with a Bow Bells accent, would attract little notice. I have promised the sum of twenty pence for two days of the boy's time. I know that Hastings will not deny any assistance he can give to M H.

Sutton has just taken himself off to the study to work more on Ferdinand, claiming that keeping in my company was making him nervous about something he can do nothing about. He insists he cannot concentrate on playing M H if he is about to jump out of his skin at every noise from the street. I understand his sentiments more than he supposes I do, but at the same time, I cannot approve of his determination to ignore the very real risks we are running here.

Chapter Fourteen

HOW I STRUGGLED to my feet, I shall never know. I found myself at the top of the garden steps, my crutches clutched in my hands, sweat standing out on my brow, and a steady, churning nausea working behind my waistcoat. The enormity of this discovery rushed in on me like a tidal wave, and I needed a short while to collect my thoughts enough to act. Somehow I composed myself sufficiently to make my way along the terrace to the door to the Terrace Suite, all the while reminding myself I might be being watched. The blood had not congealed, and the body was warm to the touch. I had to conclude Lord Brackenheath had been killed only a few minutes before my arrival, a thought that did not comfort me in the least. Good Lord, what a coil this could become, I thought as I hurried to inform Holmes of what I had discovered. I hoped no one would make the same grisly discovery I had before Holmes was able to deal with it.

I tapped on the Terrace Suite door, and when that brought no results, I slapped the frame with the flat of my hand. I did not call out for fear of alerting the killer, who might still be in the immediate vicinity; surely the situation was impossible enough without further complications.

A moment later the door was opened by Sir George Tyrell, who concealed his surprise admirably. "Good God, man, what happened to you?"

"Nothing," I said, attempting to push past him.

But he blocked my way, as impassable as a cordial bear. "Won't do, old man, truly. Not with a smear of blood on your face and the front of your shirt. Are you injured?"

"No," I said quickly, and made a swipe at my face with one hand. "I am well enough. Please, Mister Tyrell, I must speak with my employer at once."

At that Tyrell relented and moved aside. "Very well; he's over there, with the ambassador and the secretaries." He indicated the far end of the table where the men were gathered to affix the seals to the agreement.

"Guthrie," said Holmes as I approached. He was holding a fresh-lit cigar between his long fingers, and as the light fell across his face, he appeared unusually saturnine. "Whatever it is, you had best tell me about it."

"It's Lord Brackenheath," I said quietly.

"God save us, what's he done now?" Holmes demanded in exasperation. "I am losing patience with him."

I glanced at George Tyrell and said, "I fear I must talk to Mister Holmes in confidence."

To give him credit, Tyrell did not dispute this. He laid his finger beside his nose and stepped back from us, going to join the Prime Minister at the side-table where brandy was being poured.

I leaned on my crutches, grateful for once of their support. "I have just left Lord Brackenheath," I began.

"What is he up to now? Tell me the worst," said Holmes with resignation.

So I steeled myself and said, "He is lying dead near the foot of the terrace stairs. There is a knife of some sort in his back."

Rarely have I heard Mycroft Holmes swear as he did then, and I stood apprehensively by as I heard him out. He glared at his cigar. "A knife you say?"

"Yes, with a short, simple handle, of horn, I think." I tried to bring my thoughts to bear on the sight, but they slid and scattered like quicksilver. "Something like a German hunting knife, perhaps."

Holmes took a sharp breath; when he spoke, his voice was still lower than it had been. "Try to remember precisely. Tell me exactly what you saw."

Carefully I recounted my search and my discovery, trying to keep my tone level as I described the body. "I could not see it very well, sir, and I was very much shocked to find it at all."

"I suppose," said Holmes sarcastically, "we should be grateful that the killer chose that site to leave the body. If it had been thrust under one of the boxwood hedges he might not have been discovered until tomorrow, and that would make this situation much more awkward for the Swiss. And they will be upset enough as it is." He rocked back on his heels. "We must give the alarm." He scowled. "Or rather, *you* must give the alarm, as quietly as possible. We do not want any appearance of compromise, for that would call the agreement into question. It will not do to have this place in an uproar until the agreement is fully ratified." He gave a quick look over his shoulder. "I am going to say that Lord Brackenheath is not available, so that we may complete this work. It is, after all, the truth, is it not? And it will permit us to conclude our negotiations without undue delay. While I tend to this, I want you to find Andermatt and inform him of your discovery before you go to the police, who cannot be left uninformed. When you arrive at Scotland Yard, I recommend you request Inspector Cornell for the investigation. He is the soul of discretion. Barring him, Inspector FitzGerald will do." He turned away from me abruptly and made his way to Ambassador Tochigi's side, bending down to make his request.

I could not wholly conceal my dislike for this arrangement, but I realized it was the only reasonable way to proceed, given the importance of the agreement. I took a moment to muster my thoughts, and started out of the room.

"Guthrie," said Holmes quietly, "attend to your face first. You have not yet got all the blood off."

I colored up as I drew my handkerchief from my pocket and swiped at my jaw and chin. Upon receiving a nod of approval from Holmes, I resumed my departure. I had almost reached the door when Ambassador Tochigi came up to me.

"I understand Lord Brackenheath has departed," he said quietly.

What an apt way to put it, I thought with grim amusement. "Yes, sir. I am very much afraid he has."

"And his wife as well?" he inquired politely.

"No. She is still in the ballroom," I said, and realized how odd this would seem to a Japanese gentleman. "She arrived on her own, in her own carriage," I said, as if this would account for such a lapse.

"Hai," said the ambassador. "Then Lord Brackenheath may return."

"I most sincerely doubt it," I said, feeling uncomfortable again.

Ambassador Tochigi cocked his head. "If you are sure of it. He made no secret of disliking this agreement. He may not wish to be party to it at all. In which case we may proceed without delay."

"It is unlikely he will return," I said, feeling inexcusably bad for misleading the ambassador.

"Well, there are those in Japan who would share his sentiments, were they present to express them." He bowed again. "I thank you for bringing the news. It is not wholly welcome but it will permit us to get on with our duty here. The agreement is to be made public at midnight. You have made this possible."

"You are very kind, Ambassador Tochigi," I responded, thinking I was getting better than I deserved.

"Nonsense," he said, and turned back to the table where the rest of the group were gathering with the purpose of making the agreement official.

I let myself out of the Terrace Suite, the ambassador's courteous words ringing like tocsins in my ears. What would Ambassador Tochigi think of me when he learned the truth of the situation, as he must do in a matter of forty minutes at most? I realized my position could become more precarious than it was. Ambassador Tochigi could demand my dismissal for failing to inform him of Lord Brackenheath's murder. The word *murder* stuck in my thoughts like a stone in my shoe.

I found Andermatt far sooner than I wanted to, for I had not yet gathered my thoughts enough to present this unwelcome intelligence in a manner gauged to make it as palatable as possible.

"There is a spot of blood on your face, sir," said Andermatt as I came up to him in the entrance to the dining room, supervising the servants where the midnight buffet was being set out. "Is anything the matter?"

I must not have got all the blood off my face after all, and I knew it was useless to deny it was there. "Yes, Andermatt, I am afraid there is," I said, and motioned him to a corner of the room. "And I am afraid there is a very . . . untoward development you must know of at once."

"Goodness, Mister Guthrie," he said, his very blandness stirring me to a more emotional response.

"A short while ago I went in search of Lord Brackenheath. He was wanted in the Terrace Suite. I sought him first in the ballroom, but he was not there." It was a quiet enough beginning, and I was hoping I would not make a mull of it when I heard myself say, "I found him on the terrace stairs where they turn, almost at the foot in the garden. Lying dead."

Andermatt's eyes widened. "How lamentable," he exclaimed. "Are you certain he had not collapsed? Should we not summon a physician at once?"

"A physician could not help him now," I told him, and went on before I could stop myself. "He was stabbed to death."

Now Andermatt was very much distressed—although no agitation disturbed his manner—but he was breathing quickly and his neck had reddened. "Stabbed? He was murdered, you are saying. Are you certain?"

"I felt the knife in his back. The blood on my face is his." This was blunter than I had intended, but I was not able to find softer words.

"Oh, dear," said Andermatt. "I will have to inform the ambassador at once." He literally wrung his hands.

"Yes, you must." I did not like to contemplate what would come next.

"And given that Lord Brackenheath is English, it would be courtesy to summon the English police." He was thinking aloud.

"Yes, and his killer might well be English, too," I reminded him, and received a weak smile for my efforts. "The English police will know best what to do."

"Yes. Yes. That is always possible, is it not?" He looked so relieved I nearly laughed, though I did not like to be so unsympathetic to the man. "The men we have here do not often deal with criminals of this order." He made up his mind quickly. "I will authorize you to contact Scotland Yard for us, in your capacity as Mister Holmes' secretary. Tell them they are being summoned as a gesture of cooperation. And we do not have the personnel to conduct such an investigation in this embassy. Of course, this is legally Swiss business, but we do not want it said that we are unwilling to accept the aid of our host country, or that we have failed to do the most we can to ensure the protection of those who have put their trust in us." I was a little surprised at the readiness with which he made the decision, and was about to remark upon it when he said, "The ambassador leaves such matters to me. It would be lamentable if we lost prestige because of this unhappy event, and the ambassador has been at pains to be certain he maintains the highest integrity for our country. He has his hands full dealing with the management of international matters."

In other words, I told myself, the ambassador is a well-born fool with a family name who does not know or want to know anything of the daily working world. In the last several months I had met my share of those in England. "I will go there myself, as soon as you have seen the body."

"Ah . . ." said Andermatt, his eyes darting nervously. "Yes, I suppose you're right. I should summon an officer or two and have them accompany us to the body."

"Us?" I said, disliking the word.

"You will have to show me. You found him." It was nearly an

accusation. "You will have to come with me." He indicated my crutches. "A fortunate thing you have those, or you might find yourself suspected of the crime."

I could not conceal my shock. "How do you mean?"

"It is difficult, if not impossible, to wield a knife while supporting yourself on crutches. You might be able to fire a gun, but not strike with a knife. You may count yourself lucky to have been injured." His face had that sharp look now that told me he was rather more than the chief servant of the Swiss ambassador.

"True enough," I said, astonished at the rush of gratitude I felt.

"So. Wait here while I summon our guards and we will find the body." He turned on his heel and went away, only to return in less than five minutes with two uniformed guards. "We will go out the side door, beyond the Terrace Suite," he announced. "That way we will not draw attention to ourselves. We do not want to rouse the suspicions of our guests, or to disrupt the evening."

"Or alert the murderer," I added as I fell in with them.

"Precisely," said Andermatt.

The guards were carrying lanterns. Both were young men with open faces and firm jaws, and I found myself thinking that they were chosen more for their appearance on parade than for their experience in battle. Still, they were selected by Andermatt, which I was certain meant more than simple approval.

The steps were reached too quickly for my taste. I started down them, using the light from the lanterns to set my crutches easily on the stone treads.

Lord Brackenheath lay where I had left him. I saw his rictus features and flinched, using that as an excuse to move aside. "There he is," I said, knowing how unnecessary such a statement was.

Andermatt bent and touched the dead man. "Not dead long. He's cooling but not cold." He then tested the pool of blood that spread around the body; I wondered at how he came to know so much about blood and death. "Not wet, but not yet fully coagulated."

"How long dead, sir?" asked one of the guards in German.

"Forty minutes at most. With such a quantity of blood, it takes longer to congeal." He straightened up. "All right, Mister Guthrie. The corpse will be watched and no one will interfere with it. Off you go to Scotland Yard. And not a word to anyone here about what you have found."

"I have informed Mister Holmes," I said, and explained. "He was the one who instructed me to tell you. I thought that must be obvious."

"No, it wasn't," said Andermatt, and sighed. "Very well. We must rely on Mister Holmes to guard his tongue." He rubbed his chin. "All the more reason to hurry this along."

"Certainly," I said, wanting to do my utmost to help.

He bent over the body again. "I will touch nothing until the police arrive. The guards will remain posted here, so that no one will have any opportunity to touch it, or remove any objects that might be part of the murder." He leaned nearer. "Did you see the knife clearly?"

"No. I did not have much light," I said to him.

"More's the pity." He peered at the body. "I can see part of the handle. It is unfortunate the body fell back this way. The knife is concealed."

In conscience, I felt I had to explain. "The body has rolled slightly. I did it while I was trying to discover who it was."

Andermatt licked his tongue. "Necessary, I suppose, but it could have caused a problem. There is bound to be gossip." He motioned me aside, and I went with him to the start of a long avenue of roses. "Did you remove anything from the scene? Your word as a gentleman, sir."

"No, I did not. I found the body, saw the face and came away." At another time I might have been offended by his question, but at the moment, I could not blame him for making such assumptions. The whole affair was potentially disastrous, and we were all aware of it.

"Prudent of you," said Andermatt. He indicated where he wanted his guards to stand, and then said to me, "Well, be about your errand, Mister Guthrie. Your employer will tell Lord Salisbury of what has transpired so that he may excuse himself before the questions begin and the press gets wind of the murder. The sooner we commence this, the sooner it will end."

I nodded my agreement, and made my way along the garden path to the front of the Swiss embassy. How much I wished that Sid Hastings were here, but I knew better than to expect him for at least another two hours. I would have to rely on the embassy to supply a discreet driver. I went to the front and asked for a whiskey to be called. A few minutes later, I was on my way to Scotland Yard.

FROM THE JOURNAL OF PHILIP TYERS

Word has come from the Swiss embassy that M H and G will be delayed there well into the night for reasons he disclosed with care. What a truly shocking development, to have a murder during a gala reception. In regard to these unfortunate events, I have been requested to investigate the associations and connections of Lord Brackenheath, who I am informed has met with an untimely end. I have assured M H that I will do my utmost to gather all the information I can before news of his demise becomes public, as it must do in the morning.

I have informed Sutton of this development, and it is to his credit that he has not allowed himself to be troubled by this revelation. He informs me that he is now certain his little charade is useful to M H and is determined to pursue the role he is playing for as long as it is deemed necessary to protect M H. I can only laud his courage, which I did not think he possessed.

The investigation of the murder is to be offered to Inspector Cor-

nell, if he is available. His expertise and tact are both wanted in this instance. If he is not available. I suppose Inspector FitzGerald will be chosen. Either man is capable of dealing with the ramifications of this unfortunate crime, though Cornell is the more astute of the two. FitzGerald is marginally the more perceptive.

Chapter Fifteen

INSPECTOR MARCUS FITZGERALD did not like being called from his home, let alone for an event such as this one. He got into the whiskey with me, his square features and military moustache set in stern lines of disapproval, as if he thought well-born men such as Lord Brackenheath should have better manners than to be murdered at so inconvenient an hour, and in so potentially embarrassing a manner.

"I am sorry, Inspector, but I was informed that Inspector Cornell is not in London just at present." I tried my best to sound contrite, but did not manage as well as I hoped to. The pressure of the crime was pressing upon me as I knew it must upon others.

"No, he's not, worse luck," growled Inspector FitzGerald, who was Cornell's only recognized rival at Scotland Yard.

"If he were scheduled to return tomorrow, it would be another matter. But as he will not, we are depending on you to do your best, as Inspector Cornell would do," I kept on, determined to make him see the advantages to himself this case presented.

"He's gone until Friday week. The trial is expected to take that long, given the nature of the offenses." He made himself comfortable, tucked his small portfolio behind his legs, and regarded me with a mixture of philosophical acceptance and annoyance. "So, let me have your version of what has happened. There's a Peer of the Realm dead. I understand that much. The Yard didn't send you round to me in this havey-cavey manner without there being something difficult in the man's murder."

"I thought all murders were difficult," I said, feeling put-upon.

He laughed. "Lord love you, no. Most of them are simple as salt. A fellow has a quarrel with his neighbor or his family. The neighbor or relation gets even by killing him. Nothing difficult in that. All we have to do is ask one or two questions and the thing's all right and tight. As easy as shooting clay pigeons. Juries know what to make of such cases. They find the murderer guilty without trouble and the whole thing is over and done with." He regarded me with a faintly cynical smile. "This isn't going to be one of those, is it?"

"I doubt it," I answered, and proceeded to tell him of the events of the evening that led to my discovery of the body of Lord Brackenheath. I was at pains to make it clear that the circumstances were delicate in the extreme, not only because the dead man was a Peer of the Realm, but because the negotiations at the Swiss embassy were delicate and had reached their most crucial stage. I made an effort to emphasize the importance of decorum as well as integrity in dealing with the murder. Fitz-Gerald listened to me in silence, a frown deepening on his brow. "And that is the whole of it. Lord Brackenheath has been stabbed by a person or persons unknown during an important diplomatic mission. His death may or may not be connected with the mission. If it is, the honor and safety of England may well be at stake here."

"And the Admiralty and the government expect the police to take the heat for them. Saves them looking like fools," said FitzGerald with amiable cynicism. "Where do you fit into all this, Mister Guthrie?"

"I have been attending the negotiations in my capacity as personal secretary to Mycroft Holmes, who has been participating in the negotiations in an unofficial capacity." I hoped this last was not lost on Inspector FitzGerald. "On his orders I was sent to bring you to the Swiss embassy, and I am doing it to the best of my ability."

"So you are," said Inspector FitzGerald. He looked at the buildings. "And we will arrive shortly. Who knows of this . . . development?"

"I must suppose the Swiss ambassador has been informed, though I did not do it. I do not know who, if anyone, among the other guests has been told. I assume the general announcement will be delayed as long as possible." It was as candid an answer as I could give, and FitzGerald greeted it with a nod and a grunt.

"We'll find out about that directly." He pulled his watch out and squinted at the face. "I won't see my desk again before dawn, I warrant."

"Very likely not," I agreed, thinking the same myself.

As he replaced his watch, he looked nervously at me. "You say that there are Japanese involved?"

"There are Japanese at the gala. It is being given in their honor, and in honor of the Emperor's second son, who is a cadet at Dartmouth." I realized that Inspector FitzGerald had no experience with the Japanese, so I said, "Don't worry, Inspector. They speak English and they will cooperate with your investigation." I hoped devoutly that this was true.

The whiskey turned into the drive to the porte cochere of the Swiss embassy. The lanterns were all still blazing away, and I could hear the little orchestra playing *The Lancers,* and saw the movement in the ballroom as shadows on the half-open draperies. I guessed that the guests were still generally in ignorance of the death of Lord Brackenheath, for I doubted diplomatic sangfroid extended to such blatant disrespect for the dead.

We were met by Mycroft Holmes himself, who stepped up to the whiskey as it drew to a halt. "Thank you for coming so promptly, Inspector. I know we may rely on your absolute discretion in this matter. It is a most awkward circumstance, whatever the cause of the murder. I fear any premature release of information might well prove damaging for England, and I am certain you have no wish for such a development."

"Good Lord, no," exclaimed Inspector FitzGerald as he got out of the whiskey, taking his portfolio with him and tucking it under his arm. "Wouldn't want the government to lodge a complaint with Scotland Yard. And you may be certain that they would, as quick as lightning." He ignored me as I descended less handily behind him, my crutches making my movements slow and clumsy.

"If you will follow me, I will take you to where the body lies," said Holmes as if it were the most ordinary thing in the world. "The ambassador has said he does not want the evening to end in upset if that can be avoided." His smile was slight. "And his head of household, Andermatt, agrees."

"Has the body been disturbed?" asked Inspector FitzGerald, getting down to business at once.

"Not since Guthrie discovered it. He admits to having moved it sufficiently to discover the identity of the victim, but nothing more disruptive than that. A man on crutches is ill prepared to handle a corpse. He very correctly informed me of what he had found, and I at once sent him to fetch you. As I must suppose he has already told you." Holmes had set off along the path leading directly into the garden, going at a steady pace, but not so quickly that I had any effort to keep up.

"Yes, so he informed me," said Inspector FitzGerald. "He also told me that guards were posted to be certain nothing else befell the body." He let the implication sink in before he added, "I hope that there has been no attempt to tamper with Lord Brackenheath."

"None. I will vouch for that," said Holmes at once. "The embassy staff have set guards to protect the body, and to ensure nothing of the scene is altered."

"And there has been no announcement made?" asked Inspector FitzGerald. "No alarm has been given?"

"Our only announcement has been of the signing of our agreement with Japan. That is the reason for this gala, essentially. It suits our purpose to have the guests unaware of this tragedy, at least for the time being."

"I take your meaning, Mister Holmes," said Inspector FitzGerald as they came around the high bow at the end of the terrace and found the guards waiting, with Andermatt still in charge. In my absence someone had brought a stretcher to the top of the stairs, in preparation for the removal of the body. A dark blanket lay folded at one end of the stretcher. The Inspector stopped abruptly to take in the sight. "Guthrie said that there was very little light when he found the body."

"So there was," said Andermatt before Holmes could speak. "I ordered my men to bring lanterns, the better to examine the scene in the hope that some vital clue might be discovered."

Holmes stepped in. "This is Andermatt, Inspector FitzGerald. He is the head of household here for the Swiss ambassador."

"And a bloody sight more, no doubt," said Inspector FitzGerald, taking his measure of the man at once. "Well, so much the better, I reckon. It's a delicate matter, after all. Chaps of your sort might as well be in at the first." The Inspector held out his hand to Andermatt. "Inspector Marcus FitzGerald of Scotland Yard, at your service."

Andermatt's expression remained unchanged, but he extended his hand. "Under other circumstances it would be a pleasure, Inspector," he said, and nodded down at the body.

"Right you are, then," said Inspector FitzGerald. He approached the body carefully, taking care not to tread in the blood that now caked the steps.

"Stand aside, men," said Andermatt to his guards. "Let the Inspector set about his duty. Render him any assistance he may need." He then looked directly at Holmes. "I believe it would be prudent to inform Ambassador Tochigi of what has happened, now that the agreement has been ratified."

Inspector FitzGerald took his notebook from his inner jacket pocket, retrieved a pencil and began to sketch the murder scene.

"Yes, I agree," said Holmes, continuing with determination. "And Lady Brackenheath as well."

Andermatt flushed a little at his own lapse. "Yes. Of course. Lady Brackenheath must be told before anyone else learns of it." He met Holmes' eyes. "Will you tend to that? It would be better coming from you, an Englishman, than from another. It will be hard enough to bear without her having the news from . . . foreigners."

I did not know if this was true, but I could see that Andermatt did not relish informing the young woman that she was now a widow. I chided myself for the offer I was about to make, then shut such considerations aside. "Would you like me to accompany you, sir?"

Holmes looked at me with sharp eyes. "Yes, Guthrie, I would. In case she is in need of more support than I have time to give. A pity we do not know who her friends are, for we could summon one to stay with her." He gave a short sigh. "Well, there is nothing for it. As soon as the murder weapon is recovered, we will have to tell Lady Brackenheath. The sooner begun, the sooner finished, as my French grandmother used to say when I was laggard."

"You can turn the body over now, men," said Inspector FitzGerald. "I have finished my sketches. Have a care. I want to see that knife as soon as I may."

None of the guards rushed to do the work. Handling the body was awkward, for rigor mortis had already set in, and no one wanted to get his feet in the blood, though most of it was dry and dark.

"Good gracious!" exclaimed Inspector FitzGerald as he bent over the corpse. "What have we here?"

In spite of our reluctance to approach the murdered man, Andermatt, Holmes, and I could not help but give our full attention to the remark. We turned as one and watched with undisguised interest as Inspector FitzGerald held up the weapon he had been handed.

"I never saw anything quite like this. Nine-inch blade, a little curve to it, and a handle made, I think, from horn. A single wound, for all I can determine, unusual in a stabbing death," he declared as he regarded the magnificent antique dagger. "You know anything about it?" he asked Holmes.

"Yes," said Holmes, his voice sounding distant. "It is Japanese. An *aichuki* of the seventeenth or eighteenth century. It is the kind of dagger used in *seppuku*—Japanese ritual suicide."

Inspector FitzGerald wrapped the dagger in his handkerchief. "Lord Brackenheath never killed himself."

"No," said Holmes quietly, and began to twiddle his watch-fob. "But it may be the murderer—"

"Is Japanese," said Inspector FitzGerald at once, nodding. "That's fairly obvious."

Holmes gave him an exasperated stare. I could sense the torrent of thought that possessed him now, though I doubted Inspector FitzGerald was aware of it. "I reckon it a trifle too obvious, Inspector. Given this setting, I would rather suppose someone intends to implicate the Japanese. Think, man. If you were going to kill someone at a function of this sort, would you select anything so blatant as that dagger unless you intended to throw suspicion on the Japanese?"

"The Japanese are Orientals, sir, and they have strange ways," said Inspector FitzGerald.

Holmes directed his gaze to the night sky. "Give me patience." Then he fixed Inspector FitzGerald with a hard stare. "The Japanese attending this gala are not foolish men. If they wanted to do away with Lord Brackenheath, they could easily avail themselves of pistols or other, less distinctive weapons. They have pistols at their disposal, as the rest of us do. It would have been an easy thing to shoot the man." He was speaking quickly, his words crisp as new collars. "I, for one, would consider the aichuki dagger the reddest of red herrings."

"The dagger makes much less noise," the Inspector pointed out.

"My dear FitzGerald, there is a small orchestra playing dance music in the ballroom, and more than a hundred guests, all talking at once. I would think it would take cannon fire at least to gain their attention," said Holmes with deliberate sarcasm. "A pistol held near the body would not be noticeable."

"That's as may be, sir," said Inspector FitzGerald, pugnacity ill-concealed behind his deferential manner. "I am only able to evaluate what I see, and I see a man with a Japanese dagger in his back at a function where there are Japanese. I cannot think it wholly coincidental."

"Exactly," said Holmes. "It isn't a coincidence, it is a deliberate attempt to mislead you. Certainly the weapon is Japanese, and certainly this gala honors the Japanese Ambassador and Prince Jiro. But I am saying that no Japanese would use an aichuki in this fashion. It would be more reprehensible than using the Coronation Orb to bash the P.M.'s head in."

Holmes' observation had its intended result: In spite of himself, Inspector FitzGerald chuckled. "Not that there hasn't been many a King who would not have wanted to do just that." He carefully put the aichuki in his small portfolio, making a point of closing it. "This will have to be examined."

"Certainly," said Holmes at once. "In fact, I hope you will be particularly careful with that dagger, for we want no claims of tampering to be made when the details of this most unfortunate event become generally known." He tucked his watchfob back in its pocket. "I fear we must anticipate a furor in the press."

Inspector FitzGerald rolled his eyes upward. "Don't mention the press."

"But I fear I must. We need to anticipate their response and be prepared for it." Holmes nodded in Andermatt's direction. "And you will have to decide how the embassy is to deal with the attention."

"We do not have to deal with them," said Andermatt, watching his men carry Lord Brackenheath's body toward the waiting stretcher.

"It will be better for you if you prepare a statement to offer them. Appease them if you can." Holmes swung around and looked across the terrace to the ballroom. "I fear everyone who attended this gala may be considered fair game by the press."

I found myself thinking of Penelope Gatspy and had the irrational thought that I should warn her, for her own protection. I realized that such an effort was impossible, and I suspected that my employer would not want any such information being provided to Miss Gatspy, given her association with the Golden Lodge.

Andermatt was frowning, his attention on Mycroft Holmes. "I take it I am to refer no one to you, sir?"

Holmes shook his head. "As I am not actually here, officially, it would be best if my name were kept out of it. I will do all that I can to assist you and the police in their inquiries, of course, but not as anything more than an unnamed source." His smile was as fleeting as it was grim.

"As you wish, sir," said Andermatt with a look of understanding that startled me.

"All right, Guthrie," said Holmes as he saw Lord Brackenheath's body strapped to the stretcher and decently covered. "We'd best be about this wretched business."

I nodded. "Of course, sir."

"Andermatt, may we have the use of the White Salon? It is private enough for speaking with Lady Brackenheath, isn't it?" Holmes asked as we prepared to reenter the embassy.

"Of course," said Andermatt, the greater part of his attention given to his guards and the stretcher they carried toward the small, north-side entrance to the embassy. "There is brandy and port on the sideboard."

"Excellent," said Holmes, and very nearly sounded as if he meant it. "Come, Guthrie. We have work to do." And with that he strode off in the direction of the Terrace Suite.

I followed after, my pace slowed by more than my crutches.

FROM THE JOURNAL OF PHILIP TYERS

Sutton has taken up a seat in the study, and immersed himself in The Duchess of Malfi *once more. He has lit a cigar as M H inevitably does, and has read and smoked away most of the evening. This has left me the opportunity to watch the service alley, for I am more convinced than ever that the watchers are at their posts; I am determined to identify them all.*

Sid Hastings has sent word that he has returned home, for the flurry of activity at the Swiss embassy has brought a dozen policemen to keep guard on the street, and he does not want to be the object of their attention, since he would have to reveal the commission of M H. He says he will return when the police have departed, and has arranged to be informed by the jarveys working that area of the town to inform him as soon as that occurs. It may be inconvenient for M H to have to wait for Hastings, but it is preferable to having his presence noted.

I have set a joint of beef to roast, for I know when M H and G return they will not have dined and will be famished after so hectic a night. A late supper will give them the opportunity to review the events of the evening in unhurried peace, and will assure them of a good night's sleep. Fortunately I have fresh bread purchased this afternoon to serve them, and I can prepare a side dish of asparagus dressed with butter and mushrooms. It is not much, but it will serve, with port and Stilton to finish.

Sutton has decided to remain the night and will rise at M H's accustomed hour so that our employer may sleep late and restore himself to face the difficulties that are sure to confront him. I am once again impressed by the good sense Sutton displays. Who would have thought an actor would have so canny a grasp on the world?

Chapter Sixteen

"WHAT HAS MY husband done now?" Lady Brackenheath asked with ill-concealed annoyance as Enzo the footman left her in our charge in the White Salon. Her response to the interruption of her evening had thus far been one of mild vexation, and she had not accepted Holmes' offer of a chair upon completion of their introduction. As she moved about the room, her magnificent jewelry and clothing shone and glistened. In the shine of the gaslights the room was now more the color of tallow than the pristine white of daytime, though it brushed a golden glow onto Lady Brackenheath's cheeks. "I was afraid he would disrupt this occasion with some folly. You had best tell me what it is. I am prepared for the worst."

Mycroft Holmes shrugged his big shoulders and regarded her with concern. "I doubt that, if you will forgive me, Lady Brackenheath."

Her expression remained self-possessed. "He has been saying all week that he intends to compromise this agreement. I confess I was astonished at the announcement it had been ratified." She shook her head. "Don't tell me he was detained?"

"No, that is not what has happened," said Holmes with surprising gentleness. "I do think you had much better sit down."

She tossed her head, but apparently she was impressed with his demeanor, for this time she did as he suggested and took a place on a white-satin chair. "Very well, Mister Holmes. What has my infuriating husband done now?"

Holmes hesitated a moment. "There is no easy way to say this. I regret to inform you, Lady Brackenheath, that he has been killed."

There was silence in the room for several seconds. Then Lady Brackenheath shook her head. "I'm sorry. I'm afraid I did not hear you correctly. I thought you said that Lord Brackenheath . . . has been . . . has been . . ."

"Has been killed," said Holmes as kindly as he could. "Yes, Lady Brackenheath, you heard me correctly."

She stared at Holmes, shock making her face pale and blank. "But . . . how? Killed? You did say killed?"

Again Holmes measured his words carefully. "I fear this will cause you pain, Lady Brackenheath." He signaled to me to pour some brandy for her. I was grateful to have something to do, and hastened to select a small snifter and the oldest brandy. "He was discovered not quite an hour ago near the foot of the terrace stairs to the garden. He had been stabbed."

That last struck her as surely as a blow. She put her hands to her cheeks. "How?"

Holmes held out his hand for the brandy snifter. I gave it to him at once, and then chose a second snifter, and a third. "Here, Lady Brackenheath. This will help to restore you," said Holmes as he gave her the snifter.

Obediently she took the snifter and bent her head to inhale the fumes before drinking it. She coughed once, then looked at Holmes. "There is no mistake, is there? Are you quite sure?"

"That he is dead? Yes, Madame, I am sorry to tell you I am." Holmes watched her with deepening concern. "I am also certain of his identity. There can be no question that it is Lord Brackenheath who is . . . My secretary, Mister Guthrie, found him and made sure it was he before he informed me of this tragedy."

I discovered that my hands were shaking. The events of the last hour were finally catching up with me. I had been aware that the calm I had felt until then was false, but I had not thought I was as upset as it now appeared I was. I took a long sip of brandy, and let its warmth filter into my veins.

Lady Brackenheath stared at me as if I had grown a second head or all my clothes had suddenly caught fire. "What were you doing? When you found my husband?" She was still too shaken to make this an accusation, but an edge had come into her voice.

"I had been sent to find him, Lady Brackenheath. He was wanted as a witness for the ratification of the agreement." I felt as if I were a schoolboy once again, called upon to recite a piece I did not correctly know.

"I asked Guthrie to find him," said Holmes, as if offering mitigating evidence on my behalf. "Your husband had left the room in a state of perturbation some while before, and the Prime Minister had arrived, so that he was wanted to witness the signing."

"He had intended . . . to . . . refuse to witness the signing, and to make it known to the guests that he would not, and why he would not. He believes that to cause the Japanese humiliation would be sufficient to have them refuse any further dealings with England, and would save the country from itself," said Lady Brackenheath softly. "He told me yesterday evening that it was his intention to force Lord Salisbury to rescind the agreement." She drank another bit of brandy. Two spots of color appeared in her cheeks, as if she had a fever.

"Do you know why he wanted to do such a thing?" asked Holmes, as if this were an ordinary conversation and we were merely discussing the eccentricities of neighbors instead of the intentions of a murdered man.

"He hates . . . hated the Orientals, all of them. Chinese, Indians, Japanese, Indo-Chinese, Burmese, Koreans. He even included the Russians as Orientals, and his abhorrence extended to them. He was convinced that any dealings with Orientals must end in disgrace and ruin for England, indeed, the ruin of the West. Let Europe make its bargains with the East, he declared he would not allow England to fall into the same trap. He had no intention of helping England to expose her throat to the wolves of the East. He said that no Oriental could be trusted as white men could." She wiped her cheek. Until then I had not noticed her tears, nor, I suspect, had she. She reached into her reticule and pulled out the small handkerchief she carried there.

"I have heard Lord Brackenheath animadvert on the dangers he perceived in Oriental peoples," said Holmes in the same distanced voice. "And given the circumstances of his death, it is necessary to inquire further."

"He has often said that we must not make any alliances with

them for fear of ruin." She finished her brandy and held out the snifter.

Holmes gestured me to refill it. "I am truly sorry to have to pursue this matter with you at such a terrible time, Lady Brackenheath, but I fear I must," Holmes said, taking a seat opposite her. "For it is possible that Lord Brackenheath's opinions may have been a factor in his death."

"What convinces you of that?" asked Lady Brackenheath, doing her best to regain her composure, for try as she would, she could not keep her tears from flowing.

"What convinces me," said Holmes with a look of concern, "is that he made it known he did not approve of what we were doing here. And now you inform me that it was his stated intention to disrupt it, and bring it to an end."

"So he told me," she said, answering with care now that she began to appreciate the nature of the situation.

"And if he told you what form that disruption would take, I ask you to tell me what it might be. We are at a standstill. Lord Salisbury may still face unwonted pressure if the nature of your husband's intentions is left . . . to be guessed at, and the current agreement may still be compromised if Lord Brackenheath has allies who are on the same course as he in regard to our dealings with the Japanese." Holmes leaned forward. I doubted that Edmund Sutton could have been any more inspiring of confidence than Holmes was at that moment.

"Not specifically, just that it would cause utmost humiliation to the Japanese. He said that shame was something they understood. He hoped they would have to kill themselves out of disgrace. He told me that the Japanese do that." Her cheeks were rosier, but more from chagrin than the ending of shock.

"So they do," said Holmes.

I began to wonder if the choice of murder weapon was significant, after all. I would have to mention my thoughts to Mycroft

Holmes when he had finished this first interview with Lady Brackenheath.

Just then the door to the White Salon was flung open and Prince Jiro hurried in. He paused on the threshold just long enough to take stock of the situation, then approached Lady Brackenheath, one hand held out to her. "I have only just been informed. How truly awful for you. I am so very sorry that this has happened. Please accept my most heartfelt condolences." It was a most acceptable little speech, and I thought he gave it well. Many Englishmen would not manage to convey sympathy so properly.

She took his proffered hand and did her best to smile. "Thank you, your Highness. I am . . . most grateful for your consideration."

"It is the least I can do. Pray accept my expression of dismay on behalf of my father and all the people of the Empire of Japan." Again he bowed to her.

Holmes gave a soft, diplomatic cough. "It is an unwelcome turn of events."

"At the least. It is the most alarming thing. To think that a man was killed here tonight, while we were all celebrating the ratification of our agreement. It is enough to make me shudder." Prince Jiro looked over at Holmes. "The Prime Minister has departed. It was quietly done."

"So I am aware," said Holmes, apparently unperturbed by this interruption.

"Yes," said Prince Jiro, as if something had been settled. He gave his attention to Lady Brackenheath once more. "Ambassador Tochigi asked me if you would permit him to offer you his regrets for this tragedy tonight, or would you prefer he make a mourning call upon you tomorrow or the day after."

Now Lady Brackenheath was becoming flustered. "I think it might be better if he call on me before the . . . police begin their inquiries. The sooner it is done, the less significance will be assigned to it. And it would, I think, occasion less comment than a more private visit might, given my husband's sentiments." She held her handkerchief to her eyes, but it was not adequate to the task, being a confection of Belgium lace.

Prince Jiro whipped a silken square with the royal chrysanthemum mon embroidered at the corner out of his pocket and held it out to her. "Pray take it, Lady Brackenheath. I would do more if propriety would countenance it."

She took the silk from him. "Oh, thank you, Yukio," she said almost shyly. Then she became more formal. "You have been most kind, Highness, for coming to me at this difficult time."

There was a quality in his smile I had not seen before, a regard that was more than kindness, and more than admiration. I watched them closely while disguising my surveillance. The numbness of the last hour continued to fade from my mind, and my concentration faltered as I recalled with unexpected vividness the appearance of Lord Brackenheath's body when I had first come upon it. Already that seemed to have been a distant event, though it was also more real than the pristine appearance of this room.

"I will not apologize for interrupting you, Mister Holmes, for that would imply I feel I have acted inappropriately, and I have not. This is the very least courtesy I could show Lady Brackenheath in this terrible hour." He bowed slightly to Holmes. "If there is anything I may do to aid your investigations, you must inform me of it at once." He gave a crisp salute and left the room in good form.

Lady Brackenheath held the silk to her eyes, her weeping renewed. "So good of him to . . . to do this."

This obscure statement did not trouble Mycroft Holmes, who nodded once. "Let us hope that all Lord Brackenheath's friends and associates are as gracious in their sympathy." He sighed. "I must assume that it is now generally known that Lord Brackenheath is dead. Which will mean that speculation will be rife within the hour." He rose and held out his hand to Lady Brackenheath. "You will receive proper escort to your home, of course. I trust you will be prepared to receive me there in the afternoon?"

She looked puzzled, but did her best to gather her thoughts. "Yes. If it will aid you in your investigation, I will have you admitted at any hour, so long as it brings Lord Brackenheath's murderer to his deserved end." She rose, her movements more awkward than before, but still lovely.

On impulse, I went to the door and listened. "There are people coming down the corridor."

Holmes sighed. "I would suppose it is Ambassador Tochigi, come to offer his sympathy. Lady Brackenheath, it may be difficult, but I would be most truly grateful if you were willing to receive him."

"I suppose it must be done," she said quietly, her hands now folded in her lap like a schoolgirl's. I had not realized until then what a blow this must be to a very young woman to be made a widow in this dreadful manner. Burdens now fell upon her unprepared shoulders that I could only imagine. "If it is the Japanese ambassador, I will see him. If it is the Swiss ambassador, I will see him. If it is one of the English, ask if they will call on me in the morning. I will be at home to condolence visits then."

I glanced out the door and saw Messrs. Banadaichi and Minato waiting patiently. Both of them bowed as I opened the door. "Is Ambassador Tochigi with you?"

"Yes, he is," said Mister Minato.

"Lady Brackenheath will see him," I said. "She is very upset."

"Hai," said Mister Banadaichi, and moved aside to permit the ambassador to enter the White Salon.

I stood aside at the door, and watched Ambassador Tochigi approach Lady Brackenheath. When he was about eight feet away from her, he bowed very deeply, straining his superb kimono to the limits of its belts and seams. "I am profoundly sorry to learn of your husband's death, Lady Brackenheath."

She nodded to him, making a compromise courtesy of the movement. "It is kind of you to say so, Ambassador."

"I hope that the perpetrator of this terrible act will be apprehended swiftly and brought to justice without delay." He regarded Holmes steadily. "If there is any way in which we may assist your investigation, it would be our honor to participate."

"I will inform Inspector FitzGerald of your offer," said Holmes in the best of good form. "He is the one who will be conducting the inquiries in relation to this crime."

"If you say so." Ambassador Tochigi set his smile with respectful doubt. "My assistants and I are at your disposal."

Holmes sighed once. "I thank you."

"I will inform the Emperor at once about this sad affair." He bowed once more to Lady Brackenheath. "Believe me, my lady, to be appalled at the disaster that has befallen your husband."

"I believe you," said Lady Brackenheath in an undervoice. "And I appreciate your kindness in coming here."

Ambassador Tochigi cocked his head at her. "Forgive me for asking, but I must suppose you are not as much opposed to the agreement we ratified tonight as your husband was?" His surprise was as much because he was astonished that a wife might disagree with her husband as because she had been as cordial to him as she had. "Is that not most . . . unusual?"

"My father built his fortune on trade, Ambassador. In the course of his business, he gained a high regard for the peoples of the Orient, one which he taught me to share. My marriage did not change my understanding. My husband and I disagreed about many things, as is often the case with arrangements such as ours." She dabbed at her eyes with the Prince's handkerchief.

I saw a flicker of recognition in Ambassador Tochigi's eyes as he took note of the imperial chrysanthemum embroidered on the silk. He recovered quickly enough, but I was keenly aware that he had been shocked by what he had seen. I made a mental note to report my observation to my employer at our first private opportunity.

Holmes was speaking now, addressing Ambassador Tochigi as he made his way to the door of the White Salon. "I will take it upon myself, Ambassador Tochigi, to keep you informed of the progress of the investigation into the death of Lord Brackenheath. In the meantime, you may assure your Emperor that our government will stand by the terms of our agreement in spite of these developments."

Ambassador Tochigi bowed again, not nearly so deeply as he had to Lady Brackenheath. "Thank you for that courtesy, Mister Holmes. It will be welcome news in this sad time."

Lady Brackenheath gave Holmes a sudden look of distress. "This will not bring embarrassment to the Japanese, will it? Nothing so damaging that the negotiations would fail because of it?" She saw the expression in Holmes' eyes and said, "Oh, do not misunderstand me, Mister Holmes, I would not want my husband's murder to go unpunished, but I do not want to see our government placed at a disadvantage, nor do I want the Japanese to be made a scapegoat for his death. The wrong man in the noose would not satisfy honor or the letter of the law. It is only that I would be ashamed to think that Lord Brackenheath's death was the excuse used to permit this agreement to be abrogated." She sat much straighter now, and her lovely head was as calm as if it had been cut in marble. "If I may do anything to prevent a miscarriage of justice, you may be certain I will do it."

I could see that almost everyone in the White Salon believed her. The single exception was Ambassador Tochigi himself.

FROM THE JOURNAL OF PHILIP TYERS

It has passed midnight and M H has not yet returned, nor G, and there have been no more messages. Sutton and I have spent the last hour playing whist, and sipping cognac, but neither of us has paid much attention to our cards and the drink has not offered its usual soothing balsam to our senses. I am waiting some word that will allow me to know how best to proceed.

Were I not concerned that this might not cause more difficulties than our present ones, I would send word around to Baker Street, in the hope that something might be learned from that quarter. However, without M H's specific instructions, I hesitate to take such an action upon myself. I will watch with Sutton another hour and then consider once again what is best to do.

Chapter Seventeen

THE SILENCE IN Lady Brackenheath's carriage was broken only by the steady sound of the horses' hooves and the rumble of the wheels as we made our way through vacant streets toward the Brackenheath town house.

"It was very kind of Mister Holmes to spare you for this errand; I fear we cannot expect my cousin Mrs. Collington much before four in the morning. She is very willing to answer late night summons, but rousing a household, as such missives do, is another matter," said Lady Brackenheath after about five minutes of staring into a place some three feet beyond the vehicle. I had begun to wonder if our journey would be without any conversation whatsoever. "Wilcox or one of the undercoachmen will take you to your home when you have finished seeing me within doors and are satisfied as to my safety. That *is* your task, isn't it?"

"I am willing to wait for your cousin," I offered. "You should not be alone tonight, Lady Brackenheath." As soon as I spoke, I realized how inappropriate I sounded, and I resolved to make amends. "Pray have no misapprehension regarding my motives, Ma'am, but you have endured a great shock and—"

"Mister Guthrie, I have a houseful of servants, so I will not be alone." She went on as if compelled to make up for her earlier silence. "And as to the shock, in the order of things in nature, I have long supposed Lord Brackenheath would predecease me. I have been prepared for this since the day of our wedding, though I had not imagined he would die by violence."

I found these politely voiced phrases mildly off-putting, though I was aware they were the product of an evening of shock, and wished I could find a way to tell her so without giving her offense. "That's kind of you; I am willing to make other arrangements to reach my rooms."

To my surprise she laughed; the sound was soft and delicate and lacking all artifice. "Such an absurd notion, Mister Guthrie. I would have thought better of Mister Holmes' secretary. It is now what?—two in the morning, more or less? And you are in London on crutches. What odds will you take on your reaching home without mishap if my coachman does not take you? The only reasonable course is to permit me to provide you adequate transportation."

"It is not safe on the streets at this hour, no matter how carefully one goes." The words did not come easily but I had to concede she had a point. "True enough," I said to her. "But in your circumstances, you need not trouble yourself—"

She made a quick and impatient gesture. "Then you will permit me to provide you this carriage, or something smaller if Wilcox recommends it. This is the least I can do, for you have been more than kind to me. And I am certain that Mister Holmes expects some such effort on my part. I cannot think he would like to have you wandering the streets alone at this hour, with or without crutches." She did not quite smile, but the habit of good conduct showed.

"What can I be but grateful, Lady Brackenheath?" I responded, hoping to show my appreciation without any more untoward remarks.

She put her hand to her eyes briefly. "I have so little I can do. My husband is dead, and his death may cause more trouble than anyone anticipated, yet I am helpless to change any part of that. I am at the mercy of events. That troubles me more than all the rest. What I dislike most is the prospect of having to mourn the man for a year, or risk social ostracism, and to spend that year having all my friends hover about me telling me how unfortunate I am to lose him. If I must be a widow, why not now, while I have some years which might bring me happiness? For surely, he never did." I must have revealed some of my dismay in my expression, for she went on. "You knew it was no love match, of course. No one was so foolish as to think that. All the world knew the purpose. Lord Brackenheath needed money and my father wanted advancement. I was the means to seal the agreement, much as that document you all extolled this evening seals England and Japan in mutual support. Fortunately for the parchment, it has no emotions in regard to what is written upon it. I represented the binding nature of their agreement. My husband and my father were both satisfied with their . . . um, treaty. And I was more biddable in those days, for I thought my father and my husband had some concern for my welfare. Time has shown me I was in error." Then she lowered her hand and made herself calm once more. I found it difficult to think of her as a young woman, for her composure I would have expected of someone much older than she. "My spasm of self-pity is over, Mister Guthrie. I pray you will make allowances for it. The hour and the shock have loosened my tongue; be good enough to judge what I say in that light."

"Most certainly, Lady Brackenheath," I assured her, admiring her courage tremendously even as I fought a sense of condemnation of her motives.

"If my husband's living children were legitimate, I suppose I would now be the Dowager Lady Brackenheath, or some such nonsense. A dowager before I am thirty. I would not be the first, of course. Not that those bars sinister of his would recognize me in that capacity if they had the right to do so." She was giving her best effort to restore a lightness to our talking, but not with much success.

"You mean he has . . ." I fumbled for the word and regretted the question in the same breath. "I do not mean to . . ."

She supplied it for me. "Bastards? Oh, yes, a number of them. Three sons that I know of, and two daughters. There may well be more, he was not a man to be concerned in such matters. He rarely took any interest in them beyond providing for their maintenance, and that only because it would be considered wrong not to support them while they were children. Most were shipped off to Canada and America years ago, when they were of age to go, with an allowance to make the change easier. I understand one of them has been very successful in Virginia. He arrived at the end of their Civil War, a lad no more than sixteen years old, and profited from trade in household goods. He now owns an emporium and a number of shops. The others are younger and have not yet made their mark on the world, or so I have been told often and often. None of Lord Brackenheath's children were sent to Australia, of course," she added with some bitterness. "They would have been forced to mix with the dregs of society there, or so my husband often stated. He did not object to having these children himself, but he deplored others who did." She smiled; her mouth looked brittle. "I believe a small portion of my husband's estate has been set aside for these grown children. It is not a large amount, of course, as Lord Brackenheath was of a profligate nature and had little of his original fortune left when we married, or he would not have had to stoop to taking a manufactory's owner's daughter to wife." She stopped abruptly. "Dear me. What you must be thinking. I am becoming a rattle."

"Nothing of the sort; you are in need of someone willing to listen, which I am," I told her, pleased to have this news of how things stood in the family. Mycroft Holmes would want to know all this as soon as possible. I found my conscience was not entirely at ease, for I reckoned Lady Brackenheath must suppose she was speaking in confidence, yet I had an obligation to my employer that must supersede gallantry.

We were almost to her town house, and I saw that lamps flanking her door were still lit against her arrival, though all but two of the windows were dark. It was a handsome house, originally built at the time of Queen Anne and kept magnificently ever since, with a conservatory added to the ground floor in the last twenty years. Ordinarily it would be an establishment any woman would regard as the most welcome haven. Lady Brackenheath eyed it with a look that bordered on disgust. She sighed once. "I thank you for your courtesy, Mister Guthrie. I will be grateful of your kindness extending itself to keeping me company for a few minutes."

"Of course," I said, adding, "I hope your cousin will have received your note by now and will be with you presently."

"Lavinia is most dependable in these matters; she will be here as soon as may be. I know I may rely on her absolutely." She tossed her head, more in frustration than defiance. "Of all my cousins, she has never foisted her daughters on me with the expectations I could find them noble husbands in want of money. For that alone I like her." We were stopping now, and the coachman secured his horses before swinging down from the box to lower the steps for Lady Brackenheath and me. She nodded to him. "Thank you, Wilcox."

He tugged at his hat and mumbled a response as I struggled out behind her.

Lady Brackenheath glanced at the coachman and made a swift assessment. "You are burned to the socket, Wilcox. Do you wake Gregory, and have him put the greys to the tilbury so that he may take Mister Guthrie home. See to your horses at once. Then you may have an extra tot of rum before you go to sleep."

"Thank you, M'lady" was the prompt response.

I made my way up the steps behind Lady Brackenheath as the coachman got back onto his box and started the carriage around to the stable behind the house.

The door was opened by a saturnine man of middle years with an expressionless demeanor. "Lady Brackenheath," he said quietly. "Allow me to offer the condolences of the staff in this terrible hour."

Lady Brackenheath concealed an expression of fatigue and something that might have been exasperation. Given what she had said a few minutes before, this did not wholly surprise me. "You're very kind, Haggard," came her reply, as punctilious as an automaton. "As you see, I have other proofs of kindness tonight. This is Mister Guthrie, who has been my escort home, as provided by the Admiralty. If you would extend your goodness to escorting him to the withdrawing room for a glass of sherry or port? I will join him directly I have relieved myself of my wrap and my jewels."

"Your dresser is waiting for you in your suite, Lady Brackenheath," Haggard informed her. "Tomorrow first thing, we will hang the crepe and the mourning wreaths." In the low gaslight, I thought the house seemed larger and more shadowed than it must have been, though it was large enough by any standards. With the gentle assurances of the butler, I found the whole place eerie, like something out of a de Maupassant tale, or one of those evocations by the American Hawthorne.

"I depend on you for such things," said Lady Brackenheath as she went across to the stairs and began her climb.

"If you will follow me," said Haggard, addressing me with a curious blend of superiority and servility that mark the very best of servants. "I will try not to hurry you, Mister Guthrie."

"I appreciate your escort," I said as we slowly mounted the stairs to the first floor. I realized that Lady Brackenheath was proceeding to the floor above.

Haggard only nodded toward the double doors on his right. "You will find sherry, port, and brandy on the sideboard, sir," he said. "Pour what you like."

"That is very generous of you," I said, and prepared to let myself into the room. I fumbled with the latch while I balanced on my crutches, and as I did, I thought I heard a soft footfall the other side of the door. I paused in my efforts to listen, but there was no more sound, and I was almost convinced I had imagined it, or had heard something in another part of the house. I was about to call to Haggard but that worthy was already making his way down the stairs to the ground floor, and I did not want to alert the intruder—if such there was—any more than I had done already.

With great care I swung the latch down and eased the door open a crack. No other sound greeted this activity, and so I thrust it wide and used my crutches to propel myself several feet into the room. I landed noisily and struggling for balance, but still upright, which gave me a fleeting sense of satisfaction.

Although it was dark, the spill of light from the hall revealed a dreadful sight. There were chairs cut open with their stuffing pulled out like pale entrails; drawers had been pulled from their chests and their contents unceremoniously dumped on the floor; a hutch stood opened, its fragile contents in pieces. The wantonness of this destruction all but took my breath away, and made me feel my nerves stood out around me on long, wavering stalks.

A stealthy movement at the edge of my vision caught my full attention. I set my feet, and in a single fluid motion, I dropped my left crutch and grabbed the right one, sliding my hands down its staff and using it as a wide-arc bludgeon. I had the satisfaction of feeling it connect solidly with flesh and bone, and heard the obscenity cut off in mid-utterance before a flicker of an arm warned me—too late—that there were two intruders in the withdrawing room, and by attacking one I had left myself open to the other.

"Bloody—" the second muttered.

I staggered aside, hoping to avoid the blow aimed at my head, and I might have succeeded, but my ankle betrayed me, and I fell heavily beside a gutted sofa, my shoulder striking the edge of the piece on the way down, my head ending up at the edge of a fine Turkey carpet. An instant later something ceramic smashed into my forehead and I lost all consciousness.

When I came to myself, I was coughing against a dribble of brandy down my throat. I made a quick motion with my arm and tried to sit up. The jangling sound of crockery shards accompanied my movement, as loud to my ears as the rattle of gunfire. The room appeared to wriggle and I had to steady myself.

"Mister Guthrie, Mister Guthrie. For the Lord Harry—" said Haggard with more animation than I would have thought possible. He was kneeling beside me, a small glass of brandy in one hand, trying ineffectually to tilt its contents down my gullet. "Mister Guthrie? Are you all right?"

At last I was able to sit up without nausea or overwhelming weakness. "No," I replied testily. "I am not. My head feels like a bass drum in a parade, my ankle is abominable, and I am thoroughly embarrassed at my own stupidity. You cannot think worse of me than I do of myself. But nothing is broken. I will recover."

"Good Lord!" Lady Brackenheath exclaimed from the open door. "What in heaven's name has happened?" She had only discarded her wrap and all her jewelry but her earrings. I realized only a few minutes had passed since I had been struck by the second intruder.

Now it was Haggard's turn to be embarrassed. He got to his feet and made a helpless gesture at the wreckage of the room. "I had no notion, Lady Brackenheath, that anything untoward was happening in this house. I must accept full responsibility for the damage to your property."

Lady Brackenheath made an impatient noise as she came across the Turkey carpet toward me. "We will deal with the room later. I am far more concerned about Mister Guthrie. Ought we to summon a physician?"

"No need, Lady Brackenheath," I said, wanting to spare myself greater humiliation than what I had already endured. "The miscreants only wanted to escape. They were not here to threaten you." I realized how strained that sounded in this ravaged room. "If they had intended real mischief, they could easily have . . ." I felt the words desert me as the events at the Swiss embassy returned full force to my thoughts. I tried to conceal the near-panic that washed over me, but without complete success.

"Should we summon—" began Haggard, only to have Lady Brackenheath finish for him.

"The police? Yes, I suppose we must. Given the many events of this evening, they will need to know of what transpired here." Under her manner of competence, I detected a forlorn desire for quiet.

"I will tend to it on my ride back to Mister Holmes' flat, if you will order your coachman to take me to Scotland Yard on route to Mister Holmes," I offered, and, seeing the doubts springing into her lovely eyes, I added, "I can deal directly with the men in charge of the investigation. Inspector FitzGerald will want to be apprised of developments directly. The sooner he is told of what has happened here, the sooner the inquiries will be under way that will determine the association, if any, of this event and the . . . the death of Lord Brackenheath. The police must set to work at once. It is in your best interests to act quickly. The longer you delay, the greater will be the speculation regarding your participation in this night's—"

"I beg you will not say *tragedy* again," Lady Brackenheath cut me short.

"Upsets, then," I compromised. My head was the very devil, but the room had now lost the unnerving tendency to wobble whenever I attempted to move. I reached out and took the brandy from Haggard, saying to him at the same time, "If you will prepare a report on the extent of the damage, it will be very useful to the police when they arrive. The more specific you can be as to the nature of the vandalism, the more helpful your information will be." It would also, I suspected, keep him from driving Lady Brackenheath to distraction with his constant solicitousness.

"Just so, just so," muttered Haggard as he got to his feet. "I suppose it would be best to have this room fully lit so that we may take stock of all the damage. It will make matters more direct for the police, will it not?" He bowed to Lady Brackenheath, his attitude so correct it was maddening. "If I may, M'lady?"

"Certainly. Mister Guthrie's instructions are undoubtedly more useful than mine would be." She looked down at me, challenging me with her eyes. I supposed she did not like sacrificing even more of her autonomy to inquiries by the police. "Are you planning to return with the police yourself, Mister Guthrie?"

"No, I am not," I answered. "I will report the crime and see the men dispatched here. Then I must return to Mister Holmes, for we have much to do before sunrise. There are matters which cannot be handled in the usual way, for the Japanese would be offended." As I spoke, I doubted I would be able to keep going much longer. The throb in my ankle alone was fatiguing, and my headache continued to belabor the inside of my skull. "If you, Haggard, will lend me your arm, I will be on my way."

Haggard regarded me with trepidation, as if he expected me to instigate another mishap by moving. He gathered my crutches, then extended his hand down to me. "When you're ready, sir," he said as if signaling a firing squad.

I took his hand and let him haul me to my feet and shove my crutches under my arms. Much as I resented the need for them, I was glad at that instant that they were here. I adjusted my stance and then spoke to Lady Brackenheath. "I will probably return here in the latter part of the afternoon. If you have need of me before then, you have only to send word to Mister Holmes, and I will do all that I may to assist you promptly. I am very sorry for your loss."

Lady Brackenheath looked around her withdrawing room and sighed. I could see how pale she was, and I recognized the failing accents of exhaustion in her voice. "Thank you, Mister Guthrie. We will do what we can to ready ourselves for more police. I think tonight I have spent more time with the officers of the law than I have in the sum of all my life until this evening."

I could not blame her for sounding so ill used. In her position I was convinced I would feel the same as she. I made as much of a bow as my crutches permitted, and followed Haggard out of the room.

We had almost reached the foot of the stairs when Haggard said, "You must not think ill of her, Mister Guthrie. She has had much to endure."

Until Haggard said this, I had supposed he had originally been the servant of Lord Brackenheath. Now I suspected that he was part of the improved circumstances Lady Brackenheath's father had made possible. "I am certain that is so."

"Whatever became of Lord Brackenheath, you may rest assured he brought it upon himself." He lifted his already high chin. "He did not often conduct himself well."

Under other circumstances, I would have discouraged his gossip, but I was convinced I had to learn all that I could from the man now, before his prudence silenced him. "I apprehend he was something of a rake in his youth."

"Ha!" scoffed Haggard. "He never gave it up. He used to tell M'lady that he wished he could use her for stakes at the gaming tables, for he would then restore his fortunes and rid himself of a shrew at the same time."

We had reached the front door, and he held it open so that he could signal to the undercoachman to come to the kerb. I decided to take one more chance with the man. "A pity her friends could not help her."

Haggard shrugged as he lifted his arm in summons. "Once her father died, she had no staunch defender, for her only uncle is in India. Of her friends, most could not properly protest Lord Brackenheath's treatment of his wife, not without giving offense to Lord Brackenheath, which was never pleasant. A few might have had they been willing to make the effort, had the opportunity presented itself. But there would have been a scandal, which no one wanted."

"When the year of mourning is over, all her friends must hope that she finds a man more worthy of her regard," I said with the nostrums kept for such difficult occasions.

"Yes, for she may now follow the dictates of her heart." A frown came and went. "And the one who has . . ." The words straggled off. "Nothing can come of it, more's the pity." With that cryptic remark he left me waiting for the tilbury coming toward me, with nothing but my roiling thoughts and aching body for company.

FROM THE JOURNAL OF PHILIP TYERS

M H has finally come back, but only for a short while. He has announced that he will remain at his desk until dawn, when he will want a hearty breakfast and a shave before returning to the Swiss embassy and other places to continue to advise on the official investigation into the death of Lord Brackenheath. Sutton has taken the news of the extension of his engagement with goodwill, saying only that he will do all that he may to assist M H in his work.

G has not yet returned, and this news has caused M H some consternation, for he expected G to be here before he himself arrived. As there has been no word from G, M H has instructed Sid Hastings to go around to G's rooms in Curzon Street to discover if he has, in fact, gone there instead.

M H informs me that he must call upon Inspector FitzGerald tomorrow at noon, and will need a cab to carry him to that destination. I have indicated that I will make all the necessary arrangements.

I must gather together my thoughts in regard to those who are still watching this flat, and assess the material in light of the death of Lord Brackenheath. It may be that the plot against Lord Brackenheath is of long standing, or it may be that Lord Brackenheath's death is part of a greater conspiracy that must be discovered in its entirety if it is to be eradicated. That, I suppose, will be my morning task while M H readies himself to meet with the Japanese, the Swiss, and the police.

There is someone on the stairs. Let us pray it is G returning safe at last.

Chapter Eighteen

I NEARLY FELL into Tyers' arms as the door swung open. I was worn out by my climb up the stairs and I could feel my shoulders stiffening from the effort. "Good evening, Tyers," I said as I did what I could to recover myself.

"Guthrie, dear boy," exclaimed Holmes as he surged into the corridor from the study, a cigar clamped in one hand, a pen in the other. He was closely followed by Edmund Sutton, who was no longer disguised as Holmes and therefore did not give the uncanny appearance of a doppelgänger.

"Here, Mister Guthrie," said Tyers in his calm way. "Let me help you get your crutches fixed more securely, and then come into the sitting room. I have the kettle on. Tea will be ready shortly."

I found his practicality enormously reassuring, and the rush of gratitude that filled me warned me how unstrung the evening had made me. Setting aside my vanity, I permitted Tyers to assist me, and with his help, sank into a wing-backed chair with the relief of one saved from hanging. "Much appreciated," I said, doing my best to sound like an American tourist.

The laugh that greeted this was feeble, but I was pleased to have it. I put my hand to my head and felt a knot forming on my forehead at the hairline. I was pleased it had not struck the long, thin scar that angled across my forehead, for that might have caused a more disfiguring injury. Holmes noticed my self-inspection, and rapped out an order to Tyers. "Bring willow bark tea for Guthrie. He needs it more than our usual black."

Ordinarily I would have protested, but memories of my grandmother giving me that same tea when I was ill as a child stifled my objections. I nodded agreement.

Tyers hurried off to the kitchen even as Edmund Sutton came forward to check my injury. "What did he hit you with, Guthrie?" the actor asked.

"A vase of some sort," I answered brusquely. "I suspect it was porcelain." How foolish that sounded, as if the material was important.

"Good," approved Holmes, joining Sutton at my side. "Any heavier clay might have cracked your skull." He bent over me and peered narrowly at the bruise. "You are going to be very decorative in the morning, Guthrie. I'll say that for you."

I realized this was his way of assuring me that I had no reason to be worried about my injuries, which pleased me far more than it should have. I let myself relax for the first time in what felt like days, but was actually only a few hours. It was tempting to doze, sitting here in the warmth of Holmes' flat, my colleagues with me and my discomfort alleviated for the time being. But I had not completed my commission, and so I made myself alert once more. "In the carriage on the way back to her town house, Lady Brackenheath informed me of a number of things I had not known before," I began, trying not to yawn.

"What things?" asked Holmes, his voice low and thoughtful.

"For once, it turns out that Lord Brackenheath has a number of illegitimate children; most of them I surmise are from earlier escapades in his life, and are grown." I looked down at my feet, trying to determine if my ankle had actually swollen to the size of a rugby ball or only felt as if it had.

"They are known," said Holmes distantly. "They each receive a thousand pounds upon their father's death, which is not to be paid by his wife, but from the revenues of his lands, which are entailed. I reckon some or all of the paintings at Brackenheath will have to be auctioned to pay the bequest, for there is no other way for the estate to support the terms of the will without such a sale. Little as Lord Brackenheath believed it possible, he was nearly bankrupt when Herbert Bell suggested the match with his daughter, and Bell made a marriage contract with such constraints as he thought were prudent, knowing Lord Brackenheath's proclivities. It must have caused Lord Brackenheath much chagrin to have to accept the articles of his marriage contract. I also reviewed the terms of his will when he first became involved in these negotiations, as I did for the other participants, at the request of Lord Salisbury, in order to be certain there were no overriding legal constraints or mitigating circumstances upon their participation in the negotiations." I must have looked surprised, for Holmes continued, "I have access to court files, dear boy, or I would be unable to do the tasks assigned to me."

"I should have realized," I said, and looked up as Tyers brought me tea.

"Yes, you should have," said Holmes. "And would have done so had you not been otherwise occupied, in Greece, I think it was." He turned up the nearest of the gaslights and bent to inspect my face. "Battered but unbowed. You are made of stern stuff, dear boy, and that is a source of great reassurance to me."

I looked directly at him. "You need not coddle me, sir."

"Good Lord, man, I'm not coddling," he said, moving back from me at once. "I must be certain you are fit to continue this work. I cannot be forever fretting about whether you have the strength or soundness to go on. I am thankful that you have such bottom that I need not fash myself on your account." The acerbic tone he used seemed genuine enough, and yet, I suspected he was more concerned for my welfare than he wished to admit, in part because of my churlish remark. "If you were seriously injured, I would have no choice but to find other methods to deal with this coil until you recovered."

Certain now that my gaffe had offended him, I tried to conjure up something to offer him to show my appreciation for his concern. I wanted to demonstrate my capabilities, as well, to offset any doubts Holmes may have begun to have about me. It came to me quite suddenly. "Oh, sir, I nearly forgot." Which was no more than the truth. "Shortly before I found . . . Lord Brackenheath, I was in the ballroom, looking for him. I was afraid he might choose to make a public scene about the agreement, and I wanted to forestall that eventuality if I could. But when I looked for him, I did not find him. Miss Gatspy, however, found me."

"Go on," said Holmes, his curiosity engaged once more.

I had to concentrate to bring the incident back to my mind without any anticipation of discovering the body. "As I've said, I happened to encounter Miss Gatspy in the ballroom. She approached me with some urgency in her manner."

Holmes swore fulsomely, then saw the startled expression in Sutton's eyes. "She is part of the Golden Lodge," he explained, his brow darkening as he pulled his watchfob out and began to swing it in short arcs around his finger. "And I wish I knew what her interests are in these proceedings."

"No more do I," I said at once. "On that head, I could discover nothing. She had a single purpose in mind: She made a point of telling me about a man in the uniform of a Grodno Hussar—"

"I saw him," Holmes said at once. "Good looking in a Slavic sort of way: wide forehead, aquiline nose, hair the color of Russian bread, about twenty-five years old." He studied me a moment.

"Yes. I didn't notice so much about him," I confessed. "They were dancing, you see, and as I could not take to the floor in crutches—"

"And you had Miss Gatspy to distract you," Holmes said, and let it go at that.

"She is a handsome armful, and one whom it would be a pleasure to take a turn around a waltz with," I conceded as I strove to continue my report. "But that is nothing to the purpose, or bearing on her intention. She had intelligence to impart to me. She was certain the man was not Russian at all. She was convinced he was an imposter. Said he swore in Hungarian." I chuckled—it came out like a cough. "There are many ways to account for that which do not require he not be Russian, and so I reminded her at the time. I don't think she was best pleased at that."

"And who can blame her, after all?" said Holmes. His watchfob was still, wound up tight against his finger on its fine, gold chain. "Hungarian. Hungarian," he mused.

"What the devil does that agreement have to do with the Hungarians?" asked Sutton, rubbing the fair stubble on his jaw.

"It depends on what faction is involved, and who is paying for what service, and to what end. Assuming for the moment that Miss Gatspy is right and the man is Hungarian and not Russian, we have not paid much attention to them in regard to this agreement, which I begin to fear may have been an error. It has been thought that the unrest in the Balkans demanded the main thrust of Austro-Hungarian interests. Kaiser Wilhelm has had much to do with his eastern borders. But his government have been at pains to keep abreast of all international developments. I surmise they have been more interested in our Oriental ventures than has been apparent. The Turks, as well, may be more acutely concerned with this agreement than we assumed they were. What concerns Austro-Hungary and Turkey must not be ignored. There has always been a volatile situation in Hungary. At least for the last thousand years, and the cross-currents are treacherous, even for those who are wary of them." He stopped and looked toward the window. "Any sign of watchers, Tyers?"

"Not for the last hour," Tyers replied from his inconspicuous watchpost near the window.

"We must hope their sentries doze," said Mycroft Holmes with a sarcasm that bordered on the cynical. "At this time of night, it is cold enough and still enough that many would fall asleep on guard. Not the Golden Lodge, of course," he added, and went on more darkly, "nor the Brotherhood. You may rest assured that those two unholy—" He stopped himself at the penetrating sound of chimes.

I heard the clock strike the half-hour, echoed at once by the nautical clock in the parlor, and it shocked me. "Three-thirty," I remarked to the air.

"Yes, and you must rise early. There is much to attend to." His manner became brisk and the hour appeared to have no impact upon him other than a certain heaviness at the corners of his eyes.

"And you?" I asked.

"I have much to review before I speak with the Prime Minister at eight." He stretched, his long arms reaching higher than the doorframe. "My study is prepared. Do you remain here tonight, Guthrie. I don't want you out on the streets again, where anyone can have a ponk at you." He motioned to Tyers. "The tea. Make sure he drinks it, or he will not sleep well."

Tyers nodded promptly. "I will do what I can."

"No powders, mind," Holmes added unnecessarily. "And no drops." His opposition to Dr. James' Powders and laudanum was of long standing and steadfast, for he was painfully aware of what cocaine had done to his younger brother; for reasons he never made clear, Mycroft blamed himself for his brother's misfortune.

"There's none in the flat," Tyers reminded him, as he had many times before, and always with the same patience.

Satisfied on that matter, Holmes turned to Sutton. "And you, Edmund. It would be an unnecessary risk to have you depart tonight, and futile, considering the hour, for you would have to return almost as soon as you reached your rooms in order to be here when I depart. Use my bed and get some sleep; you may nap in the afternoon, if you require it, though at your age, I don't suppose . . ." He changed the subject somewhat. "I begin to fear that we are not going to be able to end your engagement in this role by midnight tonight, as we supposed, but will have to . . . eh . . ."

"Extend my run? I am pleased to have the work, and if you have more employment for me, I am glad to entertain the opportunity to show my versatility. I wouldn't be much of an actor, would I, if I could only do one thing," suggested Sutton with a mercurial smile. "I haven't finished learning Ferdinand yet, and you will make it possible for me to do it." Say what you will about actorish ways, Edmund Sutton knew how to make himself gallant when he chose to.

"Ah, Edmund, you are remarkable, as always," said Holmes, acknowledging Sutton's grand gesture. "If I were a public figure, I should have to come to you for instruction."

Sutton's color heightened at this compliment and he looked directly at Holmes. "If there is any skill I possess, it is at your disposal."

Now Mycroft Holmes looked somber. "I pray your generosity will never have to be put to the test." And with that he motioned to Tyers to get me into the parlor, and signaled that our conversation had ended for the night.

"It will be time to rise sooner than you want," said Tyers, his own eyes puffy with fatigue. "I will bring the willow bark tea to ease your hurts. You must drink two cups of it."

"I will," I promised, though I was not as certain as he that it would reduce my various discomforts enough to allow me real sleep.

"I will not wake you until Mister Holmes has left," Tyers said, intending, I am certain, to soothe me.

"Not wake me—" I protested, swinging around as much as my crutches would permit.

"He will have to deliver his report in confidence," said Tyers. "No one will attend but the Prime Minister and our employer, so that they may be wholly candid with one another." He held the parlor door open for me and let me enter ahead of him. "I will have a bath ready for you before you eat, so you can assess the extent of the damage."

"Thank you," I muttered. "I appreciate your help, Tyers," I went on in a calmer manner, "but I fear I am too upset about last evening's events to show my gratitude properly. I hope you will not be offended by any sharp answer I have given you, for you are not the cause of my rebukes."

"No, Mister Guthrie," said Tyers with a slight, indulgent smile. "You are vexed with yourself and show it this way, so that others will upbraid you as you wish to do yourself. Haven't I seen this before." He began to make up a bed for me on the sofa, working quickly. "I have your nightshirt. And I will bring you a robe. I will get them as soon as the coverlets are in place. Will you require a counterpane?"

"Whatever for?" I asked, looking at the sofa, which was from the time of the Regency, one of the few examples of the period in the flat, aside from the Napoleonic secretary in the sitting room. It was a proper monstrosity with ugly crocodile legs and curving swan arms that looked like nothing so much as Corinthian pillars that had been squashed and bent. Holmes had told me that it was supposed to have belonged to the Prince Regent himself, "And so I supposed it must be up to my weight," he had jested. At least it served as an extra bed quite easily.

I was doing my best to undress, removing the studs from my boiled shirt and placing them in the Viennese glass ashtray on the occasional table. I felt as if my clothes had become a trap, confining me, as I strove to be rid of them. Keeping myself steady as I wrestled out of my clothes took all my concentration, and so I was hardly aware of when Tyers left the parlor. But he returned carrying my nightshirt over his shoulder and a tray with a teapot and a large cup on it. I indicated my clothes strewn over the Restoration chair. "It is the best I can do."

Tyers shook his head, but not in condemnation. "Mister Guthrie," he said as calmly as he could, "I will tend to those. In the morning, Sid Hastings will go round to your rooms and bring you a fresh suit of clothes for the day. I am certain your landlady will be willing to do this for you." He turned his back as I struggled out of my underwear and tugged the nightshirt over my head. "Mister Holmes has said he will leave you a list of instructions for the morning. From what he has said, he will need you to talk with Inspector FitzGerald and Andermatt at the Swiss embassy. There is certain to be more."

"Glad to do it," I said as I half-walked, half-hopped to the sofa and slipped into the bed Tyers had improvised there.

"Drink the tea and I will lower the light in ten minutes. You must make the most of the short hours you have." Tyers had the rare ability to be concerned without seeming to cater or belittle.

"You may be certain I will," I said as I filled the cup and took a long swig of it. The taste, not very pleasant, brought back memories of my grandmother fussing over me when I was a child, ordering me to keep well under the blankets to hurry the fever breaking. She would make a strong mutton broth, too, with port wine in it, and angelica root, which she claimed would cure all but the most pernicious illness. I sensed her face hovering over me as I drained the cup and wriggled into the bed, dragging the covers up over my head as if I were still ten years old.

My dreams were not pleasant, filled as they were with bodies emerging from bundles of rags, heaps of leaves, from under fine linen napery, out of coats hung on racks. They came sliding under doors, were pulled out of upholstery, were stacked up like cordwood. There was nowhere I could flee, in this irrational world of dreaming, that I did not encounter bodies of dead men, all of whom looked like Lord Brackenheath, and all of whom had been stabbed by a simple knife with a horn handle.

FROM THE JOURNAL OF PHILIP TYERS

Finally they are all in for what little remains of the night, and my duties are finished until morning. M H is in his study with coffee and cigars to keep him alert, Sutton has retired, and G was asleep by the time I returned to put out the light. I am going to give myself two hours to rest, and then I will be up again, to get them all about their separate tasks.

I hope I will be able to catch one of the watchers today, for I begin to think their purpose in their surveillance is not well intended, and portends something more than narrow observation. What that action could be I cannot tell, which serves only to increase my apprehension. Never before have I been so certainly aware of how fortunate I am to lack imagination. In circumstances such as these, an imagination would do little more than exacerbate my fears and clothe my worries in the most convincing colors.

Chapter Nineteen

I WOKE WITH a start as I heard the rear door of the flat close and the first descending footsteps as my employer made his way down the backstairs toward Sid Hastings' cab, waiting in King Charles II Street. I sat up and tossed my coverlet aside, trying to rid my mind of the last images of my dream. The lingering impression of Lord Brackenheath's body ripping out of damask upholstery remained with me as I got to my feet and rubbed at my hair.

My ankle twinged but I refused to use my crutches yet. I

would never recover for so long as I had to guard myself against all actions of any sort whatever that might give me the slightest pain. On the other hand, I told myself with what I hoped was wry wit, I would not like to have to run a footrace for a week or two yet. I made my way around the parlor, feeling proud of my ability to do it at all. I resisted the urge to go to the window, for if the flat was still under observation, I would become a temptation for whoever was watching. I sighed once and was about to turn toward the corridor behind me when I heard Tyers' voice.

"Good morning, Mister Guthrie. Walking without crutches. Excellent. I hope you slept well?" He carried a cup and saucer. Even across the room, I realized it was more willow bark tea, this time with lemon. "I am just heating the last water for your bath. If you will permit me five minutes? With breakfast to follow in the sitting room. Mister Sutton will join you there." He set the cup and saucer down. I could see the hollows of his eyes and realized that he must have had less sleep than I.

"Good morning, Tyers," I said, adding with as much grace as I could muster, "Thank you for taking such good care of me."

"Happy to be of service," he said, and I was convinced he meant it. He had gathered up the coverlet and was quickly folding it for storage. "Mister Holmes left a note for you outlining what he wishes you to do this morning. He asks that you will not pay any attention to the items he has scratched out, for he has reassigned those duties elsewhere."

That last intrigued me, as I was certain it was supposed to do. I felt my chin and said, "While the bath is heating, I think I'll shave."

"A razor and mug are available in the dressing room. You may use the side entrance so as not to disturb Mister Sutton." He had the coverlet attended to and was preparing to leave the parlor. "Drink the tea, sir. Mister Holmes expects it."

I realized that I would have no recourse against such instruction. I took the cup and downed the tea, thinking as I did that I had not been as sore as I had expected to be. For the time being, I would be happy to give credit to the tea for it. "There. All finished."

"Very good," said Tyers from the door, and led me past the maps and brasses to the entrance to his own room; I hobbled after him as best I could, taking solace in the realization that I had not expected to recover completely at once. "The door to the dressing room is just there," he said.

I slipped in and found the mug and razor he had mentioned. As I stropped the razor, I had my first glimpse of myself in the mirror and it all but staggered me, for the right side of my face was deeply bruised and my eye stared out of a mass of muddy purple. "Good Lord!" I expostulated, and wondered how I could go into public today looking as if I had escaped a railroad wreck. I leaned nearer the mirror the better to inspect the damage.

There was a hard, low bump on my head where the crockery had struck me, but I did not think it could result in such an appearance of carnage. The skin under my fingers was tender, but nothing so sensitive as the mass of the bruise might lead me to expect. I regarded myself a short while longer, then set about preparing lather for shaving, after pouring water from the ewer into the basin I had been provided. The razor was newly honed and it glided through the suds on my face so quickly that I feared I might do myself an injury and never notice until it was too late that I had cut my own throat. That notion was so repellant that I had to pause in my labors to master my nerves. Then I went back to work on my beard, reminding myself I had been doing this for more than half my lifetime and should not balk at it now.

"Beg pardon, Mister Guthrie, but your bath is ready," said Tyers, looking in at the door. "At your convenience."

"I'm nearly finished here," I said as I tilted my head back and scraped under my chin. This morning my skin felt much thinner than usual, and I had to resist the urge to wince as I continued my grooming. Two more swipes and I was finished. I rinsed and dried the razor and presented the mug and basin to Tyers, saying, "Why did you not warn me of my appearance, Tyers? I took quite a shock when I looked in the mirror."

If Tyers thought this question mean-spirited of me, nothing in his manner suggested it. He answered in his usual level voice, "I did not think it would serve any useful purpose to do so." With that he withdrew, mug and basin in hand, indicating the way to the kitchen where "The alcove is open."

I thanked him and made my way along the corridor to the alcove between the water closet and the pantry. I pulled out of my robe and hung it on the hook provided on the door. I had a moment's qualm, as I have often had since my unfortunate sojourn in France when one of the men of the Golden Lodge had surprised me in the inn's bath and had threatened to drown me. That, I reminded myself, was in the past. I had enough on my plate as it was not to go dredging up past dubious escapades.

The water was warm enough to take some caution getting in. As I watched my skin pinken in the heat, I felt my ankle begin to relax. It felt delicious. How pleasant it would be, I thought, to loll here in the hot water all morning. But, I told myself as I reached for the bath-brush, the water would soon grow tepid and then cold, and there was work for me to do, urgent work. Much as I might want to indulge myself, I did not like the thought of leaving Mycroft Holmes without what support I could lend him.

By the time I emerged from the bath I felt much improved. My little aches had faded and the worst hurts had diminished. I was glad to be able to wrap myself in the robe and saunter—or more accurately, limp—into the sitting room where Edmund Sutton was waiting, already in his Holmes disguise, which did not serve him well as he caught sight of my countenance.

"Christ!" he burst out in a mix of dismay and confusion. He strove to recover himself. "How . . . Last night it didn't—"

"No, it didn't, last night. I may tell you I had quite a turn when I looked in the mirror," I said, doing my best to make light of it. "Rest assured it is nowhere near as ferocious as it looks."

"No doubt," he said, aping Mycroft Holmes. He continued in that manner with all his theatrical flare, "I perceive that you have permitted yourself to be drawn into antagonistic company. This may be accounted for by the untimely arrival of a party of Basque priests at Dover for the purpose of analyzing the writings of Druids. It is said there are a number of prophesies of the Roman period that have to do with the Basque role in current European politics. You must surely be aware of the historical connection between Basques and Druids, Guthrie. There are no less than four hundred twenty-nine citations of this mutual influence on record at Oxford. There may be more at Cambridge. With this renewal of Druidical activity compounded with the Basque element, your injury may be evaluated in that perspective."

"Bravo," I said, trying to summon up enthusiasm for his kind effort to entertain me.

He attempted to smile, but did not manage it well. He relapsed into his own character, his manner anxious and his words rapid. "Are you able to keep on working? Are you certain you should not lie down for the day? Should you see a physician?"

"I will do very well, thank you," I said, beginning to feel sympathy for his distress. "I had hoped you might have something in your paint-box that would minimize this, but I don't suppose it's possible." I had intended this to be a challenge to his skills and talents, and was inwardly gratified when I realized I had succeeded.

"I've never attempted anything of the sort, but it should be possible." Sutton leaned forward to study my face, his expression intent. "There's no hiding a bruise that dark, unless you were about to play *Othello* as the Moor." He sighed. "The most I can do is diminish it somewhat, so that it is not so . . . obvious." A frown puckered along the paint-emphasized lines between his brows. "I can use some yellow and a lighter shade of blue to make it look a bit . . . greyer. There is no way to mask that bruise entirely, but . . ." He glanced up as Tyers appeared with pots of coffee and tea, and a basket of scones.

"There will be baked eggs, grilled tomatoes, and good English sausage in a moment, gentlemen." He put down his items and left.

"Lord, I'm famished," said Sutton, taking his serviette and spreading it in his lap. "After last night, I'm worn to the bone." He glanced swiftly at me in the manner of a child who has been found out stealing sweets. "Not that I've done anything to match what you and Mister Holmes have done, of course."

I laughed as best I could. "I should hope not. Your necessary pretense would be in danger if you had been about the way Holmes and I have been. I, for one, am grateful to you for maintaining a semblance of normality." I was oddly touched that he should have such concern for my good opinion, for such was surely the case. "I know I could not pull off the part you play. I haven't the talent for it, nor the eye for detail you have."

Sutton looked pleased. "That's kind of you, Mister Guthrie," he said, and grinned as the rest of breakfast was presented.

I had finished most of my food when a thought struck me. "I'm a bloody fool!" I burst out, interrupting an amusing tale Sutton was telling on one of his colleagues who, in the middle of a performance of *The Merry Wives of Windsor,* had discovered that what he supposed to be could tea in his tankard was actually good whiskey.

Sutton looked startled at my outcry, yet was good enough not take offense. "You've remembered something important."

"I don't know," I admitted as I did my best to concentrate on the fleeting images that swirled in my thoughts, memories from the night before mingling with the residue of my nightmares. "It is the upholstery," I declared.

Now Sutton was rightly baffled. "What upholstery?"

"At Lord Brackenheath's house. Last night," I said, as the pictures in my mind became stronger. "Yes. *Yes!*" What had been the matter with me that I had not thought of this earlier? I asked myself. "The upholstery of the chairs and the settee was all cut into, and the stuffing pulled out." I rounded on Sutton as if he had been there with me. "Don't you see? Why would thieves do that? What purpose could they have? They had taken none of the valuable items in the room. So why did they rip open the upholstery in that wanton manner?"

"They were looking for something," said Sutton at once, grasping the direction of my reasoning. He propped his elbows on the table and steepled his fingers, just as Holmes would do if he occupied that chair. I had the eerie sensation that a portion of Holmes' nature had communicated itself to Sutton. "Why should they make a search in that place? What was the object they sought? Something small enough to be hidden in the seat or back of a chair. Something they knew would be hidden there. They expected to find it."

"That's it!" I cried, getting hastily to my feet. The vigor I had felt the lack of not three minutes ago returned to me in a rush. "I must prepare a note for Holmes," I said. "And then I must be about my errands."

"Very good," said Sutton, getting to his feet beside me. "Sid Hastings' cousin Reginald has said he will carry messages for Mister Holmes today. His cab is not familiar to the watchers, or so we hope." He reached out and clapped me on the shoulder. "Be careful, dear boy."

I had to bite back a retort that he was not to call me that, but of course, he was, to complete his performance and make it convincing to anyone who might be observing us. "The Swiss embassy first, and then Scotland Yard," I said, to remind myself as well as Sutton about where I would be.

"And the Japanese?" asked Sutton, with a curiosity that went beyond his performance. "What of them?"

"They are supposed to make themselves available at the Swiss embassy," I said, referring to the note Holmes had left me. "I am to speak with Messrs. Minato and Banadaichi while Holmes is closeted with Ambassador Tochigi and Deputy Ambassador Chavornay."

Sutton smiled briefly. "What will be the advantage of this?" He held up his hand to supply the answer himself. "You are looking for inconsistencies, or discrepancies in their reports, are you not, and possibly for an unguarded word that might indicate some knowledge of the reason for the murder."

I returned his smile. "Yes. You have the right of it." I set my serviette aside. "If you will excuse me—"

"Be about your tasks, Guthrie. I look forward to a full report at the end of the day." He picked up the newspaper and studied it. "By evening the press will be on it and the whole world will have something to say about how Lord Brackenheath met his end."

"I fear you are correct," I said, and went to dress. As I set my collar stud in place, I gestured to my face, calling out in order to be heard, "I fear I will not have time for your art, after all."

"Perhaps later," said Sutton with an anticipatory tone I could not help but find disquieting.

"Is there anything you would recommend in the interim?" I asked, fixing my cuff links in place before pulling on my coat.

"Hiding under a big hat?" he suggested impishly. "No, Guthrie," he went on as he came down the hall. "I think you may have to brazen it out."

"Not a promising prospect," I remarked as I gave a last tweak to my tie.

"No," Sutton agreed. "If you wish my help tomorrow, I would suggest allowing an extra half hour for me to do the task properly. You will have green in the bruise by then, and that can present certain problems."

"And purple does not?" I asked, beginning to feel amused by my own plight for the first time since I shaved. "I will keep this all in mind, Sutton. I hope you will forgive me for leaving without benefit of your ministrations."

I was out of the flat by ten minutes past nine, and riding in Sid Hastings' cab for the Swiss embassy. I had elected to bring a cane along with my portfolio, and I was reviewing the notes Holmes had left for me, particularly the things I was to be certain to ask Messrs. Banadaichi and Minato more than once. I was striving to commit as many of these points as possible to memory so that it would not be obvious that I was seeking out specific information, when at the tail of my eye I caught sight of a woman on the sidewalk, and for a moment I did not realize that it was Penelope Gatspy, for she was dressed in a somber dress of dark brown with a very modest bonnet on her fair, rosy hair. I rapped on the ceiling of the cab and ordered Sid Hastings to draw abreast of her so that I could speak with her.

She pretended to be unaware of my pursuit until I ordered the cab to slow so that I could step out and accost her directly.

"You should not be speaking to me" was all the greeting she offered me. "I doubt Mister Holmes would approve." Her manner softed a bit. "Oh. Your poor face."

"It looks worse than it is," I said, not wanting to be turned away from my inquiries.

"But it must have hurt terribly. First your ankle and now this, and that scar on your forehead from Bavaria. He asks a lot of you, does your Mister Holmes," she persisted. "I hope you have taken something to lessen the pain."

There it was again—*my* Mister Holmes, coming from *my*

Miss Gatspy. I dismissed her concern with a gesture. "You will not detract me, Miss Gatspy. Don't make assumptions about Mister Holmes," I warned her, and set my pace to hers, which, being brisk, demanded I have more recourse to my cane than I liked. How a woman in fashionable skirts could move along a crowded sidewalk at such a pace, I couldn't imagine. As I looked back, I could see Hastings' nephew turn and follow. If there was other surveillance, I could not discern it.

"Well," she said brusquely, "then I should not be talking to you."

"Very likely not," I agreed at my affable best, to give, I hoped, the impression of old friends meeting by chance. "But in this jumble, who's to notice?"

She stopped abruptly and turned toward me. "Good God, don't you know how close they've come already? They've—"

"Which *they* are we talking about? And close to whom? These events seem to have an unholy number of *them.*" I was doing my best to make light of it all, but my raillery only served to increase her dismay.

"Why, the Brotherhood, of course. Vickers came back to London two weeks since and has summoned men to him with the express intention of wreaking vengeance on Mycroft Holmes. That in so doing he can destroy the agreement with Japan is only an added treat to him." Her lovely eyes were bright with distress, and I could think of nothing to say that would dismiss her concerns.

"Vickers is in London?" I asked, shocked in spite of myself.

"With at least a dozen men around him." She nodded twice. We were stopping foot traffic in both directions, but neither of us paid any heed.

"They are on a mission against my employer?" I pursued. It did not seem possible to me that such a thing could happen.

"That is what we of the Golden Lodge have learned: against your employer and against the government. Vickers has someone in London who is aiding him whose identity is unknown to us, but who may be in diplomatic circles, or so we have reason to suspect, given their determination to compromise the agreement. Though with the Hungarians taking a hand in ending the negotiations, half the work of the Brotherhood will be done for them, for if the treaty is repudiated at this stage it will undermine much of Mister Holmes' credibility with the government, will it not?"

I did not know how to answer her, for it struck me that she might be using her concern as a means to elicit information from me that I might not otherwise impart. "How do you mean?" I asked, determined to be cautious.

She lost her air of flattering anxiety and replaced it with exasperation. "How can you be such a lob-cock?" That unladylike expression took me aback and I goggled as she went on. "You are the private secretary of one of the three most powerful men in England. You cannot be unaware that the government has more than a few warships riding on the terms of this agreement. Mycroft Holmes would not employ such a simpleton as that."

"All right," I said, keeping my voice as low as I could and still be heard, "I will allow that there are ramifications to the agreement that go beyond simple military support. But I fail to see how—"

"And if this agreement is abjured by the Japanese, England will be diplomatically embarrassed throughout the capitals of the world. Her enemies will make the most of it, you may be certain of that, and the confusion that would result would delight the Brotherhood as well as advance their cause, to the detriment of all," she went on with feeling. "Those who are interested in bringing chaos to the world can only look with delight upon the murder of Lord Brackenheath, for it will give the Japanese more than enough reason to withdraw from the terms of the agreement."

I shook my head, certain I had missed a crucial connection in her reasoning. "That may be so," I said. "But why are you so certain that the Japanese will respond as you suggest? Surely there are ways to protect the agreement." I stood a bit straighter, confident that Mycroft Holmes would have the resources to circumvent any trouble arising from the murder.

"I doubt even your Mycroft Holmes could undo the ravages of this scandal," she said.

First Holmes called Miss Gatspy *my* Miss Gatspy, and now she was assigning the same custodial duties to me in his regard. "What scandal?" I demanded more hotly than was wise, for several passersby glanced our way with dawning interest.

Apparently aware that she had overstepped the mark, Penelope Gatspy began walking once more, but at a more leisurely pace than before. "Surely you know?" she asked in that maddening way of all women. "You cannot be so naive that you are unaware of . . ."

"If I did know whatever this secret is," I told her with care, "I should not mention it here in the street. Perhaps you would be willing to enlighten me."

She looked up at me, the very picture of innocent femininity. She was sensible enough to speak so softly that I had to lean down to hear her. "Why, the scandal that will result when it is discovered that Prince Jiro's married paramour is Lady Brackenheath."

FROM THE JOURNAL OF PHILIP TYERS

I have received a packet of documents from the Prime Minister regarding the guests who attended the gala reception last night. Edmund Sutton and I will spend a good portion of the afternoon reviewing these notes and matching them with those M H keeps in his private files. In regard to the matter of the Grodno Hussar, I will do all I can to identify the fellow and determine his alliances, if any, beyond those implied by his uniform.

Inspector FitzGerald has sent word requesting an interview with M H when he returns from his club tonight. I have responded to the request saying that M H will receive him at nine-thirty, giving Sutton time to shed his disguise and leave, for it would not do to have

Scotland Yard too much aware of this impersonation. I assume it will be satisfactory to the Inspector to agree to the hour.

The investigation into Lord Brackenheath's death continues, but far more cautiously than it might had Lord Brackenheath been a rakish old merchant and his murder taken place at a village fête. When the governments of the world are implicated, murder shrinks in importance as a crime when weighed against the possibility of war.

The watchers are still in place, and I fear they are armed, though I cannot think they would be foolish enough to attempt an assassination on so busy a street as Pall Mall. They would attract too much attention to themselves, as well as running the danger of injuring those passing in the street. I write this and want to believe what I write, but I cannot forget Cairo, and the mayhem that reigned in the streets there. We must continue on our guard as resolutely as possible, for any other course might well lead to disaster.

Chapter Twenty

"GUTHRIE, GUTHRIE, PLEASE tell me that this is not all the result of a sordid little affaire?" Mycroft Holmes beseeched me as we rode in Sid Hastings' cab going from the Admiralty to the Swiss embassy. It was early afternoon and pleasantly sunny. "This sounds tawdry enough that my brother would wash his hands of it, despite his fascination with criminality."

"I fear it may be," I said grimly. In the forty minutes I had needed to track him down, a number of scenarios had suggested themselves to me, each more unpleasant than the last. Now I resisted the urge to impart them all to my employer, and settled only for the one that had proved to be the most nagging. "If it is reliable information."

"Why should it not be reliable?" asked Holmes with such an air of innocence that I was instantly on my guard.

"There are a number of reasons why it might not be, not the least of which is the source. I cannot discern the motive for misleading us, except to protect her colleagues of the Golden Lodge. However, that's as may be." I did not want to recite all the things that had occurred to me; I stuck to the issues immediately to hand. "Assuming that Penelope Gatspy is telling the truth and this is not an act of deliberate deception to turn us away from—"

Holmes waved my protestations away, his intellect engaged in exercise on this new idea. "A jealous lover kills the old roué of a husband to win the fair—and very rich—widow?" said Holmes, testing the hypothesis with every word. "The lover arranges for someone to kill the husband?" He shook his head. "No. Why would they do it? To what end? Either way, both Prince Jiro and Lady Brackenheath come to grief. Their liaison is discovered and they are separated in disgrace. No, I would think their best course would be in continuing secrecy."

"Then you are inclined to give Miss Gatspy's tale some credence?" I said, surprised at the prospect. "I would think that the diplomatic connection she mentioned might be the more profitable vein to mine."

"Yes, I take your point. And regarding her information about the lovers, yes, yes, I am giving the story credence," he said, musing. "And it troubles me that I cannot put my finger on why, but I know there is something I should . . ." He stared out at the traffic passing in the street, his manner abstracted. Suddenly he slapped his hand on the worn armrest. "I should have seen it!" he exclaimed. "I permitted myself to be diverted in my attention. I did not see what was directly under my nose. Or rather, *hear* it." This was the greatest self-condemnation he could express.

"Hear what was under your nose?" I tweaked, hoping to gain some information.

"Under my ear, then, to correct the metaphor." He regarded the horse ahead of us through narrowed eyes, as if he doubted its character. His watchfob was twirling around his index finger.

"How?" I asked, unable to follow his thoughts. "What should you have seen?"

"The very thing Miss Gatspy told you." His abstraction was gone. "At the Swiss embassy, last night, when Prince Jiro came to offer his condolences, he gave her his handkerchief," said Holmes.

"Yes. I remember," I said, still not aware of what he had realized. "Surely there was nothing significant in the offer—she was weeping."

"Accurate as far as it goes. But think. When she took it, she called him Yukio. I *should have known* then. I should have noticed, but—" He sighed heavily. "Miss Gatspy is right. The scandal from this could destroy all we have worked for. Like Russia and Germany, Japan also failed to build an expanded, foreign empire while the Western nations were doing so. Now, they see the Pacific Islands and China as their last chance at achieving an empire of their own. Far more than Japan, Russia is now following a policy of expansion. With this agreement we will provide Japan the ability to meet the challenge of the Czar and curb it before the Russians become entrenched. Japan will be able to confidently control the Korean Peninsula. How aggravating it is, with much of our Empire at stake, to find all we have striven for endangered by the romantic entanglement of a single Dartmouth cadet with a married Englishwoman. I am not exaggerating when I say that a public scandal of this nature could cause the Japanese Empire to sever all relations with the West, out of chagrin. Or worse, they may feel obliged to vindicate the honor of Japan by proving themselves in aggression. They might conceivably attempt to match their expansion with our own. Then again, without the Japanese influence as counterbalance, Russia, provoked by Germany and the crisis in the Balkans, may become even more voracious. With a more militant Japan we would be confronted by two powers with direct access to India and the Pacific. We could be forced to defend vital colonies in the East, and the trade routes between them. To be compelled to wage war at such a distance would make the logistical difficulties of the Crimea seem like supplying a weekend fête. The cost in materiel and lives would be staggering, and our progress might well be set aside for a decade and more."

"What should that have told you?" I persisted, going back to his first remark. "What should you have realized?"

"Lady Brackenheath used Prince Jiro's personal name when he offered his condolences. Even Ambassador Tochigi would not be permitted such a liberty. Therefore I should have realized that the two were on terms of great intimacy." His heavy brows drew together in a glower. "I fault myself for failing to pay attention to what I took to be routine courtesy."

I considered this observation, recalled the incident and my own intention to report it, which, had I not been distracted, I would have done; I added, "Do you think it was significant that he gave her his chrysanthemum handkerchief? For it seems to me that Ambassador Tochigi was very much startled to see the handkerchief in her hand. At the time, I did not assign much importance to this, for I assumed the ambassador's disputes with the Prince accounted for his umbrage."

Holmes considered his answer for a second or two. "I thought I noticed some response in him that was beyond the usual. But I supposed it was on account of the shocking nature of the crime committed. I do not think condolences are offered to a Japanese widow in the same manner as English ones." He spun the watch-fob again, letting the chain wind around his finger in the other direction.

"Is that a factor, do you think?" I inquired.

"The differences between the English and the Japanese? Of course it is. Only consider the number of times we have all of us made assumptions based on our national characters," he said with a shake of his long head as he began to pull at his lower lip. "How can we help but become entangled in this?" He settled back to regard me. "And the information I had early on from Tschersky threw me off the scent, for I—" he broke off. "We English are concerned with results, with the profit or loss created by our actions, and the cost is not always reckoned in pounds and pence. In Japan, form is as important as the result it produces. In the Japanese court it is better to fail correctly than to succeed by a proscribed method. By extension, this means that the individual has less importance than the position he holds. In this particular instance, for example, it doesn't matter if Prince Jiro loves the lady or not. He has failed to follow the correct path. It is that lapse that makes his liaison intolerable; for it will be perceived that the Prince has shamed himself, and because of this, the Emperor may suffer the loss of the faith of his people. In the Japanese mind, the Emperor is the nation in a way that hasn't been the case in the West since before Caesar conquered Britain."

"But there must be some way to address the situation that would not have such severe repercussions. I cannot think it would be prudent to allow so great a misfortune to—" I said, only to be cut short.

"I cannot think of one," Holmes responded with a shake of his head, "for it is a matter of degree, don't you know. We English value our reputations, but by comparison the Japanese make the highest stickler seem lax. The tales you have heard of young men who have failed in their appointed mission expiating their error by ritual suicide are correct. Their deaths are entirely voluntary. To lose life is far preferable to a Japanese than living without reputation, without face." His expression changed. "Can you imagine MacMillian in such a society?" His chuckle was short-lived. "The Prince will be held to that standard. Compared to such a loss of face, anything, including our current agreement, is expendable in the Japanese mind."

"I take your meaning, sir," I said at the end of this, much chastened.

Holmes sighed. "We all suffer from the same assumptions—that everyone in the world is aware of how the game is played, and they choose not to play by our rules out of spite and perversity." He regarded me thoughtfully. "You are not so blind as most, Guthrie, and for that I thank God, for you could not do the work I require if you were as limited as the vast majority of functionaries in the world." For a short while he was silent, and then he said, "At least that writer Kipling understands a little of it. He knows that there are things in India that do not fit into cozy, British boxes. And he is willing to tell stories to prove it. For that he deserves respect beyond that given most tellers of tales."

"Permit me to say, sir, that I have never regarded his works in that light. I have considered him one of those who seeks to spin tales of high adventure for high adventure's sake." I could not think of any less condemning expression of my opinion of the man's published writings.

"They may be read that way, of course," said Holmes, dismissing my criticism out of hand. "But there is more to him than you perceive, if that is all you see in him." He settled back in thought, his demeanor forbidding. I did what I could to review the events of the night before, trying to order my accounts in my mind so that I would be able to assist the police in their inquiries. Holmes' abrupt remark interrupted my thoughts. "If Scotland Yard does not know of the . . . dealings between Lady Brackenheath and

Prince Jiro, let us not do anything to put them on the trail until we can learn for ourselves the full significance of their involvement."

"Very well," I said, a little surprised at this instruction. "I will strive to make it plain we do not know anything in that regard."

"Gracious, no, I hope not," said Holmes with a rich, sardonic chuckle. "Then we should be properly in the soup. Give the matter no more or less consideration than you would give any other speculation. The police might not entertain the notion themselves for very long, as I am certain few of them believe that any Englishwoman would wish to become the lover of a Japanese, even the Emperor's second son."

"I'll contrive to follow your instructions," I said, sounding stiff to my own ears and earning a bark of laughter from Holmes.

Andermatt again admitted us to the Swiss embassy by the side door, saying as he closed the door behind us, "We will continue this irregular arrangement as long as it suits you, of course, but it would be more convenient to have you come to the front, Mister Holmes, and more appropriate to your position with the government."

"My position with the government," said Holmes drily as I came after them, "is unofficial, as you know. And as a minister without portfolio, it would be indiscreet of me to be seen here. It would also obviate the need for my double to continue my habitual patterns at my flat and my club." He shrugged. "I do not need the ceremony and the pomp to accomplish my work. In fact, I manage far better without them."

"As you wish, Mister Holmes, though it is lamentable that those less deserving of recognition are reaping the rewards of your efforts. I do not offend you with such a liberty, for it reflects more than my own opinions," said Andermatt as he pointed the way to the library, opposite the White Salon. "Deputy Ambassador Chavornay remarked upon his return from the meeting with you and

Lord Salisbury that you are the only one who appears to have a realistic grasp of the difficulties of this case. He would be honored if you would join him for a luncheon."

"Deputy Ambassador Chavornay gives me a great compliment, and upon two points," said Holmes without any appearance of boastfulness or egregious modesty. "I regret that until this investigation is concluded, my time is not my own. Please convey my respectful regrets to the deputy ambassador, and assure him that when this is resolved I will be delighted to accept his invitation." With that he bowed to Andermatt and opened the door to the library. I came after him and closed the door with dispatch.

The room was as I remembered it, minus Miss Gatspy—dark wood and heavy draperies, with deep, overstuffed chairs near the hearth, a few trestle tables with benches and stools placed next to them, with lamps opposite to provide better illumination than the windows did. Beyond them, ten ranks of shelves running from floor to ceiling, filled to overflowing with publications in German, French, and Italian, with a few in English, Spanish, Dutch, and Czech among them.

"I will need a lamp," said Holmes as he sank into one of the three chairs set before the hearth. "And an occasional table so that I may make notes." He looked at me for a moment. "I do not mean to inconvenience you, dear boy, but would you procure the table for me? Our friend Andermatt will surely be able to arrange it."

I had a fleeting question—why had Holmes not asked for it himself? But then I recalled he had not been in this room before and did not know he would require something not already here. I saluted using the handle of my cane for the gesture and hastened into the corridor once again.

Finding Andermatt took longer than I expected. I at last ran him to earth at the entrance to the servants' dining hall, where luncheon had just concluded. With all dispatch I explained my employer's needs, and received assurance that Enzo would attend to it within the half hour. With that I made my way back to the library, noticing as I went that Inspector FitzGerald had arrived with two men to assist him. I mentioned this to Holmes as I entered the library.

"Yes," said Holmes, looking down at his notebook, frowning. "That is one of the reasons I am not eager to advertise our presence, since it is well known that I am to be found every afternoon in my flat." He put down his pencil and steepled his fingers, resting the tips of his middle fingers against his chin. "Tell me, did you happen to notice if Ambassador Tochigi has arrived yet?"

"No," I said. "There was no mention of it." I was puzzled by his question and did not want to make it appear I had been lax in my duties. "I will ask, if you wish."

"It's not so urgent," he said. "They will be here in good time. And you are to talk to—"

"Messers. Banadaichi and Minato, yes, sir, I am aware of it." I had, in fact, had little else to distract my thoughts from the possible association of Lady Brackenheath and Prince Jiro.

"It will be necessary to make a few, very circumspect inquiries," Holmes reminded me. "If either of those men had any suspicions in regard to Prince Jiro's paramour, we must know about it, preferably before Scotland Yard stumbles upon it." He had that dreamy look about him which I had learned hid strenuous intellectual activity. "It is essential that we preserve as much privacy in this regard as we are able, for the sake of the agreement."

"I am aware of that, sir," I said, realizing that he was more apprehensive about the investigation of the murder than he was willing to say. "I will respect the privacy of all those involved to the very limit of the law."

"Excellent, Guthrie. I would not ask more of you." He glanced up as there was a rap on the door. "Yes?"

"Your occasional table, sir," said one of the staff with a German accent.

"Bring it in," he ordered, and motioned me out of the way.

Once Holmes had the table arranged to his satisfaction, he asked me to move one of the lamps from the trestle table for his use. I chose one with a green hood, similar to the ones found at the Diogenes Club. "Very good, Guthrie. I am satisfied. Now you might as well go in search of Andermatt to discover where you are to interview your two Japanese secretaries."

I was familiar enough with Mycroft Holmes' manner of dismissal that I could find no reason to remain. I half-bowed and took myself off, finding Andermatt this time with Inspector FitzGerald at the entrance to the Terrace Suite. Sunlight gave the room a splendid glow, though no one paid any heed to its beauty.

"Mister Guthrie," said FitzGerald, his face still shiny from being recently shaved. "How good to see you. Just the man I was looking for."

"Good morning, Inspector," I said, and attempting to make my request known to Andermatt, "I am to discuss certain matters regarding last night with—"

"Before you do that," FitzGerald interrupted, holding up his hand as if to halt a wagon in the street, "I need you to come out and show me how you happened upon the body. Why were you outside? What made you look for Lord Brackenheath in the first place?" He had a look about him, dogged and emphatic, which I knew would be folly to resist.

"I am supposed to interview the Japanese secretaries—" I began again, only to be cut off this time by Andermatt.

"They have not yet arrived, Mister Guthrie. I am expecting them directly, with Ambassador Tochigi. You may assist Inspector FitzGerald without apprehension. I will inform you when the Japanese party arrives." With that, he bowed and left us in the open doorway.

"Wonderful fellow, isn't he?" said FitzGerald said. "Now, as I recall, you were out on the terrace. Why was that, Mister Guthrie?"

I moved through the door into the Terrace Suite and resigned myself to answering his questions. "I had been sent to find Lord Brackenheath, whose presence was wanted for the official signing of the agreement. He was supposed to represent the old landed families of England, so that the Lords would be satisfied their rights had not been usurped. It also provided a broader political spectrum for the inevitable questions that would arise in Parliament, which the Prime Minister declared he wanted to forestall, and so he brought a diverse assortment of negotiators to the process. For those who cling to the vision of England at the apex of the white man's world and the envy of all other races, Lord Brackenheath was a quintessential spokesman." As I said this, the events seemed to me to be in the distant past, not unlike recalling an examination at school. "He had left this suite some time earlier; after the Prime Minister arrived, it was hoped he would present himself. But, of course, he did not."

"Why did you look on the stairs?" asked the Inspector. He had been standing still, but now he paced, going to the windows, turning, and coming back. "Did you hear something that caught your attention? Did you see blood? What was it?"

I indicated the door on the far side of the chamber leading onto the terrace. "If you will come with me, Inspector, I will do what I can to recount my movements to you." I did not wait for him, but went straight to the door. The air in the room still smelled of cigars and brandy. With relief I opened the door onto the terrace. "I was standing near the top of the steps down to the garden, where I supposed Lord Brackenheath to have gone. I was reluctant to descend, given that I was still using crutches—"

"I noticed you had a cane today, sir," said Inspector FitzGerald, as if that in itself were significant. "And the old phiz is pretty rum."

"So I have," I said, "brought a cane." His observations on the state of my face I dismissed with a lack of apparent distress. "A token of last night's adventures at Lord Brackenheath's house."

"Odd development, that," said Inspector FitzGerald, letting it hang in case I wanted to add anything.

"Doubtless. And something not to be neglected, especially if it is established there is some connection. However the murder is, I believe, the more pressing. Let's get on with it, shall we?" I favored him with a nod of readiness as we strode out onto the terrace.

Accepting my direction in the matter, he got down to it. "Had you some reason to go into the garden, then?" asked the Inspector.

"I was unsure of where I might find Lord Brackenheath, and the garden seemed a possibility," I said, trying to recall what thoughts had led to my discovery. It was all so distant and ill defined. Taking care to be as meticulous as I could, I continued: "I came to the terrace because I had been told that Lord Brackenheath had stepped out to smoke in peace."

"Who told you that?" demanded Inspector FitzGerald. He had taken up the same position I had occupied at the top of the stairs, as if to verify my account.

"I believe it was Andermatt, although I am not entirely certain, for I asked several people where his Lordship might be found. In fact, I believe Andermatt said his Lordship was in the Terrace Garden, enjoying his cigar. I was reluctant to attempt the steps because of my crutches, which you will recall I was using last night. But then I saw what I at first took to be a discarded sack near the foot of the stairs. I . . . thought it might be a bomb or something equally destructive. So I made my way down to it, and saw that while it was explosive, no bomb lay here, but the body of a man in evening clothes. I moved the body enough to ascertain the dead man's identity. I felt drying blood under my hand, and made a note of the location of his wound, and then I went as quickly as I could to inform my employer what had occurred."

"You didn't send for Andermatt?" The Inspector was instantly suspicious. He peered at me as the breeze ruffled his pomaded hair.

"Why should I?" I countered. "My first obligation here was to fulfill Mister Holmes' instructions and make myself useful to the Prime Minister. I did this."

"Most irregular. You were technically on Swiss soil, and you should have informed them first." Now he sounded more puzzled than angry. I did not flinch from his scrutiny, and was rewarded with his observation. "Not that in these circumstances I wouldn't have done the same."

"I was sent to fetch you not long after the body was identified and the instrument of his death located and taken as evidence. The scene was not much compromised." I hoped this would mollify him to some degree.

"For diplomatic shenanigans, you were quite prompt," Inspector FitzGerald allowed grudgingly. "And you have been more helpful than I expected."

"I do what I can, Inspector," I assured him.

"That's what worries me," countered Inspector FitzGerald as he motioned me away. "Don't leave the embassy. I may have need of you again."

FROM THE JOURNAL OF PHILIP TYERS

Our comparison of names has turned up little of use so far, though another packet of banking information has just been delivered, and we will have to review it promptly. Perhaps with the intelligence we may obtain there, some useful connections may emerge. Mister Coldene has assured me that the Admiralty will assist these inquiries in any way possible, for they are as determined to protect the agreement with Japan as the Prime Minister is.

Edmund Sutton has shown himself to be most apt at this, regarding all our extrapolations as a process of character study. I am quite certain he is enjoying himself, for he remarked not half an hour ago that he wishes he did not have to go across to M H's club this evening, for he would rather pursue these clues with me than perform for those silent, brilliant men. His opinion of the members of the Diogenes Club borders on the irreverent, and never more so than when his appearance as M H has convinced them. He dismisses the notion that it is his skill which makes this possible, "For you may be certain, Tyers," he said today with glee, "no actor would be fooled."

That's as may be, but I suspect he is right. He is as keen an observer in his way as is M H's brother. Neither rivals M H, but both possess abilities well beyond the ordinary.

I will shortly prepare tea. This should convince the watchers that we are unaware of them for another day.

Chapter Twenty-one

I HAD JUST finished my interview with Mister Banadaichi, who was so overset by the murder of Lord Brackenheath that he had trouble remembering to answer my questions in English, when a note was delivered to me by one of the embassy footmen. The missive was unsigned, in the German language, written in a disguised hand on very plain, inexpensive paper:

Mister Guthrie:
Not all Japanese support the agreement, just as not all the English do. Consider Mister Minato's responses in that light. If you wish to discover more, be wise and do not put him on the alert.

I stared at the letters on the page as if they were in a foreign language unknown to me. Who had written them? To what purpose? Was this a legitimate warning, or was it yet another indication of the worst intentions of those seeking to bring embarrassment to England in her dealings with Japan? I folded the note in half and placed it in my waistcoat pocket, then did my best to master myself before dealing with Mister Minato, all the while wondering if the author of the note was aware that I was about to interview the man in question. Was it luck, deliberate action, or happenstance that put the thing in my hands just before Mister Minato presented himself to be questioned?

"Mister Guthrie?" said Mister Minato from the doorway. He bowed, gauging his courtesy with care so that he would not make it appear that he was showing me one iota more honor than I deserved.

"Mister Minato," I said, half-rising and returning his bow. "Please come in."

Mister Minato looked more exhausted than Mister Banadaichi had. There were smudges under his eyes and a heaviness in his movements that made me suppose he had slept little the previous night. "Mister Holmes has been busy today. I understand the police are here, as well."

"Yes," I said, indicating the chair across the table from me. "They are. They may want to speak with you, and they may not, depending on what their inquiries require; it may be that this talk of ours will suffice." My tone was neutral, but I could not keep from watching Mister Minato narrowly, trying to discern what it was the note-writer wanted to indicate about the man—if, indeed, the note was not merely a ploy to keep me from performing my duties to the satisfaction of my employer. I recalled his earlier kindness to me, and I wondered if I was repaying him badly. Yet my failure to conduct a proper examination of the man would lead to Mycroft Holmes' having incorrect information. I did not want that to happen. I settled myself more comfortably as Mister Minato strove to compose himself. "The Swiss will send in tea, if you wish it."

"Arigato," said Mister Minato, who, having taken one look at the bruise on my face, now contrived not to stare by avoiding me altogether. "I would like to have tea, and perhaps something to eat, for I have not yet breakfasted, and it is past the hour for luncheon. I do not think well when I am hungry, but we have had no opportunity to stop for a meal. There were many demands upon us this morning, as Mister Banadaichi must have informed you. We had many unexpected matters to attend to."

"I do understand, for it is much the same with me, though Mister Banadaichi refused, saying he was too nervous to want to eat. Still, neither of us are so afflicted, are we? A light repast would be very welcome just now. It is my pleasure to oblige," I said, and rang for a footman, thinking it would be Enzo, but it was not; this fellow was French-Swiss and smug. "Tea for both of us, and a plate of sweet and ordinary biscuits, along with some cold slices of ham." As I said this, I had a sudden yearning for my grandmother's oak cakes. It was useless to ask for them, I knew, and the longing took me aback. Keeping in mind that this was a Swiss establishment, I added, "If you would, include a breakfast pastry or two, and a fruit conserve, to make up for our hectic morning? Mister Minato is hungry, as am I." It would be useless to have asked for the sirloin, baked eggs, buttered crumpets, and kippers of a good English breakfast. I realized then I hadn't the least notion what the Japanese had for their first meal of the day.

"Avec plaisir," said the footman, in a manner that suggested the opposite, and withdrew.

"Now then, let me begin so that we may get this over with," I said, addressing Mister Minato with what I hoped was agreeable candor.

"Tell me what you want to know." It would be too severe to say that he was sullen, but I detected that there was more than Japanese correctness in the reserve with which he spoke. "I will answer as well as I am able."

"So your ambassador has assured us," I said, hoping to ease his mind.

"Hai," he said, and contrived to bow from his place in the chair. "Ask me your questions."

"Shall we get down to it, then? Sooner started, sooner ended." I did not consult notes, but spoke from the items I had memorized. "When was the last time you recall seeing Lord Brackenheath alive?"

Apparently Mister Minato had devoted a lot of his sleepless hours to just this matter, for he answered promptly and with such clarity of thought as can only come, as Edmund Sutton has taught me, with rehearsal. "I was with the men from your government, the two secretaries sent to assist in the copying of the agreement. It was my duty to do so. I believe you saw me." He stared at the tabletop in order to keep from seeing the mess of my face.

"That would be—" I prompted, not wanting to make it appear I was telling him what his account ought to be.

"Two men. Mister Wright and Mister Hackett, as I recall their names. I do not recall their personal names." He sounded almost angry that I should expect him to identify the men. "They were with Mister Banadaichi and me for a few hours as the agreement was copied." He scowled as the footman came in with our tea, vowing to return momentarily with the rest of our sustenance. "These men are men of honor, are they not?"

I was not quite sure if Mister Minato meant the secretaries or the Swiss footman, but I answered, "It is hoped they are. Your memory will serve to help us make that determination."

Mister Minato remained stubbornly silent until the footman had left us alone, and then he waited for me to pour out cups of tea for us before he spoke again. "I saw Lord Brackenheath in the anteroom near the Terrace Salon. He was holding an unlit cigar, I think. He had exchanged a few words with Mister Hackett, I suppose it was; the man who knows Korean. I thought he was trying to persuade Mister Hackett to do something for him, because he leaned forward a great deal and appeared to be keeping his voice low with an effort, but what it was he wanted and how he expected Mister Hackett to achieve his mission, I could not tell."

I stirred milk and sugar into my tea and saw a concealed wince from the Japanese secretary. "Help yourself, Mister Minato, if you want milk and sugar." I could sense the tension in the man, and I wished to know the whole of it. "Is that all you recall of the exchange you witnessed, Mister Minato?"

"There is something more. In the corridor, just before the encounter I described, I saw Lord Brackenheath insult Ambassador Tochigi. I was very much shocked that such a man in such a place would forget himself so completely. That was shortly before I saw him for the last time, no more than ten minutes at the most," Mister Minato added. He was angered afresh as his recollection sharpened. "When I understood his purpose, I watched him, in case he should do anything more of an offensive nature."

"What did he do?" I asked, as I was supposed to. "What was the nature of his insult?"

"He . . . said that he knew the Emperor was not . . . entitled to hold the position he holds. He called him a murderer and the descendant of murderers. Lord Brackenheath declared that the entire Imperial family was descended from those with no honest claim to their place, and that those who served them were nothing more than panderers and assassins. He said it as if he could do so with impunity." Speaking the words was difficult for him. He gulped his tea as if to fortify himself. "He said this to make Ambassador Tochigi refute the terms of the agreement, and admitted as much."

I could only imagine the impact such words would have on a man of Ambassador Tochigi's character. "What was the ambassador's response? Did you stay to observe it, as well?"

He nodded in that abrupt manner I had come to associate with him. "He only said that he had a commission to fulfill and he would do it in spite of anything Lord Brackenheath might attempt, that such a man as Lord Brackenheath could not compromise his honor with words. Ambassador Tochigi was certain that only his failure to complete the negotiations would dishonor him." Mister Minato frowned. "Such an insult would not be tolerated if we were in Japan."

"No doubt," I said drily. "Just as in Japan you might speak against the British Crown in a way you would hesitate to do in London, or against the Russians, but not in Saint Petersburg. That, I fear, is the way of the world."

Mister Minato glared at the milk jug. "It would not be so if—" He broke off.

"If what?" I asked as blandly as I could. I sensed that I was on the edge of a chasm with this man, though why I should have such a sensation, I did not know.

He shook his head. "You are ignorant."

"Certainly. If I were not there would be no reason for this interview. And I will be less so if you will instruct me," I said, hoping I achieved the proper tone with him—enough respect to deserve an answer, but nothing servile to make him suppose he had achieved a moral victory in his recalcitrance.

"You are nothing more than a servant, no matter what work is entrusted to you. You ask questions about matters you do not understand, and you have no notion how to evaluate the answers you receive. You do not know what is truly important, or who is in the game. You only do the bidding of those who have the power to demand it of you." His dark eyes smoldered with arrogance and resentment.

"You yourself are a servant," I reminded him.

He smiled once, very quickly. The smile was not pleasant to see. "It must seem so to you." He finished his tea and permitted me to pour more. Clearly he was starting to enjoy his game with me.

"If you are not the servant you appear to be," I said carefully, departing from the list of questions I had memorized and taking a greater risk than I wanted to, "it means you are something less desirable—a spy." I let this accusation hang between us. "Surely you do not mean to tell me that you are doing such a reprehensible task as that?" I was a fine one to speak, I added to myself.

"I have the honor to serve my country, as you do," said Mister Minato. There was no humor whatsoever in his smile.

"In what capacity?" I asked, and made note that this time he had not said he served the Emperor, but his country. Even six months ago that shift in words might have got by me, but not now. I folded my hands and met his eyes directly, willing to take whatever time was necessary to get the answer.

The impasse was interrupted by the arrival of the French footman once again, bringing the food we had requested. His intrusion was a welcome one, for it broke the tension that had built up between us. I was pleased to see him for another reason: I am of the opinion that food can do much to infuse an occasion with cordiality that it might not otherwise have.

The response came more quickly than I expected. Immediately the footman left us alone, Mister Minato exclaimed, "As a patriot. How else should I serve my country?"

"Most creditable," I said, "and yet, it could mean that you are willing to promote what you see as Japanese interests beyond those of the world at large." I was goading him deliberately, hoping for a greater response.

"How can you, an Englishman, say that when England has been bent on modeling the whole world in its image?" he challenged. "You think because you are English—"

"I'm a Scot, actually," I interjected, wanting to keep him off-balance.

"The same thing," said Mister Minato.

"As the people of Hokkaido are the same as the rest of the Japanese," I added, and was rewarded with a startled look. "I have confessed to ignorance, but I am not quite so uninformed as you wish to think me."

"It would seem not," said Mister Minato, doing his best not to appear discomfited. "I did not think anyone but Mister Holmes knew anything about Hokkaido."

"How could we arrive at mutually satisfactory terms in our agreement if we had no understanding of the state of Japan and the Japanese today?" I asked as reasonably as I could, remembering as I did that Mister Minato had a very different standard of reason from mine.

"You cannot be saying that men of Lord Brackenheath's character are of the same mind." He bit into a croissant, indifference in every lineament of his attitude.

"No. Just as there are most assuredly those in Japan who do not regard this agreement with favor, as you have so eloquently illustrated." I realized he would find my manner offensive, which was my intention. "As we have men who seek to keep England from adapting to the changes in the world, so must you have the same in Japan. It cannot be avoided. Those who have done well in the past are less eager for the risks of the future than those who seek improvement in their lot. I will allow that the society of Japan is not the same on many points, but on this one, I reckon we have more in common than is outwardly manifest."

He seemed to realize he had made a mistake, and resumed a more correct demeanor. "So neither the English nor the Japanese are free of nationalism. Each of us will act honorably, I hope. And because of that, I must consider all the aspects. As I suppose you must, too." He lifted his hands slightly and shrugged. "What has this to do with the events of Lord Brackenheath's death?"

"If he was killed to stop the agreement from being put into effect, then it may have a great deal to do with it," I reminded him. "And the police are eager to ascertain the whereabouts of all those who had dealings with Lord Brackenheath last night."

He muttered something in Japanese I could not make out, then said, "I have been told to help the police if it is possible."

"Yes. We appreciate your predicament, and we will do all that we can to minimize the imposition the investigation necessitates." I poured more tea for myself and used the time it took to do this to observe him narrowly.

"This is the same ground we have gone over before," he complained, and I realized that some portion of his sullenness was an act, and that he was taking my measure as closely as I was taking his.

"Yes. I want to be certain I have it right." I paused as if to order my thoughts more carefully. "You've stated you saw Lord Brackenheath talking to Mister Hackett. How long afterwards was the body discovered, do you know?"

"Perhaps ten minutes, perhaps a few minutes more, taking the time from when you went to the exterior door of the Terrace Suite and were admitted by Sir George Tyrell." He considered his answer again. "I think it must be more than ten minutes, now I think about it. It could be a quarter of an hour."

"I made the discovery a few minutes before," I admitted, not wanting to recall the moment again. I sipped tea again, this time to give me time to banish the image of the dead man from my mind. "Well, then, shall we say you saw Lord Brackenheath a short while before he was killed."

"That would be accurate," said Mister Minato.

"With a cigar in his hand," I added. "You said you saw him holding a cigar, didn't you?"

"He had not lit it yet. I gathered it was his intention to smoke it while he was on the terrace." He did his best to avoid my eyes. "It is a terrible thing to have such a man come to that end, and in this place. The Swiss cannot be pleased."

"No more than any of the rest of us," I said pointedly. "It is our agreement that may suffer the consequences of his death."

He nodded, making it pass for a bow.

I asked my few remaining questions, then went in search of my employer. I found him outside the library door deep in conversation with Inspector FitzGerald and Ambassador Tochigi—the ambassador, once again dressed in a swallowtail coat and striped trousers, was shaking his head vigorously.

"But we must talk to Prince Jiro," Inspector FitzGerald declared. "He is a part of our investigation, and his information may be crucial to our work."

"It cannot be permitted," said Ambassador Tochigi with heavy emphasis on the *not.* "He is the son of the Emperor, and—"

Inspector FitzGerald cut him off. "Begging your pardon, Ambassador, but he is also a Dartmouth cadet, and that means he is expected to follow the orders of the—"

"Both of you," said Mycroft Holmes, making a gesture calculated to calm. "It is necessary that we have the Prince's information. I think each of you can see the need of it. But it is also necessary to make certain the Prince's dignity is not slighted. He has come to help us, not hinder us in this investigation, and he has as much reason as you do to want the criminal or criminals brought to justice." The two men with him now listened closely to him. "Would it satisfy you both if I spoke to him? I give you both my personal assurance I will conduct the inquiry in such a way that both of you are satisfied with the results. I will be careful not to embarrass him, and at the same time I will avail myself of the opportunity to learn all that I can from him that may have bearing on the case. I give you my pledge that my account will be accurate in any regard that has bearing on the death of Lord Brackenheath. I will reserve the right to withhold any information that does not."

"It would be all right with me," Inspector FitzGerald said sullenly; this was the best he could expect to achieve, and he knew it, "providing we could review in advance all the things I would need to know."

Ambassador Tochigi was more recalcitrant. "It is not right that you should question the Emperor's son. The dead man may be titled, but he is English. What can he know of the death of this man? To speak to him at all in this regard slights him." Watching the ambassador, I realized suddenly that he knew of—or guessed—Prince Jiro's relationship with Lady Brackenheath. I determined to impart my supposition to Holmes as soon as we were private.

"I will be careful not to put him at a disadvantage," Holmes assured Ambassador Tochigi. "Only tell me that I may interview him, and I will give you my word that he will be treated with full respect."

"All right," said Ambassador Tochigi grudgingly. I was certain he sensed that to continue adamant in his refusal would only draw unwelcome attention to the Prince. "But you are to hold in confidence all his answers except those he himself permits you to reveal to the police. A failure to do this will bring about a serious breach in the relations of our two countries."

"You may rely on my discretion," said Holmes at his most soothing.

"Ambassador Tochigi," said the unpersuaded Inspector FitzGerald, becoming bellicose, "that's not right. How can we do our job if the Prince forbids Mister Holmes to tell us something that may be, as I have said before, crucial to our inquiries? If you have some notion as to how we might get around this predicament, I would like to know of it."

"FitzGerald," said Holmes patiently before the Inspector and the ambassador could lock horns again. "I think I am capable of persuading the Prince when there is an issue that bears on your investigation."

"Very well, if that is how you wish to manage it," snapped Inspector FitzGerald, standing very straight, his face flushed. "I will perforce accept your terms." He glared at Holmes and shot a look of intense suspicion at Ambassador Tochigi. "I have other interviews to conduct, gentlemen. If you will excuse me?"

"A dogged man," remarked Ambassador Tochigi as the Inspector went away down the corridor.

"Doggedness is an asset in his work. Without it, he would never accomplish his purpose," said Holmes, then signaled to me to approach. "There you are, Guthrie. All through with Messers. Banadaichi and Minato, I trust?"

"Yes, sir," I said at once as I came up to him. I was leaning more heavily on my cane than I would ordinarily like, but my ankle was beginning to swell again, and it hampered my movements.

"I hope they gave you all the cooperation you sought," said Ambassador Tochigi with the slightest of bows.

"They were most informative," I said loudly enough that

Ambassador Tochigi could hear me clearly. "I thank you for making these arrangements so that we are able to conduct our interviews with discretion. Any additional attention would not be useful at this juncture."

"Certainly," said Ambassador Tochigi, and once again addressed Holmes. "I will explain your offer to Prince Jiro at once, and will send you word on his response immediately."

"Thank you, Ambassador," said Holmes, taking care to exchange bows in the proper form before signaling to me to follow him into the library. "Now then, Guthrie, what has you so exercised?"

I had not been aware of any change in my outward manner, but clearly Holmes had detected something. I made certain the door was closed behind us, and then held out the note I had received as I said, "I am convinced that Mister Minato is a spy."

Holmes stared at me for a second or two, then lapsed into a chuckle. "Good Lord, that knock on the head has muddled your brain—you mean you've only just noticed?"

FROM THE JOURNAL OF PHILIP TYERS

We have come across something, Sutton and I, that must be put into the hands of M H at once. The various records of banking transactions have at last revealed something of interest that may well indicate the reason for Lord Brackenheath's death, or an essential part of the puzzle, in any case.

Sutton has also noted that there is some question about a Russian officer who attended the gala, whose accounts have received monies from Buda-Pest as well as from Grodno. Whether this has any bearing on the events surrounding the murder I doubt, but as M H seeks to know of any and all irregularities we find, I will include it with the less pressing cases we are assembling against his return. It may be that this information may be useful when we have to deal with Austro-Hungary next February.

I will prepare a memorandum for M H on our discoveries regarding Lord Brackenheath and have Mister Coldene carry it to the Swiss embassy, as M H has informed me he will remain there through the evening. He said he will return here no later than nine, for he wishes all of us to have a good night's sleep, not only to clear our thoughts, but to prepare us for what he anticipates will be a most demanding day. I have made the appropriate arrangements with Sutton, and will send a message round to G's landlady so that she will not think anything dreadful has befallen him.

The watchers are still in place, and I have noticed that they carry sidearms, which serves to heighten my apprehension in regard to their purpose here. The man in the service yard half an hour ago had a pistol under his jacket: I saw him pat it once, which alerted me to its presence and gave me impetus to look at the others more closely with the glass, the better to discover what weapons they might have secreted about their persons. It would be very dangerous to make an attempt on M H in such a street as Pall Mall, but I cannot suppose it is impossible. I must warn Sid Hastings to have extra care when he brings M H back from the Swiss embassy tonight, for who knows what mischief these watchers intend.

Another day of it, and I shall know the role of Ferdinand as well as Sutton does.

Chapter Twenty-two

THERE WAS NONE of the hauteur Prince Jiro had displayed on his previous encounters with Mycroft Holmes. He came into the library quietly, and offered Holmes a proper salute before bowing to him in the Japanese manner.

"I am grateful to you, Prince, for making yourself available to me." Holmes nodded in my direction. "I think you've met my secretary, Guthrie?"

Prince Jiro stared at me. "I understood we would be alone,"

he said to Holmes, stiffening. "Ambassador Tochigi assured me that what we discuss will be wholly private."

"You may repose full confidence in Guthrie's discretion—I do," said Holmes placidly as he indicated one of the overstuffed chairs flanking the hearth. "Do be seated, and we can get this done as quickly as possible."

"All right," said Prince Jiro carefully. "Count Tochigi tells me that I may decide which of my answers you may release to Scotland Yard and which are to remain private." He moved as gingerly as he spoke, settling himself in the chair as if he might break a bone if he were not cautious.

"That is my understanding as well, your Highness. And you may be certain I will abide by it." Holmes sank down comfortably at once. He signaled me to remain where I was. "It is a most unfortunate thing for all of us that Lord Brackenheath's murder should take place concurrent with the publication of our agreement. And I fear we must view it as something other than a lamentable coincidence. The murder was as much a warning as a crime."

"I agree." Prince Jiro regarded Holmes with the aspect of one preparing to escape.

"And therefore," said Holmes at his blandest, "there is really no reason to entertain you as a suspect."

The Prince sat bolt upright, pride and anger warring for mastery of his countenance. "Suspect? I a suspect? How could I be a suspect?"

Holmes paid no attention to the Prince's consternation. "I will admit that for a while you did seem a possibility, but in a way your very obviousness bothered me," he went on as if nothing untoward had happened. "Upon reflection, however, I realized that you had nothing to gain and a great deal to lose if you were the one who killed Lord Brackenheath. I also could not entertain the notion that you would use that dagger for the weapon, even if you had been so reckless as to kill the man. No matter how deep your . . . involvement, you would not want to subject Lady Brackenheath to the notoriety her husband's murder must surely bring." He sat calmly and let Prince Jiro regain his composure.

"How did you know?" the young man asked nervously.

"About the murder, or about you and Lady Brackenheath?" Holmes asked him. He showed no outward sign of discomfort, though I did notice he was fingering his watchfob.

"Either! Both," said Prince Jiro, now attempting to show the same sangfroid as Holmes, though in his case it was only a façade.

"Well," said Holmes quietly, "your ambassador was aware you were romantically entangled with a married Englishwoman, though he claimed not to know her identity, which may or may not be the case." He drew out his cigar case and offered one to Prince Jiro, who accepted after an instant's hesitation. "Any doubts he might have had were banished when Ambassador Tochigi saw your handkerchief with the Imperial mon on it in her hand last night. I paid little heed to it at the time, for there is nothing remarkable in an Englishman offering a lady his handkerchief at such a coil. It was only later that I recalled your society conducts itself along other lines, and that what might be commonplace in England would be shocking in Japan." He lit the Prince's cigar, then his own. "Guthrie reminded me today that Lady Brackenheath had called you by your personal name. I will not do so, because I do not wish to offend you, your Highness." He blew out a fragrant cloud of smoke. "But that ended any doubts I might have had. It also convinced me utterly of your innocence in regard to Lord Brackenheath's death."

"It did? How did you arrive at that conclusion?" asked the Prince. I could see that his hands shook ever so slightly.

"Simple logic, your Highness. What benefit would it be to you if Lady Brackenheath were widowed? You would not be able to marry under any circumstances, so disposing of her husband would not remove an obstacle from your path, nor would it create approbation in either of your families. In fact, as matters stand now, you cannot continue your . . . association with the full glare of public attention upon the Japanese and Lady Brackenheath. Therefore you did not kill him to achieve her freedom to marry again, that being out of the question. And what had she to gain from her husband's death, had you wanted to do her a service through ridding her of an odious spouse? He rarely beat her, and they had no children he could mistreat. She is the one with a fortune, and it is wholly in her control, so gain for her played no part in his murder. As I see it, any trace of scandal—which Lord Brackenheath's murder surely creates—works, as I have remarked, against your liaison, for it draws attention to your conduct, and scrutiny to your motives, which neither of you could want. It is possible you might kill him in jealous rage, but I do not reckon you would be willing to entertain such a confrontation at an occasion when your country is being honored." He tapped a bit of the ash off the end of the cigar.

"She is not a light woman. We are not . . . amusing ourselves," said Prince Jiro with strong emotion in his voice. "She did not intend to become my mistress, nor did she ever conduct herself in such a way that I feared she was attempting to dishonor her husband, much as he might deserve it for the many slights he visited upon her." He looked directly at Holmes, and said with simplicity, "She is the greatest treasure I have ever known."

"And I will respect your regard for your alliance," said Holmes somberly. "Your privacy will be maintained."

"And what of the police?" asked Prince Jiro.

"They do not need to know of your dealings." Holmes contemplated the low fire in the hearth. "In general, I find the clandestine distressing in domestic circumstances, but given the nature of the marriage of Lord and Lady Brackenheath, I cannot suppose their vows had not been flouted many times by Lord Brackenheath, and in a manner less chary of his reputation and hers." He sighed once. "It isn't fitting to seduce a married woman, but in this instance, I do not suppose seduction was the object."

"No, it was not," said Prince Jiro. "I am not so foolish that I sought a dalliance with a married woman of quality as nothing more than a cocksman's challenge. By the time I was aware of the nature of my feelings for her, I was unable to banish them, though I tried."

"I have witnessed such affiliations in the past, and I am aware that in a man of true character, no matter how stern the will, the best-trained mind can be overset by a whim of the heart. When it is more than a whim . . ." He made a gesture to finish his thoughts.

Prince Jiro wore an expression now of frank and profound admiration. "I am in your debt."

"No debt that I am aware of." Holmes inclined his head. "I must first disabuse Inspector FitzGerald of his suspicions in your regard before I will have accomplished much to your benefit. Make no mistake about it, he is willing to believe you would stab the man with that ritual dagger because of his disparaging remarks about your country. He confuses you with the medieval nobles of Europe."

"How could he make such an error?" asked Prince Jiro, baffled now.

"Because he has not thought the matter through. Which is hardly surprising, given the length of time we have had to conduct our inquiries." He glanced at the clock on the mantle. "It is five-ten now, not yet a full twenty-four hours since the man died. Hardly time for the Inspector to assemble all the facts."

"You seem to have accomplished the task," said Prince Jiro, a bit of irony tinging his remark.

"Ah, but I am not hampered as he is with the need to investigate a crime, at least not the crime of murder. I am doing my poor best to guard the terms of a necessary international agreement in the face of the determined activities of traitors. If it were necessary for Lord Brackenheath's murder to go unsolved in order to preserve the agreement, I would be willing to leave his death in that undesirable condition." Holmes was wearing his mild expression. He was never so dangerous as when he did that.

Now Prince Jiro stared at him. "And what of the English love of justice?" he asked, more fascinated than offended.

Holmes had taken his watchfob from his pocket and was now spinning it so that it wound around his index finger first one way and then the other. I could see that he had anticipated this question and that its resolution had not been easily reached. "Oh, I am not so cold-blooded that I could tolerate seeing an innocent man wrongly convicted. Not only does that countermand my principles, it would compromise the agreement in a most inadvisable way, which would do nothing to preserve it. Agreements purchased with treason and similar exigencies are never enduring, and I would not let this one come to grief. But short of such an impasse, I would rather leave Lord Brackenheath without his personal . . . vindication, than have the agreement abjured, and permit the traitors to prevail."

"Mister Holmes," said Prince Jiro with a slight, nervous smile, "you are more like Ambassador Tochigi than you think. He shares your convictions, though he would not express them in the same language." He bowed slightly, then took on a sterner mien. "So. What do you plan in regard to Lady Brackenheath?"

"If you mean do I intend to confront her in regard to your liaison, yes, unfortunately I must. But you have my word I will discuss the whole with her in confidence so that she will not have to worry that any information in this regard shall . . . get out." He put his watchfob back in his waistcoat pocket. "Tell me, your Highness. Who else knows about your affaire with Lady Brackenheath?"

"No one," he said promptly, then added when he encountered Holmes' skeptical gaze, "Though I assume Haggard, her butler, is aware that she has a lover."

"Why is that?" Holmes asked, sitting more forward in his chair.

"She was protected, in regard to her husband, and Haggard has been with her for longer than her husband. I have met him twice, and I have thought I detected something in his manner that is something more than the usual English curiosity and reserve where we Japanese are concerned." The Prince frowned. "I do not mean to say that he ever overstepped the bounds, for that is not the case. He has shown me every regard he would extend to a countryman, and I suspect he holds Lady Brackenheath in the highest esteem it is appropriate for him to hold her."

If only my head had not been aching so furiously, I would have paid more attention to what Haggard had told me the previous night. Now I did my best to recall the whole of the matter to mind; I missed part of Holmes' next question as a result of these cogitations.

"—last time you were private together?"

Prince Jiro hesitated before answering. "Four days ago. It seems forever now. Who would have thought it would . . ." He looked away. "She went to visit an elderly cousin living in the south; she had been doing it since she first married, so there was nothing remarkable in such an expedition. Lord Brackenheath was always pleased to have her gone from their town house, for then he could indulge himself with his cronies. The cousin's place is about an hour's ride from Dartmouth, and I met her there, as I often have before."

"And the cousin was aware of this?" Holmes made no attempt to hide his interest in the matter.

"I don't know. I never met the woman, who is an invalid of advanced years." His expression grew distant and sad. "There is a folly on the grounds, a supposed ruin of a Gothic abbey, built forty years ago. We would go there. Not even the gardeners disturbed us there."

"For how long did you meet this way?" Holmes asked.

"For just over seven months." His laughter was more painful than bitter. "The first few times I thought we would freeze." He was about to say something more, then changed his mind.

Holmes did not pursue the matter. He leaned back. "And in London? Did you ever meet in London?"

"Only twice. It was so dangerous. Too many people might notice us together." As he indicated his face with a gesture. "I am not inconspicuous, not in England."

"Where did you meet, then?" Holmes looked merely curious.

"I obtained a suite of rooms not far from Covent Garden, where many men take their opera dancers and other . . . companions, paramours and ganymedes. In Japan, we have the world of wind and willow for these . . . attachments, though Lady Brackenheath is nothing like a geisha. So I had to make do with what was available. I did not like the place, but as a foreigner, my choices are obviously limited. The second time we were there we narrowly escaped an encounter with a man well-known to Lord Brackenheath. We agreed then to confine our assignations to the country." His nervousness was returning.

"Guthrie," said Holmes without turning to me, "please pour a cognac for Prince Jiro."

I rose at once to do this, and as I did, I recalled something that Haggard had said to me, as clearly as if he had spoken in my ear: *for she may now follow the dictates of her heart. And the one who has . . . Nothing can come of it, more's the pity.* As I splashed the cognac into the balloon glass, I said, "The Prince is right. Haggard does know."

Holmes stared at me. "Are you certain?"

"As certain as I may be without an actual confession from the man. And I doubt he would vouchsafe me one in any case." I handed the glass to Prince Jiro and prepared a second for Holmes. "I will have to send Haggard a note."

"Not to confirm this, surely?" Prince Jiro demanded.

"No," I said. "Last night, or early this morning, if you prefer, I indicated that I would be back this afternoon to aid the household during the police inquiries. I will not be able to do that, and I should so inform them, so that they will not suppose I forgot them." I said this as much for Holmes' benefit as for Prince Jiro's. "Unless you wish me to call there, sir?"

Holmes made a sign of impatience. "No. I need you here. You'd best have one of the embassy messengers carry a note for you. Andermatt will arrange it, I've no doubt. When we have finished our conversation you may attend to it." He accepted the cognac, and shifted his line of inquiry. "All right, your Highness. I will ask you nothing more in direct regard to Lady Brackenheath. But I must solicit information in regard to those Japanese who accompany Ambassador Tochigi."

"But you know them," said Prince Jiro, surprised by the question.

"Not as you do," Holmes observed. "You are their Prince and their countryman. You know more of their character than ever I can, and I depend upon you to impart your impressions to me as candidly as possible." He took a sip of his cognac. "It would help me most if you will let me know something of the family backgrounds of all three men."

"I should not," said Prince Jiro, his manner becoming stiff.

Holmes did not seem perturbed by this refusal. "Your Highness, I am aware that under ordinary circumstances such remarks would be most inappropriate, and I would not have to put you in this position. But these are not ordinary circumstances, and the potential for catastrophe—and pray do not assume that I do overstate the risk—is very great if there is a single misstep."

Prince Jiro nodded thoughtfully. "I will do what I can," he said at last. "And not because I fear your using your knowledge of my private dealings against me, but because, like you, I view the failure of the agreement as potentially catastrophic." He tasted his cognac. "The Swiss have the pick of so many good things."

"That they do," Holmes seconded, and it was clear that they had established an understanding. "Now, in regard to Mister Banadaichi, what can you tell me about him?"

"I know nothing to his discredit," said Prince Jiro at once. "His family is samurai, very old and much-honored. He himself has dedicated himself to the service of the Emperor, and has vowed to guard the reign of my brother."

"Is there any reason he might want to destroy this agreement? Is his family, perhaps, unwilling to extend Japanese protection to ships not their own?" Holmes made his tone flat to minimize the insult he would give Prince Jiro through the question itself.

"Not that I know of," said Prince Jiro. "But I concede it is possible. Not that anything is declared, of course. But one hears rumors, even in the Emperor's family, about the old nobles wanting to keep Japan out of the larger world. Not that they would be foolish enough to say this openly, for they would then have to defend themselves to the Emperor, and would face grave penalties for attempting to countermand the wishes of the Emperor."

"You call him the Emperor and not your father," Holmes remarked. "Why is that?"

"Because he is the Emperor before he is anything else. The same will be true of my brother one day. He will be more than my elder brother, and I will be his subject more than his younger brother." He took another sip of cognac. "I know that matters are somewhat different in England."

"That they are," said Holmes, a quick look of affectionate amusement creasing the lines around his dark-grey eyes. "Those rumors you mentioned: What do they imply?"

Prince Jiro sat a bit straighter—no easy feat given the posture he had maintained from his entering the room. "You have some knowledge of Japan, and some experience in my country as well."

"That is true," said Holmes as a matter of form.

"You then have some understanding of the traditions our heritage imparts." He noted Holmes' single nod and continued. "There are those who put the traditions before all else, and they, it is said, seek to prohibit the intervention of the West into our affairs. It is whispered that there are companies of dedicated nobles who have sworn to destroy all things that diminish the purity of Japan and the Japanese people. It has been suggested that murder and war are not beyond their scope, if either would secure Japanese preservation."

"Do you think these rumors have any basis in fact?" Holmes inquired. He did not appear to be paying much attention, which indicated his concentration was at its height.

"Yes, but to what degree, I cannot say. I am not so naive that I do not suppose that there are powers in the world which would seek to exploit such men to their own purposes. Russia, for example, I know does not wish Japan to build any alliances with England. There may well be others, such as Germany, or Austro-Hungary, for the balance of power would be upset and not to their advantage; I have heard a few suggest that the Chinese are not eager to have this agreement ratified. This does not surprise me, nor should it anyone else. The Chinese have long used their ports to control much of the Pacific and cannot welcome having that power pass to us. I do not think the Chinese will be pleased when our dreadnoughts arrive. I hope it will not necessitate a test of arms, but if it should come to that, we are prepared." Prince Jiro glanced around uneasily. "I would not be astonished to learn that they had found a way to spy on what you are doing. I know that Ambassador Tochigi is afraid that his family may be in danger for his work here."

For the first time, Holmes looked startled. "Are you certain of that? He has made no mention of it to me."

Prince Jiro ducked his head. "You will forgive me for telling you that Ambassador Tochigi would not confide this information to you."

"Why is that?" Holmes asked, though I could see he had already surmised the answer.

His answer came quickly. "Because it is known that there are agents in England who support the efforts of the nobles in Japan, and not all of them are Japanese."

FROM THE JOURNAL OF PHILIP TYERS

It is nearly time for Edmund Sutton to make his appearance at M H's club across the street. He is finishing his preparations now, while I clear up the last of our tea. Sutton is always nervous before he goes to the club, for he says he never feels more exposed than when he is in that building with all those astute men. "If they did not regale themselves with port, brandy, and cigars, I would not attempt it at all," said he. "Nor if they permitted speech, for though I can imitate M H well enough for those who do not know him well, anyone who is his long-time associate would notice at once that the timbre of our voices is not the same, no matter how accurate the accent or the idiosyncrasies; voices are often more personal than faces."

He may find fault with his impersonation of our employer, but I cannot.

Mister Coldene has come to take my message to M H at the Swiss embassy, and has said he will wait half an hour for an answer, if there is one. He informed me that there is much pressure being brought to bear on the P. M. to fix the responsibility for Lord Brackenheath's murder on the Japanese, in order to spare the Swiss any scandal, and to point the finger away from England.

I will occupy the time compiling the information we have garnered, so that upon his return M H may peruse it. It is a fortunate thing that M H has the authority to command the release of such confidential records, else it would be the work of months to uncover all we will learn in a matter of hours. The deposit of ten thousand pounds to Lord Brackenheath's personal account is the most perplexing evidence, for all our efforts have failed to disclose who made the payment and for what reason. The bank has said that it must be the result of gambling, as most of his reverses in fortune came from that activity. But the amount is so great, and so precise, that both Sutton and I are convinced that there is some more specific purpose in its presence.

When Sutton returns, we will resume our efforts.

Chapter Twenty-three

AFTER I HANDED my note for Haggard to the embassy's messenger, I returned to the library. I found Mycroft Holmes hunched over his notebook, jotting cryptic memos to himself and scowling, his heavy brows making his dissatisfaction emphatic.

"The Prince was very helpful. His level of comprehension impressed me. I wonder if he knew how much?" I said, breaking into his fearsome concentration. "I noticed that you did your best to discover his degree of concern for Lady Brackenheath. However,

I was a bit puzzled why you made no mention of Mister Minato's double purpose here."

"I must hope that what he told me of his concern for the agreement was as genuine as his deep affection for Lady Brackenheath; if it is not, telling him of Mister Minato's spying would only serve to put him on the alert," said Holmes, his attitude one of exasperation.

"Do you think it was not?" I asked. His reservations took me aback, for Prince Jiro's manner had the ring of truth to it.

"No, I am satisfied he is sincere," Holmes responded unhappily. "Which means the rot is deeper than I supposed. And inclines me to believe that the Prince himself may be in considerable danger."

"What danger? From whom?" Now I was truly alarmed. "How do you mean? What makes you think so?" There was a desolation of spirit I could sense in him that filled me with foreboding.

"I had hoped that this was the act of a few desperate men who had taken it upon themselves to seize the moment to show their dissatisfaction with the agreement"—his face now bore the hewn look of exhaustion, and his voice was a rougher growl than usual—"which of necessity meant that the man committing the crime must be English or Japanese, though I doubted the latter, as using such a dagger to murder would be an impious act for a Japanese who honors their traditions." He had finished his cigar and used his pen to illustrate his point in the air. "As it is, I am left with the unhappy notion that this was not an opportunistic killing, but part of a well-conceived scheme to undermine more than a single agreement, no matter how sweeping it might be."

"And why do you think this is the case?" I prompted him, fascinated to discover where his acumen had led him.

"The facts, lamentably, speak for themselves. I cannot convince myself that this was an impulsive act, not given what we have learned thus far," he admitted. "And I am beginning to suspect that your Miss Gatspy might have pointed the way when she brought the Grodno Hussar to your attention."

It was useless, I realized, to protest the possessive pronoun. I chose an indirect answer. "She was right about Prince Jiro and Lady Brackenheath."

"Yes," said Holmes distantly. "I know. That's what troubles me." He picked up his balloon glass and swirled the cognac around in it, his eyes fixed about twenty feet beyond the library wall. After a few minutes of silence, he addressed me with energy. "Guthrie, do you know where you can find Miss Gatspy at this hour?"

At least he had not called her *my* Miss Gatspy this time. "I'm not privy to her current direction, but I suppose I can locate her if I try." Though as I said it, I hadn't the remotest notion how. "I am willing to attempt to locate her."

"Do so, will you? And shortly. I want to know more about this Grodno Hussar she told you was not Russian." He rubbed his chin with his free hand. "Lack of sleep must be dulling my wits. I should have realized that there was more to this than meets the eye."

"But you have said that from the first, sir," I protested.

"Ah, but I have been looking from the wrong end of the telescope, or so I fear. I should not have assumed . . ." He had a sip of the cognac and went back to swirling the amber liquid in the balloon glass. "Your Miss Gatspy should be able to put me to rights."

There it was. I held my tongue with an effort. "I will be about it at once."

My departure was delayed, however, by Andermatt, who came into the library with a sealed packet. I recognized Tyers' fist on the flap as Andermatt handed it to Mycroft Holmes. "A Mister Coldene delivered this not five minutes since." He was able to maintain his attitude of correctness and at the same time showed a trace of curiosity.

Holmes broke the seal at once and pulled out several sheets of paper, with a note from Tyers lying atop them. "Strange," he murmured, and read swiftly through the material, one hand raised as a signal to me to remain where I was.

Andermatt, realizing he would not be told of the contents, bowed slightly and withdrew.

"What is it, sir?" I asked, approaching him carefully.

"I think Sutton and Tyers have come across something important, perhaps essential." He held up a sheet of banking records. "Ten thousand pounds is a lot of money."

I scanned the page, and stared at the figure. "Even a man of Lord Brackenheath's position must find that a considerable sum."

"*Especially* a man in Lord Brackenheath's position," said Holmes. "He was all but run off his legs when he married Edith Francesca Bell." He smiled slightly at me. "Oh, yes. I have learned something of the lady since last night. I have discovered she is six-and-twenty years old, that she was married at seventeen to Lord Brackenheath, that she was named for her mother—Edith—and for her father's favorite heroine—Francesca da Rimini—because he was estranged from his family and did not want to recognize them in any way. How often these brilliant men of trade have a hidden streak of romance in their souls: Have you noticed, Guthrie?" As the question was rhetorical, he went on without pause. "I learned she was the only surviving child of Herbert and Edith Bell, that she was well-educated and traveled more than most young persons do before she was married. She was used to care and attention from an early age. Edith Bell and two other children died twenty years ago of an epidemic fever. So Herbert Bell, who did not marry again, fixed all his energies on his business and all his hopes on his one remaining daughter, whom he called Francie. His ambitions for her exceeded his judgment in regard to choosing her husband, but he was at pains to secure her future and guard against Lord Brackenheath's depredations."

"And where did you glean all that information?" I inquired, knowing it was expected of me, and curious in spite of myself.

"From Lord Brackenheath's cousin, who will assume the title. He is a bookish sort of man, thirty-eight years of age, married with four children, in temperament more suited to Oxford or Cambridge than his country estate. His means are comfortable but not lavish, and he does not hanker for more. He regards his inheritance as much as a burden as an advancement. I gather he did not approve of Cousin Edward, as he calls Lord Brackenheath. It is also apparent that he does not relish untangling Cousin Edward's affairs; what he will make of the ten thousand pounds, I can't think. He was summoned to London first thing this morning, and as soon as I had finished with the Prime Minister, I had some conversation with Mister Virgil Anthony Eneas Lucie. For a man rudely awakened to so grim a purpose, he was most cooperative. He is worried about Lord Brackenheath's illegitimate children making a claim upon him. Do you know if that is apt to occur?"

"How should I know?" I asked, with a slight emphasis on *should*.

"I thought perhaps Lady Brackenheath, whom her intimates now call Francesca according to Lucie, had explained such matters to you last night." He drank more of the cognac, then stared at the small amount remaining in the bottom of the balloon glass. "This is as good as what they have at my club. I wouldn't be as sure of the port."

"She told me about the children—though I gather most of them are grown, and were given settlements as part of sending them out of England—in Canada, America, and perhaps Australia, as I recall." I thought about what she had told me on the ride to her town house the night before. "No; I tell a lie," I amended as the conversation came back to me, "not to Australia. Lord Brackenheath did not approve of the society in Australia, according to Lady Brackenheath. He did not want his illegitimate children mixing with criminals and their descendants."

"How very . . . discerning of him," said Holmes, his heavy brows forming a noticeable V as he frowned. "If he made settlements on them, he may also have provided for them in his will. What further claim do they have upon their father, other than his concern for the niceness of the company?"

"None that I know of. Certainly they cannot importune Lady Brackenheath in that regard. It is my impression that her fortune is completely protected." I thought again of how prudent Lady Brackenheath's father had been to reserve her inheritance as he had done.

"Then the only issue would be the land and the ten thousand pounds. Since the land is entailed, it is not likely that it would be worth their efforts, not while he has his cousin to inherit. And if the ten thousand pounds are a mystery to the bank, the sum must be wholly unknown to the children." He set the balloon glass down and took out a cigar. "So they are not to be considered as likely suspects in the death of Lord Brackenheath, more's the pity."

"Why do you say that?" I asked, and guessed the answer at once. "Because," I went on before he could speak, "it means that like it or not, there are international repercussions to his murder, which, had one of his bastard children killed him, would not be the case. The scandal would be a family one, not—"

"An international embarrassment," Holmes finished for me. "Sadly, that does appear to be the case. Which is why I want a word or two with Penelope Gatspy this evening. I will send you on your way directly, dear boy, after we settle one or two other points. Now," he said as he struck a match and held it to the end of his cigar, "we must decide whether or not we inform the police of what we know, point them in the direction of the illegitimate children, or inform them that the murderer is probably a foreign national who killed Lord Brackenheath for political reasons."

"Must we not tell them the truth?" I asked, startled at his observation.

"Yes, but it is a matter of how much truth, and how it is presented, that must be decided. Inspector FitzGerald is no fool, and he will suppose we are selecting our facts carefully." He blew out a fragrant cloud, his eyes narrowing as the smoke wreathed around his head. "It is understood that this is all part of what is expected in difficult cases of this nature," he went on, forestalling other protestations I might lodge. "The police know that there is more at risk than a crime going unpunished."

"But surely they are required to pursue the matter with all the vigor they can summon? Lord Brackenheath was—"

"A Peer of the Realm?" Holmes interjected. "He was a narrow-minded, bigoted, self-serving old debauchee who used his rank to protect himself from having to pay for his excesses. Had he been a ordinary Englishman, he would have been in the courts long ago. Since he was not, we must continue to shield him from the consequences of his own actions."

"In what sense?" I asked.

"My dear Guthrie, surely you must realize that the ten thousand pounds did not fall out of the sky into Lord Brackenheath's account." Again he exhaled a billow of smoke. "And since the source of the money has been deliberately hidden, we must not rule out the possibility that someone—someone who wishes to remain unknown—bribed Lord Brackenheath. What did the person offering the bribe wish to receive for his largesse? Given that the money was paid to him less than a month after he was brought onto the Prime Minister's negotiating counsel expressly to represent those who oppose any dealings with Japan except for purposes of colonization, it seems apparent to me that the money has something to do with the agreement."

"That may be so, sir," I said, not as convinced as he. "But if he had been bribed, why should he be killed? Surely the money cannot now be reclaimed?" I had meant it as a joke, but failed.

"Lord Brackenheath was killed very close to the hour that the agreement was being signed. We have been assuming that if there was a political motive to his murder, it was because he opposed the agreement, and was killed to put an end to his opposition of it. But what if he died because he failed to stop the agreement from being signed? What if this is more an issue of punishing failure than ending his attempts to thwart the agreement?" He got up from the chair and, throwing off the lethargic manner he often assumed, he began to pace restlessly.

"But that has been considered," I reminded him.

He shook his head. "No. We have thought that, assuming his murder was for his role in the agreement, his killer had to be English who wanted to implicate the Japanese. I may have been too hasty when I told Inspector FitzGerald that no Japanese would use that dagger for such a purpose. For we have made the error of thinking that all the Japanese with Ambassador Tochigi support the agreement. But"—he paused and rounded on me like a fencer preparing to thrust—"what if one or more of them do not?"

"Support the agreement?" I said, wanting to clarify my own thoughts.

"Yes. That note you received before your interview with Mister Minato has rankled with me since you informed me of it. I think that now I am beginning to perceive its implication." He made an abrupt gesture. "I do not want to speculate further until I have had a chance to speak with your—"

"Miss Gatspy," I finished for him.

"Precisely." He pulled out his watch and stared at the face. "I will return to my flat at nine. You may come there, with Miss Gatspy in tow, if she is willing to speak with me. You may bring her to my flat after nine, if you do not find her at once. If she is not located this evening, I will have the police search her out first thing tomorrow morning."

That generous allowance of time struck me as unlike Holmes. I remarked upon it. "With ten hours head-start, she might easily flee the country."

"So she might," Holmes agreed in an abstracted way as if this possibility held no interest for him whatsoever. "Tell her I will do all that I can to keep her safe if she will speak with me. And when I say safe, I include preventing the police from questioning her."

"Very well, sir," I said, uncertain how to regard this determination to circumvent the inquiries of the police.

"Guthrie," said Holmes gently as I started toward the door, my back held stiffly to accommodate the cane, "suppose, just suppose, that in solving one murder the police bring to light certain matters that would bring a bloody war. Would your sense of justice be more outraged by the unavenged death of one man, or the slaughter of innocent thousands?"

"And Lord Brackenheath was a reprobate," I said, trying not to sound too condemning.

"He could be a risen saint and the issue would be no different. The death of this one man is a tragedy—the annihilation of thousands is a catastrophe. Which would you prefer to answer for?" He inhaled deeply on his cigar. "I will see you here or in Pall Mall after nine. Come in through the service alley, on foot, and if you can make the climb without your cane, so much the better. Miss Gatspy will know how to manage."

I nodded to him once, gathered up my cane and portfolio, and went to find Andermatt, to inform him of my departure.

"I will see you tomorrow, Mister Guthrie?" he said, correct to a fault.

"I don't know yet," I replied. "In any case, I appreciate your help and your tact."

"Tact," he said with a slight smile, "is what we Swiss are famous for."

Once I was in Sid Hastings' cab, I realized I hadn't any conception of where I might find Miss Gatspy. She had never provided the slightest information regarding her current residence. It struck me as a ludicrous notion that I could spend the evening driving through the streets of London in the hope of apprehending her. As it was growing dark, I was aware no woman of quality would be abroad alone at this hour.

"Where to, Mister Guthrie?" asked Sid Hastings from his box. "You haven't said."

"Drive to Half Moon Street," I said, choosing a street near enough to my rooms to make it possible for me to determine if more mischief had been done there yet, and to make it possible for me to inform Missus Coopersmith that all was well with me, though, given the state of my face, I doubted she would be convinced. I would also be near enough to Berkeley Square to stop in at the Brackenheath town house if all else should fail. I might be able to have an additional word with Haggard. "When we arrive, I will tell you where we are next to go." I hoped that in that time I would have a touch of inspiration that would point me in the right direction.

"Right you are, sir," said Hastings and gave Jenny the office to walk on.

We had reached Piccadilly, where there was still a good number of vehicles moving on the street. I had to suppress a sudden frisson in apprehension of danger, though I brought my cane up where I might use it as a bludgeon if I were attacked again. But we proceeded without incident to Half Moon Street while I chided myself for allowing my nerves to get the better of me.

"Drive along to my rooms, Hastings," I said, watching the street carefully, tying to discern any person watching Missus Coopersmith's house. I was growing exhausted of this constant need to remain alert to all things around me. It seemed so foolish to fash myself on such a minor matter. Then I remembered the unfortunate cat and the red paint and my vigilance redoubled. "Take me to Curzon Street, and wait for me," I told Hastings, amending my orders.

"As you wish, sir," he said, and set his mare moving again.

I got out of the cab as soon as it came to the kerb. My ankle was sore, but I could walk quickly enough and only faltered when I had to climb the steps to the front door.

Missus Coopersmith was waiting as I came into the entry-hall. "Mister Guthrie. I expected you sooner than this. Well, nothing lost; you are come now," she said through the open door of her sitting room. I noticed the cat was with her, curled up on the plump hassock near the hearth. I was about to thank her for her kindness to the creature but her next words drove all that from my mind. "I have just been having tea with your fiancée."

I stared. Elizabeth Roedale? Here? After she had broken off our engagement in such uncompromising terms? I could not begin to fathom her purpose in coming to me now, and I was about to say as much when Missus Coopersmith added, to my astonishment, "Such a charming girl, and so personable," she said as she gestured for me to join them. "Pray sit with us. I know it is irregular for me to permit her to visit you, but when she explained the circumstances to me, what could I do but welcome her?"

What circumstances, my mind clamored. "And you are a chaperon," I said, trying to sound more knowledgeable than I was. I strove to gather my thoughts before I had to face Elizabeth

Roedale again: Given how difficult our parting had been, and that I had not seen her for many months, I could not imagine what demeanor was appropriate for this occasion. Yet for some reason she had sought me out, a girl so proper that the thought of calling me Paterson was foreign to her. As Missus Coopersmith smiled her encouragement, I tried to think of how I ought to greet her, how I should account for my appearance; the bruises on my face would surely distress her. I steeled myself as I went through the door.

She was dressed in full mourning, as she had been the first time I had seen her. She held out her hand without rising, and addressed me in the familiar manner of the affianced. "There you are, Paterson. At last. I was about to give you up. I have been waiting this age; Missus Coopersmith has very kindly received me in your absence."

I bent to kiss her hand, and felt myself smiling. "Thank you for coming to me, Penelope," I said to Miss Gatspy.

FROM THE JOURNAL OF PHILIP TYERS

I have done all that I can until the physician arrives. Fortunately the bullet did not penetrate as far as the would-be assassins intended, or Sutton would not have survived. As it is, he will have to rest for at least a week and very possibly more if he is to recover from his wound.

M H has been informed—Charles Shotley, the Admiralty messenger, carried my note to him at the Swiss embassy—and will, I trust, arrive shortly. He will have to be unusually careful in his approach, for it would not do to have those who lay in wait for him discover that they had shot the wrong man.

Chapter Twenty-four

MISS GATSPY AND I arrived in Pall Mall to chaos. There were doors left open and a trail of good clothing leading toward the front of the flat. No one answered my knock on the back door, and when I called out, I received no answer. With dawning fear I led the way forward, ready to strike out with my cane.

"Be careful," Miss Gatspy recommended, keeping up a few steps behind me.

"Good Lord," I exclaimed as we entered from the rear of the

flat through the pantry, for there was a pile of heavily padded material sodden with blood lying in the doorway between the pantry and the kitchen.

Many another woman might have become faint, but Miss Gatspy was made of sterner stuff. "Someone's been hurt, I should say."

I faltered, fearing that my employer had come to grief. Then, as I approached the door into the corridor, I realized that I could hear Mycroft Holmes' rumbling accents, and the steady, quiet voice of Philip Tyers.

"The physician said this isn't mortal. And he was an army doctor. He is not one to assume either the best or the worst." Tyers was backing into the hall from the study, a basin held in his hands.

"It had better not be mortal," muttered Holmes as I motioned Miss Gatspy to come after me.

"Tyers," I called out, not loudly enough to alarm, but not so quietly that it would seem I was coming into the flat by stealth.

"Oh. Mister Guthrie," he said as he turned to me. "You gave me a start." His sleeves, rolled up, showed a smattering of blood upon them.

"Who's been hurt?" I asked, and glanced over my shoulder. "This is Miss Gatspy, by the way. Mister Holmes wants to see her."

She curtsied slightly, and came nearer to listen to Tyers' answer.

"It's Mister Sutton. As he was returning from the Diogenes Club, he was shot. From the angle at which the ball struck, his assailant was on a second floor or a roof—the ground floor or the first would not create the wound." He sounded calm enough, but there was a look in his eyes that surprised me, for I had never seen this man show so much fear before.

The blood-soaked padding in the kitchen now made sense to me, and I did not like what it revealed. I was not certain where Sutton had been struck, but there was blood enough that it had to be more than a crease, and high on the body.

"Is he badly wounded?" Miss Gatspy asked before I did. "How serious is the injury?"

"He was able to make his way halfway up the stairs to the door. I had reached him by then." He looked away. "He has lost a great deal of blood, and he is suffering from the care of Doctor Watson, who may be relied upon to keep his knowledge of this attack to himself. Mister Holmes does not want his brother to learn of it, for he does not wish his brother to become actively embroiled in this matter."

"Do you think he might?" I asked, aware of the distance the two maintained between themselves.

"If he thought Mycroft Holmes were being hunted by murderers, he might," said Tyers with a shake of his head. "If only Sutton had not been about his impersonation. Still, thank God he was wearing the padding, or I am afraid he would be needing the services of a minister and not a physician now."

"Poor man," said Miss Gatspy, then added sharply, "Who is Mister Sutton."

I sighed, realizing I could not dissemble now. "He is an actor."

"An actor?" said Miss Gatspy, and then recognition dawned. "So *that's* how he does it!" she exclaimed, keeping her voice low with an effort. "I should have realized. He is Mister Holmes' *double.* Oh, very clever."

"May we see him?" I asked, aware that we had disturbed the men in the study.

"Go ahead. But do not excite him. Doctor Watson was most emphatic about that, and in his years in the army, he became expert on gunshot wounds. Any unnecessary distress will hamper Sutton's recovery." He added in an undertone, "Mister Holmes has provided a topical anesthetic from the plants he grows. He will not permit anyone to administer opiates to Sutton."

I nodded, not surprised at this restriction, for Mycroft

Holmes' condemnation of such drugs was nothing new. I tapped on the doorframe. "Mister Holmes, may we come in?"

"Come ahead, Guthrie, Miss Gatspy," he responded at once.

All the tables in the study had been pushed back to the bookcases, save the longest, which had been swept clear of papers and books, and on which Edmund Sutton lay, his upper body naked but for a mass of bandages around his left shoulder and chest. His fair head lay cradled on Holmes' rolled-up swallowtail coat. Under the smears of his makeup, he was pale, his color ashen, and he appeared to be half-asleep. His wig was on the floor, looking like a small badger about to dig its way through to the flat below. Mister Holmes, his sleeves rolled up to his elbows, bent over him like a ponderous guardian angel, wiping Sutton's brow and feeling his pulse from time to time.

"He will live," said Holmes, answering the question I could not bring myself to ask. "Though he may not enjoy it for the next several days." He looked down at Sutton. "Had I realized his risk was so great, I would not have permitted him to—"

Sutton's words were slow and indistinct. ". . . my job . . . don't blame . . . self."

"You may not blame me, my boy," said Holmes with quiet conviction. "But I blame myself sufficiently for the both of us."

"No need," said Sutton, making an effort to keep from slurring.

"You may wish to think so," said Holmes, "but I cannot. Now, Edmund, you must rest. Doctor Watson told you that this is the best thing for healing. I trust you will do as I ask and permit Tyers and me to do all that we can to assure your return to robust health."

Sutton muttered something, his eyes closing, fluttering, and closing again. His breathing was slow and steady.

"Tyers," Holmes rapped out quickly, his tone low and precise, "I want his wound bathed and the dressing changed every two hours. If there is any trace of infection, you must tell me at once. The physicians may blather all they want about laudable pus, I do not think infection of any sort in the region of the lungs is desirable. There is iodine and carbolic to keep the wound clean. And use the powdered angelica root on the dressings—it has saved many a farmer from death. I have the greatest respect for modern medicine, but in this, I bow to tradition." He folded his big arms and looked down contemplatively at Sutton. "I had rather be lying there than him."

"Your conscience would, certainly," said Miss Gatspy. "But we must be grateful you are not, for as brave as your Mister Sutton may be, he is not capable of resolving the matter of Lord Brackenheath's death." She nodded once to me. "Your Mister Guthrie has said you need information from me, and he has convinced me it is necessary for me to impart all I know. You have every reason to be grateful to him. That I am willing to discuss what I have discovered does not mean that I support your aims in the Pacific, but that the danger I perceive in Europe is greater than the course of your naval agreement would suggest," she continued in the same bracing manner as Holmes rolled down his shirtsleeves. "I am more concerned with what might happen if your agreement is compromised any further than it has been already, not with the benefits you will reap should it succeed."

"I understand the Golden Lodge has other priorities than mine," said Holmes, cocking his head in the direction of the corridor and the sitting room beyond. "It will be easier for Sutton to rest if we repair to the—"

"Certainly," said Penelope Gatspy.

Holmes turned to Tyers. "Call me if you have any need of me."

Tyers' gesture shooed us out of the study.

I was the last of the three of us out the door, and I very nearly did not hear Sutton speak my name.

"Don't let him . . . go across . . ." He was fighting exhaustion and pain, and his effort to be understood brought perspiration to his forehead.

"To the club?" I responded, returning to his side. "Don't worry about that, old fellow. No one will expect him to leave this flat for the greater part of a week. You have bought Holmes and yourself some time, for surely some member or members of the club saw you shot. If Tyers carries a message, they will know not to expect you for a few days, and by then, this trouble with the Japanese will be at an end." As I spoke, I felt a quiver of doubt that we would be able to bring it off.

"Protect . . ." Sutton insisted weakly.

"That I will. Word of honor." I saw that Tyers was frowning, and I said, "I've got to talk with Holmes and Miss Gatspy now. We will determine how best to go about things." I was about to offer a platitude for recovery, but as I was about to speak I realized that Sutton was already drifting into sleep.

"Off you go, Mister Guthrie," Tyers whispered. "I'll take care of him, don't you fash yourself about him."

I saluted and went to the sitting room where I found Holmes tying the sash of his smoking jacket while Miss Gatspy had taken a seat, not by the large table, but by the Empire secretary against the wall.

"He will be all right," Holmes informed me in such a voice as I hope never to hear from him again. There was force in his statement, and with it a desperation that made me wonder if Holmes were more apprehensive than he had first revealed. "Watson was able to cut the ball out without any major vessels being damaged, and without sacrificing the nerves in his arm. He tells me that the organs are not touched so . . ." He steadied himself. "Had he not been wearing padding, I do not like to contemplate what could have resulted."

"Yes. Tyers intimated as much when we arrived," said Miss

Gatspy in that same self-possessed manner. "But—is his name Sutton?—yes, Sutton was aware of his risk, for I am certain you would not expose him to danger without telling him of it."

"Oh, I told him," said Holmes. "I think he enjoyed it as a game, trying to elude them without being obvious about it. But I knew the flat was being watched and that it was no game. I still do not know by whom. I should have made certain he could not be—"

"Mister Holmes, you know as well as I that anyone with a rifle who is determined to kill another cannot adequately be stopped, not with the distance a rifle may be accurately fired in these days." She paused, then said with deliberate lightness, "Even I would hesitate to try to shoot one man on a street as busy as Pall Mall; the chance of success is not high. Who is to say that a carriage or a crowd of people might impede one's aim? And how is one to avoid the confusion which must necessarily follow? It is useless to think that such commotion aids flight, for it often has just the opposite result. Which is one of the reasons I must suppose you live here: You wish to minimize the opportunity for your enemies to do you harm. It is very likely that someone shooting at you would miss and fall into the hands of the law at the same time."

"Not this time." In spite of his preoccupation with Sutton, Holmes was paying attention to Miss Gatspy. "I have not appreciated you until now, Miss Gatspy." He favored her with a short bow that would earn even Ambassador Tochigi's approval as a nice mix of deference and reservation.

She paid little attention to this. "Guthrie tells me that you are finally looking beyond the English and the Japanese for the culprit in Lord Brackenheath's murder."

"I am considering the possibilities," Holmes corrected her.

"Ah." She offered him a winsome smile. "Meaning you are not convinced. Very well. I will tell you what I know, what I suspect, and what I speculate will come of those things." She folded her black-gloved hands. "I know that the Captain of Grodno Hussars who attended the gala was not Russian. His accent was not right."

"A regional variation," said Holmes. "A youth spent in different cities."

"I don't think so, for the vowels were off, and no one escapes the vowels of his childhood, no matter where they may live afterward." She did not see his nod of agreement to know he shared her observation. "And he swore in Hungarian. I told Guthrie about that, and he paid no heed."

"I am sorry to tell you that he was following my instructions in that regard," said Holmes with a faint, self-deprecating smile.

"Well, you have come to your senses quickly, and that is something worthwhile." She looked at me. "I think perhaps Guthrie shared your reservations."

"Alas," said Holmes with deliberate, sarcastic formality. "He has the disadvantage to be in my employ."

"To be sure. And you have had much to do in the last twenty-four hours," Miss Gatspy said, as if accepting an apology. "And in all fairness, when you had the opportunity to review all the aspects of the case, you knew you had not grasped the whole, at least as we of the Golden Lodge understand it. You are alerted against Russia, for it is obvious what disputes Russia has with Japan in regard to naval ventures, but there are others with as great stakes in this game. You have only to look in the shadows to find them. The Hapsburgs are pressed on all sides. The Austrian Empire has never truly recovered from the depredations of Napoleon. They have maintained their uneasy alliances at great cost. Their neighbors are either traditionally hostile, or, worse, former members of their alliance. Now that Russia and Germany are actively vying for the opportunity of defending the Balkan States, Austro-Hungary is both outgunned and viewed as a villain, prepared to usurp the lands held by the Czar and bring about ruin in Germany."

Holmes signaled his agreement with his watchfob. "You have an excellent grasp of the situation. Austro-Hungary is barely able to keep the Serbs from out-and-out revolt, and the Albanians have reached the point where they rarely pay their taxes." He rubbed at the slight stubble on his jaw. "In the rush to procure a few, last colonies, the Czar and Kaiser Wilhelm find themselves in a peculiar and very unofficial alliance. If Austro-Hungary can engender hostility between England and Japan, Russia will be free to move against Korea and Manchuria, both of which they covet. From that will come war, you may rely on it. With Russia grateful to Austro-Hungary and busy elsewhere, Vienna will still have the ability to block German advancement. And Germany will attempt to expand into those parts of China now protected by international agreement. This would make it possible for Austro-Hungary to reassimilate the Balkan States, and perhaps reclaim part of Greece. I suspect—indeed, I hope—such efforts are doomed. But this policy of distraction is almost as useful to them as a war between rivals. You no doubt recall the terms of the treaty we delivered just after you entered my employ. Through that treaty England would be compelled to enter such conflicts, and it would not be advantageous."

"I can see that," I assured him.

"Which is what makes this current agreement so very vulnerable. If the Hapsburgs could be seen to have brought about the failure of this agreement, it would provide them prestige they currently lack. If their ambitions are thwarted in this effort to restore their position, they will be open to conquest by Germany or Russia in the name of restoration of European balance, or some such twaddle. So the preservation of our agreement with Japan is essential to the stability of Europe, little as Austro-Hungary may believe it."

"That is why the Golden Lodge has taken so much interest in your dealings with the Japanese," said Miss Gatspy. "We are convinced that matters are precarious and require careful monitoring, for without it, disputes might quickly become battles, and then we should be helpless to prevent the wholesale destruction of Europe. To permit the disintegration of any European state would lead to chaos."

Holmes heard her out without interruption. "You suppose your view is the correct one?"

"Certainly. As you suppose yours is." She made no offer of appeasement. "Mine has the advantage that it includes all the known factors without any coincidences, such as the deliberate attack on you and Guthrie."

"But my opinion is no longer fixed, not as it was," said Holmes, looking in my direction. "And there is the matter of those watching me. That is where your argument is most powerful. The men who attacked the cab. The ones who shot Edmund." He sat down away from the window. "Yes, I can see how they managed it, the Hungarians, determined to break their position through putting Russia on the attack against Japan in the Pacific so that they would be able to establish themselves through all of central Europe. Given historical precedence, it is not an entirely ridiculous notion. And the English would not be in a position to stop them because our holdings in Asia and the Pacific would demand our defenses to the exclusion of intervening in Austro-Hungarian expansion while we had our hands full of both Russia and Japan from the Gulf of Alaska to the southern tip of New Zealand."

"And the selection of Lord Brackenheath as the victim was mere coincidence?" I suggested, permitting my skepticism to be apparent in the tone of my voice.

At that Holmes shook his long head. "I dislike the appearance of coincidence. You will notice I do not speak of coincidence itself, because I have found that few of them actually exist. Where there is the appearance of coincidence there is connection, no matter how hidden. The crucial issue is to discover where and how the connection may be made." He pulled out a cigar, rolled it appreciatively between his thumb and fingers. "I think it may be that you have finally shown me the way." He lit the cigar, letting the smoke rise around him. "If I had had the good sense to apply to you for information, Miss Gatspy, I might have spared Sutton the injury he has suffered for my sake."

"And you might not have," said Miss Gatspy at her most practical. "You may have only put your enemies on the alert, and thereby increased your danger. I was not able to prevent the attempt being made on your—in the guise of Mister Sutton—life, because I was not aware that your participation in the negotiations was wholly unofficial. Had I been privy to your special arrangements, I might have come to a useful conclusion."

He made a strange motion with his hands. "My dear Miss Gatspy, I am not indulging in self-pity. My position in this, as in other governmental activities, demands certain things of me which I accept. I dislike it when those I employ are made to bear the burden for me. And thus far, they have. There have been attempts on Guthrie as well as myself, as is plain to the most ignorant. First a threat was delivered to him in the form of a cat covered in paint, and then, when that did not deter him, he was injured during his work for me. Sutton's wound was not the only attempt made on my life, if I can have gall enough to describe it in such a way. These men are my greatest assets, and Guthrie is known to work for me. Therefore I cannot help but think that their misfortunes must be laid at my door." He drew in more smoke and exhaled slowly, relishing it. "I do not generally confide in agents employed by such organizations as your Golden Lodge, and in this case, it is to my discredit. But in general, I would strive to keep my dealings as . . . unobvious as possible."

"Including deliberately leading your enemies to assume that you were not personally present for most of the negotiations," said Miss Gatspy. "A clever and useful ploy in a number of ways, including reinforcing the myth that you are a wholly private man of sedentary habits, in your own way as cloistered as a monk. For the most part your ruse would seem to have been successful. Though you could not conceal your occasional departure for the Admiralty and government functions at all hours of the day and night."

"Hence the attack in Piccadilly, the other evening," I said as the final pieces fell into place in my thoughts. "We were observed leaving, and that made it possible for our opponents to follow us and arrange an ambush." I scowled as another supposed coincidence made itself apparent. "And the vandalism at the Brackenheaths' town house?"

Holmes stubbed out his cigar though he had only smoked half of it. "That is what we have yet to solve if we are to be able to salvage any of this imbroglio."

"What do you mean?" asked Miss Gatspy.

"I mean," said Holmes, turning so that he could look at her squarely, "I must determine where Lord Brackenheath's recent money came from, and what it was intended to purchase. That will tell us where to look for the culprits who brought all this about." He folded his arms. "Guthrie, you are the one best suited to this task. Lady Brackenheath has already confided in you. I cannot suppose she will refuse any reasonable request you may have on this head." He regarded me steadily. "At last we have scented the quarry. And I do not relish the chase this time."

"Because of Sutton?" asked Miss Gatspy.

"Yes, in large part. But also," he admitted more darkly, "I fear we shall uncover deeds more heinous still."

FROM THE JOURNAL OF PHILIP TYERS

Although it is nearing midnight, G and Miss Gatspy remain closeted with M H in the sitting room, finishing their arrangements for the next two days. I have only just removed the plates from the supper I served them an hour ago—a roast rack of lamb, potatoes dressed with onions, peas in a cream sauce, bread, butter, and Stilton and port to finish. I might have served hay and old boots for all the attention they gave the food.

G has prepared a stack of notes to be delivered at seven in the morning, and M H has put his signature to all of them, with the request that all confidentiality be preserved, so that the material requested may be kept under the Oath of Loyalty.

Sutton has been sleeping. He is somewhat feverish though he shows no indication of delirium. I have changed his dressings ten minutes ago, and I am certain he has not bled as much as Dr. W said he might, which is all to the good. The wound is dreadful to see, though Dr. W stitched it partially closed and will finish the job properly in two days if there is no serious infection. By noon tomorrow we should know much more about Sutton's chance for recovery.

First thing in the morning I am to send a note around to Baker Street requesting that the gaggle of mudlarks who sometimes do errands for M H's brother be set the task of identifying the men who are watching this flat. "I should have done it days ago, but I reckoned no action would be taken here," says M H as he gives me the note. "I will be their fool only once. Now I will have them in my sights. And I shall not miss."

Chapter Twenty-five

LADY BRACKENHEATH WAS in full mourning, her veil concealing her face when I presented myself in her reception room at ten the following morning. The Brackenheath town house was draped in black crepe and all the servants were in grey and black.

"Mister Guthrie," she said as she rose to greet me. She had chosen the one chair that had not been gutted. "I had your note, but why you should wish to meet in this room, at this hour, I cannot imagine. Still, I am sure you have an excellent reason, for this place . . ." She indicated the bruise on my face. "I would suppose being here would remind you too much of those events of two nights ago."

"True enough, which is why my recollection is imperfect, and I stand in need of a reminder of what has transpired," I said, and bowed enough for propriety. "I thank you for seeing me in this sad time."

"Sad," she repeated abstractly, and nodded twice. "I suppose it must be." She sat down once again, and said quietly, "There is a reason to mourn today, I regret to tell you, one for which my sorrow is genuine. I had a letter today from my . . . friend. He will not be able to see me again. That has saddened the occasion more than . . . any of this." She waved her gloved hands to indicate her mourning and the condition of the room. "He is right, of course. I would like to refute his reasons, but I know he is right. With my husband dead and attention on this house, we dare not continue. Any attempt to see each other will serve only to bring attention to us, which neither of us can afford."

"I am sorry it has turned out so . . . unhappily for you," I told her.

"Thank you. I know you are sincere, and so few would be, if they knew," she said, continuing as if remembering something from her childhood. "By the time I am in half-mourning, he will be preparing to return home. And he will be closely observed in the intervening months. Our opportunities are—"

"Yes," I agreed, taking up where she left off, "he will be watched. You both will."

There was a little silence between us. Then she said, "You asked if we had discovered anything missing. Not as yet, no, we have not. Though we do not know what we ought to be looking for. But my staff did make one disquieting . . ." She pointed to the settee. "The upholstery on the back had been slit open and then carefully stitched up again, which two of the policemen think has been there for a long time, possibly to repair damage done many years ago."

"What does Inspector FitzGerald think?" I asked. "Does he share their opinion?"

She looked startled at my question. "No, he does not. He is convinced that the cut was a recent one. He is also of the opinion that it was purposefully done, not the repair of an accident, with the intention of hiding an object. If we only knew what that object might be." As she gazed around the room as if all the furnishings were unfamiliar to her she said, "I heard him remark that these other chairs were ruined to draw attention away from the settee, to make it look as if the vandalism had no specific object when, in fact, it did. And the drawers were emptied when the object of their search was not discovered."

I stared at the mess. "When will your staff be permitted to put this all to order?"

"Not until tomorrow," she said quietly. "The funeral is tomorrow afternoon."

"It will be an ordeal for you, and I am sorry for it," I said, as was expected, though in this case I was wholly sincere. I realized that there was nowhere I could sit down. Thank goodness my ankle was steady enough that I could manage without my cane, for I had left it back at my rooms in Curzon Street.

"Yes, it will." She stared in the direction of the windows, with curtains drawn across the morning light, dark draperies tied back with black pulls. "I will have to accept condolences for the death of a man I despised, while I grieve for the man I love, who is now taken from me as surely as if he, and not my husband, had been killed. His cousin, who assumes the title, will be hard put to find virtues enough in my late husband to occupy more than a minute of his eulogy." Her expression was mild. "I know I need not dissemble with you, Mister Guthrie, and for that I am deeply grateful. It is a welcome change to know I will not be compelled to present a false—"

"Lady Brackenheath, you need not explain," I interrupted before she said more she might regret later. "Rest assured I expect no hypocritical observances from you. And I think none the less of you for your candor." I saw a question in her eyes and I made an effort to put her as much at her ease as I was able. "In this investigation, I am aware that I must do all that I can to sift through many misrepresentations and half-truths, which are more difficult to identify than outright lies. Anyone who lessens the amount of deception I must deal with earns my gratitude."

"You are gallant to say so," she said, and sat back. "Tell me what you want to know and I will give my answer with as little bark on it as I can."

I smiled at this old-fashioned expression. "Thank you, Lady Brackenheath." I looked around the room, trying to find a way to start. "This furniture—it was yours or your husband's?"

"My father provided the furnishing for this house and Lord Brackenheath's principal seat as part of our marriage settlements. At Lord Brackenheath's request, he repurchased certain suites of furniture Brackenheath had . . . parted with when he was younger. These pieces were one such suite, and the only one of those he demanded that I like." She looked at them as if they were unfamiliar creatures in a zoological garden. "I think that Brackenheath did not so much prize this furniture as he liked to make my father dance to his tune." She looked at the chair across from her. "We had them reupholstered, of course. That would have been necessary even if they had no signs of disrepair, for the colors of the fabric were faded badly."

I regarded the once-handsome suite with curiosity. "These were purchased when, Lady Brackenheath?"

"Shortly before Lord Brackenheath and I married, as were all the furnishings you see in this house." She laughed but the sound was rusty. "I have often wished I had had the selection of the furniture, for I flatter myself I would have achieved a better effect than has been the case here."

"How do you mean?" I asked, encouraging her to talk freely.

Behind her veil her features were more animated. "Oh. Well, I know it isn't the fashion, but I am fond of the Louis Quinze and the Empire modes. I like their shapes. The nearest I can achieve here is this Queen Anne. If the vandals had wanted to ruin furniture, there are a number of pieces in this house I could recommend to their attention. It offends me that this suite was the target, and it may be that it was purposefully chosen because of my liking for it. That is the sort of thing Lord Brackenheath might do, if the intrusion was arranged." She cocked her head to the side. "Is there something you aren't telling me?"

I hesitated. "Yes," I admitted after a moment.

She fixed her attention on me. "Not about . . . my friend? Nothing has happened to him? He is all right."

"As far as I know, he is well. No, my inquiry strikes closer to home. It is about Lord Brackenheath, actually," I said, and went to the sideboard. I wanted something to lean against since I could not sit down. I made myself as comfortable as I was able and then said, "How much do you know about your late husband's financial affairs?"

"Everything, I should say, since the whole of our money comes from my father and is in my control," she answered coolly. "Mister Gravesend is my man of business. He manages all the accounts, under my supervision. I will provide you his direction, if you wish it."

I had heard of Florian Gravesend—he had a formidable reputation for impeccable honesty and the ruthless advancement of his patrons—and found myself more convinced than ever that something had occurred outside the usual dealings of the Brackenheath household. "I know where Mister Gravesend has his offices," I assured her. "I will call upon him later today, if I may."

"Certainly," said Lady Brackenheath, her curiosity piqued. "I don't know what more I can tell you. Lord Brackenheath received a quarterly sum for himself, as agreed in our marriage settlements. I never asked how he spent it, for that only served to give him reason to complain of what he considered the inadequate amount of the . . . allowance."

"And what," I asked, determined to shock her into an incautious response, "of the ten thousand pounds recently deposited to him?"

"Ten thousand . . ." She started to laugh. "He would rejoice at a quarter of that. He would crow like a cock on a dungheap." Her laughter faded. "You are serious, aren't you? How can that be? Ten thousand pounds?"

"Deposited to your husband's account quite recently. In a single lump. The source so far is a mystery." I studied her response, looking for any trace of deception.

She shook her head decisively. "I don't believe it. Someone has been joking you," she said. "No one would entrust Lord Brackenheath with such an amount."

"Nevertheless, there is a deposit made to his account for that sum; we have seen the records of the transaction," I told her, hoping she would now give me her complete attention. "Mister Holmes is convinced that it is essential to discover the source of the money if any determination regarding his death is to be made." I did not want her to feel her position was not appreciated, so I added, "If making such inquiries is painful to you, then provide me the appropriate authorization and I will not bother you—"

But this was Herbert Bell's child, and she had no intentions of handing over the reins. "It bothers me only that Lord Brackenheath had found a new source of income, known or unknown," she said abruptly. "And now you are implying that the money may have bearing on his murder. Which smacks of blackmail, I must suppose. Heaven knows he might have tarnished many a reputation since his was beyond saving. And he was not one to flinch at such a despicable course." She frowned. "It would not be appropriate for me to call upon Mister Gravesend before my husband"—the word became an insult in her mouth—"is buried, so I will give you an authorization at once, provided you inform me of anything you may discover." The air of detachment was gone now. She sat straight in her chair, and her manner was animated. "Haggard will bring me paper, pen, and ink," she went on as she rose and tugged the bell-pull. "I am amazed to learn of this," she admitted as she went to the far corner of the room. "Is it possible the money was hidden in one of these chairs, and someone knew of it?"

"Possible, most certainly," I allowed, "but unlikely." I rubbed my chin where the bruise was darkest. "It is," I went on, giving her the benefit of Mycroft Holmes' speculations of the night before, "more probable that the break-in was arranged so that certain items could be removed without the nature of the trade being brought to light, and no one would ever suspect that the damage was done as part of a specific search, but would be thought to be the result of robbery and vandalism. But my employer is not convinced. That ten thousand paid for something. Mister Holmes opines that the men we surprised on our return the other night were here to collect their purchase. That they had made an earlier arrangement to find the sequestered item in a prearranged place, and were to make it appear that no one piece of furniture or item was their target."

"Not blackmail, then?" she asked, and glanced at the door as Haggard knocked. She motioned me to silence. "Come in, Haggard." She told him she wished her portable desk, reminding him, "All the writing materials in this room ended up on the floor."

"I will fetch it for you, M'lady," he said, and left us alone.

"I will want to have a word or two with Haggard, as well," I said.

"Ah?" She regarded me closely. "I will ask him to hold himself in readiness." She sighed a little, as if she had recalled something. "I will request that Mister Gravesend provide me with copies of everything he makes available to you, if that is not unacceptable to Mister Holmes."

"I should think he would be willing to have such an agreement." There was no reason I could think of why this would not be acceptable. I did not want to have Lady Brackenheath filled with second thoughts about this matter. "It may be that you will discover more than we do." She was experienced in the keeping of accounts and I was sure she would have the necessary tenacity to pursue even an unwelcome notion to its conclusion.

"I will do my best," she said, with a note of stern determination in her voice that I found at once reassuring and disquieting; I was quite certain she would continue her investigation long after ours was concluded if she was not satisfied with Mycroft Holmes' resolution of the matter.

"If you would like copies of the information we have, I will arrange for that to be brought to you after the funeral. I would not like to intrude on your sorrow." I had not the authority to do this, but I was certain that she would require it and that it would be advantageous for my employer to have her sharp eyes to review what we had found.

"Yes, and I thank you for your tact," she said, her determination increasing. "Yes, yes, please do that. I do not want to have to answer any more awkward questions than necessary." She continued, as much to herself as to me, "Either Mister Gravesend or I would seem to have grown most inexcusably lax. How very vexing, that Lord Brackenheath should have achieved such a . . . victory, and I know nothing about it."

"The sum was deposited anonymously, Lady Brackenheath,

and under very guarded circumstances. You are not to blame yourself or Mister Gravesend for his success at the ploy. In a month, the whole matter would have come to light, and you would then have been able to pursue the affair yourself, without any interference." I turned as Haggard once again entered the room, Lady Brackenheath's portable desk in his hands.

"Well," said Lady Brackenheath decisively, "you will want to be about your work quickly, Mister Guthrie. Thank you, Haggard. You may set it down on the table."

"That I will," said Haggard, and shot a quick glance in my direction. I surmised he wished to speak to me as much as I wanted to speak to him. He did not linger once he had carried out Lady Brackenheath's instructions, but left us alone again.

Lady Brackenheath sat in front of her portable desk and drew out crested paper, a pen, and her inkwell. She inspected the nib of the pen, then set to work. Her hand, I noticed, was upright and elegant, definitely feminine but firm. When she was done writing she blotted the page, then sealed the note in an envelope and put Mister Gravesend's name on it before handing it to me. "I have instructed him to lend you any assistance you might require, and to keep a full record of your dealings for me."

"That is satisfactory," I said, taking the envelope and putting it into my inner jacket pocket. "I thank you most sincerely for your help in this investigation. You have my word that your confidence will be respected."

"I hope so," she said bluntly. "I do not relish the thought of having my . . . privacy invaded by anyone, not even Mister Holmes." She held out her hand to me, and I bent over it, not quite touching her glove with my lips. "I will await the information you mentioned with a great deal of interest."

"Excellent," I said, and prepared to take my leave. "You have made my work easier than it would have been, and I thank you for it."

"Be about your business, Mister Guthrie," she said, waving me away.

As I emerged from the room, I found Haggard waiting at the foot of the stairs, doing his best not to appear anxious. I nodded to him as I descended. I still did not move as quickly as I wished to, but I made myself be careful, for the last thing I wanted now was a fresh injury.

"Mister Guthrie, if you will let me have a moment?" said Haggard as I reached him.

"Gladly," I said, "for I have a few questions I must put to you."

He indicated the corridor to the servants' part of the house. "If you will come with me?"

"You have only to lead the way," I assured him, and followed him down the passage to a room I took to be the servants' dining room. It was unoccupied just now, and I noticed that there was a cupboard against the far wall with plates lined up on it, mugs hanging from hooks above them.

"I wanted to tell you about something I remembered about Lord Brackenheath two nights before his death. Not," he added quickly, "that I wish to speak ill of the dead, but it may be that what I observed—"

"Good." I drew my notebook from my waistcoat, and my pencil, and opened it to a fresh page. "I will make a record of what you say, so that I will not have to rely on my faulty memory when I report to my employer."

Haggard was, in fact, uncertain about this arrangement, but he smiled in order to assure me of his good intentions. "If it's necessary." He stared away from me. "I must tell you that I did not admire Lord Brackenheath. I found his way of life improvident and immoral, so my remarks about him are of necessity biased."

"I thank you for being direct with me," I said. "Though I must say that I have found very few who thought well of him." I hoped this would ease his mind to some degree, and was rewarded with a slight smile for my efforts.

"Not surprising," said Haggard.

"What did you observe?" I prompted when Haggard did not continue.

He looked up at the ceiling. "It was quite late when his Lordship returned home, for he had gone from the Swiss embassy to a private club, and had remained there for some considerable time. It was nearer three than two when he came in."

"You had waited for him?" I inquired politely.

"Certainly," he said, nodding. "Many's the time I have been needed to pay off the jarvey for bringing Lord Brackenheath home." He gave a disgusted snort, then went on. "That night, however, he was driven in a private carriage. I went to admit him when I heard the wheels and horses in the street. And I . . . happened to overhear an exchange of remarks. They meant little to me at the time."

How often, I wondered, had Haggard eavesdropped on Lord Brackenheath, and what did he know of the man? I stilled my curiosity and kept to the matter at hand. "How much of that exchange do you remember?"

"Most of it, I should think," said Haggard. "It made little sense to me then. Now I begin to realize its import." He coughed once. "The other man with Lord Brackenheath was a foreigner, with an Eastern European face, wearing a cloak. He was not quite as tall as Lord Brackenheath, as I recall, but I had the impression he was younger. I did not recognize his accent, though I heard very little of it." He paused, as if in distress that he should have failed to identify the man's accent.

"No matter; it would be better to have no identification than to identify the accent incorrectly." I held up my pencil to show my readiness to continue.

Haggard made a single nod, then let himself withdraw into his thoughts. "He was wearing tasseled boots, that I remember." He offered this as a kind of compensation for his inability to identify the man's speech, and to condemn his taste. "Lord Brackenheath said that he would be ready to provide the promised copy once he had the ten thousand pounds. He was specific that the amount should be in pounds, not any other currency. At the time I thought they were discussing an outrageous wager."

"What changed your mind?" I asked, certain that a man of Lord Brackenheath's profligate habits might often discuss such amounts.

Haggard hesitated, as if concerned that he would betray Lady Brackenheath in revealing the character of her husband. "The man said the amount would be in pounds when he was satisfied the copy was in Lord Brackenheath's hands. His Lordship declared the fellow must think him a fool. 'For what's to stop you taking the copy and paying me not a farthing for my part?' he asked belligerently. The man promised the money would be deposited first thing the banks were open." He stared down at his feet. "He told the man he would hide the copy as they had agreed, and would expect the thing to be 'collected'—that was his word—while the gala was going on."

"They did not say what the copy was of?" I asked, having formed my own opinion of the matter. Given the timing and nature of his murder, it followed that the copy in question was of the Japano-British agreement. But how, I wondered, had Lord Brackenheath contrived to get his hands on a copy of the agreement when only four were made?

A clock in what I supposed was the kitchen chimed the hour—ten—and Haggard looked up. "I cannot remain long. There are duties. You understand."

"And I have duties, as well," I said, more than pleased at how this had turned out. I offered Haggard my hand and told him, "If we are able to avert any more scandal in this sad time, it will be due in no small part to what you have been willing to tell me. I thank you for what you have done." That was a slight exaggeration, but not so great a one as made me feel I was deceiving him.

"I am glad to be of service," said Haggard, escorting me out of the servants' dining room. "Anything to save Lady Brackenheath from more distress. She has endured enough from her husband. Let her be spared, now he's dead."

FROM THE JOURNAL OF PHILIP TYERS

Sutton continues feverish, but there is as yet no sign of infection, and the flesh, though damaged, has not developed any indication of fest ering. Dr. W returned a short time ago and pronounced himself satisfied at the progress Sutton has made. He promises to call again after tea.

M H has been gone for well over two hours, and has sent word back to me that he will not be back until two or three this afternoon. He has requested I be on guard for the watchers, for he has told his brother of the matter, and his brother has given his word to put his mudlarks on it at once. These watchers will be identified.

Miss Gatspy has taken a number of duties upon herself, and has left to call at the Austrian embassy, to discover what she can about Austro-Hungarian nationals currently in London. She thinks that with the knowledge of the Golden Lodge to aid her, she may discover names that might be significant in these developments.

There is another stranger delivering meat. This may be nothing worthy of my attention, or it may be important as breath. I cannot tell which, and so I will err on the side of caution, for it may be that he is up to some mischief other than watching this flat. If there is anything unwholesome in the meat he brings, I should learn of it at once, so that we will not bring death into the house all unknowingly. I will inquire of the servants in this building and a few of those nearby if they have noticed any increase in dead rats and alley cats, which might well indicate the presence of poison in the meat he brings.

Given Sutton's condition, he would not be helped by eating anything that is not as free from taint as is possible in London.

Chapter Twenty-six

"SO WHERE ARE we?" Mycroft Holmes demanded as we sat at the table in his sitting room. "You have the information from Florian Gravesend, I see."

"Yes, or lack of it. However that ten thousand was handled, it did not make its way through the standard Brackenheath accounts. The bank must have established a second one for him—their records provided do not differentiate." I held out copies of the documents in question. "These have complete transactions of the last year. Here are household salaries, here are household expenses, here is the allowance given Lord Brackenheath, here are his payments for clothes, travel, horses and carriages. Here are Lady Brackenheath's personal expenses, which I know were kept in a separate account. She maintained a close watch on the monies spent. Gravesend said as much. He also said that his Lordship resented her for doing it: Apparently he had assumed she had no experience of business and would be willing to be ruled by him once her father died." I gave Holmes another several pages. "And here are the records of their investments. As you see, no sign of the ten thousand pounds." I averted my face somewhat, for my bruise was turning green with yellow at the edges and I knew it was not a splendid sight; I did not want to subject others to what made me wince.

"Then without doubt Lord Brackenheath maintained a separate account, contrary to his marriage contract. Possibly one he had from the time of his first marriage. Or he established it during his widowed years and decided not to make its existence known. Not unexpected, but quite interesting," said Holmes as he began to play with his watchfob. "I wonder if I have been a complete fool in this?"

"You, sir?" I asked, shocked at the very suggestion, even coming from him.

His smile was wry. "Thank you, Guthrie. You restore my confidence." He returned to twiddling the watchfob and staring off as if caught half-asleep. "It did not occur to me until earlier today that Lord Brackenheath might be party to his own destruction. I had assumed he was an unsavory-but-hapless victim of others. Now I begin to think he—" He broke off as there was a rap on the door.

Tyers informed us that a message had come from Holmes' brother. "It may be urgent," he said, and handed it in, adding as he did that "Sutton has wakened."

"How is he?" Holmes demanded as I gave the note to him.

"Weak and in pain, but still without any indication of infection" was Tyers' welcome answer. "I am going to make him a strengthening broth."

"Very good, very good. Tell him, if you will, that I will come to see him directly I have finished this business with Guthrie." He then opened the note and read it, not once, but twice. "The poor chap's wandering again," he murmured, with that air of self-condemnation that infused all his dealings with his brother. He folded the note and shook off his melancholy. "Still, this is more useful intelligence than I dared hope for."

"What is it?" I asked when he did not impart the intelligence to me at once.

He sighed. "It would seem that Franz Joseph is more interested in this agreement than he has indicated in the past. His men are part of the group of watchers, at least according to my brother's urchins." He cleared his throat. "I doubt we'll be able to demand an explanation from their embassy, for if the ambassador is aware of this, you may call me a Dutchman."

"But why?" I asked, and tried to clarify my question. "What would so secret an observation gain them?"

"Secrecy, of course," said Holmes with a bland sort of smile.

"Of course," I agreed, letting my sarcasm be heard as all the frustrations and demands of the last day caught up with me in a rush. "How should I think otherwise?" I regarded him seriously. "If there is something you would prefer not to tell me, well and good, but pray do not address me as if I were an impertinent child."

Holmes glanced at me in some shock. "Why, Guthrie. I meant no offense."

"If you tell me so, then I must believe it," I said, doing a poor job of masking my temper. Then I regained my composure. I coughed once. "If there were not so great a potential for disaster as is present in this case, I would be less distressed than I am."

"No doubt. We all would," said Holmes, rubbing his chin and putting his watchfob back into his waistcoat pocket. "I did not mean to exclude you, Guthrie. It is a habit I acquired long since, and it reappears at inconvenient times." He held out his long hand to me. "Be a good fellow and excuse my ill-manners. You were right, you know. I did address you in a most inappropriate way, given what you have done for me in the time you have been in my employ."

Reluctantly I took his hand, feeling foolish. "I should not have been so hot off the mark."

"Better you should be so with me than with . . . oh, Inspector FitzGerald, for example. Or your Miss Gatspy." His heavy brows arched quizzically.

"She isn't *my* Miss Gatspy," I corrected him wearily, and attempted to return our discussion to more profitable channels. "About these records?"

He was all attention once again. "I will examine them for the next half hour, and then you may return them to Mister Gravesend, with my thanks." He chuckled at my look of surprise. "I know you are not expecting this of me. But I am aware of how sensitive Gravesend's position is and I have no wish to compromise him any more than absolutely necessary for the good of England."

"Certainly," I said, trying not to appear too confused. "I will take care of it as soon as you give me the office to do so."

" 'Stay not upon the order of your going,' " Holmes quoted, and then added, with an expression of chagrin, "Edmund would tell you it is bad luck to quote *Macbeth.*"

I heard this with concern. "I hope he continues to improve."

"And I," said Holmes with feeling. "Watson will be by this evening and will report to me on his progress." He reached for his watchfob. "I am still not satisfied about the circumstances of his . . . injury. The man who shot him will pay for his act."

I had rarely heard Holmes speak with such intense purpose. I looked down at my feet and sought for an expression that would reveal my respect for his dedication to Edmund Sutton. "I am certain you will accomplish it, sir," I said.

"Well," he said, making an effort to speak more lightly, "I suppose you will want me to get about this work. You will find a list of military men posted to the Austro-Hungarian embassy. I want you to look it over while I review these accounts."

I could not imagine what it was I should look for, and I was about to say as much to Holmes when I realized he had already put his attention onto the pages provided by Florian Gravesend. I took the list and for the next forty minutes I read the names and basic information on the Austro-Hungarians, having no notion of what I should seek to find.

"Ah!" Mycroft Holmes announced as he gathered the banking records into a neat stack. "I think I know how to begin at last."

"And where might that be?" I asked, relieved to be able to put down the sheets I had been given.

"I don't wish to offend you, Guthrie, but for the moment it is best if you do not know." He bent forward and wrote a hasty note on a sheet of paper that bore his name. "If you will be good enough to carry this to a Mister Tschersky at the Russian embassy after you return these records to Mister Gravesend, I would be most appreciative." He sealed the note and handed it to me. "It must be given to Mister Tschersky in person. He has a password to give you, and you have a countersign. He will ask if you are Robertson. You will give your name and the position you hold with me, and then you will add that Robertson is in Paris. It will not be easy to speak with Yugeny Tschersky. You will have to be very firm, for the Russians are generally suspicious of foreigners."

"I will," I said, and took the materials he handed me, and slipping them into my portfolio, I withdrew only to find Tyers waiting in the corridor.

"Just thought you should be aware, sir," he said to me in his steady way, "the Admiralty have sent guards to watch this place. They should not cause you any difficulty, but if they do, refer them to me."

"These are men in uniform?" I asked.

"Some are" was his oblique reply, and he volunteered nothing more.

"But surely such guards bring unwelcome attention to this place," I remarked, thinking it was strange that there should be such a public display.

"It must be thought that it is Mister Holmes who was wounded, not Mister Sutton," he explained gently.

I considered this as I went to the front of the flat and let myself out. I went down the stairs to the front door, my steps brisker and more confident than they had been since my ankle was sprained. As I emerged onto the street, I noticed two men in the uniform of naval officers standing conspicuously at the edge of the road. They were most certainly the guards Tyers had mentioned. I watched them for several seconds and decided that they were too obvious to be the real protection for Holmes.

Sid Hastings came up, his cab drawing to the kerb smartly. "Where to, Mister Guthrie?" he asked.

"What about going back to Mister Gravesend? That's to be our first stop." I sighed, thinking that Sid Hastings must be heartily bored with driving to the same places. "I have some material to return to him. And then we must go to the Russian embassy."

"For Mister Holmes, is it? The Russians have a part in this

coil, too, do they?" said Hastings, expecting no answer as he set his vehicle in motion.

I could not help but pay attention to the traffic as we made our way down the street. I kept wondering who was watching me, if anyone was watching me, and why they were watching. I had once before been prey to such anxiety, in Greece, in January. At the time it had seemed reasonable to me to harbor such fears. I welcomed the sense of impending danger to keep me on my mettle. But now, in London, sane, sensible London, to be so afflicted . . . It was a terrible feeling, and one that I feared might be dangerous. I sat back in the cab and did my best not to find staring eyes everywhere.

We arrived twenty minutes later at a modern building of the Gothic revival style, made of pink sandstone. The entry was very grand, through a pointed archway into a courtyard that was paved in slate. Around the courtyard the walls of the building shimmered with windows.

Florian Gravesend himself, resplendent in a superbly tailored frock coat of deepest grey, came to the front of his suite and took the copies from me, saying as he did, "I am going to call upon Lady Brackenheath this evening, to show her what we have seen. It is essential she be apprised of these developments promptly. She has already had a note from me regarding the ten thousand. I cannot anticipate what she will say when she learns the whole of this business, but she cannot remain ignorant of it."

"No, I should think not," I agreed. "She will have to decide how she is to present this information to the authorities."

"Oh," said Gravesend, affronted at the suggestion, "I don't think it need come to that."

"It may," I said, concealing the certainty that possessed me. "Given the nature of his death, Lord Brackenheath is exercising a great deal of public speculation. Or haven't you read the paper this morning? Not the *Times,*" I added.

"I don't bother with any of the rest," said Gravesend haughtily. He wanted to be rid of me.

"One more thing," I said. "Do you happen to recall if the deposit was actually made in pounds? Or was some other currency—"

"That was my first concern," Gravesend told me. "The amount was in pounds. I would have questioned it before now if it had required conversion."

"Of course," I told him, and removed myself from his presence.

The journey to the Russian embassy took rather less time than the one to Mister Gravesend's establishment. The building was in a side-street, not too far from the grander French embassy. I recognized the uniforms of the Grodno Hussars on the guards at the entrance, but not the officer I had seen at the Swiss embassy, whom Miss Gatspy had said was Hungarian. I got down from the cab and presented myself to the senior guard and informed him I had a personal message to Mister Tschersky which I was under orders to deliver by hand.

"I will see he gets it," said the senior officer, his English quite good but obviously foreign.

"I'm sorry; I didn't make myself wholly understood," I said with as much patience as I could muster, realizing that challenging them would lead to more resistance than I had already encountered. "I have been instructed by my employer to give this to Mister Tschersky himself, and no other."

This caused a level of consternation among the guards that I had not expected, and I feared they would refuse to permit me to enter the building. After a whispered discussion with an embassy functionary, two of the Hussars held me not quite at gunpoint while the functionary scuttled into the building, apparently in search of advice, or possibly, Mister Tschersky.

Behind me, Sid Hastings held Jenny still, and took the opportunity to light up his churchwarden's pipe. The guards kept watch over me, but stood at their ease. I hoped this did not presage a long delay.

Ten minutes passed before a man of more than moderate height, well-set-up, with a long head and narrow jaw emerged from the Russian embassy. His features had a distinctly Oriental cast to them, though his deep-bronze hair was curly, as was his neat moustache. He was unobtrusively well-dressed, and his voice, when he spoke, had an odd timbre to it, reminiscent of spices. He came up to me, extending his hand. "Good day to you. I am Yugeny Tschersky. Are you Robertson? I am informed you want to speak to me?"

"Yes," I said. "I am Paterson Guthrie, personal secretary to Mycroft Holmes. Robertson is in Paris. So Holmes has commissioned me to bring a letter from him to you."

The mention of Holmes' name had an effect upon Tschersky, who stared hard at me, glanced at the envelope in my hand, and then back at me. His hand, when it finally closed on mine, was firm and I could feel strength in his grip. "Mycroft Holmes," he said. "You are either a most fortunate or most unlucky man. Judging from your face, it may be the latter." He regarded me with interest as he took the envelope. "I would be happy to offer you my credentials, but, as you are undoubtedly aware, they are in the Russian alphabet and it is unlikely you could read them."

"I am sorry to tell you, you are correct," I said, thinking I would be wise to remedy this in the near future.

"A note from Mycroft Holmes," he mused, staring down at the seal. "How, I wonder, does he expect me to deal with this?"

"Until you read it, you will not be able to decide," I pointed out, startled that he should be so ambivalent about the missive.

"True enough. But it is my experience that in matters concerning Mister Holmes, there is much uncertainty, and once in his toils, it is no easy thing to get out."

"That may be so," I said, more ruefully than I intended.

Tschersky smiled suddenly. "As I need not tell you." He held up the envelope. "Tell Mycroft Holmes I have his note and I will respond to it as quickly as possible, for undoubtedly he wants the information immediately."

"Yes," I said, though I did not know what the note contained.

"I will thank you now, Mister Guthrie, for once I know what Mister Holmes wants me to do, I may have less charitable thoughts about you." With that he offered me a mock salute, turned on his heel and went back into the Russian embassy.

"Odd lot, the Russians," said Sid Hastings as he set his pipe aside and prepared to drive me back to Holmes' flat in Pall Mall.

I climbed into the cab and did my best to settle back for the ride.

FROM THE JOURNAL OF PHILIP TYERS

Sutton has been more feverish this afternoon, but Watson warned us that this was likely. There is nothing in a slight rise in fever to cause serious alarm, I am told, given there is no indication of infection. Sutton is weak but not failing. I have been able to give him some restoring mutton broth and lemonade, both of which Watson recommends. If Sutton continues to fight off infection, there is every reason to hope he will shortly be on the mend.

A note was delivered from M H's club expressing concern for his condition and assuring him he would be missed during his recuperation. I have sent a note back, following M H's instructions, informing the members of the club that it will be a few days before M H resumes his regular visits.

G returned a half hour since from the errands M H sent him upon, which he has dispatched to M H's satisfaction. G arrived hard on the heels of the Admiralty messenger, who brought another packet of records to M H. This makes three separate deliveries in one day, and I suspect it is not the last, and not limited to the Admiralty.

M H will be away from the flat this evening, having arranged a meeting with Ambassador Tochigi for the purpose of assessing the information he has garnered thus far. I have also been told to expect Miss Gatspy shortly, to take tea with him and G.

Chapter Twenty-seven

"NOT BAD FOR for a man who just had a bullet taken out of him," said Inspector FitzGerald as Tyers reluctantly led him into Mycroft Holmes' sitting room. "Where did you say you were hit?"

If FitzGerald had wanted to see Holmes nonplussed, he was disappointed: Holmes swung around and said with no trace of distress or dismay. "What an unexpected pleasure, Inspector." He put special emphasis on *unexpected.* "Do come in and have a cup with us. And something to eat. You must be getting peckish." He gestured to Miss Gatspy and me. "We'll be pleased of your company."

Inspector FitzGerald hesitated, clearly torn between his desire for conversation and his sense that this was not the opportunity he had hoped for. At last he shrugged. "Why not? I might learn something."

"So you might," Holmes agreed, and called out to Tyers. "Inspector FitzGerald is joining us. Will you bring another cup?"

"And the second pot," said Tyers, and set about it.

Holmes nodded to me, prepared to do his duty as host. "You know Guthrie, but I don't believe you have met Miss Gatspy. Miss Gatspy, this is Inspector FitzGerald."

"Charmed," he said, taking her extended hand. His eyes narrowed as he looked at her face. "But I have seen you before."

"Why, how gracious of you, Inspector," she said, on her very best behavior. "I have sometimes served as a translator at various embassies. With so much to demand your attention, what can I be but complimented that you recall me?" Her smile was winsome, her manner guileless.

I half-rose and held out my hand to Inspector FitzGerald. "How go your inquiries, FitzGerald?"

He shook my hand perfunctorily. "It is most perplexing, and not just because it is the very devil to get answers from those who might be thought of as suspects." He was growling as he pulled up a chair and sat down beside the large table where tea was laid. "I can't get most of them to talk to me. They withdraw into their embassies and no one can touch them. The rest tell me that they are not at liberty to discuss any aspect of Lord Brackenheath's role in the negotiations, though it is apparent he did not approve of it at all, if what I've been able to discover is correct."

"I think it is fair to say that he did not like our dealing with the Japanese," said Holmes calmly. "His inclusion was the work of the Prime Minister, who was eager to have all positions represented during our discussions."

"Which, I suspect, was more for show than any true dealings." Inspector FitzGerald gave a shrewd glance toward Holmes. "If we should be discussing this at all?"

"If you mean Miss Gatspy," said Holmes in the same unperturbable way, "I would suppose she knows more of the goings-on in embassies than anyone but the footmen." He refused to be provoked. "You may say what you like in front of her. She is in no position to compromise the agreement at this point, no matter what you may say to me."

I was certain I detected a warning to her in that statement, and so I added, "And as a woman working in the capacity as translator, you may be sure she is discreet."

She looked at me. "Why, thank you, Guthrie."

Holmes paid no attention. "No need, then, for roundaboutation, as my mother would have said. What is it you are seeking to find out, FitzGerald? For you did not come here for either the fare or the company. And you did not expect me to be laid out upon my bed with physicians hovering around me." Holmes sat straighter in his chair as Tyers brought a cup-and-saucer and a second pot of tea into the sitting room.

"I am seeking to find out who killed Lord Brackenheath. I would also like to know why he was killed, and if it is indicative of anything more to come." He sounded exasperated but not angry. "But my hands are tied by our government, the Swiss government, the Japanese government, and I can get nothing from the Germans, the Austro-Hungarians, or the Russians, though we know they have been sending dispatches thick as autumn leaves." He put his big hands on his knees. "What can half-a-dozen English policemen do against such massed forces as all of that?"

"You can come to me," said Holmes cordially, lifting the teapot and filling FitzGerald's cup. "And quite sensible of you, too."

Now FitzGerald seemed confused as he took the tea Holmes poured for him. "But you are one of those who is making my path difficult."

"Not out of any desire to protect those who did the killing, I assure you," said Holmes quite seriously. "I have no wish to see Lord Brackenheath's murderer go unpunished. But I would rather we root up the whole of the plant than chop off a single limb." He put his fingertips together. "And it is possible we will learn something shortly."

"How shortly?" FitzGerald demanded. "If the murderer is a foreigner, he could escape our justice handily. He need only go to a ship in the harbor and be out of our grasp."

"I doubt that will happen," Holmes soothed him mendaciously, for this was precisely the thing Holmes himself feared.

"That, Mister Holmes, does not console me." He put his cup aside, rubbed his hands together, then reached for the milk jug. "Just as it does not please me to learn you, yourself, have been shot."

I suppose this was meant to jar a comment out of Holmes, but, given FitzGerald's opening sally, it failed to do more than evoke a faint chuckle. "It is just as well that most people caught up in these events should believe it is so."

"To mask your various efforts, is that it?" challenged FitzGerald.

"Of course. In order to prevent just such an escape as the one you fear. If those behind this plot are convinced they need not deal with me, then there is a chance something might be done to apprehend them before more mischief can occur." Holmes had the expression of one contemplating a battlefield where casualties lay.

"Can it be so critical?" FitzGerald protested.

"Yes, indeed. We are gambling for very high stakes, and they continue to rise. This entire farrago has been calculated to destroy the burgeoning alliances between East and West, and without very careful strategy on our part, might still succeed. Then we should have to say good-bye to holding India, for Russia and China should both prey upon it. This would lead to danger for Australia and New Zealand, as well as our lesser Pacific holdings. Once that was lost, we might well have trouble in Africa. England would have her forces divided and in distant parts of the world, so should trouble erupt in Europe—and you may be sure it would—we would be unable to go to the help of our allies. And Franz Joseph would have his dream fulfilled."

"Do not suppose that Mister Holmes is being too pessimistic," said Miss Gatspy when Holmes was silent. "I have discovered many things in my work, and I can assure you that there could be such an unwelcome end to this case."

"The murder of a rakehell peer, bring about the total breakdown of all dealings between East and West?" FitzGerald did his best to appear gallant. "If you don't mind my saying so, Miss, many of the fair sex do not grasp the complexity of these matters. No doubt it all sounds very dramatic to you and—"

He got no farther. Penelope Gatspy was sitting upright, a flush spreading over her fair skin. "Empires have fallen for less." She continued with great precision, every word bitten as she spoke. "My dear Inspector FitzGerald, you do not appreciate my comprehension of the problem confronting us, or the potential for harm it represents. I am not some frippery girl, to think devastation and calamity makes for excitement. Nor am I of a romantic disposition, for I can discover nothing uplifting in men going to war. I see nothing noble or heroic in thousands of men slain and the countryside in ruin. I find that tragic. I deplore its very existence. And I hope that in some small way, what I do can lessen the chances of such catastrophe." She glared at him.

"Through translations?" said Inspector FitzGerald in some confusion.

She recovered herself nicely. "If nations have greater mutual understanding, it is my hope that they will not be so eager to make war."

"She has said it better than I could," Holmes told the Inspector soberly, though he reserved a quick smile for Miss Gatspy.

"Yes. Brava," I chimed in, feeling idiotic, but agreeing with her wholeheartedly.

"Listen to her, Inspector. She has more perception than you credit her with." Holmes offered the basket of muffins, saying as he did, "Rest assured, I have every determination to learn the whole of what transpired to bring about Lord Brackenheath's death. And not just for the sake of his family, or the good name of Scotland Yard."

"I don't know what to make of all this," Inspector FitzGerald admitted. "It would seem I am out of my depth."

"So it would," said Holmes with as genial a smile as I have ever seen from him.

"But I have an obligation to the law, Mister Holmes, and as I respect you for your dedication, so you must respect me for mine. I cannot step away from this case because it may be inconvenient for the Admiralty and the Prime Minister, without specific instructions from the Crown. I have my duty to perform as well as the rest of you." He sat so rigidly then that I had a fleeting impression that he was studying to be cast in stone.

"Do as you must, Inspector. As I have told you, I have no wish to compromise your inquiries. But I have obligations, too, and I must adhere to them as you do to yours." Holmes took one of the French pastries off the small platter. He bit into it with such force that some of the raspberry filling oozed out around the corners of his mouth, giving an impression of blood.

Inspector FitzGerald put clotted cream on his muffin and

took a bite, which provided an excellent excuse for him to say nothing more.

We finished tea in silence, and only after the Inspector had taken his leave did Holmes say to Miss Gatspy and me, "I am placing my hopes on Tschersky, and his fundamental grasp of the situation. If he cannot or will not help us, or if he has placed his trust in others, then I am very much convinced we will—" He did not go on.

"Your brother might turn up something," I said, by way of offering encouragement to my employer.

Holmes shook his head. "I am afraid not," he said, very seriously. "Watson has informed me that my brother is once again seeking the intoxication of cocaine. He will not be weaned from it, not for long. He claims it cures his boredom."

"But surely, with such a case as this, he would not—" I began, only to be quelled by Holmes' sharp look.

"In these circumstances, it is enough that he has set his urchins on watch for us. The boys are very adept at their work." He would allow no other discussion of his brother, of this I was acutely aware.

"Then you should have an answer from them in short order," I said, wanting to know more than we had been told.

"Yes. And with Mister Tschersky's intelligence we should be able to put the puzzle in order." He came near to looking satisfied, and then said with unusual vigor, "In the meantime, I need you to go to Lady Brackenheath again. I know," he went on, "it is not the time you would choose, nor would I if I had the opportunity to select the occasion. But it is most necessary. I wish to learn if Lord Brackenheath knew either of the secretaries sent to copy the documents. The English secretaries," he added with feeling.

I was startled at this, and said, "But surely a note sent round would be preferable. With the funeral and all—"

"A note cannot make observations or ask questions. I rely

upon you to be my ears and eyes." He sighed. "The alternative is to summon her here, but that would not be very wise, would it?"

"I suppose not," I conceded, and nodded. "Very well, I will go to call upon Lady Brackenheath and discover, if she knows, if Lord Brackenheath was acquainted with either Mister Wright or Mister Hackett."

"It may be that one of those two men began their training with Herbert Bell, for he employed dozens of clerks. If you can, get the records of employees of Bell's manufactory, to determine if either Hackett or Wright ever worked for him. Or a brother, cousin, or father. It is important that we discover this link—if it exists—as soon as possible."

Making a gesture of resignation, I rose to my feet. "I will be on my way directly." I glanced at the windows and noticed the fading glories of sunset. "I hope I shall not intrude on their evening sherry."

Penelope Gatspy set her cup aside. "I will come with you," she announced.

"No," Holmes said in a firm voice. "You will do me the honor of staying here, and lending me your aid in reviewing the last of the records delivered to me this afternoon. I need your eyes, Miss Gatspy, to detect what we might have missed."

"You mean the records of money transfers to the embassies?" She inquired. "How *do* you get your hands on these fascinating documents, and so quickly?"

Holmes wagged a finger at her. "Miss Gatspy, you ought to know me well enough by now to realize that is a question I am not at liberty to answer."

I went into the hall and took my coat, muffler, and hat from the rack near the entry. Even in the dim light, the brass urns glowed, the Arabic script around the mouths of them seeming to have movement in their shape; I wondered if our writing looked as strange to Arabs as their writing did to me. I let myself out of the flat and descended to the street, pleased that my ankle did little more than ache as I went.

An unfamiliar jarvey was driving the cab drawn by a piebald bay that pulled up for me, and I looked up in surprise, faltering.

"Sid Hastings sent me," said the jarvey. "He's called away to tend to his boy Matthew. Broke his wrist, the lad did, falling off a fence. Sid told me to pick you up."

"And how did you know me?" I asked, feeling suspicious.

"Why, Sid pointed out the address and said as you was a cove with a bruise the size of a beef chop, just turning to green. You come down the stairs from the address I was told, and half your face looks like old Stilton. Who else would you be but Mister Guthrie?" He made an impatient gesture with his whip. "You getting in, then?"

Reluctantly, I climbed into the cab and pulled the panel shut, all the while keeping a careful watch on passers-by. I chided myself for being too cautious as I gave him Lady Brackenheath's direction.

There were a number of carriages pulled up near the Brackenheath's town house, and as I got out of the cab, I told the jarvey to drive around the block to find a place to wait, for surely he could not do it here without impeding the flow of traffic in the street.

"How long will you be?" asked Sid Hastings's deputy.

"No more than half an hour," I said, confident that if I could not have a word with Lady Brackenheath in that time, I would not be able to secure a moment with her until tomorrow.

Haggard admitted me, a hint of alarm in his impassive face as he recognized me. "Mister Guthrie." He glanced over his shoulder to the stairs leading up to the first floor, and kept his voice low as he spoke to me, unwilling to announce my presence in any way. "If it is Lady Brackenheath you wish to see, it is not convenient just at present. She is receiving the condolences of Lord Brackenheath's mourners."

"Not all of them," I said, in what I hoped was sudden inspiration, "for I would conjecture he had companions you would not admit to this house."

"True enough," he said, taking my meaning at once.

"And not all of them ladybirds or roisterers," I prompted, and fell silent, encouraging him to talk.

"Not by half," said Haggard, finally indicating the corridor to the servants' quarters. He wore the look of a small boy apprehended with pockets full of sweet biscuits. "Best come with me, sir, if I take the purpose of your visit."

"And you think that might be—" I got no farther.

"I think you suppose Lord Brackenheath was not wholly innocent in his own demise." He favored me with a single, decisive nod. "And I have begun to think so, as well. He had recently taken up some dashed queer associates. Not his usual thing at all, not gamblers and rakes, but something more . . . more deliberate. These weren't flash coves, bent on debauch, but men with that shine in the eyes, if you take my meaning? like they was following a vision." He saw one of the chambermaids coming toward him, and discreetly held his tongue until the woman was past. "He had taken to attending meetings. He had been doing this for more than a month, though I thought at first he would tire of it quickly. On two separate occasions his Lordship brought men to this house such as I have never before opened the door to. I was very much shocked when I was informed that these men were his trusted companions, and to receive every courtesy."

I sensed that Haggard's indignation was still fresh, and so I decided to take advantage of it. "Do you recall anything you can tell me about these men."

"They weren't true gentlemen, and that's a fact. I wouldn't say they were rum, in the usual way. But not the sort you'd expect even a man of Lord Brackenheath's questionable character to encourage." He stared up at the ceiling as if the presence of these men lingered as an unrelenting insult to the household. "I was pleased that Lady Brackenheath never saw those men. She was away on a visit."

I had a fairly good notion who it was she saw, but I kept my thoughts to myself. "On both occasions?"

"It was the same occasion," said Haggard. "The men visited this house at a three-day interval, coming just after Lady Brackenheath left, and having their second visit shortly before she returned." He coughed for punctuation. "I thought this was more than his usual disregard for Lady Brackenheath. It seemed to me that his Lordship did not wish Lady Brackenheath to discover what company he kept."

"And why was that? What was it about them that so troubles you?" It occurred to me I was listening to the gossip of servants again, but I could not make myself believe it was ignorant or idle.

"They all had a very poor demeanor. I was much struck by it at the time of their first visit. Lord Brackenheath often kept company with break-of-day boys, but not with such commoners as these." He frowned as he strove to find a way to make his reservations more comprehensible. "Two of them had the manners of clerks, with threadbare coats and greasy hair, and not too nice in their grooming. They were the more strident in their speaking. The other two were neater and quieter, in conservative coats of better cut, apparently because they were the leaders. They spoke with public school accents. They all had the same fixed look about them, as one sees in certain fanatics." Again he thought about his answer. "They were forever muttering about the danger white men faced in the East."

Remembering the reprehensible conduct of Lord Brackenheath with the Japanese, and how Mister Minato had been loath to speak of it, I could not be entirely surprised. "These men all shared his views, I take it," I said.

"And more," confirmed Haggard. "He—that is, Lord Brackenheath—had promised to support their interests, though I have never known him to support any but his own. It may be that he was as determined to put these men at a disadvantage as he was to bring Lady Brackenheath to shame." He rubbed his jaw, his only outward sign of discomfort. "I am not like those who suppose the Orientals are so inferior that they cannot be thought quite human, as many do, for they have achieved a civilization all their own, and I have been told it is older than any we have had in England. I do not love them, either, but I have met a few of the Chinese merchants Mister Bell did business with, and I knew he had respect for them and held them in high regard as clever, industrious, and honest. And never did I hear him disparage the race as a lot of filthy opium eaters, as Lord Brackenheath has." He stopped unsteadily.

"I take it you are concerned that some of what these men wished Lord Brackenheath to do for them was disrupt the negotiations for the naval agreement. And that he was willing to undertake the task." I did not have as much time as I wished to make it easier for Haggard to unburden himself.

"That was a part of it. But he—Lord Brackenheath—spoke to a foreign gentleman after his second meeting with these men, and he took great satisfaction in boasting to this fellow that his patriotism would gain him the freedom he wanted."

"Was this the same foreign gentleman you mentioned to me on my previous visit?" How very like a good butler, I thought, to tell only as much as he supposed was necessary for the best interests of his employers.

"No. But I had the impression they were part of the same whole. The man who came here may well have been an intermediary, sent to ascertain the situation, and then the other one, in the carriage, sealed their bargain, whatever it was."

"Why did you say nothing of this before, Haggard?" I asked,

although I guessed the answer. "Surely you were aware it might have a bearing on his death?"

He looked away from me to an empty place on the far wall. "I didn't think it was called for, Mister Guthrie."

A reprimand would be useless and inappropriate coming from me. I did my best to take this with good grace. "I might have thought so, too, in your position."

He accepted this with obvious relief. "Thank you, sir. It was not my intention to mislead you in any particular. I realize now I should have imparted the whole to you earlier, but—" He held up his hand. "I may have something that will help." With that he motioned me to remain where I was while he vanished into the rooms beyond, only to emerge a few minutes later clutching something in his hand. "The strange men I spoke of? The last night they were here, one of them dropped this pamphlet. I . . . removed it from the salon." He held it out to me as a token offering of apology.

I read the title of the work and the breath all but stopped in my throat. I took the pamphlet as if I thought it might burst into flame. It was about two dozen sheets poorly printed on bad paper and it boasted a lurid illustration of a man in Oriental robes bending over a swooning English lass in a posture that Edmund Sutton would probably describe as comedic. But for all the tawdry appearance of the thing, its intent could well have been wrought in iron.

THE DANGER FROM THE EAST

A warning to all true Englishmen of the menace from the East and the seduction of Orientalism by Jeremiah Hackett an Englishmen raised in China and Japan

"I hope it will help, sir," said Haggard.

FROM THE JOURNAL OF PHILIP TYERS

A messenger has just arrived from Mister Tschersky of the Russian embassy, and M H has taken it to his study to read privately. Miss Gatspy remains in the sitting room with the various banking records being reviewed.

G is expected back directly, and then, according to M H the whole will be made clear, for he is convinced he will then be able to determine what purpose Lord Brackenheath's death was meant to serve. How he can be so confident of this I cannot tell, but in all the years I have known him, I have only once heard him make such an announcement and have it not turn out as he declared.

Sutton has improved enough to want something to eat, which is most encouraging. I have, in accordance with Dr. W's instructions, prepared a sirloin of beef, and will give him a glass of port when he is done. W says that such a restoring regimen should have Sutton back on his feet in a week at most. Sutton is not as confident as the Doctor is. He complains of pain and weakness, but his voice is stronger and he no longer has the air of one who has looked upon the world for the last time, which is most satisfactory.

Chapter Twenty-eight

"WHY DIDN'T HE give this to the police?" Holmes mused aloud as he flipped through the pages of the pamphlet.

"Embarrassment, I suspect, and an inherent desire to control the extent of the scandal," I said, having thought the matter over at some length on the way back to Holmes' flat in the cab. "Not just for Lady Brackenheath, but for the whole establishment. He does his utmost to protect the whole."

"I take it you've read it?" said Holmes, slapping the pamphlet against the palm of his left hand.

"A bit. Not the whole of it. I take it it is all on the same note." What had impressed me the most was the odd assumption on Hackett's part that the whole of the East existed only to make life miserable for the West, that the East had no goals of its own but to thwart ours. I imagined that Hackett's youth in the Orient must have been ghastly for him.

"Repulsive claptrap, isn't it?" he asked of the air. "This part about the ritual flogging of samurai warriors: What on earth was he thinking of? He lived there, and he should have known—" He tossed the pamphlet aside. "So now we know where the rot is in our establishment. We must now discover precisely what it is that Hackett was supposed to do, or may have done, to harm the negotiations. Let us hope he is as proud of his actions as he is of his writing. And someone will have to explain to my satisfaction," he went on with icy purpose, "how it happens that a man of such extreme public opinions has come to hold a post of high confidence in the government."

I felt a kind of pity for the functionary who had permitted Jeremiah Hackett to be employed in this work, for Mycroft Holmes' wrath was formidable. Then I had a second, less compassionate thought—suppose the man who had hired Hackett had done it for the express purpose of putting forward the plan to end the negotiations, that it was not accidental lack of prudence but deliberate sabotage? That possibility was most disquieting. I made an involuntary gesture of repulsion, and was only mildly surprised when Holmes took my meaning and responded as if I had spoken aloud.

"Yes, I concur. It is never welcome to think ill of those who are supposed to do our bidding, and share our interests. But history is filled with betrayals, with those who gnawed away from the heart of the state to bring it down." Holmes came and sat down at the sitting room table. "This, with the intelligence provided by Yvgeny Tschersky, makes it possible to resolve the whole matter with dispatch and—"

"You cannot have the whole of it," I protested.

He ducked his head, a sign of concession. "Not everything, no. I do not know precisely who killed Lord Brackenheath, but I am now certain *why* he was killed, and once I have determined what Lord Brackenheath's plans were when he was killed, I am fairly certain the perpetrator will become obvious." He pointed to an envelope bearing the double-headed eagle of Russia. "Yvgeny Tschersky has provided the most significant information."

"The Grodno Hussar," I said, confident that was the matter to hand. "He has been identified."

"The Grodno Hussar," he confirmed. "Who is not, as your Miss Gatspy told us from the first, either Russian or a Grodno Hussar." He noticed the pained look on my face. "Yes, very well," he interjected impatiently. "She is not *your* Miss Gatspy. But she was correct in her information from the first."

"She said the man is Hungarian," I reminded him.

"And so he is. According to the information Tschersky has provided, he is Lajos Pecs, a younger son in a minor noble house. He has gone out to make his way in the world, and, as you can see, he has achieved some success." His heavy brows raised. "Well, would you not say he has done well?"

"At what? At passing for a Russian? Evidently not," I said, my bafflement coming out in the manner of a challenge, "for we have discovered his ruse in short order."

"Yes, we have. But only because we looked for him, and had been given a timely warning as to his true allegiance. The deception was a very clever one, as this whole affair has been." Holmes was somber now, his profound grey eyes seeming to darken as he went on. "If we had not had Miss Gatspy to aid us, it might have been two or three days more before I sought out Yvgeny Tschersky, and then the damage would be done." He lifted one hand to show his opinion of the peculiarities of the fate he did not believe in.

"But we were spared that misfortune," I said for him.

"So we were. Your Miss Gatspy is a woman to reckon with." Holmes smiled deliberately.

"That she is," I said, capitulating. He could not—or would not—stop tweaking me about Miss Gatspy, and my annoyance only served to egg him on.

Holmes made an approving gesture. "Very wise, Guthrie," he said, and reached for a sheet of notepaper, his inkwell, and a pen; he began at once to write a few lines. "And I regret to tell you that there is another errand you must run for me, and that quickly. Ambassador Tochigi cannot be left uninformed. He is currently at Prince Jiro's London residence, in Standish Mews; you will find the number here on the envelope. The place is being guarded by the Swiss for the nonce. I want you to see he receives this. Give it to him personally." He finished up his note, folded it, put it into an envelope which he sealed with wax and then handed to me.

"Is there anything you wish me to tell him? Shall I wait for an answer?" I asked.

"Ordinarily I would ask you to wait, but on this occasion, I need you back here promptly. There is much more to do." He took a deep breath. "Once Charles Shotley delivers the last of the material I have requested, we'll have everything right and tight." Then he lowered his voice. "When you return, look in on Edmund, will you? He is feeling well enough to feel neglected. You may tell him where you have gone today."

"He is still improving?" I asked.

"Thank goodness, yes, he is," said Holmes quietly. "He claims he wishes to continue in his impersonation of me. I am not certain that it is wise, but . . . I must have a double, or I cannot tend properly to my duties. And it took me four years of searching to find him."

"It would be dreadful to have to search another four years," I said, striving to capture his tone of voice.

"I wouldn't make the attempt," said Holmes. "I do not think I could be so fortunate twice in my life. And so I would become a prisoner of my own mythology, and I would have to live here all the time except for daily excursions across the street and the occasional bolt to Oxford or Cambridge, or whatever place the government—" He shook his head. "All this is true enough, but the most important thing to me is that my friend, who risked his life for my sake, will not have to die for me. I don't think I could bear that."

"Amen," I added to this with great feeling.

Holmes favored me with a long stare. "Yes." He changed his stance. "You may say this does not march with what I do—for men are sent to battle and death on my recommendation. I cannot deny it. I have been given the responsibility for aiding the direction of the ship of state, and part of that burden is the knowledge of requiring deaths." The weight of this admission was in his eyes as I had never seen it before. "And that is why I strive to keep us from war, to arrange our treaties to best serve the purpose of a just peace, to resort to battle when nothing else is possible. All else is profligacy. I have no wish to be a despot, to measure my success by the number of bodies reckoned to my credit. If I thought I might do that, I would retire from public life and devote myself to horticulture."

It was a threat he had made many times before, but this time I perceived he meant it. "You have always done what you could to minimize the danger in which I have worked," I ventured.

"So you would think," he said. "I do what I can to convince myself that is true." He made an abrupt gesture. "Collywobbles, Guthrie, collywobbles," he said, explaining his sudden devastation of mood, which he briskly banished. "Get that note to Ambassador Tochigi and return here."

While I thought it likely that Holmes did have dyspepsia, I doubted it had anything to do with what he had eaten. I held my tongue, thrust the envelope into my waistcoat pocket, and again left the flat. This time as I made my way down the flights of stairs, my ankle was more tender than I liked, and as I reached the street, I could not keep from limping a bit.

Again Sid Hastings' deputy brought his piebald horse to the kerb and I climbed into his cab, giving him Standish Mews as his destination. "Right you are," he said and signaled his horse into traffic.

"I will not remain long. I will need you to wait for me." I realized if Sid Hastings had been driving, he would have made that assumption, but I was aware that this jarvey did not necessarily know to anticipate this possibility.

"That I will, then." He said nothing more as we set off, taking care to maneuver his cab through the tangle of carriages, wagons, carts, cycles, and pedestrians.

The Swiss were at the entrance to Standish Mews, the men in uniform and armed. They politely intercepted any vehicle or person turning into the Mews, inquiring what the destination might be and what purpose they had.

When I explained that I was bringing the Japanese ambassador an important note from Mycroft Holmes, I was astonished to see how quickly these officers hurried to aid me.

"But just you, sir," the Captain of the Swiss added, apologetically.

"Not the cab?" I asked, startled at the idea.

"I regret, no. It may wait for you here." He was determined

and I did not want to waste time debating the matter with him. I climbed out of the cab.

"I will be back directly. If you will pull to the end of the service alley and wait for me there, I should return in less than ten minutes." I made sure the guards heard me issue the orders.

"That is satisfactory," said the Captain.

"Good," I responded with a tinge of sarcasm in my words. I did not wait to see the jarvey move his cab, but set off down the short street to the number of the house written on the envelope I carried.

The house in question was a tall, handsome building of Restoration vintage, with elaborate columns flanking the door. It had the look of unfaded elegance that is not often seen in such establishments. I knocked on the door and was promptly admitted by another Swiss officer, who directed me up one flight to the first floor. "There are guards on the floor above the first, as well as another five with the servants below-stairs."

I trod up to the first level and knocked again. This time it was Mister Banadaichi who admitted me. He was in Japanese dress and his bow was more formal than usual. "Mister Guthrie," he said as he rose.

"Good afternoon," I said, glancing around. The flat was as handsome as the exterior of the building, its furnishings a curious mix of Japanese and Restoration. The effect was not unpleasant once the eye grew accustomed to it. "I have a note from Mister Holmes for Ambassador Tochigi," I said.

"I will tell him so," he said, and held out his hand.

"Mister Holmes has charged me to give this to the ambassador personally," I said, hoping he would not take offense. "If you will tell him I am here, I will discharge my commission and leave you to your work."

At this Mister Banadaichi scowled, and was about to speak when Mister Minato appeared at the end of the corridor. Unlike his fellow secretary, he was in a dark English suit of clothes, the muffler pulled up around his lower face, which surprised me a little as I had not thought the weather so brisk.

"Mister Guthrie," said Mister Minato with the slightest of bows, and then his extended hand. He was not reaching for the note, as Mister Banadaichi had, but to shake my hand.

"Good to see you," I said, and began to explain my errand to him.

"I comprehend," he said, cutting me short as he loosened his muffler. "I will inform the ambassador at once of your arrival and your mission."

"Thank you," I said, and watched him go down the corridor to one of the closed doors.

"Is Prince Jiro here?" I asked Mister Banadaichi, as much to make conversation as anything else.

"No," said Mister Banadaichi in disapproving accents. "He has gone to the Admiralty. They asked him to help them in their inquiries. To send for the Emperor's son!" He was much offended by this development, and made no effort to conceal his indignation.

"Well, Emperor's son he is, but he is also a Dartmouth cadet. He has a sworn obligation to the Royal Navy. And I should hope he would want to help resolve the matter of Lord Brackenheath's death, seeing as it had direct bearing on an agreement he publicly supports." I hoped this would provide a little break in his resentment, but I had not realized the depths of his emotions.

"That is nothing!" declared Mister Banadaichi. "That is a formality, less binding than the proper conduct of good hospitality."

"He may see it in that light," I said. "I doubt the Admiralty do." In fact, I supposed that Prince Jiro found his oath more binding than Mister Banadaichi could like, or he would have found an excuse not to go to the Admiralty when he was sent for.

"It is still wrong," muttered Mister Banadaichi as Mister Minato appeared in the hall once more, beckoning me to come.

"I do not say my colleague is wrong in his thinking," said Mister Minato as I reached him, "but I do think he often mistakes form for substance, as you Westerners would say. It is a failing of the Japanese, regretfully." He smiled once as he rapped the door again with his knuckles. "It is a difficult thing, cobbling an agreement together. So much can go wrong."

"Sadly, yes, it can," I agreed, and wondered what his purpose might be in making such a concession.

A crisp command in Japanese ended our brief discussion. The door was opened from the inside by a small, balding man in dark silk robes with such an air of austerity about him that I could not help but believe that he was some kind of monk or priest. Mister Minato said something to him as he bowed, and we were admitted to the room which had clearly been turned into Ambassador Tochigi's study, for neat cases of scrolls and books lined the walls, and a low writing table was set near the window.

Ambassador Tochigi himself was rising from his knees. He was also in a kimono and he bowed to me with great dignity. "It is good to see you faring so well, Mister Guthrie. You have something for me, I believe."

"Yes, I do," I said, taking the envelope from my waistcoat pocket and handing it to him. "Mister Holmes instructed me to hand it to you myself, and I am pleased to do this for him."

Again Ambassador Tochigi bowed as he took the envelope. "I will give it my full attention at once, and will provide what assistance I can without compromising my Emperor. Please assure Mister Holmes of that, if you will?" With that he bowed again and paid no more heed to me than if I had vanished in a single clap of thunder. I did not know what next to do and was relieved when Mister Minato plucked at my sleeve. I did my best to bow properly, then all but backed into the hallway.

"You did that quite well," Mister Minato approved. "If there is any response required, we will make sure it is taken directly to Mister Holmes." He indicated the door where Mister Banadaichi still lingered, his face set in severe lines. "It has been a difficult time for all of us, has it not?"

"Yes, that it has," I said, aware that there had been other times that were as difficult during the previous year.

"Let us hope it will be over soon," he said as we reached the door. He bowed to me, and, after a moment, so did Mister Banadaichi. "Thank you for all you have done to advance the agreement."

"And you," I said, a bit puzzled by his odd affability. I put it up to Japanese customs, which were quite unfamiliar to me. I shook his hand, offered the same to Mister Banadaichi and was rebuffed, so I bowed to them both. "Until we meet again." That was a safe farewell the world over.

"Dozo. Sayonara," said Mister Minato, and closed the door on me.

I walked down Standish Mews pondering that exchange, and at the same time doing what I could not to put too much significance into my observations, for in such tense times, behavior could alter a great deal and have no particular importance. Still, I had the definite impression that I had discovered something crucial to the matter of Lord Brackenheath's death, but I could not satisfy myself as to what it was. I nodded to the Swiss Captain and turned toward the service alley, where the cab was waiting. I lifted my hand to signal the jarvey, wishing I knew his name. I was a bit startled to realize I did not.

The man on the box did nothing.

Alarm spread through me, and I hastened toward the cab and only then noticed that the reins were tightly looped around the break to keep the sweating horse from bolting. The jarvey remained in his box, unnaturally erect.

Little as I wanted to, I reached up and tugged on the hem of his coat, already knowing what would come next.

He listed, and would have toppled from the box had I not sprung to the boot and held him in place. I smelled the blood before I saw it, and the terrible wound which had been concealed by his muffler until his head lolled back toward my shoulder.

"Lord," I whispered, and forced myself to think so that I would not remain exposed for one instant longer than necessary.

FROM THE JOURNAL OF PHILIP TYERS

Mister Shotley has come again, and now M H is shut in his sitting room, the whole of his concentration fixed on what he has found in his perusal of the records provided. He has declared that only G or an emergency is to interrupt him. "For I have almost got it, Tyers," he exclaimed after he had looked through the new material.

Edmund Sutton is feeling much more himself. He has asked for a copy of Coriolanus *with the intention of learning the play while he is recovering. In a few more days he will want me to read it with him while he fixes the role in his head.*

G should be back by now, though he is only ten minutes later than M H assumed he would return, and that is not significant at this time of day.

Chapter Twenty-nine

GATHERING MY WITS, I got myself into the driving box and, propping the corpse against my shoulder, I reached for the reins with the intention of moving the cab into the street. I had just released the brake and put the sweating horse in motion when a figure in a vast cloak and floppy-brimmed hat appeared beside the cab and grabbed for my trouser-leg.

Not again, I thought, and positioned myself to kick the dastard's head.

The cloaked figure looked up, the rim of the hat falling back to reveal familiar features. "Get down from there!" whispered Miss Gatspy. "Now!"

I stared at her, wondering how she came to be here, and at the same time fearing that the jarvey's untimely demise might be laid at her door. But why would she do such a thing? "What on earth?" I exclaimed.

"Guthrie!" she expostulated, "this is no time to . . . That man was sent to kill you and then to make it appear the Japanese had followed you and murdered you. He has one of those ritual daggers with him, the same kind that killed Lord Brackenheath. He would have used it before you reached the end of the block." Her tugging became more emphatic. "He has some of his fellows on the street. You are not safe. They will try to—" She broke off as the crack of rifle fire cut through the rumble of traffic. The dead man lurched as the bullet thudded into him.

I had all I could do to hold the horse. Thoughts of Edmund Sutton's wound came unbidden to my mind.

"Guth-rie!" Miss Gatspy insisted. "Get down! Now!"

For an instant I had an inclination to take the time to bestow the dead man with some dignity, for I thought it callous to abandon him in the street. But then a second shot came, and the horse lost all patience and broke into an uneven canter that laid the jarvey out in the box. As we hurtled into the crush of traffic, I realized I could do nothing more that would not lead to greater danger. I scrambled out of the box, braced myself as best I could, and leaped free.

On landing, my ankle all but gave way, and I could tell it would once again mean using a cane for a few more days. I cursed myself and the shooter angrily, and was still condemning the world at large when Miss Gatspy hurried up to me, her arm raised imperiously to halt the clarence heading directly for me. She seized my arm and pulled me out of the road and into a doorway.

"What is going on?" I demanded.

"I told you," she said with remarkable calm. "That man was sent to kill you and make it appear you were a second victim of Japanese treachery. He is part of the group who have dedicated themselves to ending all agreements between East and West." She glanced over her shoulder, and then took a firm hold of my arm. "We can't remain here. They will be looking for us directly."

"To finish the job?" I ventured, then said, "The jarvey said Sid Hastings sent him. He knew my name and . . . he had a description." An unwelcome notion intruded. "You don't think that Sid Hastings—"

"Inspector FitzGerald's men have just been to Sid Hastings' house and discovered his daughter was being held captive by the same agents who ambushed you and Mister Holmes. They had promised to kill the child if Sid Hastings did not aid them." She shook her head. "The poor man was beside himself."

"Small wonder," I said, and tried to imagine how I should feel in his situation.

"The men they caught talked. Boasted, in fact. They were certain that they had succeeded and that nothing could stop their agents now. They are precisely the sorts of fanatics the Brotherhood turns to its purpose, all but blind with their own purpose. But Mister Holmes thought there might be time enough to thwart their plans and save you. That is why I came after you, to keep them from reaching you. Had you delayed your departure by ten minutes, you would have learned of this as I did." She quickly darted out from the doorway and hurried after a group of carters taking their leisure at the corner of the street. I followed after her as quickly as I could, my hands thrust deep in my coat-pockets in the hope of making it appear I carried a pistol.

We reached the corner of the street and I heard the sound of rifle fire again, but few others did—I must suppose it was because hey were not listening for it. I half-expected to feel the lead tear nto my body.

"This way," ordered Miss Gatspy, and slipped down the alley wenty feet beyond the corner.

As I continued in her wake, the hairs on the back of my neck nce again settled down. I had not realized until then that they had isen. I was not able to run, my ankle being too much put upon for hat, but I did achieve a shambling sort of skip that allowed me to eep up with her. "You say these men confessed?" I asked, short of reath but filled with curiosity.

Her voice was low, but loud enough to carry to me. "According to FitzGerald they were eager to tell all they had done, congratulating themselves on their achievement. He said they showed no evidence of shame or remorse. They revealed their entire conspiracy, smug in the certainty that you would be killed and the apanese implicated in your death. They were confident that they would be condemned for their role in all this, but they were satisfied to die if it would end England's agreements with Oriental countries. In fact, Inspector FitzGerald reckons they want to be martyrs to their cause." She moved along quite handily, the cloak flapping around her, hiding her sex and making her appear larger than she was.

"Good Lord!" I exclaimed. "Are these the men Lord Brackenheath was consorting with?"

"Apparently so," she said. "FitzGerald had not learned the whole from them, and Mister Holmes pines that they will cease to speak when they learn they have failed." We were at the junction of another alley. Both seemed equally dark and unpromising. Miss Gatspy indicated the backstairs of a three-story establishment, motioning me to sit there in the deepest shadows. "Come. Quickly. They are following us."

I was not as certain of that as she, but I was glad of any excuse to recover myself somewhat. "As you wish." I let myself be led away into the under-stairs hollow, behind the dustbins, to crouch there, trying to breathe through my mouth so my panting would not give me away, and so I would be less cognizant of the odor around us.

"Be very still," Miss Gatspy whispered into my ear: I felt the brim of her hat brush my face. "These men are relentless in their pursuit."

For an answer I nodded, and waited, while numerous questions burgeoned in my mind, not the least of which was—who of these men was responsible for the death of Lord Brackenheath, and why had they killed him, since he was part of their company? What made them willing to kill him? Perhaps they believed they needed a body to convince the English of Japanese perfidy. But if that were so, why should they need to kill me? Lord Brackenheath's death was a far greater scandal than ever mine would be. Every time I thought I had it sorted out, I found out I had not.

About two or three minutes after we found our hiding place, I noticed a pair of men in dark, nondescript clothing coming along the alley in a cautious-but-lethal manner. I had had no inkling that they were so close. Both of them carried pistols. This observation did not offer any reassurance of safety, and I was relieved now that Miss Gatspy had been so particular in selecting our hiding place, however noisome.

"Here," Miss Gatspy breathed, and I felt her slip a stiletto into my hand. Though I doubted it could do much against a pistol, I accepted it, certain that to have some weapon was better than having none.

We watched the men advance, both of us taut with anticipation of a fight, both of us hoping the men would pass us by and leave us undetected. What troubled me now was the fear that this might be a blind alley, so that the men would have to come back this way in order to continue their search, which would double our risk and increase the likelihood of discovery. I would have said as much to Miss Gatspy, but even so little sound was fraught with hazard. I contented myself with securing her hand in mine and giving it an encouraging squeeze.

The nearer of the two said something to his fellow in a language I did not recognize, but I suspected must be Czech or Hungarian, given the nature of the sound of it, and the spiky endings to words. It was neither Polish nor Russian, for I knew those tongues when I heard them. The second man gave an abrupt answer; by the way he delivered it, he was ordering his companion to be silent.

At the far end of the alley there was the sound of a closing door. Both men swung toward it, and one of them laughed.

Seconds went by with the slowness of glaciers moving. It would have pleased me to scream or swear or protest this situation in some more drastic way. As it was, I distracted myself by counting my heartbeats, and memorizing the characteristics of Miss Gatspy's hand in mine.

At last the two men moved away from our hiding place, continuing down the alley toward the next alley, which I trusted led back to the street.

"Keep low," Miss Gatspy advised under her breath as she peered out from our hiding place. "We will try to make it through to the Brompton Road. I doubt they will be able to pursue us in so busy a thoroughfare."

"Or so we pray," I added for her as much as for myself. Then, keeping low and moving quickly, we rushed out of our hiding place and down the alley. I hated the dragging of my foot, afraid it would be loud enough to bring the two men down upon us again.

To my astonishment we reached the street without mishap. I did what I could to neaten my appearance, and then stepped from the kerb to signal a cab while Miss Gatspy kept watch for our enemies. My first two attempts to halt a cab failed, but the third proved successful.

The ancient jarvey handled the ribbons expertly, drawing up smartly and opening the panel with the butt-end of his whip. He almost balked when he saw Miss Gatspy rush up to join me, but shrugged as I tossed him a shilling. As we climbed in, the two men we had seen in the alley rounded the end of the street, and with a cry hurried after us.

"White slavers," I explained mendaciously to the jarvey. "I've only just released my cousin from their clutches. We must escape them."

"White slavers! And in the Brompton Road," said the jarvey with utter condemnation as he put his vehicle in motion, directing his horse into the stream of traffic with the ease of decades of practice. "Fine thing it is, when white slavers can kidnap English girls off the street!"

Behind us the men made a futile attempt to reach the cab, but were shortly left behind.

"And where are you going?" asked the jarvey when he was satisfied the two men were lost behind us. "Just name the train station, and you're safely out of London before they know you're gone."

"We have friends in town." I gave him the number of Mycroft Holmes' flat in Pall Mall.

"Friends indeed," said the jarvey with an appreciative whistle. "Pall Mall friends. Those white slavers had best look to their futures in the lockup."

"Amen to that," I said, and leaned back against the squabs, my bones feeling fragile after the heady rush of excitement that had filled the last half hour.

"Thank you, Guthrie," said Miss Gatspy.

"I rather think the shoe is more on the other foot," I responded at once. "It strikes me that I have the greater debt." My emotion was sincere, though I did not like the suspicion that filled me, that the driver of the cab I had found with his throat cut had been dispatched by Miss Gatspy herself.

"Nonsense, Guthrie," she said in a rallying manner, but with an underlying sternness. "I was doing nothing more than what I am trained to do, what I am sworn to do. You, on the other hand, have been willing to adapt your needs to mine without any preparation, and with nothing more than your senses to go on." She frowned as she looked out into the street. "I am sorry that it has all been so . . . hectic. First the attempt on Sutton and now the one on you."

"But neither succeeded," I pointed out, taking more satisfaction in saying this than perhaps was wise.

"Both came too close, if you ask me," said Miss Gatspy, and her frown deepened. "I don't know what I shall do if those men are not apprehended. They represent a terrible threat to the peace in Europe. To have such dangerous assassins abroad in England . . ." She looked back as if worried that they might be behind us, preparing to renew their predation.

"That's as may be," I said to her, wanting to reassure her, and myself, that we had got free of danger. Apparently my confidence was well-founded, for we arrived in Pall Mall without further ruction. I gave the jarvey an extra half-crown for his efforts, and he tipped his battered hat as he left Miss Gatspy and me standing before the entrance to Holmes' building.

"I will be grateful when all this is over," Miss Gatspy said as we began our climb up the stairs. "Those men are frightening, even to me."

"They do seem unusually dedicated to their cause," I agreed, wanting to match her sangfroid, and almost achieving my aim.

"With the Brotherhood to aid them, as we of the Golden Lodge know they do, they are probably the most dangerous group in all of England and Europe at present. Your Mister Holmes must share my conviction." She had put her arm through mine and I could feel her indignation as acutely as if she had grabbed me by the lapels.

My leg was sore again by the time we reached Holmes' door. I rang the bell in a spirited style, as much to hide my exhaustion as to summon Tyers with all due alacrity.

"We have been expecting you this last twenty minutes," said Tyers, unruffled as ever. "Inspector FitzGerald is expected to return momentarily." He stood aside to admit us, and to take the cloak and hat Miss Gatspy held out to him.

"Thank Mister Sutton for me," she said with a dazzling smile. "I should have never been able to manage without it."

Tyers only nodded. "Mister Holmes is in the sitting room," he said, bowing slightly in that direction. "He has opened the port against your return. The Twenty-one."

"Wonderful," I said, for Mycroft Holmes had an enviable cellar, and that vintage was one of his rarer treasures. I allowed Miss Gatspy to enter the room ahead of me, thinking as I did that I had enjoyed her company in spite of all we had endured together.

Holmes was sitting in his preferred chair, his back to the large oaken table. I noticed that his secretary was standing open, and from this I surmised he had recently dispatched a letter or memo; I wondered to whom it might be. He smiled, his profound grey eyes glinting with what I believed to be satisfaction. *"In buon' punto,* as the Italians say," he greeted us. "And not a moment too soon. Good. Guthrie, dear boy, you appear to be limping again. I trust you have suffered no permanent injury?"

"My ankle is troubling me a bit," I conceded, making a show of testing it. "Nothing to mention."

"And Miss Gatspy. I am truly grateful for your timely concern on Guthrie's behalf. I must suppose you prevented any misfortune?" He gestured to chairs as his way of inviting us to sit down.

"I doubt the false jarvey thought so," I remarked as I chose the more over-upholstered of the chairs.

Holmes turned an inquiring glance in Miss Gatspy's direction. His tone was light, but his eyes were serious. "Why is that?"

She shrugged, but I saw that she was a little pale. "He had to be stopped. I attended to that." She brushed at the front of her dress in an unconscious display of repugnance. "Luckily his coat absorbed most of the blood."

"Ah," said Holmes with a nod. "Then you will be in need of this," he went on as he leaned forward toward the butler's table where the decanter stood waiting, flanked by good crystal. He poured out a fair portion for Miss Gatspy and handed it to her. "Here. If you will permit us to have the first toast?"

She accepted the glass and bowed her head. Her fair, rosy hair shone like the crown of an angel. "If that is your wish."

"Most certainly," said Holmes, handing me my glass, and then taking care of his own. He held the port up to the light. "Marvelous color. I think you will find this quite worthwhile." He offered his toast. "To Miss Gatspy. Without her, this whole case might have had a far less desirable conclusion."

I raised my glass in salute, and then Holmes and I drank. When we were done, Miss Gatspy took her first sip, and then said, "You speak as if you think the case is concluded."

"Oh, yes," said Holmes. "I should think it is. Unless matters go sadly awry, Inspector FitzGerald should be bringing the principal culprit back here even as we speak."

"And who would that be?" I asked, thinking that more than one of the participants in the drama might qualify for such a position.

"Why, Mister Jeremiah Hackett." He looked startled. "I realize you have had much to do in the last few days, but since you are the one who put the crucial information in my hands, I was certain you knew—" He stopped. "I supposed you had the whole of it." He had another taste of port. "Dear me." He contemplated his port, twirling the stem of the glass between his thumb and fingers. "But then, you were not here when Inspector FitzGerald arrived, were you?"

"No. But Miss Gatspy has told me some of what transpired." I lifted my glass to him. "And you have managed once again to save the day."

"With your help, my dear Guthrie. Without you, I should not have been able to salvage the agreement." Holmes dismissed my half-spoken protestation with a wave of his hand. "It should not have taken so long. I blame myself for the delay in finding out the whole." He sipped his port. "When Jeremiah Hackett is brought here, we will learn the whole at last."

"Did he kill Lord Brackenheath?" I asked, still trying to piece together all I had learned in the last hour.

"Good Lord, no," said Holmes. "That was done by Mister Minato." He scowled as he spoke. "And I fear he will answer for it."

"Mister Minato?" I repeated, and was gratified to see Miss Gatspy looking as stunned as I was.

"Certainly," Holmes said with a suggestion of sadness. "He discovered that Lord Brackenheath was to have smuggled out a copy of the agreement—I must suppose that Mister Hackett had made one—"

"That he did," I said, recalling the observation that the ink was wet and much reduced shortly before the ratifying of the agreement. "Or someone did."

"Hackett is the likely choice," Holmes said, and went on, "Hackett must have passed the copy to Lord Brackenheath, who then planned to leave the reception for an hour or so. He planned to leave through the garden so his absence would not be missed. He was to have hidden the copy of the document in the upholstery at his house, the which his fellow-conspirators were to discover and to conceal with the appearance of burglary. But because Lord Brackenheath was killed before he could do this—and you may believe that the men sent to this task have excoriated Lord Brackenheath for allowing himself to be murdered—the document was not in place."

"But there was no such document found on the body," I reminded him.

"And we must thank Mister Minato for his foresight in removing it. He is a most astute young man, with a clear sense of duty." He cocked his head. "You are wondering how I am certain it was Mister Minato, aren't you?"

"Well, Mister Banadaichi might also have done it," I said, and saw Miss Gatspy nod in support of my remark.

"But Mister Banadaichi was with me and Ambassador Tochigi in the Terrace Suite for more than half an hour before you found the body." Mycroft Holmes did not have to say anything more; theirs was an impeccable alibi.

Miss Gatspy had a sip of port, then said, "I suppose there is no reason to suspect Lajos Pecs, the Hungarian masquerading as a Grodno Hussar? Might not he have killed . . ." She stopped. "No. He was in the ballroom. I saw him."

"Yes. But he is not entirely blameless in this affair. He had arranged for the carriage to take Lord Brackenheath back to his town house, and to return him to the reception. He was also the one who arranged for Lord Brackenheath to be paid for his treason." Holmes' expression was severe. "I have had word from Yvgeny Tschersky that he has apprehended Pecs and will be holding him for the crime of imposture of a Russian officer. Franz Josef will be outraged, but he will not dare say anything, for that would expose Austro-Hungary's role in all this." He looked up as the doorbell sounded. "Ah, excellent. FitzGerald at last."

FROM THE JOURNAL OF PHILIP TYERS

Mister Hackett has just been taken away in restraints, all but raving, declaring himself a patriot and a defender of England. He would seem to be proud of all he did to bring the naval agreement with the Japanese to ruin. He insisted that his years living in the Orient made him aware of the danger they represented to the world.

Inspector FitzGerald has agreed that the man is to be charged with his fellow conspirators, but that the Hungarian men sent to assist them are to be captured as quietly as possible and sent back to Vienna under armed guard, for to put them on trial would bring about a compromise of the Japano-English agreement that would render it useless.

Miss Gatspy has assured M H that the Golden Lodge will render all the assistance they can in this endeavor, and M H has said he would welcome this assistance.

Sutton is feeling well enough to join M H and G at dinner. Miss Gatspy has also been persuaded to remain, so it will be a celebratory occasion. I have put a rack of lamb to cook, and must now attend to the peas and onions.

Epilogue

DRIZZLE MARRED THE morning as Ambassador Tochigi presented himself at Mycroft Holmes' flat two days later. He furled his umbrella, handed it to Tyers, and bowed to Holmes, holding out a long, narrow box wrapped in elegant silk of a mottled, dark reddish-brown color. After the usual exchange of pleasantries, he said, "Mister Holmes, you are to be congratulated for your handling of this entire investigation." He was in Occidental dress, his swallowtail coat correct to the most stringent demands, his waistcoat a dark-grey, his trousers black with the required stripe. His coat, which Tyers had offered to take, was of good Scottish wool, and tailored in Bond Street.

The weather had made my ankle ache, and so I was a few paces behind Holmes as he went to greet the unexpected arrival.

"Why, thank you for saying so, Ambassador," said Holmes, indicating the door to his study with a thrust of his jaw. He held the box with both hands, not wanting to appear unmindful of the gift. "If you wish we may be private here." He and I had just come from the sitting room where Holmes had been going over Inspector FitzGerald's most recent arrest reports.

I heard Edmund Sutton move about in the parlor, and hoped that he would not let his curiosity get the best of him. It would be unwise for the ambassador to meet him, no matter how much Sutton wanted to thank him for the kimono the ambassador had sent yesterday as a token of gratitude. It struck me forcibly that this visit could not be for the same purpose, and I had to suppress a qualm.

"It will not be necessary. I have only a few matters to discharge, and I am not apprehensive about the reliability of your staff." He indicated the package. "It was Minato's wish that you be given that." He bowed again. "I am told those responsible for the attempt to subvert the agreement have been detained."

"Most of them," said Holmes. "All those in Mister Hackett's organization have been taken in charge as of last night. There are fifteen in all, thirteen men and two women." He said this with a confidence that surprised me, for when we had reviewed FitzGerald's report not ten minutes since, he had expressed grave doubts as to whether all the culprits were in custody.

"I will so inform the Emperor. He will be most pleased to know that England is so willing to protect her agreements." His face remained grave.

"We are also investigating a few other groups of similar goals to the one Mister Hackett belonged to, in case Franz Josef has plans to turn them into Austro-Hungarian dupes," said Holmes, his voice growing stern.

"Very good. This will be welcome to the Emperor." Again he bowed, and said, "It was a good death. His honor is restored."

A stricken expression crossed Holmes' face. I could not fathom why, but he seemed truly appalled by this last remark. "Thank you for telling me," he said quietly, and bowed, Japanese style, to the ambassador. "I am sorry it had to happen."

"Yes. Honor must be vindicated, no matter how unworthy the cause. A most inauspicious necessity." With that he turned back abruptly to the door, his umbrella at the ready, and departed.

Holmes continued to stare at the box in his hands.

"Holmes," I said, beginning to feel some consternation at the solemnity of his face. "What is it?"

He shook his head once, and with an expression more dazed than thoughtful, he went into his study. A moment later, he called out, "Come here, Guthrie."

I made haste to join him, for I was increasingly troubled by his sudden change in demeanor. "What is it, sir? Shall I have Tyers fetch you—" Suddenly my afternoon engagement to take tea with Miss Gatspy, about which I had been half-thinking most of the morning, did not seem at all important. Whatever had caused Holmes such distress required my immediate and full attention.

He held up his long hand. "No. I will do." His voice, a low rumble at the best of times, became so deep it was nearly inaudible. "But keep me company; sit down while I open this."

The silk fell away, and I noticed that the color was mottled, like a large stain on white. I disliked the suspicion that was coming over me. "That's not—"

"Blood? Yes, I fear it is," said Holmes distantly, and opened the box. "Poor Mister Minato," he said as he looked down.

There, in a bed of pale silk, lay an aichuki. The blade was still tacky with blood.

"God in Heaven!" I exclaimed in dawning horror. "And the wrapping?"

"He wore it as a belt, when he did . . . what he did," said Holmes in a still, distant voice.

"You mean he actually—?" I could not bring myself to say the rest.

"Committed ritual suicide in expiation of the killing of Lord Brackenheath," said Holmes, putting the box with its ghastly contents on the desk.

"But why?" I asked. "He was protecting his country, trying to preserve an important agreement from ruin at the hands of a greedy, debauched—"

"Lord Brackenheath was stabbed in the back with just such a dagger. The death was doubly dishonorable in Minato's eyes, because of form." He looked once more at the aichuki.

I recalled the parting remark Mister Minato had made the last time I had seen him: It had been about form and substance. Like the Western man I am, I thought at the time that he was putting the emphasis on substance, as I would myself. But I was wrong. In the end, form made demands of him that resulted in this. "It seems such a waste," I said, disliking the subtle twinge of guilt that went through me.

"So it does," said Mycroft Holmes, and closed the box.